W9-AQA-297

A Worthy Heart

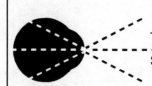

This Large Print Book carries the
Seal of Approval of N.A.V.H.

A WORTHY HEART

SUSAN ANNE MASON

THORNDIKE PRESS
A part of Gale, Cengage Learning

Charles County Public Library
www.ccplonline.org

 GALE
CENGAGE Learning·

Farmington Hills, Mich • San Francisco • New York • Waterville, Maine
Meriden, Conn • Mason, Ohio • Chicago

GALE
CENGAGE Learning·

Copyright © 2016 by Susan Anne Mason.
Thorndike Press, a part of Gale, Cengage Learning.

ALL RIGHTS RESERVED
This is a work of fiction. Names, characters, places, and dialogues are products of the author's imagination and are not to be construed as real. Any resemblance to actual events or persons, living or dead, is entirely coincidental.
Thorndike Press® Large Print Christian Historical Fiction.
The text of this Large Print edition is unabridged.
Other aspects of the book may vary from the original edition.
Set in 16 pt. Plantin.

LIBRARY OF CONGRESS CATALOGING-IN-PUBLICATION DATA

Names: Mason, Susan Anne, author.
Title: A worthy heart / by Susan Anne Mason.
Description: Large print edition. | Waterville, Maine : Thorndike Press, 2016. | © 2016 | Series: Courage to dream ; book 2 | Series: Thorndike Press large print Christian historical fiction
Identifiers: LCCN 2015047573| ISBN 9781410487735 (hardcover) | ISBN 1410487733 (hardcover)
Subjects: LCSH: Large type books. | GSAFD: Christian fiction.
Classification: LCC PR9199.4.M3725 W67 2016 | DDC 813/.6--dc23
LC record available at http://lccn.loc.gov/2015047573

Published in 2016 by arrangement with Bethany House Publishers, a division of Baker Publishing Group

Charles County Public Library
www.ccplonline.org

Printed in Mexico
1 2 3 4 5 6 7 20 19 18 17 16

*To my mother-in-law, Barb,
who has been such a cheerleader
in my life,
especially with respect to my writing!
And to my mother, Irene,
who doesn't quite understand this whole
publishing thing but is happy for me
anyway!*

"Fear not: for I have redeemed thee, I have called *thee* by thy name; thou *art* mine."

Isaiah 43:1

1

June 1914
New York City

"There she is! The Statue of Liberty."

The eager cry of a child caused a ripple of excitement among the crush of passengers as the steamship inched its way into the New York Harbor.

Maggie Montgomery craned her neck to get her first glimpse of the famous landmark. When the crowds shifted enough for her to see the giant arm holding the torch aloft, a thrill of anticipation shot through her, as sharp and biting as the wind that tore at the kerchief covering her hair. America's symbol for freedom. For new life.

Maggie's new life.

She clutched her brother's arm. "Can you believe it, Gabe? We've made it to America."

Gabe nodded, his gaze fixed on the wonder of the immense statue before them. " 'Tis a grand sight, to be sure." He spoke in a reverent whisper almost drowned out by the wind.

She squeezed his coat sleeve, knowing her brother was as moved as she. Never in her wildest imaginings had she dared envision this moment — that her long-held wish to travel and see other parts of the world could actually come true. Now here they were on an extended trip to visit their older brother, Rylan, and his family in New York. What adventures would await her here?

Gabe took her by the elbow. "Let's move to the other side and get a look at the dock. Maybe Rylan will be there waiting for us."

Being a big lad, Gabe had no trouble maneuvering Maggie and himself to a spot at the far side of the rail. Maggie could feel the anticipation rushing through the passengers as they chatted and laughed — many, like Maggie, seeing the tall buildings of New York for the first time.

Breathtaking was all Maggie could think. So different from their tiny village in Cork. The vastness of the scene before her made her feel as insignificant as an ant on the ground, and though grateful for Gabe's arm around her waist, anchoring her to the rail, she couldn't suppress the shiver of nerves that ran through her body.

Gabe pulled her closer. "Are you cold, love?"

"No. Just excited." *Nervous, more like.* But Maggie wasn't about to let her overprotective brother in on that tidbit of information. "It's been so long since we've seen Rylan. I hope he'll recognize us." She paused to look into Gabe's gray eyes, so similar to her own. "Do you think he's changed?"

The stiff wind whipped Gabe's dark hair about his forehead. He'd stuffed his cap into his coat pocket, since it would never stay put, battered by the ocean breeze. "No fear of that. Now that he's married to the love of his life and has adopted wee Delia, I think Rylan will be his same jolly self."

The fact that Rylan and Colleen had taken in one of the children from the orphanage Rylan directed made Maggie love her brother all the more. "Delia must be seven or eight by now."

"Just the right age to be impressed with her Aunt Maggie's beauty and spunk." Gabe tugged playfully at a loose curl that had escaped her head covering.

She swatted him. "Away with you. I'm no beauty. Not by New York standards, anyway." She smiled. "I've been reading some American magazines to prepare me for what the ladies wear over here." She plucked at

11

the sleeve of her serviceable brown overcoat. "I'm afraid I'll be painfully out of style."

"Not to worry. You'll have Colleen and the other O'Learys to help with your wardrobe. I'm sure they won't mind lending you a dress or two." Gabe grinned, revealing dimples in each cheek.

Maggie's heart swelled with love for her handsome brother who had long been her protector. She knew Gabe had not been keen to come on this voyage, that he was doing it at the request of their mother. The rest of her family had all agreed that she and Gabe would stay in America until the end of the summer. Long enough, her mother hoped, for Gabe to forget about the political uprisings in Ireland. And long enough for Maggie's former beau to forget about her and get on with his life.

In the emotional aftermath of her failed betrothal to Neill Fitzgerald, Mum had given Maggie the money for her passage without a moment's hesitation. But when the time had come to go, leaving her mother had been the hardest thing Maggie had ever done.

"Hey now, why the sour expression?" Gabe elbowed her. "You look like someone kicked your cat."

She gave a discreet sniff and lifted her

chin. "Just missing home is all. 'Tis a far cry from this, isn't it?" She gestured to the ever-nearing shoreline.

"That it is." Gabe gave her another squeeze and a knowing look. "Mum will be fine with Paddy and Claire and the grandkids. You have nothing to feel guilty about."

Nothing except the secret she held close to her heart. But no use dwelling on that now.

Loud shouts from the upper decks created a wave of movement among the crowd.

"Looks like we're docking. We'd best gather our bags."

As soon as the crew lowered the gangplank, the eager passengers scurried to disembark. Swept along with the rush, Maggie clutched her bag with one hand and Gabe's arm with the other. How would they ever find Rylan in all this confusion?

Her legs shook with her first steps on solid ground in nearly seven days. She concentrated on staying upright, scarcely able to take in the scope of the wharf and the crowds of people bustling about her. The rancid odor of raw fish and ripe bodies met her nose.

Gabe guided her to an open spot by a wall, setting their bags on the ground beside her. "Wait here and rest a minute. I'll try to find Rylan." He took his cap out of his pocket and slipped it over his unruly hair. "Don't move 'til I return. Promise?"

"I promise." She had no intention of going anywhere, content to watch the flurry of activity on the docks — the men unloading the ship and the rest of the passengers pouring off. Maggie untied the knot of the kerchief under her chin, pulled it off, and stuffed it into the pocket of her coat. How she yearned for a bath and a shampoo for her hair. She'd kept her long, dark curls braided and wrapped tight to her head for the whole voyage, fearful of contracting lice or some other hideous contagion.

"Maggie! Is that you?"

Maggie's head swiveled in the direction of the elated voice. A wide smile broke over her face while unbidden tears of joy filled her eyes. "Rylan!"

Her older brother bounded toward her, heedless of the bags and the crush of people, and scooped her into his arms. She squeezed him hard as he kissed her on both cheeks.

"Ah, Maggie. You're even lovelier than the last time I saw you." Rylan wiped moisture from his eyes.

Maggie loved that her exuberant brother never tried to hide his emotions, but experi-

14

enced every one full out. "You're a charming liar. I look a wreck after a week on that bobbing cork." She laughed out loud at the sheer pleasure of seeing him again. "You, on the other hand, look wonderful. Marriage must agree with you."

He winked and grinned. "With a wife as beautiful as my Colleen, how could it not?"

She gave him another hug. "I'm so happy to see you. I've missed you something terrible." She pressed a kiss to his cheek. "I can't wait to see my sister-in-law and my niece." She'd met little Delia three years ago when Rylan had brought his new family to Ireland on his rather unconventional honeymoon. After finalizing Delia's adoption, Rylan and Colleen took the little girl with them everywhere.

"And Colleen is just as eager to see you." He straightened and scanned the immediate area. "Where is Gabe? He shouldn't leave you alone."

"Searching for you. Did you not see him?"

"No." He frowned. "I hope he's not run into any trouble. There are some unsavory characters around here, looking to pick the pockets of unsuspecting travelers as they disembark."

"No need to fear, brother. My pockets are still intact."

Rylan grinned and turned to clasp Gabe in a huge hug.

"It's been far too long." Gabe clapped Rylan on the back.

Rylan nodded. "You have no idea how good it is to have family on this side of the ocean. Come on. Colleen will be worrying if we don't get back soon."

The men picked up the suitcases, and the threesome set off toward the main street leading into the city. Feeling steadier, Maggie soaked in every detail of the colorful surroundings — the magnificent buildings, so tall she couldn't find the tops, the vibrant clothing in many different styles, and the interesting speech patterns of the people passing by.

They'd traveled about two blocks when Rylan stopped. "We'll catch the streetcar here. It will take us within a block of my home." He set the luggage on the ground beneath a sign. "Since we don't own a motorcar, we walk or take the streetcar."

"No need to explain, Ry. You know we walk everywhere at home."

Maggie smiled. "A streetcar will be a luxury for me."

As is this whole trip.

The only thing marring her excitement was the persistent niggle of guilt that continued to plague her. Everyone believed she was here for a summer sojourn, but in truth she had no intention of returning to Ireland. The opportunity to come to America, to escape the restrictions of her small village and to seek her fortune in the big city, was a dream Maggie was not willing to sacrifice. Even if it meant leaving her beloved mother behind forever.

Twenty minutes later, after an unsettling ride on a tram car that jostled worse than their ship over the waves, Gabe helped his sister step down. He set his bag on the ground and paused a moment to catch his breath.

The sights along the route had made Gabe's pulse race in a way he hadn't anticipated. With the political unrest increasing in Ireland, he hadn't wanted to leave home. The only reason he'd agreed to this trip was to ease his mother's anxiety about Maggie traveling alone. Perhaps unfairly, Gabe had been prepared to detest everything about New York, yet he'd almost fallen off his seat when they'd passed a local fire station and he'd caught a glimpse of a gleaming red fire truck inside the open door. Other than spending time with Rylan and his family, Gabe looked forward to learning how the

New York Fire Department operated. He hoped to bring ideas back to his rather rustic station in Cork. Any methods of improvement would be welcome in their small town.

After a few minutes of walking, Gabe slowed when Rylan stopped at the foot of a cement staircase.

"This is it," Rylan announced, starting up the steps to a tall, brick house.

Compared to their mother's cottage back in Ireland, Rylan's home seemed as large as a castle. Yet Gabe wouldn't trade the lush green meadows surrounding their thatched house for anything. He scanned the street lined with row upon row of similar structures and not a blade of grass in sight. Where did Delia run and play?

"Quit gawking and get in here," Rylan said with a laugh.

He pushed open the front door, and they entered a long, narrow hallway. Quick footsteps sounded in the distance, and almost immediately a girl ran toward them.

"Mama, hurry up. They're here!" The blond tyke raced over to Rylan and launched herself into his outstretched arms.

Rylan beamed at the girl. "You remember Uncle Gabe and Aunt Maggie, don't you?"

Delia nodded, ducking her head. "I remember Aunt Maggie 'cause she's so pretty."

Gabe held back a snort.

Maggie ignored him and plucked the child out of Rylan's arms. "Not as pretty as you, sweet girl. What I wouldn't give for hair as fair as yours." She rained kisses on the girl's cheeks, causing an eruption of giggles.

Rylan winked as Colleen came up beside him. "There's my lovely wife. I was beginning to think you'd been captured by leprechauns."

Colleen swatted her husband's arm. Three years of marriage had not dimmed her fiery hair and violet-blue eyes.

"Hush," she scolded her husband as she stepped forward to hug Gabe.

He kissed her cheek. "Grand to see you again, Colleen."

"We're so pleased you could come and visit. Rylan gets so lonely for his family."

The love shining on her face made Gabe's breath catch. What would it be like to have the devotion of such a fine woman? So unlike the fickle Brigid, who'd thrown him over for another firefighter. Gabe turned his thoughts firmly away from his ill-fated romance and concentrated on his brother's family.

Colleen hugged Maggie. "You must be

exhausted after your voyage. Make yourself at home in the parlor, and I'll boil the water for tea."

Rylan took their overcoats and hung them on a hook, then led them through a door on the right into a cozy living area where a cheerful fire burned in the hearth. A sofa and two armchairs flanked the fireplace.

Maggie plopped onto the settee, little Delia still clinging to her neck.

"Can I get you a nip of Irish whisky?" Rylan asked.

Gabe shook his head. "No, thank you. One too many hangovers cured me of that vice. Tea will be lovely."

Rylan took the seat opposite Gabe. "How was Mum when you left? Was she really all right with you two coming here?"

"Aye. She wished she could come, too, but her health still isn't the best. Paddy and Claire will look out for her while we're gone. Tommy and Eileen will help, as well."

A trace of sadness crept over Rylan's features. "I wish I could get away for a month or so to go home for a visit, but the orphanage is bursting at the seams lately, and I wouldn't leave Colleen to manage on her own."

"Oh? Any news we should know about?"

Maggie winked at Rylan over Delia's blond curls.

Gabe had half-expected to see Colleen ripe with child when they arrived, yet her slim figure belied the arrival of a niece or nephew anytime soon.

A frown darkened Rylan's brow. "No, and it's a bit of a sore subject, so I'd appreciate it if neither of you mentioned it, unless she brings up the topic."

"So, Rylan," Gabe said, taking the opportunity to change the subject, "any chance you can get me a tour of the nearest fire station tomorrow?"

"Is that all you ever think of?" Maggie rolled her eyes. "Can you not forget about fires for once?"

"Not when it's in Gabe's blood, sister dear." Rylan stood to poke at the fire. The logs hissed as a flame shot upward. "As a matter of fact, I know Chief Witherspoon quite well. He inspects the orphanage on a regular basis. I could arrange a tour, if you'd like."

"That would be grand. The sooner the better."

Rylan laughed. "Being cooped up on that boat has made you itchy, I see. Not to worry. I'm sure I can spare a few minutes tomorrow to take you over."

A thrill of excitement quickened Gabe's pulse. With inside knowledge of New York's renowned stations, Gabe could return home a hero and hopefully earn a promotion at work.

That thought brought a smile to his face and made this unwanted trip to America a great deal more bearable.

2

The harsh clank of metal echoed through the damp corridors of the New York Penitentiary as the cell door closed behind him. Squaring his shoulders, Adam O'Leary prepared for his last walk through the center aisle of the prison. He should be filled with joy, ecstatic over his release from incarceration after almost three years. Instead, a nervous ball of dread swirled in his stomach. How would he face his family — his highly religious, morally superior family — after being tried and convicted for his crimes?

The musty stench of unwashed bodies followed him through the corridor until he reached the last barrier. The guard before him rattled his circle of keys and selected one to unlock the door, then ushered Adam through. They continued on to a large outer room with a high counter and several long benches.

"I hate to say it, O'Leary, but I'm going

to miss your ugly mug around here." The man known to Adam only as Sarge gave a slight twitch of his lips, which Adam supposed passed for a smile.

Adam nodded and fixed him with a sincere gaze. "Thanks, Sarge. For everything. You made life in this hole a little more bearable." Adam stuck out his hand, not sure if Sarge would take it. But the man's huge paw swallowed Adam's and pumped it hard.

"Best of luck on the outside, lad. And try to stay out of trouble this time."

"I'll do my best."

Sarge gave him one last clap on the shoulder before leaving Adam in the charge of the officer at the desk. After Adam had signed the required papers, the man handed him a plain brown package containing his worn leather wallet and pocket watch.

"You've been provided with enough money to purchase a one-way train ticket once you reach the mainland." The officer pushed a few bills across the counter. "The patrol boat will meet you at the dock to take you over. Don't let me see you back here again." The gruff warning didn't match the sympathy visible in the man's eyes.

"I've no intention of coming back, sir. Thank you." Adam folded the bills into his wallet and tucked the wallet into his back pocket. The weight of the leather made his trousers sag around his hips, emphasizing the weight he'd lost since coming here. He hoped Mrs. Harrison's good cooking would remedy that in short order.

If his father allowed him home again.

Adam pulled on his jacket and tugged his cap over his shaggy auburn hair. A haircut and a proper shave would be most welcome right now. Grimly, he gathered the small bag that contained his only other clothing, tipped his cap to the officer, and headed out the main door.

Less than one hour later, Adam stepped off the patrol boat and onto the East 34th Street pier. Brilliant sunshine momentarily blinded him as he made his way down the walkway toward the street. On the corner of First Avenue, he paused to get his bearings, unused to the rush of people, cars, and horses on the streets. A streetcar bell clanged as it went by, a sound Adam hadn't heard in ages. The clear blue sky and long streets beckoned him. Instead of the street-car, he'd walk to the station and take the next available train to Long Island.

He strolled for several blocks, relishing the freedom to venture as far as he liked without a guard watching his every movement. Being able to enjoy the fresh air without having to sweat and toil at splitting rocks seemed decadent. He walked in the general direction of the train station, but his steps slowed as the neighborhood sights became familiar. Drawn almost against his will, he picked up his pace until he found the address he sought.

Adam stopped across the street from the tall, brick building on Lexington Avenue and simply took it in. An engraved brass sign proclaimed it to be St. Rita's Orphan Asylum. Going from memory, Adam noted a few subtle changes to the building, which he attributed to his sister and her husband, Rylan, the new manager. Cheerful flower-pots stood guard at the foot of the cement staircase leading to the main door. Window boxes spilled colorful blooms from the first-floor windows. Colleen always did love fresh flowers.

Fighting an inner tug-of-war, Adam crossed the street. He had no intention of intruding on Colleen, but the lure of possibly catching a glimpse of her won over. From an open window, the voices of young children drifted outside. High-pitched cries of glee created a wave of longing in Adam. Had he ever been that carefree? Even as a ten-year-old boy, he'd rarely laughed or indulged in senseless playtime. Unlike the orphans housed within these walls, Adam had been given every advantage in life, yet despite their circumstances, they sounded happier than Adam had ever been.

He pushed back a spurt of regret, imagining his vivacious sister inside, tending to the children's needs. He wished he could find the courage to march up those stairs, grab her in a hug, and tell her how much he'd missed her these past years. But his uncertainty about the welcome he'd receive held him frozen in place. Despite the few letters he'd received from Colleen during his prison term, Adam did not have a clear picture of her feelings toward him. Would she embrace him or throw him off the property? He wouldn't blame her if she did the latter, considering he hadn't even attended her wedding. If he'd known at the time that he would lose his freedom a few weeks later during a raid at the Lucky Chance Saloon, he would certainly have made a different choice.

Only one of the regrets that haunted him now.

He stuffed his hands in his jacket pockets and moved reluctantly away from the entrance, prepared to walk on, but excited cheers coming from the side of the building drew his attention. He followed the noise down a side alley to the back of the building, where a large iron gate barred his way. His height gave him the advantage of being able to see over the adjacent hedge.

"Run, Billy. You can make it!" a tall lad shouted at another boy, who rounded what appeared to be bases made from burlap sacks.

At the far end of the grassy area, a dark-haired woman hiked her skirts to her knees and raced after the ball. With one swift movement, she scooped it up and hurled it back to a boy waiting at second base. Despite her Herculean effort, the runner made it safely to his goal. Several groans competed with the cheers.

The woman laughed as she made her way back. "Nice job, Billy. Whose turn to bat?"

The strong Irish lilt to her voice captured Adam's interest. She sounded as though she'd just stepped off a steamship from Ireland.

A tiny blond girl ran over to the woman and tugged her skirt. "Miss Montgomery, I need to use the restroom."

Miss Montgomery crouched in front of the tot and took her by the hand. "What's your name, darlin'?"

"Sarah."

The woman waved at one of the older girls

across the yard. "Can you take Sarah inside, please?"

"Yes, miss." She came forward to take Sarah by the hand, and they moved out of Adam's sight.

"Can Mr. Rylan come out and play with us?" A boy with tousled hair bounced over to talk to Miss Montgomery.

"Not right now. I'm afraid he's working." She crossed her arms in front of her, a mock scowl creasing her pert nose. "Are you saying I'm not good enough for you?"

The boy grinned. "You're not bad . . . for a girl."

With an exaggerated growl, no doubt given for effect, she took off in pursuit of the tyke. He squealed and ducked around her. So fascinated was Adam as he watched the enchanting young woman, he realized too late that the boy was headed straight for the gate where Adam stood. Quickly he ducked behind a tall hedge on one side of the gate. Had they seen him?

Loud whispers froze Adam in place. There was no point in running. He'd only be spotted leaving the scene of the crime, and the last time he'd tried that, he hadn't fared too well.

The gate creaked open, the hinge squeaking in protest. A swirl of skirts rushed

29

through the opening, and before Adam could take a breath, the woman stalked over to stand in front of him.

"Is there something we can help you with, sir?" Though the question seemed polite, her facial expression, as well as her tone, dripped with suspicion.

Her eyes, a cool shade of gray steel, mesmerized him. He blinked and straightened from behind the greenery. "No, thank you, miss."

She fisted her hands on her hips. "What are you doing, spying on us like that?"

Oh, she is a feisty thing. Though he towered a full head above her, she showed not one iota of fear. Adam shifted his weight from one foot to the other. How could he explain what he'd been doing? "I apologize if I caused you any concern. The sounds of the children drew me over." He tugged the brim of his cap and gave a quick nod. "Good day to you."

The woman scanned him from the top of his cap, which couldn't conceal his unruly hair, past his over-large clothing, to the toes of his worn shoes. What must she think of him? A down-on-his-luck hobo in need of a handout? His heart thumped in his chest — for not an entirely unpleasant reason. For the first time in years, he felt fully alive,

30

every sense attuned.

She pinned him with a fierce glare, as though intending to give him a further tongue-lashing, but instead she lifted her chin. "Don't be loitering around here or I'll be forced to call the constable."

"No need, miss. I'll be on my way." He longed to ask after Colleen, but that would put his sister in the awkward position of having to explain who he was and why he didn't go inside to speak with her.

With a reluctance he couldn't explain, Adam turned and headed down the alley toward the main street, wishing he could have met the lovely Miss Montgomery in another time — before he'd ruined his life.

Maggie's feet glided over the plush carpeting that lined the main corridor of the orphanage. "I never dreamed an orphanage would be this beautiful," she said to Colleen as they walked.

Maggie had waited outside with the children, unexpectedly joining in their game of softball, while Colleen had taken care of a pressing matter relating to the grocery order for the kitchen. Now Maggie gave her full attention to the tour of the building that Colleen had promised.

Colleen smiled. "Believe me, I know how

you feel. The first time I came here, I pictured rats running through the halls and hordes of children dressed in rags."

Maggie laughed out loud. "I'd say you had a vivid imagination."

"You'd be right." Colleen chuckled as she pushed open the door to one of the rooms and ushered Maggie inside. "The couple who donated this building to the nuns insisted on the best furnishings and decorations. They wanted the unfortunate children who'd lost the most important people in their lives, as well as their homes, to feel nurtured and loved here."

"From what I've seen so far, the children seem to appreciate all they have."

"Most of them do." Colleen ushered her through another door. "This is the common room. We use it for anything from prayer services to musical performances."

Every detail of the large room faded the moment Maggie spied the large upright piano. Pulled by a force beyond her control, she crossed to the magnificent piece and ran her fingers lovingly over carved swirls in the mahogany surface.

"This was donated by the same couple. The woman was an accomplished pianist, or so I'm told. Do you play?"

Maggie looked up to see Colleen watching her with a curious expression. "Aye. The piano and the organ." She brushed the keys with reverent fingers, her senses tuned to the soft timbre of the notes that emerged. "To make extra money back home, I gave lessons to the children whose parents could afford it."

Colleen lifted a brow. "I don't remember seeing a piano in your cottage when we were there."

"The pastor lets me use the one in our church. I didn't realize how much I've missed playing."

"Feel free to use ours whenever the children aren't doing their lessons. Speaking of which, let me show you the classroom."

Reluctantly, Maggie tore herself away from the piano, promising herself she'd try it out the first chance she got, and followed Colleen to the next room.

Maggie took in the rows of desks, shelves of books, and the chalkboard up front. "It's grand. Nicer than our schoolhouse back home." A sudden longing for her country school and the students she taught rose in her chest.

Colleen fairly glowed with pride. "It *is* nice, isn't it? I'm sure, as a teacher, you'd like to take a closer look."

"I would indeed." Maggie walked to one

of the bookcases and ran her fingers over the spines. A tall cupboard at the far end caught her attention. "May I?"

"Of course."

Maggie opened the doors to find a treasure trove of items: pencils, pens, bottles of ink, stacks of paper, rulers, and containers of chalk. She inhaled the scent, which reminded her of her own schoolroom, and a pang of homesickness gripped her. She hoped her students were faring well without her.

Colleen adjusted the blind on one of the windows looking out onto the street. "Maggie, would you be willing to assist in the classroom while you're here? We can always use extra help, especially with the younger children."

Maggie clasped her hands together. "I was hoping you'd ask. I'd be delighted to, if the nuns won't mind."

Colleen smiled. "Sister Veronica will welcome you with open arms. Lucky for you, Sister Marguerite is mostly retired now. She was a force to be reckoned with in her day."

Maggie grinned and shut the doors to the storage closet. "I do believe Rylan regaled me with one such tale — something about you and an ink spill?"

Pink bloomed in Colleen's cheeks. "I can't believe he told you that story."

Maggie winked. "I think Rylan fell in love with you that very moment. Or perhaps it was while he was helping with your waylaid wagon and you both ended up covered in mud."

Colleen set her hands on her hips. "I see I have no secrets left at all. Wait until I see that man tonight. He'll get a piece of my mind." But her huff of laughter gave away her pretense.

Maggie followed her back out into the corridor. "You and Rylan are so fortunate. To have each other and to share this important work together." A spasm of wistfulness tugged at Maggie. "I hope I'll be as lucky one day."

Colleen patted her arm. "I'm so sorry your engagement didn't work out. But you're barely twenty. You've lots of time yet."

Thoughts of Neill Fitzgerald — thoughts Maggie had tried hard to leave on the shores of Ireland — came rushing to mind, bringing with them a wave of regret over the way their relationship had ended. It seemed marriage to Neill was not her destiny. "Maybe so, but meanwhile, I'll fill my time helping children. It's my life's calling, I feel certain." That and her music. Maybe she could teach the children to play a few simple songs while she was here and inspire a love of music within them.

She glanced at Colleen in time to see a shadow of sadness drift across her features. "Lately I've been thinking about my life's calling, as well." Colleen paused in the foyer and gripped her hands together in front of her skirt. "These children may be the only ones I get to nurture." She gave a small shrug. "Don't misunderstand me. I'm extremely grateful for Delia, but I can't deny the longing for a babe of my own."

Maggie squeezed Colleen's arm. "I'm sure every woman has the same desire. I'll make sure to double my petitions to heaven on your behalf."

"Thank you. The more prayers the better." Colleen squared her shoulders and seemed to pull herself together. "We should bring the children in for lunch. They get cranky when they're hungry."

As Maggie followed Colleen toward the back exit, she suddenly remembered the stranger at the gate.

"I don't wish to alarm you, Colleen, but I found a man watching the children at the back gate earlier. I shooed him on his way. Still, I thought it best to warn you."

Maggie recalled the man's shaggy red hair

and unkempt beard and the quiet desperation he exuded. Yet something behind the desperation — a type of yearning or regret — had spoken to her, and she hadn't felt frightened.

A slight frown marred Colleen's features. "It might have been a parent attempting to catch a glimpse of the child they had to leave here for one reason or another. I'll tell the other adults to be diligent in watching the children when they're outdoors."

"Aye. I suppose it couldn't hurt to be careful."

Irish Meadows. Never had two words summoned more love and more hatred with one breath.

Adam slowed his gait as he neared the long, winding lane that would take him to his parents' Long Island residence — his childhood home. If he had anywhere else to go, he'd head there in a heartbeat. However, not only was he without funds, he couldn't bear to hurt his mother again. If she found out he'd been released from prison and hadn't come to see her, she'd never forgive him.

He straightened and forced back the dread threatening to swamp him. No matter what fit of rage his father decided to unleash on him, Adam would endure it for his mother's sake.

When he reached the two brick pillars and the connecting arch that defined the property's entrance, disbelief stalled Adam's feet once more. A new sign swung under the ironwork, one that made bile rise in Adam's throat.

Irish Meadows: O'Leary and Whelan Enterprises.

Ripe anger surged through Adam's veins. That gold-digging snake had actually done it. Coerced Father into making him a partner in their family business. Gilbert Whelan, the orphan boy Adam's parents had taken in, had usurped Adam's place in the family. Adam squeezed his hands into fists. If he were here right now, he'd cheerfully knock Whelan into the next pasture.

Adam continued through the entranceway, trying to quell his indignation with the words the prison chaplain had made him repeat over and over. "God grant me the wisdom to accept the past and the courage to face the future with a clean heart."

Adam took in a deep breath and slowly released it. Nothing would change the past that had cost him his freedom. But Adam *did* have the power to change his future. And letting go of old resentments would be the first step toward achieving that goal.

As he got closer to the house, his palms grew damp. In truth, he personified the prodigal son, returning home to beg a lowly position on his father's farm. If Adam had to shovel out stalls, or feed the beasts, or even sleep in the barn, then that's what he'd do. Anything to earn back his mother's trust and respect. He couldn't bear to think of the pain his actions had caused the one person who had loved Adam unconditionally his whole life.

Yet right at this moment, Adam's courage faltered. If he could be sure of catching Mama alone, he'd march right through the front door. But the thought of his father's perpetual scowl had Adam wanting to put off that encounter a while longer.

The warm sun heated his back through his jacket as he bypassed the house and headed straight to the gleaming white fence that surrounded acres of meadows to the east and defined the oval racetrack in the center. The soil had been freshly tilled, most likely by head trainer Sam Turnbull, who loved to rise with the dawn and groom the track each morning.

With grim determination, Adam averted his gaze to keep from seeing the willow that shaded the far pond — a horrible reminder of the unspeakable tragedy that had further fragmented his fragile relationship with his father.

The thunder of horses' hooves over the soft earth brought his attention back to the track. Thankfully, the trainer raced by without a glance in Adam's direction. Maybe it was a leftover habit from prison, where staying anonymous had become a matter of survival, but Adam automatically kept to the shadow of a maple tree and wound his way to the far barn — his haven as a boy.

The smell of wood shavings and hay uncurled the knot of tension in Adam's stomach. He inhaled deeply, breathing in comfort from the past. When his eyes adjusted to the dim interior, he made his way past the stall doors. At this time of day, all the work horses would either be out plowing the far fields where his father grew hay to feed the livestock or grazing in the west meadow. Adam walked past Sam's quarters to the small room that contained the workbench.

A lump of emotion jammed Adam's throat. Nothing had changed since he'd left. The same well-used tools sat neatly to one side on the scarred tabletop. Adam ran his fingers lovingly over a piece of wood Sam was in the process of sanding. How many years had it been since Adam had created a new piece of furniture? Or refinished an old one? He hadn't indulged his passion for woodworking since before he'd left Irish Meadows. Before he'd gotten sucked into the mire of the criminal world.

He picked up a few woodchips from the table and sifted them through his fingers.

"So you've come home at last." The gruff voice of Sam Turnbull sounded in the doorway behind Adam.

Adam dropped the chips and turned to face the man who had been both mentor and surrogate father to him.

"Hello, Sam. It's been a long time." Unsure of the welcome he'd receive, Adam wiped the sawdust from his palms and waited.

"That it has, son." Sam moved forward and, without hesitation, clasped Adam in a tight embrace.

Adam inhaled the familiar scent of wood shavings and horseflesh, unable to remember the last time anyone had hugged him.

Sam cleared his throat and stepped back. "When did you get home?"

Adam quelled the urge to laugh. Sam made it sound as though Adam had been away on an exotic trip instead of locked

41

away in the bowels of the earth. Adam met Sam's quiet gaze. "This morning. Took the first train I could get."

"How'd they treat you in there?"

"Well enough."

Sam scratched his graying goatee. "Look, Adam. I'm sorry I never came to visit. . . ." He broke off.

"It's okay, Sam. I didn't expect anyone to."

Sam released a breath. "Your mother will have Mrs. Harrison cooking a feast for you." He squinted. "Does she know you're home?"

"Not yet. I couldn't face them right away." Adam ran a hand over his unruly hair.

"I imagine you could use a hot bath and a clean set of clothes."

"I could."

"As far as I know, everyone's out for the day. Why don't you go in and freshen up before you see them?"

A wave of relief slid through Adam. "I think I'll do that." It would be easier to face his father feeling more like his old self, instead of a vagrant.

Sam laid a hand on Adam's shoulder and walked with him through the barn.

At the main doorway, Adam hesitated, then forced himself to ask the question he must. "Do you know if my father needs any help in the stables?"

Sympathy swam in Sam's brown eyes. "You'd have to ask Gilbert. He's in charge of the hiring now."

Of course he is. The irony hit like a sucker punch to his gut. Was this more of God's punishment? Having not only to let go of his anger toward Gil, but to grovel at his nemesis's feet for a lowly position on the farm he'd always hated? Adam forced himself to remember the cold, steel bars that had caged him within the dank prison walls. At Irish Meadows, at least he'd have open air, green grass, and blue skies. If it meant prostrating himself, then so be it.

Adam managed a tight smile for his old friend. "I'll talk to Gil later."

"It's great to have you back, son."

Adam nodded and swallowed the ball of dust in his throat as he headed out the door.

If only his father would share that same sentiment.

3

Adam finished dressing, praying no one would discover him here in his old room. The maids, per their usual schedule, were busy elsewhere at this time of day, and as expected, when his family members had returned home from their day's activities, they had gone directly to the parlor to await the summons for dinner.

Standing before the mirror, Adam adjusted the cuffs of his jacket and studied his reflection. A bath and a quick trim of his auburn hair and beard, as well as a clean set of clothes, had rendered him almost presentable. Nevertheless, unrelenting nerves pitched in his stomach. How would his family react to his homecoming? Mama would certainly be overjoyed — as would his younger siblings. Adam only prayed their happiness would temper his father's reaction.

He pulled out his pocket watch and

checked the time. Dinner would be served any minute. Adam squared his shoulders, and with one last fond glance around the familiar bedroom, which his mother had kept exactly the same as before he'd left, he closed the door and headed downstairs to greet his family.

The sound of animated voices met Adam's ears as he neared the bottom of the main staircase. He paused a moment to drink in the elegance of the house — the mahogany banister, the large chandelier overhead, and the marble entryway. Growing up, he'd taken this luxury for granted, but now that he'd experienced cement-block walls and iron bars, his home seemed like a king's palace.

His father's booming laugh rang out into the hallway. Adam cringed, imagining how the man's good humor was about to change.

Halting at the parlor door, Adam peered into the room and simply stared. His father sat in his favorite armchair by the fireplace, newspaper raised in front of his face. Adam's youngest siblings, Deirdre and Connor, sat on the sofa on either side of his mother.

Adam's chest constricted as he took in the silver threads now winding through her fading auburn locks. Tiny lines bracketed her eyes and mouth, further indications of the passing years. A twinge of guilt pushed at his conscience, knowing the pain he'd caused her, which in all likelihood had added to those lines. If it took the rest of his life, he'd make it up to her — one way or another.

Steeling himself, Adam entered the parlor.

"I hope I'm not late for dinner." He added as much false gaiety to his tone as he could muster and pasted a weak attempt at a smile on his face.

For several seconds the room stilled, and four pairs of eyes turned to him. His father's newspaper fluttered to the floor while his mother gasped. Instant tears flooded her eyes.

"Adam! You're home." Deirdre was the first to recover, and in her usual boisterous fashion, she ran to throw her arms around him. Poised on the brink of adolescence, she still wore her reddish hair in braids that hung over her shoulders.

"Hi, Dee-Dee." He lifted her slight frame off the rug and gave in to the pleasure of returning her embrace. "How's my girl? You've gotten so tall since I last saw you."

"You've gotten skinnier." She frowned at him.

"Didn't much like the food where I was

staying." Though Adam kept his attention on his sister, he grew increasingly aware of his father's stiff posture and his mother moving toward him. Connor hung back, as though unsure how to react.

Adam set Deirdre on her feet to focus on his mother, a storm of emotion rioting through him. "Mama. It's good to see you," he managed to get out.

"My boy is home." Tears dampening her cheeks, Mama grabbed him for a hard hug. Her frame shuddered as she wept in his arms. "We've missed you so much."

Adam's chest ached. "I've missed you, too." His thoughts flew to the one time she'd come to visit him in prison, against his father's express orders. Seeing his upright mother in that hovel of a place had broken something in Adam. He'd vowed then and there that if he ever got out, he would make something of his life so she would never again have to witness him in a state of such degradation.

Mama stepped back and wiped her face with a handkerchief. "Why didn't you let us know you were coming? We'd have prepared your favorite meal. Made sure your room was ready."

"I'm sorry. It all came about so fast, and there wasn't time. Besides, I didn't want

47

anyone making a fuss." He smiled at her, ever his greatest defender.

Connor came forward, now a lanky teen with the family's trademark auburn hair. The boy shook his hand. "Welcome home, Adam."

So serious for a fifteen-year-old. "Thank you, Connor. You've grown, as well. Almost as tall as me now. Though I still may be able to best you at arm wrestling."

The boy's mouth tugged upward. "I don't know about that. I've beaten Gil a few times." His smile faded, as though he suddenly remembered Adam's strained relationship with Gil.

With considerable effort, Adam kept his expression pleasant, ready to make the first effort at burying the hatchet. "I'm glad to hear Gil's been keeping you in line."

At last, Adam focused his attention on his father, who now stood by the fireplace. His stony countenance did not inspire optimism. It seemed it would be up to Adam to make the first move.

"Hello, Father. You're looking well."

"Can't say the same for you. I guess prison will do that to a man."

Adam ignored his mother's harsh intake of air. "Yes, sir. It will." He swallowed and shoved his hands into his pants pockets. "If it's not too presumptuous, I'd like to join the family for dinner, and afterward, I hoped we might talk — in private."

The man's expression did not change, save for the tick in his jaw. Adam sensed his mother nervously awaiting her husband's decision.

"Very well." Father bent to retrieve the discarded newspaper and laid it on the coffee table. He straightened, directing his gaze at Mama. "Kathleen, do we know if Gilbert is joining us for dinner tonight?"

"I believe so, unless he's told Mrs. Harrison otherwise."

Adam looked around, suddenly realizing his other sister was missing. "What about Bree?"

Mama smiled. "She's at college for another week."

Footsteps echoed on the hall tiles, and Gilbert rushed through the door. "Sorry I'm late. Hope I haven't kept everyone waiting." He froze when he spied Adam. "Adam. This is a surprise."

Adam took in the expensive cut of Gil's jacket, along with the glitter of gold cufflinks, and fought back a bitter flare of resentment. *This should have been my life. He stole it from me.* "Hello, Whelan."

The use of Gil's surname, which as a child

had always rankled him, still found its mark. Gil's jaw tightened. "I didn't realize you were being released so soon."

"Good behavior does have its rewards."

An uncomfortable silence filled the room. Mama cleared her throat and looped her arm through Adam's. "Come, let's adjourn to the dining room. I'm sure dinner will be served any moment."

Adam allowed Mama to lead him down the hallway to the dining room, mentally preparing to swallow a large piece of humble pie for dessert if it meant he could stay.

The children's ward at Bellevue Hospital rang with laughter, a sound that warmed Aurora Hastings to the core. For a few brief moments during her visits here, these children could forget their pain and enjoy a little fun. Aurora loved her volunteer duties at the hospital almost as much as the hours she spent helping at St. Rita's orphanage. The more time she spent with these misfortunate little ones, the more she became convinced that nursing was the career she was born for. The path God intended for her life.

Aurora continued reading the story, making sure to exaggerate her facial expressions and keep the tale entertaining. When she closed the book at the end, a collective groan went up from the children.

"Can we have one more story, Miss Hastings? Please?"

She'd learned when to end the sessions, knowing the children would always beg for more, but that too much would exhaust them. "I'm afraid not. But I'll be back soon, and I'll have a new book next time."

She made her good-bye rounds, hugging each child, trying to make them feel special, if only for a moment. Then she waved and let herself out of the ward into the main corridor. With a sigh, she leaned against the wall, allowing the pinch around her heart to recede. It always took a few minutes to shrug off the sadness that clung to her after seeing the little ones in pain, alone in their beds. How she wished she could take them on an outing to the park or on a picnic. But she lacked the authority and the means to make that dream a reality.

"Miss Hastings."

The male voice halted her inner musings. She turned to see Dr. Reardon coming toward her, and a rush of pleasure filled her.

For the past several months, Dr. Reardon had been acting as a mentor of sorts, allowing her to observe the nurses interacting with his patients in order to determine if

Aurora herself might make a good nurse. If all continued according to plan, she hoped to apply to Bellevue's nursing program in the fall, and Dr. Reardon's recommendation would add considerable weight to her application.

Philip Reardon stopped beside her, his cheeks slightly flushed. "I'm glad I caught you before you left."

Aurora gave him a welcoming smile. "What can I do for you, Doctor?"

"I have an interesting case on the second floor. I thought you might like to observe the treatment we're trying." He seemed a bit nervous, fiddling with the stethoscope looped around his neck over his white coat.

"I'd like that very much." She shifted the books in her arms, noticing again what an attractive man he was.

He wore his brown hair short and sported a neatly trimmed mustache. His eyes, the color of milk chocolate, exuded warmth and compassion, some of the traits she most admired.

Philip Reardon was a man her father would approve of as a suitor. A man dedicated to his profession. A man, Aurora had to admit, she was beginning to see as more than just a mentor.

"Wonderful. Are you ready now?"

"Yes. I've just finished with the children. I can spare a few more minutes before I head home."

Dr. Reardon's beaming countenance hinted at more than just a professional courtesy. Could Philip be forming a different type of admiration for her? Though not an unpleasant notion, Aurora found herself hesitant to start something that might damage their working relationship. At present, she needed Philip far more as a supporter than a suitor.

She fell into step with him, and they headed toward the stairs.

"So, have you told your parents about your plans to enter the nursing program?" he asked as they reached the second floor.

A band of tension cinched her neck. "I'm afraid I haven't been brave enough yet." She glanced over at him. "I'd rather face a thousand infectious diseases than make Papa angry."

Dr. Reardon only chuckled. "I understand. Your father is rather intimidating."

"To say the least."

He shot her a sideways glance. "I would think that you'd want to apprise him of your plans. If he sees how serious you are about your career, he might stop nagging you to find a husband."

"Either that or he'll double his efforts to pair me with someone," Aurora replied. "You're right, though. I will have to tell him one day soon."

Dr. Reardon stopped outside of a private room and turned to face her. "If it's not too presumptuous, I would be happy to speak to your father. Perhaps if I explained what a fine nurse you'd make, he might see your desired career in a more favorable light."

Aurora hesitated. It would be so easy to accept his assistance. But she needed to handle her father in her own way. "I appreciate the offer, and maybe at some point I will take you up on it. But I'm a grown woman, and I need to learn to deal with Papa as an adult." She gave a light laugh. "The first of many battles I will face in my career."

A glint of respect glowed in the doctor's eyes. "I have a feeling you will do just fine, Miss Hastings."

A telltale warmth crept through her cheeks as she basked in his approval. Having a man admire her for her talents was a refreshing change. Most men saw her only as the beautiful heiress to the vast Hastings fortune, not the least concerned with Aurora's opinions or her intellect.

The image of Gilbert Whelan flashed

through her mind, and with it the usual pang of regret. After Gilbert's betrayal and the ugly ending to their engagement, Aurora had sworn off romance and marriage altogether. Now, three years later, the pain had receded to a tolerable level, but she would never forget the harsh lesson she had learned at his hand.

Dr. Reardon opened the door and ushered her into the patient's room. Aurora had no doubt that Philip's interest in her had nothing to do with her father or her family's financial status. She and Philip shared a bond of mutual respect and a common interest in healing the sick — a solid basis for a lasting relationship.

Still, for now, she'd bide her time. Keep any budding feelings in check until she had her recommendation and a guaranteed acceptance to Bellevue's nursing program.

Maybe then, with her future secure, she'd be willing to open her heart to the possibility of romance.

His father's study hadn't changed in the three years since Adam had been here. Each book, each racing trophy, the neat stack of papers on the corner of his father's desk — all could have been frozen in time. Adam inhaled the familiar scent of his father's after-dinner pipe and braced against the bittersweet wave of nostalgia. As a boy, he would sneak into the study to sit in Father's chair and dream of being grown up enough to smoke a pipe with him.

"Brandy?" His father held up the crystal decanter, one eyebrow raised.

Was that a question or a dare?

"No, thank you." Adam took a seat on the wing chair near the hearth and adjusted his jacket. He still wasn't used to this restrictive clothing. Prison garments hung like gunny sacks on most of the inmates.

In the two minutes it took his father to pour himself a drink, Adam rehearsed the little speech he'd prepared. Father lowered his hefty frame onto the chair opposite him and took a long swallow of the amber liquid.

Adam cleared his throat. "For the record, I would like to formally apologize for any embarrassment I caused our family. I will forever regret the disgrace I've inflicted on the O'Leary name." He bent his head over his knees and stared into the flames that danced in the fireplace. "I know I don't deserve a second chance, but I'm here to throw myself on your mercy."

His father did not speak or move a muscle.

Adam's veil of courage slipped a notch. Still he soldiered on. "Since I am in need of a job, I hoped you could use another stable hand. I'm willing to start at the bottom. Do whatever it takes to earn my way back into the family's good graces."

His father drew deeply on his pipe and blew out a stream of smoke. His blue eyes shone as cold and slick as marble. "Do you have any idea how I felt when I found out what you'd done? That you'd provided inside information about my clients' horses to gangsters?" His eyes narrowed. "How could you betray me like that?"

Adam hung his head, wishing he had an explanation, yet even he didn't completely understand his actions. "Part of it, I'll admit, was jealousy over Gil. The college graduate come back to share his intelligence with us lowly peasants. As though he were the salvation of Irish Meadows." The bitterness tasted sour on his tongue.

You must let go of your resentment. His mentor's words rang in his head.

Father slowly lowered the pipe. "Why have you always hated Gilbert? What has he ever done to you?"

Was he blind? Or simply unaware that he'd treated his ward like the golden boy who could do no wrong?

Adam shook his head. "Hate is not the word I'd use. Resent, maybe."

His father slammed his palm down on the arm of his chair. "If you'd shown the least bit of interest in the business —" He squeezed his eyes shut in an obvious attempt to control his anger. "I promised your mother I wouldn't fight with you, and I plan to keep that promise." He got up and walked to the window. "Since Gilbert is an equal partner now, I need to discuss this with him. If he agrees, you can start in the barn — on a trial basis."

Adam mentally railed at the irony that Whelan now held the key to Adam's future. No employer would hire a man fresh out of prison, and Adam needed a way to earn money if he were ever to save enough to start his own business.

One step at a time . . .

He rose and walked to the desk. "Thank you. You won't regret it, I promise."

His father turned from the window to pin him with a hard stare. "You've caused your mother more grief than I ever wanted to see her go through, especially after losing Danny . . ." His accusing gaze made Adam want to squirm. "Don't give her reason to shed one more tear."

Adam's heart squeezed with guilt. "I won't."

"I think for now it would be best if you

58

slept in the barn. I don't want Connor and Deirdre influenced in any negative way. Especially Connor. He's at a critical age right now."

A flash of the old antagonism surged through Adam's veins, and he fought to supress it. To ignore the sting of being deemed unworthy to share the family home. He swallowed his pride, thinking sadly of his comfortable bed upstairs, and moved toward the door.

"Oh, and Adam? Next weekend marks Brianna's graduation from Barnard College. Your mother is planning a big celebration. It would be better for everyone if you remained out of sight. We don't want Brianna's accomplishments overshadowed by your rather untimely return."

Raw anger pasted Adam's mouth shut. With a curt incline of his head, he strode out of the room, using all his willpower not to slam the door behind him.

Aurora approached the large Simmons estate, thankful that the suffrage meeting was being held at Mrs. Simmons's tonight, since it was only blocks from the hospital. Aurora could easily walk without having to involve the family chauffeur in her clandestine outing.

Aurora knocked on the ornate wooden door and went over her plan for the evening, firming her resolve not to let some of the more vocal women get to her. She was here to find out about the latest developments in the suffrage movement, and if that meant putting up with idle gossip, then she would simply ignore the loose tongues of the ladies present. Aurora wished to possibly learn of larger meetings in the area, where career women met to support one another, hoping she might join a group of like-minded women.

The housekeeper answered her knock. "Good evening, Miss Hastings. Please come in."

"Thank you." Aurora removed her wrap and handed it to the woman, who then showed Aurora to the parlor.

Plump Mrs. Simmons sat perched on her Queen Anne chair, holding court among the other women who regularly met to discuss women's rights.

"Good evening, Aurora. So glad you could join us." Mrs. Simmons beamed a smile that brightened her features and caused her chin to jiggle.

"Thank you. It's good to be here." Aurora crossed the plush carpet to sit on one of the available chairs, taking in the faces around the room.

"We have a guest with us tonight," Mrs. Simmons announced. "Colleen's sister-in-law, Maggie Montgomery, is visiting from Ireland. Welcome, Maggie."

The young woman smiled. "Thank you, Mrs. Simmons. You've all made me feel most welcome."

The charm of her accent intrigued Aurora. Too bad Maggie was related by marriage to the O'Learys. Ever since Colleen's sister Brianna had stolen the affections of Gilbert Whelan, the whole O'Leary clan left a bitter taste in Aurora's mouth. One she was still trying hard to put behind her.

"Are you feeling well, Aurora dear? You look pale."

Aurora straightened her spine against the back of her chair. "I'm fine, thank you."

"You haven't picked up some dreaded disease volunteering at that hospital, have you? Your dear mother and I have both warned you —"

"I am perfectly well, I assure you." Aurora managed a wide smile, which she hoped would convince the others of her well-being.

"Very good. Let's get started." Mrs. Simmons pulled a sheet of paper from the side table and adjusted her reading glasses on the tip of her nose. "The first order of business is a piece of good news. The National Federation of Women's Clubs has voted to formally endorse the suffrage campaign."

A murmur went around the room.

"The backing of this well-respected group can only mean good things for the suffrage movement. The vote for women in New York is getting closer than ever."

Aurora's pulse jumped. This was indeed good news. She made a mental note to learn more about this federation.

One of the women, Mrs. Pinkerton, crossed her arms over her ample bosom. "I, for one, will be glad when we can meet without fear of censure, not only from men, but from other women, as well. How can they not be behind women's rights?"

Mrs. Simmons raised an eyebrow. "As widows, my dear Harriet, we are fortunate not to have to submit to a husband's demands. Many others, such as Aurora, must defer to the head of the household."

"Yes, indeed." Mrs. Pinkerton leaned forward. "We are all aware of Arthur Hastings's view on a woman's place in society, as I'm sure Aurora can attest."

All heads turned toward Aurora, and she fought the urge to sink into the floor. As much as she supported the movement, Aurora abhorred being made a living example of the need for women's freedom.

"Hasn't your father's primary goal been to marry you off as soon as possible — despite the humiliation of Gilbert Whelan's rejection?" Mrs. Pinkerton's cheeks puffed out. "I still can't believe he threw you over for that rather plain O'Leary girl —"

Colleen Montgomery flew to her feet, cheeks crimson. "May I remind you that the 'O'Leary girl' you're speaking of is my sister, and that Gil is soon to be my brother-in-law?"

Mrs. Pinkerton's mouth flapped open.

Colleen strode to the middle of the room. "Please accept my apologies, Mrs. Simmons, but I feel the need for some fresh air."

Maggie rose, as well, a confused expression on her face. "Lovely to meet you all." She gave a half curtsy, then followed Colleen into the hallway.

With all eyes trained on Aurora, the room became too suffocating to bear. The last thing she wanted to think about was her failed betrothal to Gil. And Aurora doubted she'd learn anything of further value this evening. She pushed to her feet. "I'm afraid I must leave, too, Mrs. Simmons. I do hope you'll invite me to the next meeting."

Mrs. Simmons followed her out into the

hallway. "I'm so sorry, my dear. I will speak with Mrs. Pinkerton and make sure she learns to curb her tongue. I'll also send my apologies to Colleen and Miss Montgomery." Mrs. Simmons shook her head as she handed Aurora her wrap.

Despite the beginning of a headache, Aurora attempted a smile. "It's not your fault. When I see Colleen next, I'll make sure she understands that."

"Thank you, dear girl. You really are a gem."

Aurora entered her Manhattan family home, removed her hat and wrap, and handed them to the butler.

"Is there anything else you need, miss?" Denby stood in the foyer, awaiting dismissal.

"No, thank you, Denby. I believe I'll ask Mrs. Forrester for some tea before retiring."

"Very good, miss." He bowed and moved silently down the hallway.

Ten minutes later, seated in the parlor with a steaming cup of tea, Aurora breathed a quiet sigh, grateful that the worst of her headache had faded. Moments later, she heard the front door open and the voices of her parents echoing in the entryway. She looked up as they entered the room.

Her mother's pleased expression held a

hint of surprise. "Aurora dear, you're up late this evening."

Aurora set her cup in the china saucer. "I got in not long ago."

Her father moved to the sideboard, where he uncapped the crystal decanter of brandy. "Wasting your time at that hospital again, I presume." He poured the liquid into a glass.

Aurora straightened her back against the cushions of the settee. "I don't consider volunteering with the children a waste of time, Papa. On the contrary, I find it to be rewarding for everyone involved."

Papa shot her a disapproving look and merely grunted.

Aurora turned to her mother, who took a seat beside her. "How was your day, Mama?" She could always count on Mama to diffuse an awkward conversation.

Her mother smiled, creating a smattering of lines around her eyes. "I had lunch with Agnes Barnes and spent the afternoon in the garden. A very pleasant day."

Papa lowered his substantial frame into his favorite armchair and set his glass on the side table. "I had an interesting day." He paused. "James O'Leary came into the bank to see me."

Aurora froze, her hand suspended in mid-air. Except for Colleen, whom she saw at

65

the orphanage and at suffrage meetings, Aurora avoided the O'Learys like a contagion.

"How are James and Kathleen?" The regret in Mama's voice caused Aurora a slight twinge of guilt. Aurora knew Mama missed her friendship with Mrs. O'Leary, and that she had distanced herself out of deference to Aurora.

"They are both well." Papa paused. "James invited us to a party . . . at Irish Meadows."

Shock raced through Aurora's system, causing her hand to tremble on the teacup. "That man has some nerve after what he did to us." Even after all this time, the memory haunted Aurora. Out of a misguided sense of loyalty, Gilbert had gone along with James O'Leary's scheme to woo Aurora in order to obtain Papa's favor for a bank loan, yet in the end, Gil's conscience had won out and he had broken their engagement. Aurora's feelings had been crushed, but in truth her pride had taken a worse beating. "Please tell me you turned him down."

Papa cleared his throat and cast a glance at Mama. "On the contrary, daughter. I accepted the invitation on behalf of all of us."

Aurora's mouth fell open, and she set down her cup with a rattle. Papa hadn't associated with James O'Leary since the whole betrothal debacle, so why would he consider going to Irish Meadows now?

"Surely you agree with me, Mama?" Aurora looked to her mother for support, but Mama merely shrugged.

"It's up to your father, dear."

Papa lifted his glass. "James and Gilbert have both apologized more than once for that unfortunate episode. Time and distance have allowed me to put the incident aside. I hope you are mature enough to do the same."

Under her father's intense scrutiny, Aurora dared not let her dismay show. Refusing to attend would only make her father more insistent that she go. She shifted on her seat and held her tongue.

"James's daughter is graduating from college, and they are throwing a big celebration in her honor."

Aurora's stomach dropped. In addition to facing Gil again, seeing Brianna O'Leary would be sheer torture. She may have forgiven Gil for his part in the plan, but to expect her to attend a celebration for the woman who had stolen Gil's affections was too much. "Papa, if you wish to attend, that is your prerogative. But I will not pretend, in front of Gil and the whole O'Leary clan, to be happy for —"

Her father's scowl, along with the downward droop of his handlebar mustache, put a halt to Aurora's tirade.

"The O'Learys are a prominent family in the community — one we cannot afford to ignore." He glanced over at her mother, who remained silent. "There will be many influential people in attendance, including, I'm sure, a fine selection of eligible young men. You *will* join us next Saturday."

Aurora bit back a bubble of indignation. *I don't care about eligible men,* she wanted to shout.

But good breeding and manners would not allow her to disrespect her father in such a fashion. She swallowed her outrage and lowered her gaze to the floral carpet. "Very well, Papa, I will go, but I can't promise anything more than that."

4

Gabe followed Rylan into the heart of the 42nd Street fire station and fought to keep his jaw from dropping at the sheer size of the space. In the main bay, several men polished the gleaming chrome on two fire trucks. Rows of hooks housed helmets, overcoats, and other firefighting gear. Large boots sat underneath a bench in neat formation, ready for wear at a moment's notice. It was obvious the captain of this crew ran an organized ship. If only Gabe could find a way to spend some time here, he could learn how an American fire station operated.

"Rylan! What brings you here on this fine morning?" The loud male voice boomed out over the bustle of the room. A burly man strode toward them, grinning at Gabe's brother.

"Good morning, Oliver." Rylan moved to shake the large man's hand. "I'd like you to meet my brother, Gabriel, visiting from home. Gabe, this is Chief Oliver Wither-spoon."

His bushy brows rose. "Home? As in Ire-land?"

"Aye." Gabe tried not to wince as the chief gripped his hand and pumped hard.

The big man's eyes actually misted over. "Ah, I miss home something fierce. Twenty years I've been here, but I can still smell the green grass on a rainy day."

"I know the scent well."

"Gabe is a firefighter back home. He asked if I could arrange a tour of the station while he's here."

"For a fellow countryman? I'd be hon-ored."

Rylan stayed for the first few minutes of the tour, but once Chief Witherspoon headed to the firemen's quarters above the slick brass poles, Rylan bid them good-bye. Gabe, already feeling right at home with the friendly Irishman, was pleased to stay longer and view every last nook and cranny of the station.

As the tour came to an end, they passed a large portrait of a serious-looking gent sporting a large mustache and dressed in a well-cut suit and bowler hat. With the picture claiming an obvious place of promi-nence, Gabe wondered what connection this man had to firefighting.

"That's Arthur Hastings." Chief Wither-spoon answered his unspoken question. "He owns the Hastings Bank and Loan. Arthur donated enough to get us our first motor-ized engine." He jabbed a finger toward one of the vehicles.

Gabe whistled. "She's a beauty. I'd love to have the chance to ride on her while I'm here." He clamped his lips shut, realizing how presumptuous he'd sounded.

Chief Witherspoon laughed. "All the men fought to see who'd be the first to ride her. I'm sure one of them will be happy to take you out for a demonstration one day."

Over a cup of coffee, the two discussed fire-dousing techniques, hoses, and prob-lems with water pressure. Gabe learned of the difficulties the department faced servic-ing the tall buildings in the city, since the ladders often weren't able to reach higher than the sixth story.

Over their second cup of coffee — a remarkably palatable beverage for a fire sta-tion — the conversation turned to Ireland.

"Is it true what I've been hearing?" the chief asked. "That civil war is brewing back home?"

Gabe's stomach clenched at the reminder of what he was missing. The fact that the unrest might have heated up even further in his absence, that he might not be there to join in the fighting, ate at Gabe's peace of mind. "It's true. To be honest, it's why I hated to leave. If there's a war, I want to be the first to sign up to fight for my homeland."

Gabe expected the man to heartily agree with him; however, the chief's ruddy cheeks sagged. "I guess I've been away too long. My wish is simply for peace. The only family I have left is a brother, who's happy to stay on his farm and not take sides in the cause."

"There'll be no peace until the English are out of Ireland." Gabe pressed his lips into a grim line to keep from further comment. He'd learned to be cautious about sharing his political views.

Chief Witherspoon rose from his chair. "Well, let's hope the problems will all die down and life can go on in peace."

Gabe bit back a retort. Peace could never be if things were left to die down. Not with the English holding all the power. But he held his tongue and swallowed the last dregs of coffee, summoning the courage to ask the question he'd been holding back since he'd first stepped through the double doors. "Chief, I don't suppose you'd be needing any help at the moment?"

A wide grin split Chief Witherspoon's weathered face. "A man with your experience? We'd never turn down that kind of expertise. And when there's no fire to fight, we'll have you buffing engines or polishing boots."

Gabe pushed to his feet on a giddy rush. Anything to keep occupied and help speed along the time away from home. He shook Chief Witherspoon's hand. "I'd gladly do any chores you have for me. After seven days on a boat, I'm itching to get to work."

The chief's eyes twinkled. "I hear you, lad. Not to worry, we won't let you sit idle. See you bright and early tomorrow, then."

Maggie craned her neck to stare up at the high spires of St. Patrick's Cathedral, which towered over the other nearby buildings on Fifth Avenue. Never in her life had she seen such a magnificent example of architecture. She could scarcely imagine what the interior might look like.

A stiff breeze whipped Maggie's skirts around her ankles, urging her to action. Today she would take concrete measures toward carving out her future here in America. She'd told Rylan and Colleen she wanted to do some sightseeing on her own, and she'd had to fight a prickly battle with her brother to let her go. Thank goodness he'd promised to take Gabe to the fire station or he would have insisted on accompanying her. The fact that her main destination was the cathedral had finally made Rylan relent.

Taking a breath to combat the flutter of nerves in her stomach, Maggie crossed the street and climbed the cathedral's steps. The sculpted-brass doors opened easily under her hand. On reverent feet, she moved into the sacred space, the vastness of the interior causing her jaw to drop. Massive columns lined the aisles all the way to the front altar. Her tiny church at home could fit in one alcove of this mighty worship area.

She exhaled softly, moving over the gleaming floors to the center of the church. Vaulted ceilings and ornate carvings captured her attention, but still she didn't see the item she sought. Grateful to note that a mere handful of people dotted the pews, she turned in a slow circle and looked up toward the rear balcony. Her heart leapt in her chest. The telltale cylinders of the pipe organ rose straight to the ceiling. She had to get nearer, to run her fingers over the beautiful instrument.

Fighting the urge to dash to the back in

search of a staircase, Maggie paused to admire the statues and paintings, as well as the amazing stained-glass windows along the outer walls. At last, she made her way to the rear vestibule, where she found a small door, behind which rose a narrow, circular staircase. With breathless anticipation, she climbed the curved steps to the upper balcony. There, alone and unguarded, sat the magnificent organ.

Maggie clasped her hands together and moved slowly toward her target. It was ever so much larger than the one she'd learned on in St. Colman's Cathedral back home. What would it sound like? She ran reverent fingers over the wood and, before she could stop herself, slid onto the bench. Obviously a tall person played this instrument, for the height of the seat meant her feet barely skimmed the pedals below. Awed, she scanned the rise of immense pipes above her, and then finally, unable to resist, she ran her fingers over the keys. She startled when the full sound emerged, echoing through the space. Her heart pounded as she waited for someone to appear and scold her for touching the piece, but after several seconds with no activity, she dared play on.

A thrill of pure pleasure shot through her as her fingers worked the rows of keys. She pulled out a few of the stops, and the swell of the music filled her soul. At last, she reluctantly slowed to a halt on a sigh of delight.

"I wondered who was playing my organ."

Maggie swiveled on the bench to find a man watching her, arms crossed over his chest. She swallowed and got slowly to her feet. "I couldn't resist trying the keys. It's so much grander than anything I've ever played on."

He stepped closer, and the slight lift of his lips helped her relax.

"Not a problem, my dear. My name is Frederick Unger. I'm the organist here. And who might you be?" The man's English was flawless save for a hint of a European accent.

"I'm Maggie Montgomery, visiting from Ireland." She gave a shy smile. "I've missed playing since I left home."

He came closer still, and she saw his hair contained a great deal of gray, his eyes a merry twinkle. "Do you play for your church?"

She shook her head. "Our parish is far too small to warrant an organ. But sometimes when I'm in the city, I play the one in the cathedral. The organist at St. Colman's taught me a few bits and pieces, and the rest I learned on my own. It wasn't much different from the piano."

One gray brow rose. "I'd say there's a huge difference. You must have an innate musical ability to pick up the organ like that."

Her laugh echoed in the cavernous space. "So my mum always tells me." She moved toward the exit, and Mr. Unger fell in beside her.

She snuck a sideways glance at the man. "I was hoping to speak to someone about possible employment. Would you happen to know if any churches in the area might be in need of an organist?" The thumping of her heart belied the casual inquiry.

"Are you looking for work here in New York?"

She paused at the top of the stairs. "I am. I'd love to stay in America, but to do so I'd need a job."

He regarded her thoughtfully. "I don't know of anything at the moment. Where could I reach you if I hear of something?"

She bit her bottom lip. Rylan would have her head on a platter if he knew she was talking to a strange man, let alone telling him where she was staying. But her instincts told her Mr. Unger was a God-fearing gentleman. "You could contact my brother,

Rylan Montgomery, at St. Rita's Orphan Asylum. He's the director there and can get a message to me."

Mr. Unger held out his hand. "It was lovely to meet you, Miss Montgomery. Perhaps we'll see each other again."

She shook his hand, calloused from constant practice at the keys, no doubt. "Thank you, Mr. Unger. It was a pleasure indeed to play your organ. I hope I get the chance to do so again."

Instead of going right back to Rylan's, Maggie's elation carried her farther up Fifth Avenue to the entrance of Central Park. The sight of some familiar greenery for the first time since leaving Cork drew her in, yet at the same time caused a clutch of homesickness that tightened her throat muscles. She hadn't realized how much she'd missed the smell of grass and the sounds of nature. Mum's garden would be in full bloom right now, and every morning she'd be out tending it. All alone. Without Maggie's help.

She pushed aside the brief tug of melancholy and turned her focus to the beauty that surrounded her, strolling down the maze of paths until she came to a bench in a more secluded area. She sat down, content to breathe in the comforting scents of grass and budding roses while the sun warmed her face. Overhead, a pair of sparrows darted in and out of the branches, almost as though playing hide-and-seek.

"Hello, Maggie."

For a moment, she thought her visions of home had conjured up the familiar voice. She turned her head slowly, her heart beginning a slow chug in her chest.

The very man she'd come to America to avoid stood on the walkway before her. Instead of his usual simple shirt and trousers, he wore what looked like an expensive suit and tie. His hazel eyes, reddish-brown hair, and the distinct scar on his chin were the only features that made him still recognizable.

A million thoughts swirled through her muddled mind as she rose from the bench. "Neill? What in heaven's name are you doing here?"

He took a tentative step forward. "I came to find you."

"Whatever for? I thought I made myself plain enough the last time we talked."

He gestured toward the bench. "Could we sit for a minute so I can explain?"

Maggie could only nod as she sat back down. Never would she have believed that Neill would leave their town. He'd ridiculed her desire to travel and see other parts of the world, saying she was a dreamer and needed to learn to live in the real world. Yet here he was. She clasped her trembling hands together on her lap and waited for him to speak.

Neill joined her on the bench. He removed his hat and fingered the brim. "I owe you an apology, Maggie, for the way I handled our . . . disagreement. I let my temper get the best of me and for that I'm truly sorry." His eyes shone with sincerity.

Maggie had no doubt he actually regretted his burst of rage and the words he'd hurled at her. He was always sorry after their fights, but it never stopped him from repeating the behavior the next time they argued.

She inclined her head. "I accept your apology, though I'm having a hard time believing you'd cross an ocean to give it."

A fierce expression animated his face. "I love you, Maggie. Can't you believe that? I've loved you for as long as I can remember, and I'm willing to do whatever it takes to prove it." He threw out his arm. "Even sail around the world."

Words of response scrambled in Maggie's brain. She'd learned the last time she'd tried to rebuff him that being blunt only served to trigger his anger.

He reached out to take one of her hands in his, caressing it with his thumb. "I didn't appreciate how much traveling meant to you. When I learned you'd gone, I decided to come here myself and share your journey with you."

Maggie couldn't bring herself to tell him that her journey didn't include returning to Ireland. She wasn't ready to reveal that to anyone just yet.

"Neill, I thank you for your apology. It means a lot that you're willing to understand my point of view."

A spark of hope lit his eyes.

"But," she continued softly, "I haven't changed my mind . . . about us."

When his jaw tensed, she braced for him to raise his voice.

But instead of shouting, he seemed to sag. "You love me, too, Maggie. I know it. If you'll just give me another chance, I'll make it up to you. I swear."

Part of her wished it could be that easy. That she could resume their engagement and continue their former plans for the future. But it had never been *her* future. Never *her* dream. The only thing that had mattered to Neill was working in his father's pub and one day taking over for him.

Maggie's teaching, her love of music — none of that mattered to him. When he'd told her she'd have to quit teaching after the wedding and work in the kitchen of the pub until the babes came along, that had been the final death knell on their relationship.

"Nothing's changed, Neill," she said firmly. "I won't give up my music or my teaching, and I certainly have no desire to work in a pub." Especially not The Jaded Shamrock, a rather bawdy place where the men harassed her any time she went in.

His eyes darkened, the first sign of his temper slipping. "A wife is supposed to support her husband and work by his side as a helpmate."

Maggie curled her fingers into the material of her skirt, inhaling to control her emotions. "What about a husband supporting his wife? Wanting her to be happy?" The sharpness of her tone split the air. All the resentment of the last few weeks in Ireland bubbled back to the surface.

He opened his mouth, then quickly clamped it shut. Yet the anger in his eyes told her everything she needed to know. Neill had not changed, not one bit. It was pride, not love, that governed his actions. His pride could not handle losing her.

"I can learn to compromise, Maggie. But you have to be willing, as well. Marriage is about give and take."

Gently but firmly, she extracted her hand. "That it is. And one day when I marry, I will be happy to compromise." She paused, shifting slightly away on the bench. "The problem is that I don't wish to marry *you.*"

Neill's eyes glazed over. A chill raced up Maggie's spine, and she jerked to her feet, clutching her handbag in front of her. She scanned the area, thankful to find a couple strolling toward them. Neill wouldn't dare unleash his temper on her in public.

Sure enough, he got to his feet, seeming to collect himself. He straightened his vest and his tie. "Well, it looks like I have my work cut out for me. But make no mistake, Maggie, I will win you back. By the time we set sail for home, you'll be mine once again."

Maggie fought for calm she didn't feel. "You're wasting your time. I've no wish to see you again."

Before he could argue further, Maggie fell in step behind the couple as they passed and followed them out of the park. She dared not look back, lest it give Neill the slightest bit of encouragement.

A chill of unease stayed with her all the

way home, leading Maggie to fear she might not be rid of Neill that easily.

5

From behind an elm tree at the side of the house, Adam watched the steady stream of cars and carriages arriving for his sister's graduation party. He couldn't deny that it hurt to be banned from the festivities. Not that he'd miss the crowds of impeccably dressed people, all fawning over one another with false niceties — but he would have liked to congratulate Brianna on her achievement. Of all his siblings, Adam had thought his tender-hearted sister would be the one to welcome him home and help ease him back into the family fold.

He stepped farther back into the shadows to ensure no one would see him. Assured of his anonymity, he continued to study a group of people alighting from a familiar car driven by Sam Turnbull. Sam often drove Father's Model T when required to chauffeur family members, and tonight was no exception.

Rylan Montgomery emerged from the rear door and held out his hand. Colleen followed, resplendent in her evening gown, and gave the man a loving smile. Regret — sharp and biting — rose through Adam's chest. As children, he and Colleen had been close — until Adam had taken a path that had destroyed his family's trust.

Another figure stepped from the car. Adam jerked to attention, every sense tuned to her presence. He recognized her immediately: the girl from the orphanage, the one the children had called Miss Montgomery. Suddenly, it all made sense. The dark hair, the Irish accent. This woman was not an employee, but a relative of Rylan's.

She straightened and ran a hand over her flared skirt. Her dark-as-midnight hair cascaded over her bare shoulders in a fall of curls. Even at this distance, her beauty stole the breath from Adam's lungs.

What would it be like to be waiting inside with his parents and be properly introduced to this fetching creature? To kiss her hand, ask her to dance, hold her in his arms?

The fantasy took hold for a moment, shimmering like a mirage just out of reach, then faded into the background. Such would never be the case. He had forfeited the right to woo a respectable woman.

His hand curled into a fist at his side. Why had he let his antagonism toward his father get so out of hand, to the point where getting back at him had been worth ruining Adam's own life? What an immature fool he'd been.

Unable to look away, Adam watched until Miss Montgomery moved out of sight toward the front entrance. Then he blew out a disgusted breath and slunk off to the shadows of the barn — back with the animals where he belonged.

The O'Learys' brick mansion was grander than any house Gabe had ever seen, from the white pillars that framed the double front doors to the crystal chandelier gracing the entranceway.

Over the years, Gabe had heard his mother speak of her distant cousin, Kathleen O'Leary, who lived in America, but never had Gabe pictured the woman living anywhere as posh as this.

From the rapt expression on Maggie's face, it appeared she was as awestruck by the grandeur as he. Gabe smiled to himself. His little sister had never looked more beautiful, her hair fashioned in an intricate sweep of curls and ribbons. Wearing the green silk dress she'd borrowed from Colleen, Maggie resembled a maiden from a fairy tale.

On the other hand, Gabe felt like a stuffed turkey, trussed up in one of Rylan's fancy suits. He'd choose to wear fire gear over the tight cravat at his neck any day. As a rule, Gabe didn't mind socializing, but he preferred a cozier spot, such as Declan's pub back home, where he knew every man, woman, and child. Not a huge room like this with close to a hundred strangers.

It occurred to him then that Maggie had been very quiet all the way into Long Island and even now seemed unusually subdued. Normally on such a grand occasion, she would have been chattering away about the elegant guests and the striking décor.

"Are you feeling unwell, Maggie? If so, I'd be happy to take you home."

She blinked up at him. "I'm fine. Why?"

"It's not like you to be so quiet."

Her glance slid away. "I've a lot on my mind, is all."

Before he could determine what sort of things might be plaguing her, Colleen came to usher them across the crowded parlor to the piano situated near a set of French doors that opened onto a terrace. A distinguished-looking man stood beside a woman whose resemblance to Colleen was unmistakable.

"Mama, Daddy." Colleen's excited voice cut through the murmur of conversation humming in the room.

The woman's features flooded with pleasure. "Colleen." She rushed forward to gather her daughter in a warm embrace, then allowed Rylan to kiss her cheek.

Rylan gestured behind him. "Kathleen and James, this is my brother Gabriel and my baby sister, Maggie."

Kathleen came forward to hug both Gabe and Maggie. "It's so wonderful to meet you." She took Maggie's face in her hands. "Why, Maggie, you look just like your dear mother at the same age. We were as close as sisters until I came to America with my family."

Maggie smiled. "I know. Mum talks about you often."

Kathleen turned her attention to Gabe. "And you, young man. You're as handsome as your brother. The same dimples, too, I see."

Gabe grinned, finding it impossible to resist her cheeriness. "A Montgomery trademark."

James O'Leary stepped forward to shake Gabe's hand. "Good to meet you, lad. Are you enjoying your visit to America so far?"

"Yes, sir. New York is a fascinating city."

Kathleen looped her hand through her husband's arm. "Gabe, I understand you're staying in Colleen and Rylan's attic room. If you'd be more comfortable here, we have more than enough space and would love to have you."

A movement across the room caught Gabe's eye. The shimmer of jewels and a flash of golden hair riveted his attention. Gabe forgot to breathe as the most beautiful girl he'd ever seen turned her head and met his gaze.

Maggie elbowed him in the side. "You didn't answer Kathleen's question."

"Ah, sorry. I got distracted by all the . . . beauty surrounding me."

Maggie gave an impolite snort.

"Thank you kindly for the offer, Kathleen, but I'm volunteering at the fire station a few blocks from Rylan's, so it's best for me to be close by."

The arrival of a smiling young woman with red hair and green eyes interrupted them. She rushed forward and threw her arms around Colleen.

Colleen returned her embrace with enthusiasm. "Congratulations, Bree. We're so proud of you."

After introductions to the guest of honor,

Maggie became engrossed in a lively conversation with Brianna and Colleen. Looking past them, Gabe scanned the room for another glimpse of the golden-haired girl he'd spied across the way.

Disappointment slid through him when he couldn't locate her. Perhaps she'd been a figment of his imagination. He shook his head to clear his foolish imaginings.

The crowd shifted, and Gabe found himself standing alone. He used the opportunity to slip out the French doors onto the stone terrace. Once outside, he inhaled the fragrant night air, scented with flowers from the garden below. Here, with room to breathe, the invisible fingers of tension began to fade away.

He crossed to the stone balustrade and stared over the grounds below. How his mother would love the multitude of flowers blooming in Kathleen's garden. He wished that she'd been well enough to make the ocean voyage with them.

Gabe pushed back thoughts of home and walked the length of the balcony, suddenly desiring a stroll among the greenery. He descended the shallow steps to the garden path and continued along the winding trail, drinking in the wonderful scents. In the dimming light of dusk, the colors appeared muted. He'd love to return in the daytime to see the blooms in all their vibrancy.

A loud crack split the silence, bringing Gabe up short.

"Take your hand off me this instant."

There was no mistaking a woman's distress. He rounded the corner to find a man and woman engaged in a struggle. The man had his hand wrapped around the girl's arm, an angry red welt marring his cheek.

The woman's back was to Gabe, leaving him unable to ascertain her facial expression. He didn't relish the idea of intruding on a lover's quarrel; nevertheless, he couldn't leave without ensuring her safety.

Seemingly oblivious of Gabe's presence, the man glared at the girl. "What did you think I intended when I invited you out here? Intellectual conversation?"

She struggled against his grip. "I took you at your word. That you wanted a stroll in the garden."

"No one could be that naïve."

Gabe stepped out of the shadows. "Excuse me. Is there a problem here?"

The man's head whipped up. "A simple misunderstanding," he snapped. "None of your concern."

Gabe turned his attention to the woman and had to fight not to gape. It was the girl he'd seen inside earlier. Her porcelain skin showcased wide, slightly fearful eyes and perfectly bowed lips. Hair of the palest yellow sat in a halo of curls around her head. Gabe swallowed in an attempt to unstick his tongue. "Are you in need of assistance, miss?"

The man dragged her along the path. "She is not."

"Yes, I am. This man is accosting me."

The note of panic in her voice aroused Gabe's protective reflexes. "You will let her go immediately."

The man stopped. "Or what?"

"Or I will make you," Gabe said calmly.

The man sneered, scanning Gabe from head to toe. "You think I'm afraid of an Irish dandy?"

With considerable effort, Gabe held on to his temper. The man was clearly trying to gain the upper hand with insults, but Gabe refused to give him the satisfaction. "You still haven't removed your hand from the lady's arm."

The man gave a low growl and lunged at Gabe, who neatly sidestepped him, sending him sprawling into a nearby bush.

Gabe moved back to the girl, who stood rubbing her arm. "Are you all right?" he asked.

"Yes, thank you." Her eyes widened. "Watch out behind you."

Gabe whirled, but not in time to avoid the man's fist, which plowed into Gabe's jaw. An explosion of pain radiated through his cheek as he reeled backward. Gabe shook his head, regained his footing, and charged forward. As much as he'd hoped to avoid a physical set-to, it seemed this oaf needed further persuasion to leave the girl alone. Thankful for his firefighter training that kept him in good condition, Gabe ducked under another attempted punch. Then, in one swift movement, he hauled the fellow over his shoulder and, spying a water fountain a few feet away, strode over to dump the lout into the shallow pool.

"Cool off in there a while, and maybe next time you'll respect a lady's wishes."

The man sputtered and thrashed in an attempt to right himself.

Gabe returned to the girl. "I'd best escort you inside before he comes after us again." He held out his arm to her.

She nodded and slipped her hand into the crook of his elbow. Together they made their way to the back terrace. At the French doors where Gabe had exited, he paused. The girl's slender hand trembled on his arm. He glanced down, trying to ascertain her emotional state.

"Do you want to go inside? Or is there someone I can get for you?" As much as Gabe wanted to be the one to help her, he realized he was a stranger to her.

She shook her head. "I can't face my father right now."

The sight of tears standing in her startling blue eyes made Gabe's stomach muscles clench. "Tell me what to do. Just please don't cry."

He pulled a handkerchief from his pocket and handed it to her. She dabbed it against her cheek and sniffed, then gestured to a bench farther down the terrace. "Could we sit for a minute? I don't think Jared will come back, now that he's drenched. He's too vain to be seen in such a state."

Gabe escorted her over to the bench. "This Jared, is he a suitor of yours?"

She took a seat, arranging her pale blue skirts around her. A frown formed tiny ridges between her brows. "No. Just a family acquaintance. Though my father would be happy if he were a suitor."

"Why is that?" Gabe couldn't imagine any father wanting a man like that for his daughter.

"Papa wishes to marry me off. He insists on introducing me to potential husbands whenever the occasion arises."

The sorrow in her tone and the slump of her shoulders made Gabe wish he could sweep away all her problems. "Why would he be needing to marry you off? I can't see how you'd have trouble finding a husband. Unless you've got an extra leg hidden under your skirt."

Her mouth gaped open. Then, just as Gabe had hoped, she threw her head back and laughed. The sound lightened his heart.

"No extra leg, I promise."

"Whew, that's good to know." He grinned at her. "My name is Gabriel Montgomery, by the way."

"Aurora Hastings."

He looked into her eyes. "Aurora. A fitting name for one who lights up the room like the sun."

Aurora stared at the handsome Irishman sitting beside her. If any other man had paid her such an outrageous compliment, he'd have sounded foolish. But coming from him, the words made her heart tap dance in her chest.

A rosy hue infused his cheeks. "Forgive me. I've no right to speak to you like that."

"I don't mind," she said softly. "I like the way you talk. Did you come to America recently?"

"Aye. A couple of weeks ago. I'm here with my sister, Maggie. We're visiting our brother Rylan for the summer."

Aurora blinked. "Rylan Montgomery?"

"That's right. Do you know Rylan?"

"I do. He's doing admirable work with the orphans." A blush heated her cheeks. "I volunteer at St. Rita's whenever I can."

"I'm glad my brother places so high in your estimation." Gabriel grinned, his teeth flashing white in the glow from the interior. "But wait until you meet my sister. She's more stubborn than our mule back home, as the rest of my brothers can attest."

Aurora laughed, deciding there was no need to mention meeting Maggie at a suffrage gathering. "How many brothers do you have?"

"Three. Tommy, Paddy, and Rylan. Maggie is the youngest. She's had to endure us all constantly trying to protect her."

Aurora gave a soft sigh. "I always wished I had brothers and sisters. I used to envy my friends fighting with their siblings."

He cocked his head, still holding her gaze. "An only child?"

"Yes. Which is another reason why my father is so . . . controlling."

"I see. Well, clearly he has terrible taste in

suitors, if Jared is anything to go by."

She shook her head. "Jared is not the only ill-suited man my father has paired me with. But that's a story for another time." She gave an apologetic shrug. "As much as I'm enjoying our talk, I should go back inside." With reluctance, she rose from the bench.

Gabe stood with her.

"I don't think I thanked you for helping me." She frowned and pointed at his jaw. "He didn't hurt you, did he?"

"That little punch? Hardly noticed it."

She bit her lip to keep back a giggle. Ladies did not giggle, as Papa so often admonished her.

Gabe took her hand and bent to kiss it. Flutters vibrated in her stomach.

"It was lovely to meet you, Aurora. I hope I'll see you again."

Aurora's breath swirled in her strangled lungs. "I hope so, too."

As he escorted her back into the noisy parlor, Aurora gave herself a mental shake. No point in getting foolish notions about a man who lived an ocean away.

Her future was here in New York. And if things continued in a favorable way, it might include a relationship with a handsome doctor who shared her passion for medicine.

A solid, dependable man. Not a charming

Irish rogue.

Her life had no place for a man like that.

6

After making sure all the horses had been fed and watered and had clean straw in their stalls, Adam made his way to Sam's workshop. Knowing he'd never sleep a wink while the party went on without him, Adam planned to soothe his wounded pride by working on a chest he'd started. Sam had been kind enough to supply the materials, giving him a quick refresher course in the finer aspects of furniture-making. It hadn't taken long for Adam's fingers to remember the feel of the wood or the ease of the lathe in his hand.

When footsteps sounded in the corridor some time later, Adam lifted his head from his work. Sam must be up late tonight. Or perhaps he couldn't sleep, either. The door to the workshop creaked open. Adam froze, and the sand block slipped from his fingers.

Miss Montgomery stood in the opening, a vision in green silk, her dark hair arranged in a fancy upsweep with several enticing strands left to curl over her shoulders.

When her eyes met his, her mouth fell open. "You're the man from the orphanage. What are you doing here?"

Adam brushed the sawdust from his hands as he attempted to recover his equilibrium. "I work here." He came around the table toward her but halted at the wariness in her eyes. "I'm sorry if I caused you any concern. I heard the children's laughter and couldn't help watching them play for a minute."

She squinted at him. "Perhaps I over-reacted. But you did look like a tramp with all that long hair."

He smothered a laugh. "Good thing I've since had a haircut."

She grinned at him, visibly relaxing. "A big improvement, to be sure."

He leaned a hip against the bench. "What are you doing here — in the barn, I mean?"

She flushed as she lifted her chin. "I came to see the horses. The guests were praising the quality of Mr. O'Leary's animals, but to be frank, they seem rather ordinary to me."

With effort, he kept his lips from twitching. "That's because these are the work horses. The thoroughbreds are kept in the main stables."

Her eyes widened. "The building to the left?"

"That's the one."

She threw out her hands. "I can't believe they have a place so luxurious for animals. Back home in Cork, it would be a palace fit for a king."

Adam couldn't tear his gaze from this charming creature. Her guileless honesty was a refreshing change from the girls he'd met over the years — all trying to impress him with their looks or their family's wealth.

"You're from Ireland, then?"

"Aye. Visiting my brother. My name's Maggie Montgomery."

"A pleasure to meet you, Maggie. I'm Adam." No need to divulge his surname. He could be an anonymous stable hand to her. A man with no shameful past, no criminal record. "And is the party not to your liking?" He moved closer in measured steps, as though approaching a skittish filly, afraid to scare this rare woman away.

She clasped her hands in front of her. "It's grand, of course, but I'm afraid I'm not used to so many people. I needed a little . . . breathing room." She glanced around him to the table where he'd been sanding. "Are you a woodworker?"

"I do this as a hobby in my spare time."

He paused, hesitating to answer. "I'm . . . a stable hand." He waited for her demeanor to change, for her to distance herself from him. But instead she came closer, her face awash with curiosity.

He pointed to the ground. "You might want to mind your dress. It's dirty in here."

She glanced down at her feet then, where the hem of her skirt brushed the sawdust on the floor. "Aye. If it were my own dress, I wouldn't mind, but I borrowed this from my sister-in-law." A look of regret shadowed her features. "I suppose I should be getting back . . ."

"Would you like to see the horses before you go?" What mad impulse made him offer that? He should stay as far away from Maggie Montgomery as possible. For her own good, if nothing else.

Her eyes, the color of gray heather, brightened, and a smile created enticing dimples in each cheek. "I'd love to."

Adam untied the work apron from his waist and placed it on the bench. "Allow me to escort you." He held out his arm for her.

Her light laugh trilled over the room. "You don't strike me as a stable hand. Have you always worked with horses?"

The irony of that question burned in

Adam's chest. Three years ago, he'd abhorred everything to do with horses. Now he was their caretaker. "I was raised with them."

"How lucky for you. I've always wanted my own horse. The closest I came was a donkey named Tiger. He pulls our cart when we go into town to shop."

Adam guided her out the side door that led to the main stables. "You said you were visiting a brother. Do you have a lot of family in America?"

"Only Rylan. Another brother, Gabe, came with me. My two oldest brothers, Tommy and Paddy, are married with families back home. They're taking care of my mum while we're here."

Adam found he could listen to this girl's lilt forever and never tire of it.

They reached the main stables, and Adam held the door open for her to enter. He flicked the switch and the electric lights came on to illuminate the space.

Beside him, Maggie gasped. "I've never seen anything so lovely. You must be excited to work here every day."

"It's a living."

She gaped at him as though he'd sprouted horns, then her look of incredulity softened. "Ah, I see the problem."

"You do?"

She nodded, studying him. "Your true love is furniture-making, not horses, and you'd rather be doing that."

Adam stopped dead in the center of the corridor. In the few minutes she'd known him, Maggie Montgomery had pegged the very core of his conflict with his father. James O'Leary could never accept the fact that his son didn't share his passion for horses. Woodworking was for lower-class, working citizens. Not the heir to Irish Meadows.

"You are a very wise woman, Maggie."

"So my brothers often tell me." She smiled at him. "Don't worry, Adam. If you give it time, I'm sure you'll eventually get to do what you love best."

"I hope you're right." He forced his feet to move forward. "Allow me to show you the number one horse in the stable. One that recently won the Kentucky Derby."

"I'd love to." She took his arm again, but before they reached the mahogany-and-brass enclosures, the main door burst open.

Adam swiveled to see who would be entering at this hour, and his stomach sank to his work boots. His father's scowling face blotted out everything else.

"What in tarnation is going on here?"

Maggie felt Adam stiffen beside her, and he slowly removed her hand from his arm.

"Just giving Miss Montgomery a tour of the stables, sir. Nothing to make a fuss about."

Maggie frowned. Why would anyone make a fuss about that? And what was Mr. O'Leary doing out here? Surely, he hadn't missed her among all his prestigious guests.

A flurry of further footsteps sounded, and Rylan appeared in the open doorway.

"Ah, Maggie, there you are. We've been worried about you."

"Maggie, is this man bothering you?" Mr. O'Leary's frown was enough to frighten years off the growth of a child.

She pulled herself up to her full height. "Not at all, sir. He's been most kind, offering to show me the horses."

Mr. O'Leary shot Adam a withering stare that Maggie did not understand. Even if Adam had violated some rule that stable hands could not interact with guests, Mr. O'Leary's reaction seemed extreme.

Rylan motioned to her. "Come back to the house, Maggie. Gabe and Colleen are in a fret about you."

Shame pooled in her chest. "I'm sorry. I didn't mean to worry anyone." She turned back to face Adam. His countenance had changed completely. Gone was the pleasant stable hand who had indulged her whims. In his place, a fierce, scowling man glared at Mr. O'Leary. Maggie started at the open animosity vibrating between the two men.

"Thank you so much, Adam," she said. "I'll have to come back another time to see the horses."

His features softened as he looked at her and nodded. "It was my pleasure, Maggie. I hope you enjoy the rest of your stay in America."

"Thank you." Why did it feel as though she'd never see him again? And why did that bother her? "Good luck with your furniture-making."

Two red flags stained Adam's cheeks. Maggie hoped she hadn't said anything that might get him in further trouble with Mr. O'Leary.

Rylan took her by the elbow and practically dragged her outside. She quickened her pace to keep up with him. Just before they reached the house, Maggie pulled her arm free.

"Do you mind telling me what's got your knickers in such a twist?"

An unusual scowl creased Rylan's forehead. "You can't go wandering off like that, Maggie. You're not in Ireland anymore. Things are different here."

"I only wanted some fresh air and to see the magnificent horses everyone was talking about. Is that a crime?" A cool evening breeze teased the curls on her bare shoulders, and she shivered, wishing for her wrap.

"You should have taken an escort. Girls — *ladies* — don't go walking places alone. It's more dangerous here."

She peered at him. "Are you implying that Adam is dangerous? Because you couldn't be more wrong."

Rylan let out a slow breath. "He's a criminal, Maggie. You're not to speak to him again."

Her mouth dropped open, her mind emptying of all logical thought. "Do you make it a habit to learn the history of all Mr. O'Leary's employees?"

With a hand to her back, Rylan led her up the stairs to the porch that surrounded the house. "Adam is not just a stable hand. He's Colleen's older brother." He leaned in close beside her. "Adam was released from prison a little over a week ago."

Maggie's knees wobbled. She sank onto a wicker chair, unable to absorb his statement. "I don't understand."

Rylan took a seat beside her. "No one is willing to hire an ex-convict, so Mr. O'Leary allowed Adam to work in the barn, but it doesn't mean he trusts him. There's a lot of bad blood between them." Rylan blew out a weary breath. "Trust me, Maggie, it would be best if you forget you ever met Adam O'Leary."

"What do you think you were doing with that girl?"

Adam stared at his father's reddened face. "I was about to show her the horses, like she asked. Why are you making this into something sinister?"

"Don't you realize that simply being seen with you could ruin her reputation? Or do social niceties not matter to you anymore?"

Adam clamped his lips shut. Although he hated to admit it, his father had a point. "I'm sorry. I didn't think . . ."

"That's half your problem, boy. You never think before you act. You certainly never consider the consequences of your actions on others. Ruin your life if you must, but leave the rest of us out of it."

From the apoplectic look on his father's face, Adam feared the man might suffer another angina attack. Perhaps coming to work here had been a huge mistake. No matter what Adam did, it was the wrong thing. His presence had created nothing but tension between his parents, and the last thing Adam wanted was to cause his mother more unhappiness.

"You're right. I don't know why I ever thought this could work." Bitterness dripped from Adam's words.

His father stilled for a moment. "I think it would be best for everyone involved if you found another position. You can stay on here until then."

A harsh laugh escaped Adam. "That could take years. Don't worry. I'll be gone in the morning." He strode across the hardpacked floor, boots slapping the ground.

"Don't leave without saying good-bye to your mother," his father called after him. "Make her believe you have a better offer somewhere else."

It galled Adam to have to concede to his father, but for his mother's sake, he would do it. Anything to make up for the pain he'd caused.

Adam gave a stiff nod and exited the building, but instead of going to his quarters, he walked to the fence surrounding the racetrack. He leaned his elbows on the top rung and hung his head, focusing all his attention on the simple act of breathing in and out.

A few minutes later, he sensed a presence beside him.

"You look like you've seen better days." Sam's sympathetic voice allowed the tense muscles in Adam's back to unclench.

"Had a lot worse, as well." Images of dreary days spent caged in a cell flashed behind his eyes. He let out a loud sigh. "This arrangement isn't going to work, Sam. No matter what I do, my father is ready to hang me from the nearest tree without a trial."

Sam laid a hand on Adam's shoulder. "I'm sorry, lad. I've enjoyed having you back, sharing my barn with you."

Adam glanced over at him. "Me too."

"Where will you go now?"

"I have a friend in the city. Maybe he can give me a new perspective on things."

Sam's bushy brows bunched together. "I hope you're not going back to the thugs who got you into this mess."

Adam shook his head. "Trust me. I've learned my lesson in that regard. This is a friend who visited me in prison. John's a good man — wise beyond his years. He's used to dealing with people . . . in my situation."

Sam pushed away from the fence and tugged his hat on tighter. "I have a brother with a ranch out in Wyoming. I could send you there, no questions asked."

A lump formed in Adam's throat at the man's simple faith in him. He nodded. "Thank you, Sam. I hope it doesn't come to that, but it's good to know I have another option."

Sam squeezed Adam's shoulder with one beefy hand. "Good luck, son. And let me know if you need anything."

With that, Sam ambled off across the path to the barn.

Adam remained outside, knowing sleep would elude him for a long while. The vivacious features of Maggie Montgomery danced before his eyes as he stared out into the darkness, taunting him with dreams that could never be.

How had Adam ever thought coming back to Irish Meadows was a good plan? His father was not a man inclined to put the past behind them — not even for Mama's sake. Time and distance might provide the only solution to Adam's dilemma.

As his mind continued to run in circles, Adam turned to the one source of peace he'd found in prison.

Lord, I know I'm supposed to love my father,

but does it have to be so hard? Help me to find it in my heart to forgive him, and he me. Help me to be humble and accept the consequences of my actions. And if You're handing out miracles, allow me to make amends to my family . . . if that's even possible.

Adam forced himself to recall John Mc-Nabb's last visit to the penitentiary and the vow Adam had made in John's presence — that he would take whatever steps necessary to atone for his mistakes and make peace with his family. That he would commit to doing God's will and start his life anew with a gracious heart. To do so, John had said, Adam would need to let go of his resentment and set aside his pride.

As the morning's first rays broke over the horizon, Adam set his jaw with renewed resolve. If it took him the rest of his days — if he had to shovel manure from here to eternity — he would make his mother proud of him again. And in doing so, Adam hoped he might one day earn the respect of his father — at last.

7

Early-morning steam rose off the sidewalk to greet Adam as he trudged down Park Avenue, the collar of his jacket pulled up against the slight chill in the air. He turned onto 11th Street, peering from beneath the brim of his cap at the various buildings he passed. Finding a church shouldn't be too difficult, though Adam wasn't entirely sure what John's church would look like. Much different from St. Patrick's Cathedral, he imagined.

At the break of dawn, Adam had gathered his few possessions and, not wishing to awaken his mother at that hour, had left a note for her with the housekeeper. Perhaps his actions had been cowardly, but he couldn't bear to face Mama until he had a new plan in place for his life. Not to mention he hadn't wished to cross paths with his father again. So Adam had taken the earliest train from Long Island into the city

114

and walked in the direction of John's church.

Adam hiked several more blocks until he came to the address John McNabb had made him commit to memory and then slowed to a stop in front of the Shepherd of Good Hope Church. This early in the morning, the gray stone building appeared deserted, and for the first time since leaving Irish Meadows, Adam's courage faltered. What was he thinking, coming to this holy place? Surely the walls would shake and crumble with outrage should he step inside. Yet how else would he find John?

A soft mist drizzled down from the leaden clouds. Adam shivered and blew on his cold fingers, shifting his satchel to his other hand. He climbed the steps and tried the front door, only to find it locked. The information carved on a wooden sign indicated the first service started at 8:30 in the morning. Surely John would open the church before then. Adam would simply walk around the block a few times until he noticed evidence of activity inside.

On his second time around, he was gratified to spy a light shining through the side windows of the church. Adam squared his shoulders and climbed the stairs again. This time, under his stiff fingers, the latch gave way and the door creaked open.

Adam froze. Would the sexton appear and demand he leave? When no movement sounded, he continued through another set of doors into the main worship area.

At the front of the room, a tall man placed a Bible on the lectern. When he lifted his head, he caught sight of Adam. "Can I help you, sir?"

Adam stepped into the open. "Hello, John."

Shock, then pleasure, flitted across the man's features. "Adam? Is that you?" He walked briskly down the main aisle of the church, reaching out to give Adam a hearty handshake. "I hadn't expected to see you so soon. Everything's all right, I hope?" His brow furrowed, creating wrinkles on his prominent forehead.

"Could be better. Do you have a few minutes to talk? I know it's your busiest day . . ."

"Of course, of course. Come back to the rectory and have a cup of coffee."

"I could use one. Thanks."

He followed John out the side door and across a narrow walkway to a small brick house. John opened the front door and motioned Adam to follow him in.

Children's voices and the clatter of dishes

met Adam's ears. He hesitated on the threshold. "Your wife won't mind?"

"Not at all. Come and meet my family."

The man's simple acceptance — taking a criminal into his home to meet his wife and children — humbled Adam.

During his prison visits, John had quoted Bible verses and spoken of his convictions, but now Adam saw that John's words weren't mere utterances to sway a fallen sheep. This man lived his faith.

Adam tugged off his cap, set his bag on the mat, and entered the homey kitchen.

"Anne, we have a guest. This is Adam O'Leary. Adam, this is my wife and our sons, David and Michael."

An attractive, brown-haired woman moved away from the sink to smile at Adam. "Nice to meet you, Mr. O'Leary." She laid a hand on the shoulder of the younger boy at the table, who appeared to be about four or five.

"You, too, Mrs. McNabb. I'm sorry to disturb your breakfast." He glanced at the cast-iron frying pan on the stove, where the enticing aroma matched the sizzle from the pan.

"Nonsense. You must join us." She removed the bacon and brought the refilled platter to the table.

Before he could protest, John pulled out

one of the ladder-back chairs for Adam. "Have a seat, and I'll get that coffee."

Adam sat down and, mindful of the boys' curious stares, tried to soften his features, fearing his scowling countenance might frighten them.

John set two steaming mugs of coffee on the table and gave his wife a pointed look.

She nodded. "Boys, come along and get dressed for church." She smiled at Adam. "We'll give you time to talk. There are biscuits and jam to go with the bacon."

John kissed his wife's cheek. "Thank you, honey."

Adam remained silent while John served two plates of food and took a seat across from him.

"So how can I help?" John said quietly.

Adam shoveled a bite of bacon into his mouth and chewed before answering. "Things didn't work out with my father. I lasted a week as a stable hand before he accused me . . . of inappropriate behavior. I had to leave."

John set down his fork and shook his head. "I wish I could say I'm surprised. The unfortunate truth is that you're going to have to deal with society's prejudices. It will take time to prove your trustworthiness and earn back people's respect. Just remember

God is with you, no matter how others treat you."

Simply listening to the man speak in his calm, straightforward manner brought a measure of peace to Adam's soul. It called to mind the wonderful talks they'd shared when John had visited him in prison. His simple acceptance and nonjudgmental attitude had drawn Adam to him and slowly awakened Adam's faith. A faith that was now being tested.

"Did you take my advice and have that talk with your father?"

Adam swallowed some biscuit. "Not exactly."

John took a drink of his coffee, eyes steady over the rim of his cup, waiting for Adam to explain.

"I was hoping to prove myself on the job first, and then when the time was right, broach the topic."

John nodded. "I can understand wanting to work your way up to that particular conversation." He set his mug on the table. "So what are you going to do now?"

Adam's throat went dry. He gulped down a quick sip of scalding black coffee. "That's why I'm here. I was hoping since you work with inmates, you might have some advice as to where to start." He couldn't help the frustration that seeped into his voice.

John slathered jam onto a biscuit. "Let me talk to a few men in the congregation. See if any of them needs help or knows of anyone who does."

"I'll do any type of manual labor," Adam said quietly. "Nothing is too menial."

"Do you have a place to stay in the meantime?"

"Not yet."

John frowned. "Don't you have a sister here in the city?"

"I do. But after what happened yesterday, I know I wouldn't be welcome." From the way Rylan had practically dragged Maggie away from him, Adam suspected he wouldn't want him anywhere near his wife, either.

John released a soft sigh. "I wish I could offer to take you in. Though my wife is a tolerant woman, I'm afraid she'd never agree to it, even if we had the space."

"I understand." Adam finished the last piece of bacon and pushed his chair back. "Don't worry. I'll find somewhere to sleep."

John rose, as well. "There is a storage room in the church basement. It's not much, but I could set up a cot for you there."

Adam straightened his shoulders. "Only if

I can work in exchange for the room. I won't accept charity."

John looked ready to argue with him, but then nodded. "All right, we could always use help with repairs around the church."

Though Adam realized John was likely inventing jobs to save Adam's pride, he appreciated the man's offer. "Very well."

In the hallway, a clock chimed the hour. John moved to take his plate to the sink. "We can discuss all this later. Right now I must get ready for the service." He moved toward the door.

"Will I see you in church?" The question was gentle, no coercion involved.

Adam hesitated. Was he ready to go back to church? To face people's censure, knowing others would not be as accepting as John?

"Not today. But one Sunday soon, I promise." Adam pulled his cap from his jacket pocket and tugged it on. A measure of relief flooded his tense muscles. At least he had a place to lay his head. The rest would come in time. "Thank you, John. You have no idea how much your support means to me."

"I'm happy to help in any way I can." John walked Adam to the door. "But I will ask for one thing in return."

"Name it."

"Go and talk to your sister and brother-in-law. Clear the air with them as a first step toward making amends with your family."

Adam hesitated, but finally nodded. "You're right. I owe Colleen a long-overdue apology." He opened the door, then faced the clergyman. "I thank you, John, for your hospitality and your help. I won't let you down."

Maggie straightened the quilt on her side of the bed she shared with Delia and crossed the wooden floor, careful not to awaken the sleeping child. Out in the hall, she huffed out a small sigh. Between her encounter with Neill the other day and last night's discovery about Adam, Maggie felt more than a little unsettled.

She'd decided to say nothing to Gabe and Rylan about Neill, knowing they would both overreact to the situation, and in doing so, would severely restrict Maggie's freedom. Plus, Maggie wanted to spare Gabe the knowledge that their trip to America might have been for nothing. Not only had Neill not accepted the demise of their relationship, he'd turned around and followed her here. She still couldn't quite grasp the enormity of his actions. Back home, Neill watched every penny he spent and funneled most of his earnings back into the family pub. How he'd come up with the money for his passage across the ocean, she had no idea. She only prayed that Neill would soon realize that Maggie had no intention of resuming their engagement and head back to Ireland. A small voice inside her, however, told her he might not be finished trying to change her mind.

The unbidden image of Adam O'Leary intruded upon her thoughts, begging a comparison between the two men. Though not handsome in a classical way like Neill, Adam exuded a masculine ruggedness that Maggie found riveting. The hard planes of his face, shadowed by a neatly trimmed auburn beard, told of unspoken hardships — a weariness of the world, so to speak. And now she understood why. He'd endured time in prison.

By all rights, Maggie should be repulsed by a common criminal, a man who resorted to illegal methods to achieve an end. Yet her soul ached for him. After her two encounters with him, she simply couldn't perceive Adam as evil. Above all else, Maggie prided herself on her intuition about people, and rarely had she been mistaken. Her instincts told her that Adam O'Leary was a good man.

As she descended the narrow staircase to the kitchen, Maggie decided she would ask Colleen more about her mysterious brother as soon as the opportunity arose.

She found her sister-in-law at the stove, stirring a big pot. Dirty dishes on the table told Maggie that some of the family had already enjoyed the porridge Colleen was tending.

"Am I late for breakfast?"

Colleen turned to smile, her bright hair gathered in a roll at the nape of her neck. "Not at all. We were up early this morning. Rylan and Gabe went to check on things at the orphanage before church." Colleen ladled oatmeal into a bowl. "There's milk and honey on the table."

"Thank you. Have you eaten?"

"I have, but I'll join you for tea." She carried the teapot to the table and poured two cups.

Maggie sat and took a mouthful of oatmeal. Her stomach churned with nerves as she wondered how to broach the topic with Colleen. From all accounts, her brother was a sore subject in the family. Maggie would need to tread with caution.

"Remember the strange man I caught

watching the children at the orphanage a few days back?"

Colleen frowned. "Yes."

Maggie paused. "Turns out that man was Adam."

Colleen's gaze widened. "It was?"

"Yes. I recognized him the moment I saw him in your family's barn, although I didn't know he was your brother." She poured a little milk into her tea. "Now I understand the longing on his face."

Colleen set down her cup with a thump and bit her lower lip in an obvious attempt to contain her emotions.

Maggie reined in her impatience at wanting to blurt out a hundred questions at once and waited while Colleen dabbed the corner of her apron to her eyes.

"Were you and Adam close as children?"

"Very close." Colleen gave a wan smile. "You might say Adam and I were the black sheep of the family. Before I met Rylan, I was quite a schemer and" — she lowered her gaze to the table — "not the most scrupulous of girls. Rylan changed all that."

"I'm sure you weren't as bad as you imply. Otherwise you wouldn't have captured my brother's heart."

A soft look stole over Colleen's features. "He saw the good beneath the bad."

Funny that Maggie sensed the same about Adam. Wisely, she held that thought back. "And Adam?" she asked gently. "What set him on a path to prison?"

Colleen shook her head and sighed. "Adam and Daddy never got along, and things got worse when Daddy took Gil in as his ward. Gil shared Daddy's love of horses in a way Adam never did. Adam became . . . resentful of Daddy's preference for Gil over him."

Maggie stiffened on her chair, incensed on Adam's behalf. "How could a father favor another child over his own flesh and blood? That doesn't make sense."

Colleen stirred a spoon of honey into her tea. "To be fair, Adam made it hard — always getting into trouble at school, avoiding his chores, pulling tricks on Gil and Danny."

"Who's Danny?"

A shadow of sadness dulled Colleen's vivid blue-violet eyes, making Maggie wish she'd held her tongue.

"Danny was our younger brother. He drowned when he was eight. His death only complicated matters, since Daddy blamed Adam for the accident." Colleen clamped her lips together as if to hold back any further comments.

"I'm so sorry. How did your poor mother cope with such a tragedy?"

"She took it very hard, but Mama's a strong woman." Colleen sighed. "The one thing she couldn't do, however, was fix Daddy and Adam's relationship."

Maggie swirled the oatmeal in her bowl with her spoon, not quite brave enough to look at Colleen with her next question. "How did Adam end up in jail?" She hated to press the issue, but she needed to know.

Colleen swiped at her damp cheeks and pushed away from the table, chair legs scraping. "Gambling." The terse word echoed in the silence of the kitchen. "And associating with gangsters. Adam provided inside knowledge of Daddy's clients and their horses to a group of thugs involved in backroom betting." She moved to the counter and began to scrub the sink, her hands flying with hard, fast jerks.

Gambling? It didn't sound like such a terrible thing to Maggie. Gambling was a common activity in the pubs back home. Even some of the constables bet on a game of football or a horse race now and then.

"I'm very sorry for all the sorrows your family has had to endure. I hope I haven't offended you by prying."

"Of course not, Maggie. We're family."

Colleen stopped scouring and wiped her hands on a towel. "Besides, I think it only fair to warn you about Adam. You should know that he's fallen far away from the moral upbringing of his youth. I don't know if he'll ever be accepted back into our family again." She smoothed a hand over her dress. "Now if you'll excuse me, I must go and awaken Delia."

The sorrow on Colleen's lovely face as she left the kitchen was enough to make Maggie regret bringing up the topic at all. She stirred the lumpy mess of oatmeal in her bowl, her appetite now vanished, and let out a sigh.

Colleen had made herself quite clear on the topic of her brother. No matter how sorry Maggie felt for Adam, he was not to be trusted.

She needed to put the man out of her thoughts for good.

Adam mounted the steps of the stylish brownstone and knocked on the door. Nervous perspiration gathered between his shoulder blades. He tugged off his cap and waited for either his sister or Rylan to answer the door, hoping they hadn't already left for church.

He knocked a second time, half relieved

when no one appeared, and was about to slink away when the squeak of the door stopped him.

A small blond girl stood staring at him with frank blue eyes. "Who are you?"

"My name is Adam O'Leary. I'm looking for Colleen . . . ah, Mrs. Montgomery."

She cocked her head to one side, contemplating him. "My Mama used to be Miss O'Leary. Are you related to her?"

Adam blinked. He'd only been away for three years. How could Colleen have a daughter this age? Then he remembered the adopted child Colleen had mentioned in her letters.

"Colleen is my sister," he answered carefully. "Is she home?"

"Delia, who's at the door?" A feminine voice echoed down the corridor.

"It's your brother."

The childish simplicity of her statement struck a soft chord in Adam's heart. Would Colleen allow him in, or would her Irish temper flare and leave him on the end of a good tongue-lashing?

Colleen opened the door wider and stood staring. "Adam?"

He attempted a smile. "Hello, Colleen. You're looking well." In the years since he'd seen her, she'd matured into a beautiful woman.

"What are you doing here?" She scanned the street behind him, as if a gang of hooligans would jump out at her.

"May I come in? I'd like to speak with you if you have a moment."

She hesitated, placing her hand on the girl's shoulder.

"It won't take long, I promise. Then I'll leave you in peace."

She gave a small sigh. "All right. Come in."

When he crossed the threshold, she closed the door behind them.

"Adam, this is our daughter, Delia. Delia, this is . . . your Uncle Adam." The slight catch in Colleen's voice gave away the emotions she was trying to hide.

"Hello, Delia. It's nice to meet you." He gave a small bow to the girl, who giggled.

"I have lots of uncles now."

"Delia, we'll be leaving for church in ten minutes. Run up and change into your good dress."

"Yes, Mama." The girl gave him one last look and scampered off.

"Come into the parlor. As you heard, we don't have much time."

Sorrow threaded through Adam's chest.

There would be no warm hugs, no words of welcome from his sister. At least she'd agreed to hear him out. He could be grateful for that much.

Adam followed her into the cozy sitting room, so different from the elegant parlor at Irish Meadows but just as appealing in its own way. They each took a seat on opposite ends of a camel-hair sofa.

He curled his fingers over the wooden armrest. "So you have a daughter?"

She nodded, smiling. "We adopted Delia from the orphanage. She's very special to us."

"I can see that. I bet she gives you a run for your money."

Colleen's lips twitched, and for a brief second, a familiar twinkle of mischief glimmered in her eyes. "That is truer than you know."

He laughed, but immediately sobered. "I'll get right to the point of my visit. I came to apologize for any problems I may have caused last night. I had no idea —"

"It's all right, Adam. Maggie explained how she ended up with you in the barn. It wasn't your fault."

"That's kind of you to say. But truth be told, I should have sent her right back to the house. I hope she suffered no . . .

repercussions?"

"Other than Rylan's scolding, no. Her reputation is intact."

"Thank goodness." He leaned forward over his knees, urgency making him nervous. "I also came to apologize for any embarrassment my incarceration may have caused you." He held her gaze. "More importantly, I wish to say how sorry I am for missing your wedding. I regret that more than you know."

Moisture formed at the corners of her eyes. "I won't deny it cast a cloud over the day, especially for Mama."

"I am sorry, Colleen. For what it's worth, I want you to know that I've changed, and I plan to work hard to make it up to the family." He paused to draw a breath. "Heaven knows, I don't deserve your forgiveness, but if you feel so inclined, it would make me a very happy man."

The clock on the mantel ticked out the seconds. At last, Colleen nodded. "I can forgive you, Adam. But I'm not the one whose forgiveness you need." She gave him a direct look. "That would be Daddy."

Adam held back a snort. "I doubt that will ever happen."

She surprised him by reaching over and taking his hand. "Try, Adam, please. For our family's sake, you need to make peace."

A band of guilt threatened to choke Adam. If only it were that easy. But he had a strong suspicion that nothing he said or did would make any difference to James O'Leary. "I'll do my best. But I can't guarantee our father will listen."

Colleen smiled. "I've missed you, Adam. More than I even realized."

"I've missed you, too." He cleared his throat and rose. "Well, I'd best let you get on with your day. Thank you for hearing me out."

Her skirts swished as she stood. "I understand you won't be working at Irish Meadows any longer. What will you do now?" A concerned frown marred her perfect complexion.

"The prison chaplain is going to see if anyone in his parish would be willing to hire me." He attempted a reassuring smile. "Don't worry. I'll find a job somewhere."

They made their way to the narrow front entrance.

"Wait." Colleen put a hand on his arm to stop him. "The caretaker at the orphanage is getting on in years and can't keep up with all the work anymore. Maybe Rylan would —"

He squeezed her arm to stop her. "I appreciate your offer, but the last thing I want is to cause problems between you and your husband."

Sadness stole the shine from her eyes. Her silence told him she couldn't dispute his words. "How will I reach you if I need to?"

"Through Reverend John McNabb at the Shepherd of Good Hope Church. Take good care, Colleen."

She surprised him again when she reached out to gather him in a hug, and he had to fight to keep his emotions contained. As he stood back, his gaze moved to the hall behind them.

Maggie stood as though frozen, her hand on the newel post of the staircase.

Delia ran past her, tiny feet thudding on the wooden floor. "Are you coming to church with us, Uncle Adam?"

Adam couldn't tear his gaze from Maggie's stricken face. "I can't today, sweetheart. Maybe another time."

His stomach twisted as he forced his attention away from Maggie's haunted eyes. What was she thinking? Did she hate him — now that she knew him to be a criminal?

Adam shoved his cap on his head, gave Colleen a quick nod, and pushed out into the street. But no matter how fast he walked, he doubted he'd be able to banish Maggie's look of anguish from his mind any time soon.

8

Gabe whistled as he polished the chrome of the motorized fire truck in the bay, satisfied that by the time he finished, the shine would be enough to blind Chief Witherspoon.

"Hey, Irish. You can knock it off now. That spot won't get any cleaner." Will Spack, one of the firemen who was a few years older than Gabe, tossed a wet sponge at him. It smacked Gabe in the chest and landed in a puddle on the cement floor.

After his second week at the fire station, Gabe knew most of the men well enough not to take offense at their jibes.

"You're just worried I'll make you look bad," he shot back.

Jerry O'Donnell poked his head from around the side of the truck. "Got that right, Montgomery. Spack's worried the chief will fire him and hire you instead."

A tiny thrill shot through Gabe's torso. What would it be like to be a permanent firefighter here, a true member of this team that worked tirelessly to keep their city safe? The thought of his beloved mother made the image evaporate faster than the splotches of water on the cement. He could never cause her the pain of losing another son to America.

That, as well as the unrest at home, made staying here impossible.

"You lads hungry?" Chief Witherspoon's booming voice rang out from the upper level, where the firemen's quarters were situated. "There's a pot of stew up here courtesy of Mrs. Witherspoon."

Jerry gave a loud whoop and charged toward the stairs.

Gabe laughed and bent to retrieve the sponge, dumping it along with his rag into the bin against the wall. He wiped his wet hands on his trousers, already salivating in anticipation of the tasty meal.

Then the gong of the fire alarm split the air. The entire crew froze to listen to the numbered sequence of bells, and then suddenly burst into action. Gabe stopped to watch the frenzy of activity.

The chief pushed by him. "Don't just stand there, Montgomery. Suit up."

"I'm going?" Adrenaline licked through Gabe's veins.

"We need every man available. Looks like we're heading to Arthur Hastings's house."

Gabe pushed back a rush of concern as he moved to the hooks on the wall, where he grabbed some spare gear. "How do you know it's the Hastingses?" He stuffed the helmet on his head, grateful he'd been wearing boots while he washed the truck.

"Their house takes up a full city block. It has its own alarm code." The chief jammed on his helmet. "Come on."

The men jumped onto the truck, and seconds later they roared out of the station, bell clanging.

If they weren't responding to a potential tragedy, Gabe would have been thrilled down to his boots to be riding the motorized engine for the first time. Instead, he tried to prepare for what was to come. He'd learned that the Arthur Hastings whose picture was in the fire station was indeed the father of the lovely girl he'd met at the O'Learys' party. Anxiety churned in Gabe's chest at the thought of her family's home burning. He prayed she was out for the evening, nowhere near the danger.

They rounded a sharp bend. Spack wound the siren, which wailed through the streets, causing pedestrians to jump out of the way and then turn to watch.

Gabe clutched the side of the truck as they careened onward. As soon as they came to a stop in front of a mansion, the men leapt to the street and began to unwind the hose. Chief Witherspoon ran to the front door, where a woman in uniform stood, wringing her hands.

"Hurry, please," she called. "Miss Aurora is upstairs."

Gabe's head snapped up from where he wrestled with the equipment.

"Where's her room?" Chief Witherspoon barked.

"At the back, second story, middle room."

The chief shouted orders. "O'Donnell, bring the ladder around the back to the middle window. Spack, Jackson, get the hoses."

Gabe didn't wait to hear more. From firsthand experience, he knew that hesitating, even for a moment, could cost someone's life. He charged through the front door, ignoring everything else. Thick smoke drifted through the marble entry, yet Gabe found the staircase with no trouble. Taking the stairs two at a time, he mentally recited the rules of fire rescue from his training at home. He thundered past the landing until he reached the second floor and turned down the hall, counting rooms as he went.

When he reached what he estimated to be the center of the building, he started opening doors. On the second try, he found a decidedly feminine room. A fit of coughing momentarily delayed him, and his eyes watered from the sting of smoke. Still, he was thankful not to find evidence of flames as he entered the room.

"Miss Hastings?" he called out. Despite the circumstances, he couldn't help feeling like a cad being in the woman's bedchamber.

A large four-poster bed dominated the room, its curtains pulled closed around it. Gabe yanked the material aside. Sure enough, a sleeping figure lay beneath the quilts. He shook her shoulder, chiding himself for feeling so awkward. If this had been a stranger, he wouldn't have hesitated a moment to carry the anonymous victim to safety, but picturing the beautiful Aurora, he couldn't allow himself the liberty.

Finally the woman stirred and rolled over, blond curls tumbling over her forehead.

"Miss Hastings. The house is on fire."

"What?" She came to life slowly, then gave a slight scream.

He tried to imagine how she must feel, awakening to a strange man in her room wearing a helmet and fire gear. "Aurora, you must hurry."

She sat up, clutching the bedding to her neck. "How do you know my name?"

"It's Gabriel Montgomery. We met at the O'Learys'."

"Oh." She stared, then blinked twice. "My robe is on the chair." She pointed across the room.

He snatched the wrap and handed it to her, turning his back as she put it on. Seconds later, he peered over his shoulder to see her belting the robe and stepping into a pair of slippers. Without a word, he took her by the arm and ushered her into the hallway. The smoke had thickened considerably. "Try not to breathe too deeply." He kept his arm around her as they made their way down the staircase.

Once they got outside, they both coughed as they took in great gulps of fresh air.

The housekeeper rushed forward. "Oh, thank goodness, miss. I was so worried."

"Mrs. Forrester. Did everyone else get out?"

"They did. I'm so sorry I didn't make it upstairs. The flames in the kitchen were too much —"

Aurora laid her hand on the woman's arm. "Don't worry. I'm fine."

Gabe moved closer. "Excuse me, but I

need to go and help the others."

"Of course, thank you." She shivered slightly.

"Under no circumstance are any of you to go back into the house. Understood?" Gabe leveled them with a stern look until they nodded.

Though reluctant to leave, Gabe knew where his obligation lay. He grabbed a hose and followed the others around the side of the house to the back, where the main burn still smoldered, and moved to help the other men tackle the fire.

Twenty minutes later, Chief Witherspoon declared the fire contained. Thankfully, the firefighters had managed to keep the blaze to the kitchen, though the rest of the residence had suffered damage from the smoke. But all in all, they had been very fortunate.

The chief sent two men to make a thorough check of the entire building to ensure everyone had gotten out and that no other hazards existed.

As they lugged the hoses back out to the truck, the chief threw Gabe a stern glance. "I think we need to discuss the way we handle victim rescue here."

A twinge of guilt flared. Gabe had acted on impulse — not always a good thing.

The chief crossed his arms. "That being

said, I'm glad you were able to get Miss Hastings out unharmed. I'm sure her father will be very appreciative."

Relief whooshed through Gabe's muscles. "If it's all right, I'll make sure the ladies are faring well after their shock."

The chief's bushy eyebrows rose. "Be my guest."

Gabe ducked his head to hide the flash of heat that stole across his cheeks. There was nothing out of the ordinary in his actions. He'd do the same for anyone he rescued from a fire.

The fact that one of the women made his pulse sprint faster than a spark hitting an accelerant had nothing to do with it.

Nothing whatsoever.

A terrible chill invaded Aurora's whole body until she couldn't contain the tremors. It was silly, really. No harm had come to her. The house, for the most part, remained intact. So why did she feel the urge to sit on the ground and weep?

Because you've got no one but the house-keeper to comfort you.

Her parents' extremely busy social life meant Aurora was often left home alone with only the servants for company. Like tonight. Mama had invited her along but, tired after a long day and nursing the remains of a headache, Aurora had opted to stay home and turn in early. Most times, Aurora could bear the loneliness, content with the companionship of her cat.

Petunia!

Alarm rushed through Aurora. Had her pet been injured?

She ran back toward the house, only to be barred by two firemen coming out from the foyer. "You can't go in there, miss. Not until the chief gives the all-clear."

"But my cat . . . I have to find her."

"We can't let you risk injury for an animal."

She tried to duck around them, but they remained immutable. "Please, she's very important to me. . . ." Tears choked her airway as she imagined her dearest companion lying unconscious somewhere in the house, overcome by smoke.

"Miss Hastings? Is someone else inside?" A frowning Gabe Montgomery appeared at her side.

A wave of relief swept through her at a dizzying pace. "It's my cat. Please. I have to find her."

He put a gloved hand on her shoulder. The sturdy weight of it steadied Aurora's nerves.

"I'm sure she got out. Most animals instinctively find an escape route in a fire."

"But she sleeps in my room. The door was closed until you came. What if she's trapped and she's in trouble?" The thought of her dear pet perishing from the smoke was more than she could bear. Tears slipped down her cheeks. "Please, you have to make sure she's all right."

A frown creased Gabe's forehead under his helmet. He glanced around and then blew out a breath. "I'll go back if you promise to stay here."

He seemed so impossibly large in his fire gear. Large and safe and trustworthy. She nodded and wrapped her arms more firmly around her middle. "I promise."

Mrs. Forrester appeared. "I'll stay with her, sir."

He started off, but paused. "What does the cat look like? Please tell me it's not all black." The soot on his face added a comedic touch to his pained expression.

For a moment, despite her anxiety, Aurora was tempted to giggle. "She's pure white, so she'll be easy to spot."

He grinned. "That's good news. I'll be back." He bounded off before she could catch her breath.

"My, isn't he a charmer?" Mrs. Forrester

sighed. "If that's how they make them in Ireland, maybe I should book my passage on the next ship."

Aurora gave a nervous laugh, swiping the remaining moisture from her cheeks. Though still worried, she felt a huge weight had been lifted. For some reason, she trusted Gabe to find Petunia.

Aurora paced in front of the house as she waited, praying for their safety. Considering how many rooms the home contained, it could take ages to go through the whole building. Would Gabe really do that?

At last, he strode out the front door, a disheveled ball of fur in his arms.

"You found her!" She rushed forward to gather Petunia into her arms, burying her face in the cat's fur, which reeked of smoke. The stunned creature trembled, but once in Aurora's arms, seemed to settle.

Aurora looked up at Gabe. Three streaks of blood dripped from his cheek. "Did she do that?"

He gave a rueful grin. "Miss Petunia wasn't too happy with the idea of coming out from under your bed."

Aurora shifted the cat to one arm. "I'm so sorry. She must have been terrified. Normally she's very friendly." She reached out to gently wipe away a streak of blood with her thumb. "Thank you. That was above and beyond the call of duty."

He grinned, and two dimples appeared under the soot. "Haven't you heard that firemen are required to rescue cats? It's in the training manual."

A laugh escaped before she could check herself. And for the first time in a long, long while, Aurora didn't feel so alone.

9

"Mr. Montgomery will see you now." Mrs. Taft, a tall, austere-looking woman, led Adam along the carpeted hallway of St. Rita's Orphan Asylum.

Adam had been stunned when Rylan had called John's church and asked to see him. What could his brother-in-law want? Remembering the way Rylan had dragged Maggie out of the barn away from him, it didn't give him a great deal of hope for this meeting.

Adam fingered his cap and kept pace with Mrs. Taft, taking in the tasteful décor with some surprise. He'd expected an orphanage to be rather stark and uninviting, not as cheery and welcoming as this.

When they reached a door marked *Director,* Mrs. Taft gave a brief knock, announced Adam's arrival, and then retreated down the hall.

Adam tugged on the hem of his wool vest

and hoped his hair wasn't too unruly. Memories of the first time he'd met his distant cousin came rushing back. Rylan, who'd been studying to become a priest before he'd met Colleen, had been gracious, affable, and nonjudgmental. Adam breathed a quiet prayer that he would still harbor the lessons of his Christian training and would be able to forgive Adam's past. So much of his future relationship with Colleen would hinge on Rylan's attitude.

Adam stepped into a comfortable room lined with bookcases and wooden cabinets. Rylan sat behind a large mahogany desk, sun streaming in from the window behind him.

He looked up with a slight smile. "Adam. Thanks for coming. Please sit down."

"You wanted to see me?" Adam took a seat on the wooden guest chair.

Rylan folded his hands on the desktop. "Yes. Colleen tells me that your job at Irish Meadows didn't work out."

Though said without rancor, Rylan's words still stung. Adam kept his gaze even. "No surprise really, given my history with my father."

Rylan nodded. "I won't begin to judge your relationship with James. That's between the two of you. However, Colleen has asked if we might have a job for you here."

Though it galled him to have to beg for work, Adam swallowed his pride. He would do whatever necessary to ensure he never set foot in a prison again. "I'll take whatever work I can get."

Rylan studied him, mild curiosity in his gaze. "What about this church where you're staying? Are you working there?"

Adam clasped his hands together over his knees. "I'm doing repair jobs in return for lodging. Reverend McNabb was a great mentor to me during my time in prison. He's helping with my transition back into society."

"I'm glad you have a friend looking out for you." Rylan's brown eyes remained sympathetic. The fact that Adam sensed no animosity in Rylan came as a big relief.

Rylan picked up an ink pen and tapped it on the desktop. A frown creased his forehead. "Colleen has put me in a difficult position with her request. I have a responsibility here, not only to the children, but to the nuns, the staff, and the volunteers, as well."

A sinking sensation settled in Adam's stomach as his optimism faded. "I understand. No one wants an ex-con around." He pushed up from the uncomfortable chair, anxious to be out in the open, free from the confines of the room. "Thank you for speaking with me, Rylan. And thank Colleen for me." He moved around the chair toward the door.

"Wait. You didn't let me finish."

Adam paused, then turned to face Rylan, who came out from behind the desk.

"As a Christian, I'm a firm believer in God's unconditional forgiveness — and in second chances. To that end, I have a compromise in mind, one I hope will suit both our needs."

Adam swallowed, afraid to allow the bubble of hope to rise. "What sort of compromise?"

"Our caretaker, Mr. Smith, is getting on in years and can't do a lot of the heavy work, especially the outdoor maintenance. If you'd be willing to do odd jobs as needed, doing your best to stay away from the children and the staff, then I think we could work something out."

A dizzying wave of relief sped through Adam's system. With the income from the orphanage, he might be able to get back on his feet much quicker than expected. "That would be more than fair. Thank you for your generosity."

He held out his hand, hoping Rylan would

accept it.

Rylan made no move toward him. "One more thing. I have to ask you to stay away from Maggie. I won't risk her reputation being ruined. Do I have your word?"

Adam's chest constricted at the thought of Maggie's lovely face. Though it pained him to admit it, Rylan was right. Adam had nothing to offer such an amazing woman. He released a slow breath. "Agreed."

Rylan moved forward then and shook his hand. "Come back tomorrow and I'll have a list of jobs to be done."

It was more than Adam had ever dared hope. "Thank you, Rylan. I appreciate it."

As Adam retraced his steps down the hall of the orphanage, elation warred with disappointment. He lifted a quick prayer for the fortitude to keep his promise to Rylan, yet in order to do so, he would have to stay far away from the tempting Miss Maggie.

Gabe stuffed his hands in the pockets of his trousers as he turned onto Madison Avenue. The sudden attack of nerves told him this might not be the smartest thing he'd ever done. In all likelihood, Chief Witherspoon would object to Gabe's impromptu visit to the Hastingses' manor. Yet back home, if one of their neighbors had suffered a fire, the whole community would have come together with enough food to feed the British army and all other sorts of care packages for the victims. Surely it wasn't out of the ordinary for him to go by and check on the state of the house . . . and its occupants?

The mere thought of seeing Aurora again quickened Gabe's pulse. Though he'd met her but twice, it was more than her breathtaking beauty that had captured Gabe's attention. Her sweet demeanor, the way she loved her family, worried about her cat, and showed concern for her housekeeper only added to her appeal.

The image of Brigid's cunning green eyes and sharp tongue came to mind. Her flirtatious ways, ones Gabe had mistakenly believed to be solely for his benefit, had flattered his ego. But nothing about Brigid's fickle affections and brash kisses could compare to the genteel, refined Miss Hastings. He could barely remember what Brigid looked like — because now when he closed his eyes, all he saw was Aurora.

For the first time since leaving home, Gabe experienced a twinge of regret over having to return to Ireland at the end of the summer. If he were able to stay longer, he might have time to see if something would develop between them. His steps slowed as he reached Aurora's home and once again took in its grandeur. Reality became a cold splash of water. What manner of fool was he? A girl of Aurora's wealth and cultured upbringing would want nothing to do with a poor firefighter from a tiny Irish village.

He ran his fingers over the coins inside his pocket. Their familiar jingle calmed his nerves. He was here to do the neighborly thing, nothing more. He'd inquire as to everyone's health and then head back to the station. If the chief had no need of him today, he'd see if Rylan could use a hand at the orphanage.

Before he lost his nerve, Gabe climbed the stairs to the front door and clapped the brass knocker.

Seconds later, the housekeeper answered the door, her face smudged with dirt. Gabe stared in surprise, sure this was not the normal manner in which the woman presented herself to callers.

"Hello, I'm Gabriel Montgomery, one of the firemen from last night."

She smiled, dirt creasing her cheeks. "I remember you, Mr. Montgomery. I'm Mrs. Forrester, the Hastingses' housekeeper. I'm glad to have the chance to thank you again in person."

Gabe shifted on the doorstep. "No need

for thanks, ma'am. We were only doing our job."

"You have no idea how you saved my sanity. I'd have never forgiven myself if anything had happened to Miss Aurora. I just couldn't brave the smoke to go up those stairs." Her chin began to wobble.

"That's a very common reaction to the threat of fire. Nothing to be ashamed of." He cleared his throat, still a bit raw from the smoke. "Would Miss Hastings be home by any chance?"

The woman shook her head. "As you can tell, we're in the process of cleaning the debris from the kitchen, and Mr. Hastings moved the family to a hotel until they head out to their summer home on Long Island."

Gabe drew in a full breath, half relieved and half disappointed that he wouldn't see Aurora after all. "Well . . . I just wanted to make sure she suffered no ill effects."

Mrs. Forrester smiled. "Not at all. Miss Aurora's right as rain. Even that pesky cat is fine."

Gabe laughed. "Please convey my best wishes to the family. Good day to you." He tipped his cap to the woman and slowly retraced his steps back to the fire station, determined to put Aurora out of his mind. Perhaps the good Lord was sending him a message. If so, it was probably better that he didn't see her again.

The station, normally a hubbub of activity, seemed unnaturally quiet as he made his way toward the chief's office at the rear of the building. He'd raised his hand to knock when a feminine voice met his ears.

"I wanted to come by and personally commend Mr. Montgomery for his bravery last night."

Gabe's pulse kicked up a notch. Aurora Hastings sat across from Chief Witherspoon's desk, hands clasped daintily on her lap, a covered basket at her feet.

"I appreciate the sentiment, Miss Hastings. However, I'm afraid Mr. Montgomery violated proper procedures —"

Her back stiffened away from the chair. "I hope you're not planning to discipline him, because I truly believe he saved my life — and that of my cat, as well."

Gabe bit back a groan. He knew that if the chief found out about Petunia, Gabe would be in even more trouble.

"You mean to tell me he went back . . . for a cat?" The screech of his superior's voice raised the hairs on the back of Gabe's neck.

He had no choice but to step into the room. "Excuse me, sir. I couldn't help but overhear —"

"Montgomery," the chief bit out, apparently doing his best to curb his temper. "Miss Hastings came to thank you for your heroics at the fire."

Aurora got quickly to her feet.

Gabe swallowed and looked down into two blue pools of concern. Was it his imagination or was she offering a silent apology for saying too much?

"No need for thanks, Miss Hastings. I was happy to help." He gave her what he hoped to be his best smile.

A pink hue flooded her cheeks. "Oh, I brought you this as a small token of our gratitude." She bent to pick up the basket at her feet and handed it to him. "It's for all the men who helped save our home," she added hastily.

His hand brushed hers as he took the basket from her, and he let his fingers linger a moment longer than necessary.

"They're scones and tea cakes from the local bakery, since our kitchen is out of service at the moment."

He lifted the cloth to peek underneath and sniffed in appreciation. "Thank you for your thoughtfulness."

"I'm sure my men will enjoy them." The chief's countenance had relaxed, but the determined gleam in his eye told Gabe he was in for a lecture about rescuing pets.

"May I escort you home, Miss Hastings?"

She hesitated, glancing over at his boss. "If I'm not taking you away from your work . . ."

Gabe waited for the chief to say yay or nay. The man huffed out a sigh and waved a hand. "Off you go. But I want to speak to you when you return."

"Yes, sir." It would be worth the impending reprimand to spend time with Aurora. He turned to offer her his arm.

She beamed at him. "I'd be delighted to have your company, Mr. Montgomery."

Aurora had never felt so self-conscious walking the streets of her neighborhood before. Many times she'd gone out accompanied by a man who wished to court her, but never had she worried about what to say, how small her steps were, or if the wind mussed her hair. This morning she'd wanted nothing more than to see Gabe again, yet now that she had his undivided attention, her mouth seemed pasted shut. Strolling beside the handsome fireman, Aurora clutched her reticule and wished she were one of those chatty types who could talk about anything to anyone.

"I understand your family is staying at a hotel for a few days, and then you'll be off to your summer home."

Aurora glanced at him sharply. "How did you know that?"

One dark brow rose in a sheepish manner. "I went to your house earlier to see how you — um, to see how your family was faring. The housekeeper told me."

"Oh. That was kind of you to come by." She gave a light laugh. "I suppose we both had the same idea." Only Aurora wasn't sure his motives were the same as hers. She fought to retain her composure.

"I believe Mrs. Forrester mentioned Long Island. Is your home anywhere near Irish Meadows?"

"Yes. We're practically neighbors."

"So that's why you were at their party. Are you friends with Brianna and Colleen, then?"

Aurora's reply stuck in her throat. She wet her lips and tried to formulate a polite response. After all, Gabe was related by marriage to the O'Learys. "Brianna and I served on a few church committees together."

She stared straight ahead as she walked, conscious of his gaze on her.

"Why do I get the feeling there's something you're not willing to say?"

Aurora raised a hand to clutch her hat as a quick wind threatened to snatch it from her head. Gabe moved to shield her from the dust swirling around them until the gust died down.

"Thank you." She shook out her skirts and continued on. "You're right. My relationship with the O'Leary family is . . . complicated." She took two more steps. "For a short time, I was betrothed to Gilbert Whelan."

Gabe stopped mid-stride. "Brianna O'Leary's fiancé?"

"Yes." Aurora kept moving forward, forcing him to keep pace with her.

"Forgive me, but he seems an unlikely match."

"Papa didn't think so. Gil worked at his bank after he graduated from college. Papa thought the sun rose and set on him. He was quite distraught when Gil broke our engagement."

"I imagine you were, as well."

She sighed. "For a time, I did fancy myself in love with Gil, but it turned out he had feelings for Brianna."

"Why did he court you if his affections lay elsewhere?"

"As I said, it's complicated. Gil did it to

160

please Mr. O'Leary, who wanted leverage with my father." Aurora lifted her chin. Why had she told Gabe of her humiliation at the hand of the O'Learys? She blinked, stunned when Gabe reached for her hand and pulled her to a halt.

"A woman as lovely as you should never have to suffer being a pawn in a man's game. You deserve to be cherished and respected." A flush spread across his cheeks as though he regretted his words.

She stared, not sure what to say. "You're being polite, but thank you. Don't worry, I've gotten over it." *Mostly.*

He resumed his place beside her, and they continued on their way in silence for a piece.

"So what do you do for fun, Aurora?"

Visions of the children at the hospital flew to mind, and she smiled. "I volunteer at the Bellevue hospital. Mostly in the children's wing. Papa doesn't approve, but he tolerates it as a whim I'll get over once I'm married and settled down."

Gabe guided her around a corner onto 34th Street. "That seems like a worthy pursuit."

"Oh, it is. If you could see the children, how much they enjoy being read to and played with — it does my heart good to hear their laughter."

At his unblinking gaze, she suddenly felt foolish for revealing her innermost feelings.

Then a slow grin bloomed on his face. "It does *my* heart good to see you really smile for once. I'm happy you've found something that brings you such joy." He took her elbow as they stepped over a curb. "And what do you plan to do out in Long Island for the summer? Will you volunteer at the hospital there?"

Her back muscles stiffened. "I'm not going to Long Island. Papa doesn't know it yet, but I've made arrangements to stay with a friend in the city. I can't bear to leave my patients here."

"Your patients? You sound like a doctor." A teasing light glowed in his eyes.

She hesitated, then leaned closer. "May I share a secret with you?"

"By all means. I'm good at keeping secrets."

"I plan to enroll in nursing school this fall. One of the doctors is allowing me to observe the nurses when I'm there. So far, he seems pleased. I haven't fainted once."

Gabe gave a hearty laugh. "That's a good thing. We wouldn't want you to be fainting at the sight of blood."

She giggled. "Definitely not."

He sobered. "I consider nursing a most

noble profession. It takes a special type of person to tend the sick."

"I want to do something worthwhile with my life. Not simply spend my days hosting parties and social engagements." She sighed. "I fear I have a battle ahead to convince Papa."

They arrived at the Vanderbilt Hotel, and Aurora stopped in front of the ornate doors. "This is it. Thank you for keeping me company."

"It was my pleasure." He stepped closer to allow a man and woman to pass. "Aurora, you are one of the most admirable young women I have ever met. I will be praying that everything turns out as you hope." He winked, and her heart bumped against her ribs. "You might try bending the Lord's ear, as well, to help change your father's mind. You'd be amazed at what a little prayer can do." He lifted her hand to his lips. "I hope we meet again. Give my best to your family."

"I will. Thank you."

He paused, her fingers still wrapped in his. "If you don't mind me asking, does becoming a nurse mean you never wish to marry?"

Her breath tangled in her lungs as his gaze met hers. "I'm not opposed to marriage," she said slowly. "I believe if God intends me to marry, He'll bring the right man into my life at the appropriate time."

A smile stretched across Gabe's face. "A very wise answer, Miss Hastings." He gave a tug on his cap. "Good day to you."

Whistling a jaunty tune, he turned and sauntered down the street.

Aurora watched him go, a vague sense of unrest plaguing her. When speaking of a husband just now, she hadn't given Philip Reardon a single thought. Instead, her imagination had been filled with Gabe's impish grin and charming Irish lilt.

What that meant, she didn't dare consider.

She'd leave it up to God to determine.

10

Adam let himself in the back door of the orphanage and attempted to shake off the feeling of being an unwelcome intruder. In keeping with Rylan's stipulations, he'd purposely waited until the parade of children had left the premises before venturing indoors. As far as Adam knew, the only people who should be inside were Mrs. Norton, the cook, and old Mr. Smith, who was cleaning the dormitories upstairs. Even the nuns were out at a special church service.

So when Adam heard the unmistakable sound of music, he paused in the hallway before cautiously moving toward the room where he remembered seeing a large piano. The sound became more intense, and the wood of the door vibrated beneath Adam's hand. Whoever was playing had had a lot of training. From the little he'd learned about piano from his mother, an accomplished player in her own right, he recognized the composition. If he wasn't mistaken, the piece wafting out was either Bach or Beethoven.

But his curiosity would not be sated until he discovered who was playing. He nudged the door open enough to peer inside. Across the room, Maggie sat at the piano, her eyes closed. An expression of near ecstasy glowed on her face as her hands flew over the keys. The power of the music combined with the breathtaking beauty of the artist mesmerized Adam. He stared, drinking in the scene until he felt like a voyeur. When the tempo changed to a slower pace, he moved away and let the door close without a sound. Then, before he could be discovered spying on Rylan's sister like a besotted fool, he made his way to the utility room to get the tools he needed to fix the two broken desks in the classroom. As he descended the stairs to the basement, the haunting melody stayed with him, as did the ethereal beauty of Maggie's face.

How Maggie had missed this feeling — the joy of the notes resonating within her as they burst forth from her fingers. Her confidence grew while she played, forgotten bliss surging through her as the emotion in her music touched her soul. She had long equated the rapture of music with the rhapsody of God's great love for her.

Thank You, Lord, for this marvelous gift. For the healing power of music.

When her fingers at last began to ache, she reluctantly moved away from the piano. Past experience had taught her not to push herself too hard when she'd been away from the keys. She needed to ease back into daily practice.

After closing the lid on the magnificent instrument, Maggie rose slowly from the bench, careful not to put too much weight on the foot she'd injured during a game with the children the previous day. She limped toward the classroom, purposely ignoring the twinge of pain. As much as Maggie had wanted to join Colleen and the children on their outing, her swollen ankle had made it impossible.

Instead, Maggie consoled herself by taking advantage of the time alone to play the piano, and she planned to familiarize herself with the material in the classroom — in particular some intriguing books about American history. If she wished to become a teacher in America, she'd have to learn the country's history. No time like the present to begin. She hoped to impress the nuns with her eagerness to learn, as well as with her time volunteering in the classroom. If she obtained a reference from the good sisters, maybe she could find a position in one of the local schools by the fall. That, coupled with any possible work playing the organ, and she should be able to stay in New York.

The door creaked as she entered the classroom, unusually silent without the bustle of children. Afternoon sunlight streamed through the high windows, casting beams of light over the desks.

The books she wanted were stored on the top shelf of the far bookcase, likely to keep the children from damaging the teacher's resources. Maggie huffed out a determined breath and dragged a stool over. She stretched to reach the top shelf and pulled out one book, sending a cloud of dust into the air above her head. Obviously these resources weren't used very often.

The urge to sneeze hit hard. She wiggled her nose to control it and reached farther for another volume.

"What in tarnation are you doing up there? Trying to break your neck?"

Maggie squealed and jerked on her perch, putting undue weight on her weakened foot. The book slipped from her grasp. She made a grab for it, vaguely conscious of Adam charging into the room. Her ankle buckled, and for one blinding moment, she feared a sprained ankle would be the least of her worries.

As the book hit the floor with a resounding *smack,* strong hands gripped her waist, lifting her off the stool. Before she could utter a warning, Adam set her firmly on the ground. She gasped at the searing pain that shot through her leg, causing her to stumble, her face coming into contact with the scratchy wool of Adam's vest.

He gripped her by the elbows and lifted her, holding her weight off her injured foot. "Steady there."

Through her haze of pain, Adam's calm voice soothed her. The man everyone had warned her about held her gently in his arms until she had regained her equilibrium enough to raise her head.

"My ankle," she whispered. "It's sprained."

"But you barely touched the floor."

"I hurt it yesterday, and I think I twisted it again."

He scowled. "Why would you climb up there on an injured ankle?"

"Just stubborn, I suppose." She attempted a laugh to cover her discomfort and moved farther away, keeping her weight on her good foot. "Thank you. I think I can manage now."

Adam bent to retrieve the fallen book, wiping the dust from the leather cover. "Is this what you risked life and limb for?" The slightly baffled expression on his face made her feel foolish.

"Aye. Thank you." She took the book, tucked it under one arm, and then paused. "What are you doing in here? I thought you worked outside." Maggie had been amazed that Rylan had hired Adam — even for outdoor work.

"Rylan asked me to repair two of the desks while the children were out."

She took note then of the toolbox he'd dropped inside the door when he'd rushed to her aid. "Oh . . . well." She swallowed, trying not to think about him holding her moments earlier. "I'd best let you get on with your work. Thank you again for your assistance."

He stood studying her, unblinking. "I heard you playing the piano earlier. You have an amazing talent."

The intense blueness of his eyes unnerved her as much as his hands on her waist had. She shook her head. "I'm afraid I'm rusty. It's been a while since I've played."

One brow quirked. "If that's rusty, I can't

imagine you in full form."

The compliment left her off balance in more ways than one. She started to move away and almost went down as her ankle faltered. Once again, Adam caught her in a firm grip. Every sense heightened, rendering the pain in her foot null and void. His male scent, a mixture of soap and the outdoors, swirled around her. She made the mistake of looking up, and the emotion smoldering in his eyes tripped her pulse. Her gaze shifted to his full lips, surrounded by the trim beard and mustache. Her fingers ached to touch his jaw, to discover if the facial hair was coarse or soft. To pull his face close and . . .

Suddenly he stiffened and set her away from him. "You'd best go and rest that foot."

Mortification burned up her neck. Had her thoughts shown on her face? She stepped back and smoothed her skirt. "I will. Thank you."

Turning, she limped away with as much dignity as she could muster.

Adam folded his arms over his chest, trying to ignore a mad desire to scoop up the stubborn woman and save her from hobbling like a cripple. But he'd already broken one rule, albeit by accident, just by being in the same room as Maggie. Still, her injured expression chafed at him. "Maggie, wait a minute."

She whirled around with amazing agility for one with a sprained ankle. "Yes?"

"I didn't mean to sound harsh. It's just that . . . well, I'm sure your brother mentioned the condition of my employment here."

When she shook her head, he continued. "I'm to stay away from the children . . ." He paused for effect. "And more specifically, from you."

Her eyes darkened to the color of wet steel. "Rylan has no right to dictate who I can or cannot speak to."

"As a brother concerned for your welfare, he does."

She threw out her free hand, disgust evident on her face. "I am sick to death of my brothers trying to protect me from everything. As if I have no mind of my own."

For a moment, Adam thought she might stamp her foot in frustration.

Instead, she tilted her chin. "I'm sorry if Rylan made you feel . . ."

"Like a leper?" He gave a rueful smile. "I *am* a leper, Maggie. A man who's spent time in prison is not welcome many places. It's the price I have to pay, and I accept it."

It was the first time he'd acknowledged to her that he was an ex-convict. He held himself still, waiting for her reaction.

To her credit, she didn't flinch or look away. The only change in her demeanor was a hint of regret that passed over her features. "I'll not do anything to jeopardize your position here. But I won't ignore you if we run into each other." She moved a step closer. "Deep down, you're a good man, Adam O'Leary. One who's made a mistake and is trying to make up for it. I would never hold that against you."

Too taken aback to utter a word, Adam watched her hobble away.

Maggie's words stayed with Adam for the rest of the afternoon, long after he'd finished the minor repairs on the two desks. Her compassionate reaction to his incarceration proved what an amazing woman she was, which only made it harder to put her out of his mind.

Adam blew out a sigh and hefted a pair of pruning shears. He'd moved outside to trim the hedges surrounding the orphanage property, a taxing job that caused a film of sweat to dampen his back. As he paused from his task, a rustling noise on the other side of the fence caught his attention. Was someone in the alley between the orphanage and the neighboring building? He'd noticed a strange man passing by the orphanage several times in recent days. If it was the same man, Adam would make sure the fellow realized he wasn't welcome here.

Adam set his tool on the ground and quietly opened the gate to peer out. The swish of a skirt accompanied a flash of purple from someone passing on Lexington Avenue. A niggle of suspicion pulled Adam toward the street. A woman in a purple dress cast a furtive glance over her shoulder.

Adam stiffened the moment he recognized her. Jolene Winters worked in the saloon that Adam had once frequented — and she did not just serve drinks. What was she doing on this side of town?

She stopped, and for a moment Adam wondered if she'd seen him. But then she turned and hurried off. Something about her actions bothered Adam, though for the life of him he couldn't say why. Just seeing the blatant reminder of his past made the bile roil in Adam's stomach. Shaking off a feeling of foreboding, he headed back to continue his work.

At the gate leading to the rear of the orphanage, Adam halted. A piece of colored cloth protruded from beneath the foliage.

He frowned. Why hadn't he noticed this earlier?

Adam bent to tug at the material, which looked to be an old quilt. Finding it unyielding, he knelt to use both hands. An innate sixth sense raised the hair on the back of his neck, warning him to take care. As gently as possible, he pulled the bundle out into the open. Palms moist, he peeled back the fabric and stared uncomprehendingly at the sleeping face of an infant. Adam swallowed. He *hoped* it was merely sleeping. He pressed a tentative finger under its chin, relieved to find the skin warm and a light pulse beating.

He raised his head to scan the area. Had Jolene left this child? Was it hers — or perhaps one of the other saloon girls' offspring? With no one in sight, Adam lifted the fragile bundle and reluctantly went in search of Maggie, praying she'd have some idea what to do with a baby.

In the orphanage's main floor parlor, Maggie sat with her sore ankle raised on a footstool and attempted to concentrate on her book. The words on the page blurred before her, their meaning lost. For reasons she dared not examine, her encounter with Adam O'Leary had left her restless and unable to settle her mind.

Annoyance at Rylan for demanding that Adam avoid her chafed at her pride, yet she couldn't completely fault her brother for attempting to shield her from a man he considered a criminal. Still, she was a grown woman who could take care of herself. Surely there was no need to ban Adam from her presence — unless Rylan feared she would form an unwelcome attachment.

Her heart gave a traitorous thump. In all honesty, she couldn't deny her fascination with Adam — an attraction unlike anything she'd ever felt for Neill. In the months they'd courted, she'd discovered Neill's outward good looks and charming personality hid a controlling nature, one that eventually drove Maggie away. She shivered. No, Maggie would take a gentle man like Adam any day over the likes of Neill.

Somewhere in the outer area of the building, a door slammed. Maggie tensed, waiting for the giggles and voices of the children, but nothing except the thump of heavy footsteps met her ears. Footsteps too vigorous to be Mr. Smith's. And Adam had left the building over an hour ago. Mrs. Taft, the receptionist, had left for the day, and as far as Maggie knew, she was alone.

Surely Neill wouldn't dare . . .

She straightened on her seat, willing her nerves to settle. The footfalls passed her door and continued toward the classroom. She held her breath, waiting, until she heard the classroom door open and close.

Unable to remain seated a moment longer, Maggie limped to the parlor door and cracked it open. She poked her head out, surprised and relieved to see Adam in the middle of the corridor. He stood, clutching a cloth bundle in front of him.

"Maggie." His expression of relief was evident even at a distance. He turned and strode toward her. "I need your help. Someone left an infant by the back gate."

Maggie's mouth fell open. "A babe?"

He nodded. "I discovered the blanket sticking out from under the shrubbery."

With a reverent breath, she took the bundle from him, cradling the head in the crook of her elbow, and peered down into the perfect little face. "How precious."

"Do you think it's all right? Should we fetch the doctor?" Anxiety oozed from his words.

"Let's take a closer look." She went back into the parlor and laid the baby on the sofa. Very carefully, she unwrapped the covering. The child was dressed in a plain cotton gown. "I'll have to check the diaper area, in case you're squeamish."

He shot her a wary glance, but then shrugged. "Go ahead."

As Maggie lifted the gown and opened the diaper, the infant began to squirm.

A minute later, Maggie smiled as she re-pinned the cloth. "It's a wee girl. She's perfect, though she's very young and her nappy isn't wet, which isn't always good. I remember my sister-in-law always checking the twins' nappies, saying a dry one could mean the babe was dehydrated." She wrapped the piece of quilt around the now-whimpering child and lifted her to her shoulder. Maggie stood and rocked the little one as she had her own nieces and nephews many times. Soon the baby relaxed into a slumber.

"You seem to know how to handle an infant." Adam shuffled from one foot to the other, mangling the cap in his hand.

"I have four nephews and two nieces, so I've had a fair bit of experience." She looked up at him. "This babe is only a few weeks old. We'll have to find a way to feed her since she's sure to be hungry soon." A wave of sadness engulfed her. "Who would leave such a precious child under a bush? Her mother must have been desperate."

Adam stiffened. His jaw became a hard line.

She stilled. "What is it?"

He muttered under his breath as he paced the carpet, raking his hand through his hair. At last he stopped in front of her. "I may have an idea where to find the mother."

A sense of foreboding snaked up her spine. "Where?"

His brows thundered together. "I'll explain later. But first I'm going to fetch a doctor. I couldn't live with myself if anything happened to the child." He jammed his cap on over his now-messy hair. In two strides he reached the door, then paused. "Will you be all right here alone with her?" His gaze moved to her foot.

She blinked, amazed to realize she hadn't felt any pain as she rocked the infant, though she'd likely pay for it later. "We'll be fine. Off you go." She gave him a smile of encouragement, a secret thrill warming her insides that he'd thought about her welfare and the baby's before considering any repercussions for himself.

"I'll be back as soon as I can."

Maggie lowered herself and the baby to the sofa, feeling oddly bereft when she heard the main door shut.

Twenty minutes later, noise erupted in the

179

hall once again. Maggie's pulse sprinted. She told herself it was simply relief for the child's sake, but she couldn't deny a rush of anticipation to see Adam again.

When she heard the patter of many feet accompanied by childish chatter, a wave of disappointment hit hard. For a short time, it had seemed that she and Adam existed in their own little world.

"Maggie?" Colleen peered into the room. "We're back. How is your ankle?" She stopped right in the middle of the room, her focus aimed on the bundle in Maggie's arms. "Is that a baby?"

"It is." Maggie hesitated to say more, worried to confess Adam's part lest she cost him his position. Yet Colleen and Rylan would find out soon enough.

The color drained from Colleen's face, and for a moment Maggie feared she would fall to the floor in a faint. It occurred to Maggie then how difficult this might be for Colleen, desperately wanting a baby of her own.

"May I hold it?" Colleen's voice was a mere whisper.

"Of course." Maggie held out the baby to her. "It's a girl — very young, from what I can tell."

Colleen cradled the child like a piece of

delicate china. "How . . . where did you get her?"

"Someone left her under the bushes by the gate." Maggie hobbled across the room and sank gingerly onto the sofa.

Colleen sat beside her and lay the baby on her lap.

Maggie's words seemed to penetrate, and Colleen snagged her with a piercing look. "What were you doing outside? You were supposed to rest your ankle."

Maggie bit her lip. "Adam found the baby and brought her inside. He's gone to fetch the doctor to check on her."

Loud voices sounded in the hallway. Maggie recognized Rylan's voice but couldn't make out what he was saying.

The voices trailed off, and Rylan entered, followed by a man carrying a doctor's bag. Maggie watched the door, waiting for Adam. When he didn't appear, she knew Rylan must have sent him away. Her heart squeezed at the unfairness of the situation.

Rylan moved immediately to Colleen's side. "Someone left a baby?"

"Yes. Isn't she beautiful?" Colleen breathed reverently.

"She certainly is." He gave Colleen a tender smile. "Dr. Reardon is here to examine her."

While the man opened his bag, Maggie slipped into the now-empty corridor. Repressing a sigh of disappointment, she limped toward the back of the building, trying to determine which way Adam would have gone. She passed through the kitchen and exited through the back door.

At the far side of the yard, pieces of shrubbery flew in all directions under the ferocity of Adam's shears. Maggie shored up her courage and made her way gingerly across the grass. Her pulse bumped hard when he trained angry eyes on her.

"Go back inside. You shouldn't be out here."

She hobbled closer. "Did Rylan take you to task for talking to me?"

He turned back to his work. "He expressed his . . . feelings on the matter."

Maggie grimaced. Why was her normally fair-minded brother being so hard on Adam? "I'm sure when I explain —"

"Don't bother." Adam clipped harder, shoulder muscles straining. "I broke our agreement. He has every right to fire me if he chooses."

Alarm and outrage slammed through her. "I won't let him. When he learns how kind you were with the baby —"

Adam whirled around. "Stop it, Maggie.

Stop making me out to be some kind of saint. Pretend I'm invisible like the rest of the world."

Tears filled her eyes, and her throat grew tight. She swallowed hard. "I'm sorry, but I don't think I can do that."

Her gaze fused with his. She willed him to see that she believed in him, that she shared his pain.

Raw agony glowed in his eyes for a moment before a shuttered look came over his features, as though he'd drawn a curtain between them. "No good can come from associating with a known criminal. If you want to make something of your life, you'd best remember that."

Maggie struggled for an argument to change his mind, but he'd turned back to his clipping, leaving her emotions as slashed as the foliage on the ground. She began to limp away, but her concern for the child made her stop. "You said you might know where to find the babe's mother. Will you try?"

He clenched his jaw, then finally gave a tight nod without looking at her. "It may take a day or two."

At his unyielding profile, Maggie gave a resigned sigh. "I'll let Colleen and the doctor know."

11

Why had he ever mentioned he might know who'd left the baby at the orphanage?

In the shed at the back of John's church, Adam hammered nails into a piece of wood with a force that reverberated up his arm. John had given Adam the leftover lumber from a recent church renovation project to build furniture with in his spare time. But even the intense physical labor could not take away the dread plaguing Adam at the idea of returning to the very place he'd been arrested. Only the thought of an innocent child in need of its mother, as well as Maggie's huge imploring eyes, made refusing her request impossible.

He could not let either one of them down.

Later that morning, Adam got off the streetcar several blocks from his destination, intending to walk the rest of the way. Respectable men didn't frequent the type of establishment he was headed to. And the one thing Adam craved almost as much as his mother's forgiveness was respectability.

He tugged his cap low over his forehead, glad that a haircut now rendered his auburn hair almost unnoticeable beneath it. His beard might be a giveaway if anyone saw him, though back when he'd frequented the saloon, Adam had worn his face clean-shaven.

With his shoulders hunched and hands stuffed in his pockets, he made his way to the rundown saloon. At the entrance, he paused, noting the peeling paint and rotting wood. Like a man facing the hangman's noose, he opened the door and stepped inside.

It took a moment for his eyes to adjust to the dim interior. The familiar odors of stale beer and cigarette smoke made his stomach lurch. The same scarred tables sat in pre-cisely the same arrangement as he remem-bered. An old man slumped in a chair at one of the corner tables. To the far left, Marty, the bartender, lifted his head. His eyebrows rose to his thinning hairline.

"O'Leary? Is it really you?"

Adam cringed at the sound of his name echoing in the near-empty room. He moved toward the bar. "It's me."

Marty set the glass he'd been drying on

the counter with a thump. "We heard you were doing time."

A muscle pulsed in Adam's jaw. "Got out a few weeks ago." He scanned the room. "I'd appreciate it if you kept that news to yourself."

Marty gave a knowing nod. Although he worked in this seedy establishment, Marty kept his nose clean of the illegal activities that occurred here. "Fair enough. Can I get you a drink?"

Adam took in the rows of bottles lining the shelf behind Marty and held back a grimace of distaste. How many times had he overindulged and woke the next morning with little memory of the night before? *Lord, forgive me.* "No, thanks. That's another vice I've given up."

Marty wiped his wet hands on a stained apron at his waist. "What brings you by, then?"

Adam leaned forward and lowered his voice. "I'm looking for Jolene. She still work here?"

Jolene had served drinks to the patrons in the saloon — in addition to the extra favors she'd performed in the rooms upstairs.

Marty hesitated. Adam could almost see beads of sweat forming on his brow.

"Funny you should ask. She disappeared

186

for six, seven months. Then two days ago, she showed up again, asking for her old job back."

"Did Max give it to her?"

Marty shook his head. "Not in the tavern. But . . ." His gaze swung to the door leading to the back room, where Max and his cronies hatched their deals. Adam only prayed that they'd still be sleeping off the effects of the night before.

"I think Max may have given her a job upstairs . . . if you get my drift."

Adam's focus flicked toward the back staircase, and he flinched. Would he be forced to climb those stairs and find her? Every fiber in him balked at the thought.

"She's not there now, if that's what you're thinking. But Fran is. She may know something more."

Marty had a point. Fran and Jolene had been best friends as well as coworkers. If anyone would know where Jolene was staying, Fran would.

"Did I hear my name?" A feminine voice sounded from around the corner.

"Hey, Frannie," Marty said. "We were just talking about you."

Adam turned to see a girl who, despite the heavy makeup adorning her wan face, looked ten years older than the last time he'd seen her. Faded brown hair wisped out from her topknot, framing shallow cheeks. A low-cut red dress, highly out of place for the middle of the morning, hugged her thin frame.

She sashayed over to Adam. "Well, if it ain't Mr. High-and-Mighty O'Leary."

"Hello, Francine. How have you been?" As much as it pained him, he had to be friendly if he wanted to get any information from her.

"Just fine, sugar. Have you finally decided to take me up on my offer?" She rubbed a hand down his sleeve.

Discreetly he pulled back, hoping his distaste didn't show on his face. "I've come to ask a favor," he said in a low voice.

She smiled suggestively and leaned closer. "Anything for you, honey."

Adam swallowed. "Is there somewhere more private we could talk?"

"Sure thing." She winked at him.

He threw a desperate glance at Marty.

"You can use my office." Marty motioned to a narrow hallway. "Second door on the right."

"Thanks, Marty."

Adam led Francine to the dingy space that served as Marty's office, which in reality was more of a storeroom. He pulled the door almost closed behind them, not wanting their conversation overheard.

"Have you seen Jolene recently?" he asked without preamble.

Francine's expression hardened. "What business is that of yours?"

Adam prayed for the words to convince Francine to confide in him. He tried to soften his stance and his manner. "Look, Fran, I think Jolene may have gotten into some trouble. I'm trying to help, that's all."

She bit her painted lip, staring at him with hard brown eyes. "Why would you want to help Jolene?"

"Didn't I always treat you girls with respect?" He kept his tone steady.

"Yeah, you were a real gentleman." She didn't make it sound like a compliment.

Adam weighed his choices and opted for the truth. "I saw Jolene outside St. Rita's orphanage the other day. I think she may have left a baby there."

Fran's gaze skittered away. She folded her arms across her waist and took a few steps across the room.

Adam followed her. "Did Jolene have a baby?"

No response.

"Did you?"

She whirled around. "I'm not that stupid."

"Then who?"

The woman clamped her lips shut, her foot tapping on the warped floorboards.

"Come on, Fran. There's a little girl whose life may depend on me finding her mother." A slight exaggeration, but one he hoped would accomplish his goal. He didn't know much about babies except that they fared better with their mothers, and holding that fragile life in his arms had made Adam feel responsible for the little girl's well-being.

Sure enough, a flash of sympathy softened Fran's sharp features. "Is the baby okay?"

"For now, but she'll have a better chance if she's with her mother."

Fran pulled a rickety chair over and sank onto it with a shuddering sigh. "You're right. It's Jolene's. She asked me not to say anything. She needs her job here, and if Max knew about the baby, he might not hire her."

"Did he?"

Fran nodded. "She starts tonight." She raised tormented eyes to Adam. "I don't know how she's going to do it. She's still weak from the birth."

Adam bit back an oath. "Did Jolene want to keep the baby?"

Fran gave a sad smile. "She'd give any-thing to be able to keep her. But she has

190

nowhere to live, no way to earn money other than . . . this." She spread out her hand to indicate her cheap gown.

Adam nodded. "If I had the means to change that, I would. Being fresh out of jail, I'm having a rough go of it myself."

"So the rumors were true."

"Yes, and I'd prefer that Max not find out I was here." Adam paused. "Will you tell Jolene what I said? She can reach me at the orphanage."

Fran rose and smoothed out her skirt. "I'll tell her. But I can't promise anything more."

Adam nodded. "Fair enough. Take care of yourself, Francine." He moved to the door. "Tell Marty thanks."

Before she could reply, Adam strode down the hall and out a side door that led to the alley. He adjusted his cap, glanced around to make sure no one saw him, and walked out to the street, where he took his first full breath since entering the saloon.

Seated at Colleen and Rylan's dining room table for Sunday dinner, Maggie passed the bowl of peas to Gabe. He grinned and gave her a saucy wink. She studied him as she spooned gravy onto her potatoes. For someone who hadn't wanted to come to America, her brother seemed extra cheery lately.

Something told Maggie that the change in his demeanor might be due to more than his volunteer work at the fire department.

She had a feeling it involved a woman. If so, perhaps Gabe may not be in such a hurry to leave at the end of the summer, after all.

Colleen reached down to coo at Ivy — as she'd started calling the babe — in the wicker basket at her feet. Since the child had arrived, Colleen hadn't let her out of her sight. Nor would she allow Ivy to stay at the orphanage, despite Sister Veronica's assurance that the child would be fine with them.

"This baby needs constant care," Colleen had told her. "And I'm more than willing to provide it."

Rylan's troubled expression as he watched his wife told Maggie that he was as worried as she about Colleen becoming too attached to the infant. If the mother came back to claim her, or if some couple adopted the wee darling, Colleen would be heartbroken.

Colleen straightened, obviously satisfied that Ivy was content, and beamed a smile across the table. "Do you need help with the potatoes, Delia?"

The girl struggled with the serving spoon. "Aunt Maggie can help me." The girl sent

Maggie a pleading look.

"Of course I can."

Since the baby's arrival, Maggie sensed Delia feeling left out and tried to pay extra attention to her niece whenever possible.

Colleen plucked a roll from the basket. "I understand the Hastingses have moved into a hotel while repairs are being done on their house."

Maggie noted with interest the way Gabe perked up at the mention of the name.

Colleen handed Gabe the basket. "Poor Dorothy and Aurora. I can't imagine what this has been like for them. Did you know their cook was responsible? She forgot a pot on the stove when she went to bed."

"They were all lucky the woman sounded the alarm so quickly. The whole house could have burned down." Gabe's grave tone matched his expression.

"I think Dorothy will be looking for a new cook after this. And speaking of cooks, Mrs. Norton has hired a woman part time for the orphanage kitchen. Rylan managed to rearrange the budget to allow her some assistance. So Mary will be starting tomorrow."

"I'll be sure and introduce myself, then." Maggie buttered a roll, hoping this new cook would be half as good as Mrs. Norton, who supplied the Montgomerys with much of their baking.

A knock sounded on the front door.

Rylan frowned "Are we expecting anyone?"

"Not that I know of."

When he excused himself to answer the door, Maggie's appetite deserted her. What if Adam had found Ivy's mother and the woman had come to claim her child?

The murmur of male voices reached her ears.

Seconds later, Rylan appeared in the doorway. "Colleen, Adam is here. He'd like to speak with you."

Maggie's heart jumped into her throat. *Oh Lord, help Colleen face whatever it is he's found out.*

Colleen rose from her chair. "Maggie, will you watch the baby for me?"

"Of course."

Delia hopped off her perch. "I want to see Uncle Adam."

"Not tonight, Delia." Rylan's unusually stern voice stopped Delia cold. "Finish your dinner, please. We'll be back in a few minutes."

With a mutinous frown, Delia climbed back onto her chair while Colleen followed Rylan out of the room.

Gabe set down his fork. "What do you think that's all about?"

Maggie held back a sigh. "I'm afraid Adam may have word about . . ." She gestured to the baby, not wanting to say too much in front of Delia.

"Oh. Then I hope it's good news." But his expression told her he had the same doubts as she.

Maggie couldn't manage to eat another bite. Every sense remained attuned to the room down the hall. She had to know what was going on in that parlor.

"I think we need more gravy." She lifted the container and pushed away from the table.

"Maggie." Gabe's warning growl failed to stop her. She'd grown used to ignoring her brothers.

"Keep an eye on the children," she whispered as she passed his chair.

Instead of entering the kitchen, Maggie stopped outside the parlor door, thankful it wasn't fully closed and that she had no trouble making out Adam's deep voice.

"Did Maggie tell you about the woman I saw in front of the orphanage the day I found the baby?" he asked.

"No, she didn't." Rylan's tone was suspicious.

"I recognized the woman. She worked in a saloon I used to frequent."

There was a pause, and Maggie strained her ears to hear more.

A weighty sigh sounded. "There's no easy way to say this. The woman is a prostitute."

Colleen gasped. Maggie's stomach dipped as she tried not to imagine how Adam was acquainted with such a woman.

"I went to find her, but she wasn't there."

"You went back to that place?" Colleen practically hissed.

"I didn't want to, trust me. But I did it for the babe. She needs her mother."

"Not a mother like that."

Maggie cringed at Colleen's tone, which hovered between disdain and hysteria.

"As Christians, aren't we supposed to treat everyone with respect?" Adam's calm question filtered out into the hall. "Having made my own mistakes, I cannot presume to judge Jolene for her actions."

Jolene? So he knew her by name, then. Maggie's pride at Adam's nonjudgmental attitude warred with a sudden surge of jealousy. Had he known Jolene as more than friends? She didn't dare consider the possibility.

"If this Jolene is such a paragon, why did she leave her innocent baby under a bush?"

"Come now, darlin'." Rylan's soft voice tugged at Maggie. "Let's hear the rest of what Adam came to tell us."

"I spoke with another woman at the saloon who admitted the child is Jolene's. Jolene wanted to keep her, but her lifestyle is not exactly conducive to nurturing an infant."

Maggie's heart broke for the woman, trapped by her circumstances with no way to change them, forced to give up her child.

"I left word where Jolene can reach me. Other than that, there's not much more I can do."

"Do . . . do you think she'll come back for Ivy?"

"Ivy?"

"That's what I've called her. Seems fitting since you found her in the foliage."

A low chuckle sounded. "It's a lovely name, Colleen."

Maggie couldn't stand it. She had to peek around the doorframe. When she did, the compassion on Adam's face almost brought her to tears.

Colleen sniffed. "Do you think she'll want Ivy back?" she asked again.

Adam shrugged. "You never know. It might have been a hasty decision, one she may later regret." He lay a hand on Colleen's shoulder. "Don't get too attached, Colleen. Not yet anyway."

Colleen crumpled the handkerchief between her fingers. "I'm afraid it's too late. I love that little girl, and I intend to keep her."

"Are your eyes dropping, Aunt Maggie?"

Maggie jumped at Delia's voice by her elbow. Gravy sloshed over the side of the container and onto her dress. "Delia! You startled me."

The girl stared up at her. "Daddy says it's not polite to eyes drop."

Rylan appeared in the doorway. "That's right, Delia. Your Aunt Maggie knows better than to *eaves*drop, too."

Heat scorched Maggie's cheeks as her focus moved past Rylan to the amused expression on Adam's face.

Colleen appeared beside her husband. "Maggie has every right to know what's going on. After all, she was the first one to look after Ivy."

"Thank you, Colleen." Maggie attempted to gather her dignity and threw her brother a frosty glare. "Now if you'll excuse me, I have some gravy to clean up."

Adam bit back a chuckle as Maggie stalked off to the kitchen with Colleen close behind. "I imagine Maggie was a handful as a child."

Rylan rolled his eyes. "You have no idea how many hours my mother spent on her knees over that one." He gave Adam a rueful smile. "I pity the man who becomes her husband. He'll have a time reining her in."

The two men shared a grin, then a movement at the door claimed their attention.

A dark-haired man entered the parlor, so similar in looks to Rylan that Adam knew he had to be his brother.

"Colleen said to tell you she's putting the baby to bed." He paused inside the door. "You must be Adam. I'm Gabe."

Adam nodded. "Good to meet you."

Gabe came forward to shake his hand. "Colleen's told us you're working hard to get your life back on track, and I commend you for that."

"Thank you." Adam stiffened, bracing for the comment that was sure to come next.

"I'm happy Rylan could give you some work to tide you over." Gabe paused, a slight frown whispering over his features. "By the same token, I'm sure you understand why we have reservations about any type of . . . connection . . . between you and our sister. 'Twouldn't be proper for a young lady to associate with a criminal."

Although the words were spoken in a gentle manner, Adam felt as though he'd been sucker-punched. *A criminal.* That would be the label he'd wear for the rest of his life — no matter what he did to redeem himself. The two men standing shoulder to shoulder in unity told him as much.

"I understand," he said quietly. "Be assured I would never do anything to harm Maggie or her reputation." He tugged his cap back on. "Good evening, gentlemen."

Adam couldn't fault Gabe or Rylan for their caution. He'd feel exactly the same if any of his sisters were to strike up a friendship with someone like him. Still, it didn't erase the sting.

He didn't dare glance into the kitchen on his way out of the house lest he catch sight of Maggie. Not wishing to see her in this raw state, he pushed out the front door and down the stairs to the walkway below, only then allowing himself to breathe.

When the door opened behind him, he steeled himself for another confrontation.

"Uncle Adam? You didn't say good-bye."

The tiny voice caused prickles of guilt to erupt in Adam's chest. He spun around to see Delia standing on the steps, hurt shining in her wide eyes.

"I'm sorry, Delia. I guess I was in a rush." He held himself back from scooping her up in a hug, in case Rylan was watching from

one of the windows. He wouldn't appreciate Adam interfering with his daughter any
more than his sister.

"Is my daddy mad at you?"

The question snatched the air from Adam's lungs. Her perceptiveness reminded
him that children often knew far more than
adults gave them credit for. "It's a long
story." He sat down on one of the stairs,
surprised to feel a small hand on his shoulder.

"I like stories."

Her sincere blue gaze bored straight
through to Adam's heart. He owed this
child an explanation, and only the truth
would do. "Do you know what prison is?"

She nodded solemnly. "It's where bad
men go."

Bad men. Somehow that label hurt more
than being called a criminal. "Not everyone
who goes to jail is bad. Some just made a
mistake."

"Did you make a mistake, Uncle Adam?"

He held her gaze. "I did. And I went to
jail as punishment."

A movement preceded the sudden weight
in his lap. Delia's arms wound around his
neck, and she pressed a kiss to his bearded
cheek.

"You're not a bad man. If you were, I'd

be afraid of you."

A boulder-sized knot clogged Adam's throat. He kissed the top of her head, blond wisps of hair tickling his nose. "Thank you, sweetheart." Reluctantly, he unwound her arms from his neck. "But we have to honor your daddy's wishes. You'd best go inside before he gets worried."

"Okay." She paused, hand on the railing. "I love you, Uncle Adam."

Another dagger stabbed him. "I love you, too, Delia. Be good for your mommy and daddy."

She gave him a sad nod, as if knowing she wouldn't see him for a while, then quietly went back into the house.

12

Aurora stepped outside the ward on the second floor of the hospital and inhaled deeply, seeking relief from the pungent smells inside. She'd been observing the examinations of two polio patients, and between the body odors and the antiseptic scents, Aurora couldn't wait to breathe clean outside air.

She started down the tiled hallway but stopped when Dr. Reardon came up behind her.

"Miss Hastings, if you're not busy, would you be able to accompany me to St. Rita's? I'm scheduled to do a follow-up examination on the new infant there, as well as check on a few other children."

Aurora turned to face him. This was the first time Dr. Reardon had ever asked her to join him outside of the hospital on a patient visit. Whenever she went to the orphanage, it was strictly to visit with the children — never anything medical. "I'm flattered you would want me along. Is there any particular reason?"

Was it her imagination or did he blush?

"I thought it would be good experience for you."

She still questioned his motivation, but it didn't really matter. She'd been meaning to make a stop at the orphanage, especially after he'd told her about the newly arrived baby. "I'd love to go along."

"Wonderful. Meet me outside in five minutes."

The ride in Dr. Reardon's motorcar proved quite enjoyable. He was a skilled driver and maneuvered through the streets with ease. When he stopped in front of the orphanage, he hurried around to open the door for her and offered a hand to help her alight. She looked up at him and caught the unmistakable flash of attraction in his eyes.

His hand lingered on hers, and for an instant she thought he might lean in and kiss her. Her heart gave a lurch, but she freed her hand and moved forward, almost tripping on the curb.

"Careful there." Dr. Reardon caught her by the elbow.

She clutched the sleeve of his jacket, her breath coming too fast. The fresh scent of soap and wool invaded her space as she struggled to regain not only her balance but her equilibrium, as well.

A chuckle sounded from somewhere behind her. "Hello again, Miss Hastings."

The familiar Irish lilt made Aurora's heart gallop. She turned to see a grinning Gabe Montgomery on the sidewalk.

"Gabriel. I didn't expect to see you here." She wished she could do something to cool her flushed cheeks.

"Are you certain you're all right, Miss Hastings?" Dr. Reardon's concerned face inched closer.

She pulled back, putting some distance between them. "I'm perfectly fine, thank you, Doctor."

Gabe came to stand beside her. "What a lucky coincidence to run into you here." Something akin to pure merriment danced in his eyes.

If only Dr. Reardon wasn't watching her as intently as a scientist viewing a specimen in a lab, she might be able to talk in a coherent manner.

"I'm accompanying Dr. Reardon to check on the children. Dr. Reardon, this is Gabriel Montgomery, Rylan's brother."

The doctor's face brightened. "Ah, yes. I see the resemblance. Good to meet you, Mr.

Montgomery."

"Likewise, Doctor."

They climbed the stairs and entered the main door of the orphanage. Aurora was surprised, and somewhat dismayed, when Gabe followed them in. How was she supposed to be professional and concentrate on the children with Gabe shadowing them?

Aurora removed her gloves and hat and left them in the cloakroom, wishing for a mirror so she could check her appearance. With the tips of her fingers, she smoothed her hair in place and followed Dr. Reardon down the main corridor to the small room he used to see patients. Colleen sat on a chair inside the door, a swaddled infant in her arms. While Dr. Reardon greeted her, Aurora turned to Gabe, who sauntered along behind them.

"What are you doing here?" She didn't intend to sound so annoyed, but she needed her wits about her, and Gabriel Montgomery kept her totally off-kilter. The fact that he'd caught her in a somewhat compromising position with Dr. Reardon did not help matters.

"I'm here to see my brother." He cocked his head to one side. "You don't seem pleased to see me. I could take great offense at that."

Aurora worked to contain her frustration. "I'm not *un*happy to see you. It's just . . ." She waved a hand toward the doctor.

"Miss Hastings, I'm ready to begin." Dr. Reardon's frown made Aurora's stomach sink. Already she'd disappointed him.

"I'd best let you get on with your work." Gabe bowed over her hand. "I'll be seeing you tonight for dinner anyway."

"I beg your pardon?"

One brow rose over eyes that appeared to dance an Irish jig. "Did your father not tell you? He's invited me to dine with you at the Vanderbilt Hotel this evening."

"Oh," she replied weakly. "I guess I'll see you later, then."

As she watched him walk away whistling, Aurora pushed aside the thread of unease winding through her system. Hopefully Papa only intended to thank Gabe for his bravery, but knowing her father, he most likely had an ulterior motive.

One that Gabe might not enjoy in the least.

Adam put the finishing touches of varnish on the pew he'd repaired and then stood back to admire his efforts.

John let out a low whistle as he approached. "You certainly have a way with wood."

"Thank you." Adam allowed the pleasure of the compliment to flow through him. It felt good to be appreciated even for such a simple task. He wiped his hand on a clean rag. "Tell me, John, have you heard if any of your parishioners need any work done?"

John's smile faded. "Unfortunately, all the people I've spoken with have nothing at the moment."

The response wasn't unexpected, yet Adam felt the rush of disappointment nonetheless. He'd been clinging to the hope that someone would be willing to give him a chance — as a favor to John, if nothing else. "Well, thanks for trying. I appreciate it."

He'd have to keep his job at the orphanage a while longer — a slow form of torture being so near Maggie and unable to speak with her. As much as it pained him, Adam knew Rylan and Gabe were right. He had no business talking to Maggie, never mind daydreaming about more. The sooner Adam could distance himself from her, the better.

John walked to the pulpit and placed a book on the dais. "I hope you don't mind, but I looked at some of your work out in the shed."

"I don't mind."

"The pieces are excellent, Adam. Good enough to sell to the public."

"Thank you." Adam replaced the lid on the can of varnish and wiped his brush on a rag.

"Have you ever thought of opening your own business?" John came back and bent to help him pick up the newspapers protecting the floor.

"Thought of it? It's been a dream since I was a child. But my father wouldn't hear of it. He deemed it too lowly a profession."

"So you turned to crime instead. A logical jump."

Adam stiffened until he realized John was teasing him. "You know I never started out to break the law. By the time I realized what I'd gotten involved in, it was too late to get out."

John sobered. "I know."

"Too bad a person's intentions don't count for anything."

"Indeed."

They exited through the rear door and crossed the property to the shed where Adam stored his creations.

John opened the door. "Seriously, Adam, these pieces should be shared."

"I plan to share them." Adam set down

his equipment. "This cedar chest is a wedding gift for my sister Brianna. She's to be married at the end of August."

"It's lovely." John bent to run his hands over the cradle Adam had nearly finished. "Is this for her, as well?"

"No. It's for the abandoned baby Colleen is looking after. She has no real bed for her."

"That's very thoughtful. Especially since her husband hasn't been the most welcoming to you."

Adam put the varnish tin on the shelf. "Rylan has given me work, which is more than most people would do."

A deep frown lined John's forehead. "But he hasn't been very forgiving. He's warned you away from his sister as if you're some type of monster."

"You can't blame him, John. He's only trying to protect his family. My own father has treated me worse."

John straightened. "Speaking of your father, have you done anything more in that regard?"

The cords in Adam's neck cinched, and he rubbed a hand over them. "Not yet. Maybe I'm not ready to know the truth."

John crossed his arms in a pose that told Adam he had a few more tidbits of advice to impart. "You once told me that suspicions about your father have bothered you for years. Like it or not, Adam, you *need* the truth so you can put the pain of your childhood behind you once and for all."

Adam released a weighty sigh. "You're right . . . as always."

"And you're good for my ego." John clapped a hand on Adam's shoulder. "Why don't you take the rest of the day off? You could probably catch the next train to Long Island."

John was right. Adam had put this off long enough. "Thanks. I think I will."

Once John had left, Adam took extra care to ensure everything in the shed was tidy, and then, with no excuses left, he closed the door and prepared for the walk to the station.

The train ride to Long Island and the subsequent walk to town gave Adam time to firm his resolve that the course of action he was about to take was absolutely necessary to his peace of mind.

His first stop was a long-overdue visit to the cemetery behind the small church he used to attend with his family. Adam walked through the rows of graves, clutching a handful of wilted daisies he'd picked along the way, and finally halted at the familiar spot where the ornate gravestone of his little brother evoked a host of unwelcome memories.

How Adam used to resent coming here every year on the anniversary of Danny's death. It seemed designed as a form of torture to remind him once again how he'd failed his family.

Daniel James O'Leary, age eight.

Adam's throat tightened at the flashes that invaded his mind. His brother's mop of dark hair — the only one in the family to share their father's coloring — the dusting of freckles across his nose, the impish grin that always meant he was up to no good.

"I should have taken you swimming like you asked, Danny, instead of running off with my friends. I should have been a better brother to you."

His eyes stung as the stark truth penetrated Adam's soul. He'd been jealous of his brother — jealous that their father showed Danny more affection than he'd ever showed Adam. Jealous that Danny looked like their father, while he did not.

Adam forced himself to be brutally honest. Neither Danny nor Gil had deserved Adam's resentment. Even Gil had done nothing to warrant Adam's hatred, his only crime being an affinity for horses that matched James's. In reality, the true source

212

of Adam's anger had been Father himself.

Adam bent to lay the daisies at the base of the large stone. With one knee on the damp grass, he recited the prayers his mother used to make them say, for once finding comfort in the words. When he finished, he traced the carved stone letters with one finger, silently pleading for forgiveness from his brother.

"You deserved so much better, Danny. It should have been me who drowned. Then you'd be here to fulfill our father's dreams."

"Is that you, Adam O'Leary?" Reverend Filmore strode across the grass toward him.

Adam swiped a hand over his eyes as he jerked to his feet, working hard to contain his emotions. "It is, Reverend. How are you?"

"I'm well, my boy. It's good to see you again." He shook Adam's hand.

Had the man not heard where Adam had been for the past few years? Surely not, or he wouldn't be so happy to see him.

Reverend Filmore folded his hands over his stomach. "What brings you here on this fine afternoon?"

"Just paying respects to my brother. It's been a long time since I've been . . . home."

"It has indeed. Staying with your parents, are you?"

"No. I have a place in the city."

"Glad to hear you're getting back on your feet. Well, give my best to your parents."

Adam fell in step with him as he headed toward the church. "I'm not sure if I'll see them today, sir. But I do have a matter you might help me with."

Reverend Filmore turned to peer at him through his spectacles. "What is it, son?"

"I'd like to see my baptismal record."

The pastor came to a halt, and for a brief moment, Adam feared he might refuse.

But at last the man nodded. "Follow me. I keep the records in my office."

It didn't take long for the man to find the ledger in his bookcase and bring the volume over to his desk.

"What year would you be looking at?"

Adam swallowed. "I was born in November of 1889." *If what I've been told is the truth.*

Reverend Filmore flipped through the book until he came to the right time. He ran his finger across the yellowed pages and stopped at an entry near the middle of the page. "There it is, my boy. Your mother liked to have her babes christened within a few weeks of their birth."

Adam held his breath as he attempted to focus on the script.

Adam Francis O'Leary, christened this 24th

day of November 1889. Date of birth: Novem-
ber 18, 1889. Mother: Kathleen Agnes
O'Grady. Father: James Francis O'Leary.

Nothing out of the ordinary there. Did he really imagine there would be a different name for his father? He let out his breath.

"Is there anything else you need?" Reverend Filmore regarded him with a curious stare.

"Actually, there is." Adam still wasn't convinced that he was indeed James's son. "Would my parents' marriage be registered here?"

Reverend Filmore straightened, his expression suddenly wary. "Were they married in this church?"

"I believe so, yes."

"Very well. Let's have a look." He moved to the bookcase, pulled a different volume off the shelf, and laid it on the desk.

His pulse thrumming in his veins, Adam peered over the reverend's shoulder while he scanned the pages, moving backward through the months. At last his finger stopped at the name O'Leary.

"Here it is."

Adam scanned the date in the left-hand column. *March 25, 1889.* He pressed his lips together, doing a quick calculation in his head. Eight months. He sucked in a breath and stepped away from the desk.

"Come now, son. There's nothing to be embarrassed about. You were likely born a few weeks earlier than expected. If not . . . well, your parents wouldn't be the first couple who didn't wait for the wedding night, if you catch my drift." He closed the book with a soft thud.

Adam drew himself up to his full height. "I'm sure you're right."

Reverend Filmore accompanied Adam out of the office and rested a hand on Adam's shoulder. "Talk to your parents, son. It will ease your worries."

Adam replaced his cap as he exited the building. If only it were that easy. "Thank you, Reverend. I'll keep your advice in mind."

"Make it fly, Aunt Maggie." Delia's squeal of delight sounded over the rush of the wind.

Maggie smiled. "I'll try, but you have to help me. Hold the string up high while I run." She lifted the bedraggled-looking kite over her head and began a slow trot across the grass, careful not to trip on her skirt.

She'd promised Delia she'd take her to the park and fly the kite they'd constructed the day before, and today, since there was a slight breeze blowing, Maggie hoped she'd be able to get it off the ground.

When the wind seemed favorable, Maggie released the toy to the elements. It dipped and bobbed, seeming to hover in midair, and then pitched upward on a current.

Maggie rushed back to help Delia with the string if necessary. "That's it. You're doing a fine job."

The paper-and-wood kite managed to maintain the tautness necessary to stay suspended. Delia bit her lip in concentration, holding the string as though it might fly away without her.

Craning her neck, Maggie watched the kite's fledgling journey and laughed out loud with sheer delight. For some reason, her thoughts turned to Adam, wishing he were here to share his niece's joy.

"That's a fine-looking kite you have there."

The small hairs on the back of Maggie's neck rose. She whipped around to see Neill standing beside Delia.

Delia grinned up at him. "Aunt Maggie helped me make it."

"Well, you're a lucky girl to have such a nice aunt." Neill stared at Maggie as he spoke.

Delia scrunched her nose. "You sound just

like her. Do you come from Ireland, too?"

"I do indeed."

What was Neill doing here? When Maggie hadn't heard any more from him, she'd decided he must have given up and returned home. Now here he was again. Had he been watching her all this time?

Her heart thumping an uneven beat, Maggie stepped forward and laid a hand on Delia's shoulder. "Delia, this is Mr. Fitzgerald. He's a friend from home." She shot him a warning look over Delia's head. "Neill, why don't we sit on the bench while Delia flies her kite?"

"I'd like that."

A mixture of irritation and dread swirled in Maggie's stomach as she took a seat on the wooden bench. She glanced around the small neighborhood park, grateful to see another family out for an evening stroll.

"What are you doing? Following me around?"

"How else am I to win you back if you won't see me willingly?" His gaze grew earnest. "Won't you tell your brothers that we're still courting? Then I can call on you properly at the house." He grabbed her hand in his. "Let's have some fun together, Maggie. We can explore the Museum of Natural History together. Take the ferry over to the Statue of Liberty."

For a mad moment, she was taken back to their childhood, when she and Neill, along with a group of neighborhood friends, would race over the meadows, climb trees, and explore the abandoned barns out in the country. But they were children then, and too many things had changed. She sighed and removed her hand from his. "A few days of sightseeing won't change the fact that our lives are on two different paths."

He stiffened, the enthusiasm fading from his features. "What do you mean? We both love our town, both want to raise a family there. I've got a good business that provides a stable income. We'll live above the pub until we can afford our own house."

Maggie shook her head. "I can't marry you, Neill. Though I'm fond of you, I don't love you like a wife should love her husband. I'm afraid nothing is going to change that."

His features hardened. "That's not true, Maggie."

She sighed. There was only one way to make him understand. "I'm not going back to Ireland."

Creases appeared on his forehead. "Not until the end of the summer. But once you have this wanderlust out of your system, you'll be ready to come home and settle down."

"Aunt Maggie, look."

Maggie rose from the bench and squinted at the kite as it careened around the sky in a crazy pattern. She waved at Delia. "You're doing great, sweetheart."

With a silent prayer that Neill would accept the end of their relationship once and for all, she turned back to him. "I'm not going back," she repeated. "I'm staying in New York for good."

Neill shot to his feet, disbelief in his eyes. "You can't be serious."

"I am. I —"

Without warning, he grabbed her roughly and kissed her. At one time, back when she'd actually thought they might make a life together, she'd found his kisses pleasant enough. But today his hard mouth brandished punishment as well as possessiveness.

She shoved him away from her and swiped a hand across her lips. With considerable effort, she reined in her temper. "Forcing yourself on me will get you nowhere. Now, please do us both a favor and don't contact me again."

Maggie lifted her skirt and rushed back toward Delia, just in time to see the kite swoop from the sky and plummet to the ground below.

Delia laughed and ran toward the fallen toy. "Did you see how long it stayed up, Aunt Maggie?"

Maggie forced a smile to her lips. "I did. You're an excellent kite flyer."

As they gathered up the length of string, Maggie glanced behind her to the bench. Neill stood glaring, a look of hatred in his eyes. He jammed his hat back on his head and stalked off down the path.

"Can we try it again?" Delia asked.

All the energy seemed to drain from Maggie's body, leaving her as limp as the kite in her hands. "Maybe tomorrow, sweetie. I think I've had enough for today."

Adam pulled out his pocket watch and checked the time. The train back to Manhattan wouldn't leave for another two hours, which gave Adam plenty of time for a quick trip to Irish Meadows. He stiffened at the thought of facing his father, not prepared for that battle just yet. But a visit with Brianna was long overdue. If Adam's luck held out, perhaps he could talk to her alone.

Twenty minutes later, Adam strode up the road toward his parents' home. He skirted the main entrance and made his way to the servants' door, where he ducked inside a small hallway leading to the kitchen. Pausing to remove his cap, he listened for any sign of Mrs. Harrison at work in her domain. The telltale clatter of pots and pans told him she was indeed there.

"Are you going to lurk in the doorway all day or come in and say hello to your old cook?"

Adam startled at the woman's ability to know the moment someone came near her kitchen. He stepped into the room. "Hello, Mrs. Harrison."

She wiped her hands on her apron and came forward, her round face beaming beneath her white cap. "Why, Adam O'Leary, you are a sight for these weary eyes." She wrapped him in a tight hug, and once again Adam was struck at the manner in which servants at Irish Meadows seemed more family than staff.

"How have you been keeping, Mrs. Harrison?"

"Not bad at all. If you're looking for your parents, I'm afraid they're out for the day."

He breathed a sigh of relief. "Actually, I was hoping to speak with Brianna, if she's home."

"You're in luck. She got back from the library about an hour ago."

"Adam?" The sound of his sister's voice preceded her footsteps into the kitchen. "It *is* you. I thought I heard your voice." Brianna rushed forward to envelop him in his second hug of the day.

Her loving acceptance humbled him. "It's good to see you, Bree. You look wonderful." She had indeed matured into a lovely woman, her cinnamon-colored hair tamed into a tidy roll at the back of her neck.

When she pulled back, moisture rimmed her eyes. "How are you doing? Mama won't say a word about you for fear of upsetting Daddy."

"I'm fine." Adam glanced at Mrs. Harrison and the other maids who scurried about the kitchen. "Could we talk in private?"

"Of course. Why not your old room? No one will bother us there."

He nodded and winked. "Afraid Gil may come looking for you?"

She cast him a scathing glare as she swept toward the servants' staircase. "I may be marrying the man, but he won't stop me from talking to my own brother. Come on."

Adam laughed, following her upstairs. "I'm glad to see you've developed a backbone at last."

She peered over her shoulder. "It was

223

either that or follow Daddy's orders for the rest of my life. Not much of a choice."

They walked along the second-floor hall to Adam's bedroom at the far end. Once inside, Brianna took a seat in the armchair by the window while Adam grabbed his old desk chair and straddled it. He glanced around the room, trying to ignore the rush of nostalgia twisting his insides.

"So what is it?" Bree asked without preamble. "I can tell something's on your mind."

"You're right." He frowned, looking past her out the window.

"This better not be about Gil. Now that we're getting married, I expect you to put your ridiculous animosity aside once and for all."

He chuckled at her ferocious defense. "You'll be happy to know that I'm working hard to do just that. I realize it was never Gil's fault that our father preferred him over me."

"Oh, Adam." Sympathy shone in her green eyes as she laid a hand on his arm. "I've never understood why Daddy treated you so harshly. I thought maybe he had greater expectations for you, being the eldest."

Adam held back a snort. "That's part of it, I'm sure." He ran a hand through his

hair. "Can I ask you some questions —
without you asking anything in return?"

She gave him a wary frown. "What
about?"

"About our parents. Do you know anything about how they met, or their courtship?"

Her brow cleared. "Of course I do."

"I figured if anyone did, it would be my
romantic sister."

She laughed and smoothed the material
of her striped skirt. "Mama and Daddy met
at the mercantile our grandparents owned.
Mama was there one day when Daddy came
in with his father to buy supplies. Apparently she stole Daddy's heart right away."

Adam pondered this for a minute. "How
old was she?"

"About seventeen."

"Did they have a long courtship?"

"I think it was quite quick, if I remember
Mama's stories." A dreamy expression stole
over her face. "They were married in the
same church as I will be soon."

Needing to move, Adam pushed up from
the chair and walked to the four-poster bed.
Absently, he fingered the blue-patterned
quilt that had adorned his bed since childhood. "What about other suitors? Wasn't
Mama promised to someone else when she

met Daddy?"

Brianna's fair brows came together. "You're right. Mama's father had an agreement with a friend of his, a Mr. Drake, that she would marry his son." Brianna tapped a finger to her lips. "I don't know the son's name. But I do know Mama didn't much care for him. As soon as she met Daddy, she knew she could never marry anyone else." The dreamy look returned.

"Do you know anything more about the Drakes?"

Her smile faded. "Not really. What's this about, Adam?"

He set his jaw. "I said no questions, remember?"

She rose from the chair, hands fisted on her hips. "That's not fair —"

"Did Mama say anything about her twenty-fifth wedding anniversary this past winter?"

Brianna's mouth fell open for a moment. "I didn't realize . . ." She stared at him. "You'll be twenty-five this fall, won't you?"

"Yes."

"Then it must have been their twenty-sixth anniversary." She worried her bottom lip with her teeth.

He sighed, unwilling to disillusion his sister. "You're probably right. Must have my dates mixed up."

Brianna grew pensive. "I wonder why no mention was ever made of it last year. How odd."

He moved toward her and settled his hands on her shoulders. "Do me a favor and forget I asked. It's not important. Besides, you have your own wedding to concentrate on now."

His ploy worked, and her features brightened immediately. "I can't believe it's almost here. I'm finally going to be Mrs. Gilbert Whelan."

A whisper of tenderness for his sister curled around his heart. "You really love him, don't you?"

She beamed at him. "I do, Adam. Gil's kind, caring, and so thoughtful. You'd see that if you'd give him a chance."

Adam swallowed his bitterness and managed a nod. "For your sake, Bree, I'll try my best."

13

Gabe stood in the attic room at Rylan's house and peered at his reflection in the warped full-length mirror. He had to bend to see the top of his hair, which he'd slicked back with some type of pomade Rylan insisted all the stylish gentlemen in New York wore. Gabe attempted to adjust his bowtie but finally gave up getting it any straighter.

He turned to collect his wallet from the nightstand and noticed the letter still sitting there. With a heavy heart, he picked up the envelope, the weight of the words it contained adding to his unease. His mother had written of the increasing unrest at home and her worry that if things should escalate to civil war, his two older brothers would join the fight. What would happen to his mother if Tommy and Paddy left? Just when Gabe had been entertaining the idea of extending his stay in America, circumstances at home begged his presence.

Mentally, Gabe berated himself for getting caught up in the ease of life in America. His work at the fire station and the beautiful Aurora had pulled his attention from the plight of his fellow countrymen. How could he forget the strife happening back home? From now on, he would keep that at the forefront of his thoughts — that and his intent to get back home as soon as possible.

He sighed and slipped the envelope under his pillow. He would put this worry out of his mind for now and try to enjoy the evening with Aurora and her family.

Gabe descended to the main level and entered the kitchen.

Colleen turned from her position at the stove. "My, you look handsome. Rylan's suit is perfect on you."

Gabe gave a mock bow. "A sacrifice I'm willing to make to eat at the famous Vanderbilt Hotel." *And to impress the lovely Aurora.* The mere thought of sharing a fine meal with her in a date-like setting made his pulse gallop.

Colleen laid a wooden spoon on the stovetop and wiped her hands on her apron. "Why do you think Mr. Hastings invited you to dinner?"

"I'm sure it's to thank me for helping save

his . . . house from the fire." Wiser to keep Aurora out of the conversation. No use giving his sister-in-law fodder for her overactive imagination.

"But why you? Why not Chief Witherspoon or the other firemen?"

Gabe shifted in his brother's shoes, which pinched at the toes.

"Did he not tell you, my love?" Rylan strode into the kitchen with Delia perched on his shoulders. "Gabe rescued Aurora from her room. No wonder the man wants to thank him."

Rylan swung Delia to the ground. "Go get washed for dinner, sweetheart."

Gabe tugged at his bowtie, uncomfortable under Colleen's speculative stare. A whimper sounded from the basket on the kitchen table, and Colleen moved to scoop up the baby.

Gabe had never been happier to hear an infant cry. "Well, I'd best be off. Don't want to be late."

"Heavens no. What would Aurora think of you then?" Colleen's laughter followed Gabe out the door.

By the time he reached the impressive entrance to the Vanderbilt Hotel, where wealthy patrons swept past him through the massive main doors, nerves swamped

Gabe's stomach. What was he doing pretending to belong in such luxury? He came from a small village where most of his friends lived in thatched cottages, farmed sheep, and met in the pub for a pint after dinner.

Gabe squared his shoulders and, with as much confidence as he could muster, walked into the lobby, where the ornate splendor flabbergasted him. Gleaming marble and crystal reflected light off every surface. Men and women sat on the elegant settees and strolled about the spacious halls. Gabe shook off his awestruck demeanor and headed to find the dining room.

The maître d' lifted his nose at Gabe. "May I help you, sir?"

"Yes, thank you. I'm expected for dinner with Mr. and Mrs. Hastings."

The man inclined his head. "Very good. Follow me."

Conscious of all eyes in the room watching him, Gabe fought the urge to straighten his tie again. They weaved through a maze of tables until at last the man stopped. "Here is your party, sir."

"Thank you." Gabe wondered if he was expected to tip the man, but since he had no ready cash, he focused on the people at the table.

Mr. Hastings, a short, stout man with a handlebar mustache — exactly like in his portrait in the fire station — rose to shake Gabe's hand. "Mr. Montgomery. So glad you could join us."

"Thank you for the invitation, sir." Gabe shook his hand, resisting the temptation to gawk at Aurora as she and her mother came toward him.

"Allow me to introduce my wife, Dorothy."

Gabe bowed over the older woman's hand. She was handsome for her age, with tidy brown hair swept back from her face and twinkling blue eyes. Gabe could see where Aurora got the bones of her beauty.

"And of course you've met my daughter."

Aurora's beaming smile lit up the room. She looked as beautiful as a painting in a yellow gown, her golden curls arranged atop her head.

"It's grand to see you again, Miss Hastings. You ladies look lovely this evening."

Mrs. Hastings tittered like a young girl. "My, my. Such a charming accent."

From the corner of his eye, Gabe caught the irritated expression on Mr. Hastings's face.

Aurora's mother laid a hand on his arm. "I'm so glad I can finally thank you in person, Mr. Montgomery. You have no idea how worried we were about our daughter when we received word of the fire."

Gabe fought the heat creeping into his cheeks. "Thank you, Mrs. Hastings. I'm only glad I was there to help."

They took their seats, and a waiter appeared instantly, as though he'd been lurking around the corner, waiting for his cue.

"Please allow me the liberty of ordering for you, young man. I'm sure you're not used to restaurants such as this back in your country."

Gabe waited a beat until Mr. Hastings spared him a glance. "I will defer to your good opinion, sir."

"We enjoy the duck here. The cook does an excellent job."

Though Gabe would have preferred a thick steak, he didn't contradict his host.

After the orders had been placed, Mrs. Hastings made a fairly obvious attempt to direct the flow of conversation, asking Gabe many questions about life in Ireland. With each response, Gabe got the distinct impression from the scowl on Mr. Hastings's face that he was saying something terribly wrong. Why had the man invited him here if he clearly disapproved of Gabe?

Only Aurora's rapt attention made the

dinner bearable. Gabe couldn't help but wish they were sharing the meal alone, at a private table.

When they'd finished a delicious dessert of crème brûlée, Arthur Hastings patted a napkin to his mustache and cleared his throat. "So tell me, Gabriel, when do you return to Ireland?"

The man couldn't have been more obvious if he'd ordered him aboard the next ship leaving the harbor. Gabe's attention swung to Aurora, who had gone pale. He tried to reassure her with a smile. "My sister, Maggie, and I are here for the summer. We have return passage for the end of August."

A shuttered look came over Mr. Hastings's features. "How lucky for your family that you're able to manage such a long visit. I'm surprised your employer is willing to hold your position for you."

Gabe set down his teacup with a noisy *clink.* "I guess that's the advantage of living in a town where everyone knows one another. Mr. Connors is not just my employer; he's one of my best friends and more than happy to keep my job for me."

An uncomfortable silence descended.

"That type of community sounds wonderful," Aurora said too cheerfully. "We have a similar close-knit feeling in our Long Island neighborhood where we spend the summer."

Gabe smiled again, to let her know he was grateful for her attempt to lighten the mood. "Aye, I witnessed that the night of the O'Learys' party. Though our houses back home are nowhere near as grand as Irish Meadows."

"More like cottages, aren't they?" Condescension dripped from Mr. Hastings's voice.

Gabe's hand stilled on his fork as he fought back a sarcastic retort.

Aurora leaned forward, her eyes darting from her father to him. "I'm sure your home is lovely, Gabe."

"Oh yes," Mrs. Hastings added. "I've heard the scenery is breathtaking. I hope to travel to Ireland one day when Arthur retires." She laughed, as if not expecting that day to come anytime soon.

"I doubt you'll ever get Papa on a ship across the ocean, Mama. Not after the *Titanic*."

"You're right about that, daughter." Mr. Hastings pushed back his chair and got to his feet. "I believe I must call it a night." He turned and extended his hand. "Thank you again for all you did for my daughter during the fire, Mr. Montgomery. I wish you a pleasant stay and a safe trip back to Ireland."

Did Gabe imagine the implied threat in the strength of his grip and his unsmiling countenance? Why bother to buy him dinner and thank him for his service if he obviously found Gabe so distasteful?

Gabe tensed. Could his admiration for Aurora be evident to her father? Perhaps the real reason for this invitation was to send a clear message to Gabe that his daughter was off-limits.

Gabe retrieved his hat from the vacant chair beside him and bowed to Mrs. Hastings and to Aurora. "Good evening, ladies. Thank you for the pleasure of your company."

Mr. Hastings clapped a hand on Gabe's shoulder. "I'll walk you out. Dorothy, Aurora, I will see you upstairs shortly."

Gabe swallowed and wished he could loosen his tie. Before following Mr. Hastings across the room, he allowed himself one last look at Aurora, whose misery shone in her gaze. Not wanting to leave her upset, he winked at her, gratified to see her lips tilt and an attractive blush steal over her cheeks. "I hope to see you again, Miss Hastings."

"Likewise, Mr. Montgomery." A worried

frown still creased the space above her pert nose.

With reluctance, he forced himself to walk away. He found Mr. Hastings waiting in the lobby and approached him with caution, unsure what to expect. "Thank you again, sir, for an evening I shall not soon forget."

The man did not smile. "Just so we're clear, Mr. Montgomery, I expect this to be the last time you have any contact with my daughter. While I appreciate your . . . concern . . . for her well-being, I'm sure you realize that any type of friendship between you would be inappropriate."

A burst of indignation heated Gabe's veins. "What about it would be inappropriate?"

The man raised a brow, clearly taken aback by Gabe's challenge. "There's no point in forming attachments when you live halfway around the globe. Besides, I expect to announce Aurora's betrothal to a suitable candidate by the end of the summer."

The flame of Gabe's temper burned higher. Only supreme self-control held his tongue in check. The man was, after all, Aurora's father, and Gabe would do nothing to cause her grief.

"You've made your position very clear." Gabe set his bowler on his head and adjusted the angle. "I'll not seek Aurora out, but if I happen to run across her during my travels, I will not ignore her." He tipped his hat. "Good night."

He strode out the main door before Mr. Hastings could say another word. Once outside, Gabe immediately ripped off his tie and stuffed the offending piece of material into his pocket. The cool evening air washed over him as he stalked away, frustration pumping with every step. When he happened to glance at one of the windows as he passed, its surface reflected a person Gabe barely recognized. The manicured man in the glass was not him. With a growl, he raked his fingers through his stiffened hair until he managed to dislodge some pieces, which fell over his forehead. What a farce this whole night had been. Dressed like a dandy, trying to pretend he was something he was not — for all the good it had done.

The image of Brigid's face came to mind. No, he was done twisting himself into knots to impress a woman. It wasn't worth it.

This was just the thing he needed to put his goals into perspective. He could not afford to be distracted by a passing flight of fancy.

His homeland and his family needed him

far too much for that.

Aurora paced the plush carpet of the hotel suite, sure the steam of her anger must be escaping from her ears. Never had she been more humiliated by her father's boorish behavior. His tone throughout the evening had dripped with condescension. Surely Gabe must have noticed it, too.

Aurora stopped at the window and pushed aside the curtain, straining to catch a glimpse of Gabe as he walked home. In the darkness, she couldn't distinguish one figure from another. With a sigh, she returned the curtain to its proper place. What could be keeping Papa? Had he stopped at the men's lounge for a brandy? It was entirely possible.

No matter, she would wait as long as it took. Thank goodness her mother had claimed exhaustion and gone straight to bed. Aurora wanted to talk with her father alone, without her mother's constant efforts to keep the peace.

The door to the suite opened, and her father entered. He removed his hat and set his decorative walking cane in the stand by the door.

"Aurora, I thought you'd have retired by now."

She moved toward him, allowing her anger to compensate for the sudden rush of nerves. "I wish to speak with you, Papa."

He tugged his vest into place and strode across the room to the small table near the fireplace, where he picked up his favorite pipe. "What about?"

She folded her arms in front of her. "About the rude way you treated Gabe."

"In what way was I rude to Mr. Montgomery?" He lit a match and applied the flame to his pipe.

"You know very well how. Your condescending attitude was humiliating — to Gabe and to me. Why did you ask him to dine with us, only to treat him like a peasant?"

He leveled her with an unapologetic stare. "That is precisely the reason. In case the young buck had any ideas about you, I felt it my place as your father to make sure he knows his."

She'd expected him to argue, to claim he'd done nothing wrong. But to hear him actually admit his shameful scheme left Aurora speechless.

Papa blew out a stream of smoke. "And in the event that all my subtle hints went unnoticed, I made sure Mr. Montgomery got my point quite clearly on the way out."

She curled her hands into fists at her sides. "What did you say to him?"

"Just what I'm about to tell you. You are to have no further contact with that young man. He is off-limits to you."

A squeak of protest escaped Aurora's constricted throat.

"To make sure he understood, I told him I would be announcing your betrothal by the summer's end." Papa pulled his pipe from between thinned lips. "Enough is enough, Aurora. You have wasted your life for the last three years. It's time to grow up and choose a suitable husband. If you can't do it, I'm sure I can come up with someone."

He settled on the sofa and opened his newspaper, effectively dismissing her.

Aurora stood, angry breath heaving in her chest. She longed to lash out, to scream her outrage until her father was forced to listen. But there was no use arguing with Papa when he was in this stubborn frame of mind. Instead, Aurora retreated to her bedroom and flung herself on the bed to contemplate her next course of action.

Come the morrow, she would talk to Dr. Reardon and push ahead with her application to nursing school.

And when the time was more favorable,

she'd break the news to her father.

Moonlight illuminated Maggie's way as she descended to the main level of the silent house and entered the empty kitchen. Not wishing to brighten the whole room, she lit a single candle and set the holder beside the stove.

She had no idea of the time, only that she'd been tossing and turning for what seemed like hours. Thoughts of Neill had plagued her since their encounter in the park, and she'd come to the unhappy conclusion that since it appeared Neill had no intention of returning to Ireland, she could no longer put off telling her brothers.

Tomorrow when they were all together, she would break the news.

The clock in the parlor chimed the hour. Maggie counted the tolls, surprised to find it was only eleven o'clock. She took a bottle of milk from the icebox and poured a small amount into a saucepan, setting it to heat on the stovetop. Hopefully some warm milk would allow her to fall asleep before midnight.

The front door opened, and seconds later Gabe appeared in the kitchen. "Maggie." He looked startled to see her up.

"That must have been some dinner to be

coming home at this hour."

Instead of smiling, Gabe frowned. "I've been walking for hours. Not that it helped clear my mind any."

Maggie took in his disheveled hair and clothing, and a thread of worry invaded her heart. She lifted the pot from the heat. "Did you not enjoy your evening with the Hastings family?"

Gabe ran a hand through his already-messy hair. "Not really, no."

Rylan had told her that Mr. Hastings wanted to thank Gabe for rescuing his daughter. What could have gone wrong? Maggie took out two mugs and divided the warm milk between them. "Did the Vanderbilt Hotel fail to meet your expectations?"

Gabe sank onto one of the kitchen chairs. "The hotel is beautiful."

"Was Miss Hastings not appreciative of your heroics?" Again her attempt to tease Gabe into a better humor fell flat.

He sent her a heated glare. "Aurora was perfect. Her father, on the other hand, was a pompous boar." He picked up his cup and drained the contents in one gulp.

Maggie sat down and waited for him to elaborate.

"It seems Mr. Hastings's purpose in inviting me to dinner was to lord his wealth over me in an attempt to warn me away from his daughter." He thumped the mug down on the table.

Maggie took a thoughtful sip of the warm drink. "You're only here for the summer. Why would he be worried about that?"

A flush infused Gabe's cheeks.

"You wouldn't be daft enough to start something with her, would you?" Her traitorous thoughts flew at once to Adam. It seemed she needed to take her own advice.

"What's the point since we're leaving?" A nerve ticked in his jaw. "I just hated the way the man treated me like I was lower than a servant."

She laid a hand on his arm. "Well, I, for one, know what a fine man you are. You did his family a favor. Let that be the end of it."

Gabe's stubborn gaze slid to the far wall, telling Maggie that it was *not* the end of it. Not by a country mile.

Just as it wasn't the end with Neill. Why were affairs of the heart so complicated?

For a moment, Maggie considered confiding her worries to Gabe, but from the grim set of his mouth, she decided it was not the right time. Best to approach her brothers when they were in a good humor.

With any luck, she would tell them tomorrow — before Neill had a chance to accost her again.

14

What was it with him and strays?

"First a baby and now a dog." Adam kicked a stone off the path as he strode up the sidewalk toward St. Rita's. As if he wasn't already irritated enough, this hound had been following him since he'd left John's church, and no matter how many times Adam tried to chase the thing away, it stayed on his heels, a discreet enough distance away that he couldn't do much about it.

When Adam turned down the side alley of the orphanage, the silly thing slunk in behind him, its bone-thin frame shaking. Adam scratched his beard and then peered over the back gate to make sure none of the children were around.

"I suppose it's not fair to take my foul mood out on you. Come in for a minute, and I'll see if Mrs. Norton has some scraps for you, but then you have to go."

Foul didn't begin to describe Adam's disposition over the past few days. He'd yelled at Maggie to leave him alone, and she'd looked at him with eyes sadder than this mongrel. He knew he'd hurt her feelings, but in the long run, it had been for her own good. Any type of friendship with him could only lead to disaster, and he would do nothing to cause her harm.

The talk he'd had with John McNabb before leaving this morning had further darkened the cloud of gloom hanging over him. Adam had made the mistake of confiding in John what he'd learned about his parents' marriage and the fact that he still couldn't shake the bone-deep suspicion that James was not his real father.

"Why don't you just ask your parents?" John had suggested mildly. "Better than all this crazy speculating."

Though not happy at the prospect, Adam had been forced to agree. "Perhaps you're right. I'll never be at peace if I don't find out one way or another. But I'll need to figure out how best to approach it." He could hardly burst into Irish Meadows hurling accusations. That would only alienate his family further.

What he needed was a logical plan of action.

A loud whine brought Adam's thoughts careening back to the dog at his feet. "Right, scraps. Wait here."

He mounted the back steps leading into the kitchen. Though Mrs. Norton loathed the very sight of him, Adam hoped she'd take pity on the poor dog and give it something to eat.

When he entered the room, cap in hand, ready to grovel if need be, a younger woman turned from the sink, her round, plain face breaking into a welcoming smile. The enticing aroma of baking bread met his nose, and despite having had a decent breakfast, his stomach growled.

"Hello. Is Mrs. Norton around?"

"I'm afraid she's out on an errand. Can I help you?"

"I'm Adam, the outside caretaker, and —"

"I know who you are." The girl winked at him. "I'm Mary, the new assistant cook."

Adam swallowed. "Nice to meet you, Mary." Obviously no one had filled her in on his background. "Would you happen to have any scraps or bones you don't need? There's a stray dog out back who's in need of food."

Her countenance brightened. "I'm sure we have something. Let me check."

"I'll be out back." Adam hurried out the

door, in case Rylan or Maggie happened along. He walked to the small shed in the yard and pulled out a pail and a bag of cement mix. While the children were out, he'd fix the cracks in the front stairs. The mangy mutt followed every step he took.

Soon the back door opened, and Mary waved at him. "I've put a few things in this bowl for him."

Adam strode across the yard to take it from her. "Thank you, Mary. I hope this won't get you on Mrs. Norton's bad side." He tried for a congenial smile, but his mouth refused to cooperate.

"Oh, no. Mrs. Norton won't mind. Just bring the bowl back when he's done."

It took the dog only a few seconds to scarf down the table scraps, and when he was finished, Adam filled the bowl with water and let him drink his fill.

"You know, if you had a bath, you might not be bad-looking under all that filth." Adam couldn't help but recall the day he'd gotten out of prison and how much better he'd felt after some grooming.

He took a metal bucket from the shed and returned the bowl to the kitchen, grateful to find Mary wasn't there at the moment. He filled the bucket with water, grabbed a bar of lye soap and a clean rag, then headed back outside. Adam half thought the dog might have disappeared after his belly had been filled, but the mutt had found a spot to lie in the shade. Adam approached with the water, and still the hound didn't move. With stoic calm, the animal endured the cold bath and scrub of lye. Adam had just congratulated himself on a job well done and had started to douse the animal with a pail of rinse water, when the dog suddenly objected to the whole process. He bolted away, knocking the pail from Adam's hand, soaking his boots with the remaining water.

"For the love of St. Patrick," Adam grumbled, bending to right the pail.

The mutt bounded back, gyrating to shake the excess water from its coat. The spray drenched Adam's face. He sputtered, wiping the deluge from his eyes and beard. He squinted at the animal, who, with its tongue lolling, seemed to be grinning at Adam.

A decidedly feminine giggle sounded behind them.

"Who's giving who a bath, I'd like to know."

Adam snapped to attention at the voice he'd know anywhere. He glanced over to see Maggie's gray eyes dancing with merriment. Embarrassment heated his neck as he retrieved the rag he'd intended for the dog and swiped it over his own face. Dark patches of water marred his shirt and trousers. Suddenly he found himself wishing for his former wardrobe — fine suits and shirts, silk ties, and highly polished shoes. Maybe then he could hold his head up with a measure of pride when in the company of this beautiful woman.

"Whose dog is this?" Not appearing to mind the wet fur, Maggie stroked the mutt's head. His ropey tail beat a happy refrain on the grass.

"He's a stray."

"And why would you be bathing a stray? Have you nothing better to occupy your time?" With a saucy grin, Maggie tugged the towel from Adam's hand and bent to rub the cloth over the dog's coat.

Heat pricked the back of Adam's neck. He directed his glare to the offending creature, who now sat, the picture of docility, basking in Maggie's administrations.

"My, he's a handsome lad," she said. "Look at this lovely chestnut fur."

Adam almost growled, ashamed to find himself steeped in jealousy over a homeless animal.

"How did he get back here? Surely he didn't climb the gate." Maggie straightened, pushing her hair from her face.

Adam stared at her long, dark curls. What would it feel like to run his fingers through those tresses? With effort, he pulled his gaze back to the dog, who did indeed look much better. "He followed me here and seemed hungry . . ." Adam stopped, realizing how foolish he must sound.

Maggie grinned at him. "Oh, so you fed him and gave him a bath? A sure way to get rid of him."

He shrugged. "What can I say? I felt sorry for the mutt."

Her fingers stilled in the dog's fur. "Which proves my point, Adam O'Leary. You're a kind man with a big heart."

Speechless, he could only gaze into her eyes — so honest and clear, reflecting the beauty of her soul.

She cocked her head to one side, studying him. "I think a dog will do you a world of good."

He straightened, scowling. "I do *not* need a dog. I've no place for him where I'm staying." He held her gaze. "Which is on a cot in a church basement." She needed to realize the type of life he was leading.

Maggie smoothed her dress. "Well, Delia's been wanting a dog. Perhaps I'll speak with Rylan tonight and see what he thinks."

"He might make a good guard dog for the

orphanage." Adam frowned. "Which re-
minds me — you might want to tell Rylan
I've noticed a strange man lurking around
at odd times of day."

Maggie shivered and pulled her shawl
closer around her, her eyes suddenly wary.
"When?"

"Early one morning last week, and another
time later in the day. Why?"

She shrugged but didn't meet his eyes. "I
may have seen him, too."

Adam's protective instincts roared to life.
"Maggie, you need to make sure you're not
alone when you go out. The city can be
dangerous."

She raised her chin. "I'll be fine. Now,
you'll have to excuse me. I need to let Rylan
know I'm back from my walk." She reached
down for one more pat of the dog's back.
"Take care of yourself, Adam."

"You as well, Maggie." He stood, watching her until she disappeared into the orphanage.

Seconds later, the press of the dog's wet
nose against his hand brought Adam back
to his senses. A ragged breath escaped him.
He really needed to find a different place to
work — somewhere he wouldn't have to
face this constant reminder of something
that could never be.

The next day, when Adam returned to finish his repairs, he was surprised to find the dog sitting at the base of the stairs, tail wagging. Perhaps feeding the mutt hadn't been the smartest idea.

"What am I to do with you?" Adam huffed in mock exasperation as he bent to rub the animal's ears.

He took a closer look at the dog. Someone must have fed him again this morning. His eyes were clear, and the edge of hunger had disappeared. He appeared contented — happy even.

"Glad one of us has found a home." Adam promised himself he'd see if Rylan would like a shelter built for the animal, in the event that he became a permanent fixture at the orphanage.

After mixing water with the cement powder to form a patch for the cracks, Adam returned to the front stairs with a trowel and began to layer on the mixture. A movement farther along the sidewalk caught his attention. He stiffened as he recognized the man who had been loitering around the orphanage of late.

"You there," Adam called out. "Is there

something I can help you with?"

The man hesitated for a moment, but instead of retreating, he came closer. His expensive clothing told Adam he wasn't simply a vagrant in search of a handout, though the jagged scar on his chin gave Adam pause.

"Perhaps you can. I'm looking for a woman by the name of Maggie Montgomery."

Adam's stomach muscles tightened as he straightened. The distinct Irish lilt made Adam wonder if this was perhaps yet another brother. "What do you want with her?"

The brown-haired man moved closer to the stairs. "So you know her, then?"

At Adam's side, the dog let out a low growl.

"I might. What business do you have with her?" Every warning sense in Adam's body went on alert.

The man smiled. "I'm Neill Fitzgerald, Maggie's fiancé."

The trowel laden with cement slipped from Adam's fingers and landed with a loud *plop* on the walkway. Surely Maggie would have mentioned a fiancé. Then again, this dandy could be lying. "She never said she was engaged."

Fitzgerald merely laughed. "That's Maggie for you. Would you know if she's here? I understand her brother runs this orphanage."

The muscles in Adam's jaw tightened. He wished he could find a fitting excuse to lie to the man, to tell him Maggie was nowhere around. But he'd made a vow that, once he was out of prison, he would live in truth. Could he lie now, for no reason other than a vague feeling of distrust, which might have more to do with jealousy than any other rational feeling? He sighed and wiped his hands on the rag hanging from his pocket. "I'll see if Mr. Montgomery's in." He pointed to the stairs. "You can wait here."

Since staff were expected to use the rear door, Adam rounded the back of the orphanage and hoped Rylan would understand why he deemed it necessary to enter the building with Maggie inside. The children, he believed, were on an outing, and the nuns would likely be in chapel for their prayer time.

As quietly as possible, Adam made his way to Rylan's office. He knocked once, and when there was no answer, he opened the door and peered inside. The room lay shrouded in darkness. It appeared Rylan had gone out, as well.

Adam hesitated. Should he let this man in to see Maggie? Or should he ask him to come back another day? Though Adam preferred to wait until he could speak with Rylan, Adam realized Maggie had the right to make her own decision in the matter. It was possible she might want to see this man.

He weighed his options and then reluctantly went to find her.

Seated at the piano in the common room, Maggie brought the piece she'd been playing to a close. The tune was more complicated than she'd remembered. In any event, the composition wouldn't be suitable to teach the children. She flipped through the pages of music, hoping to find a simpler piece.

The *creak* of the door alerted her to someone's presence. A flare of disappointment shot through her. Likely Mr. Smith wanted to mop the floor while everyone was out. She'd anticipated having more time to linger over the keys before the children returned.

"I'll be out of your way in two shakes." Maggie swiveled on the bench and froze. The sheets of music fluttered from her fingers to the floor.

Neill moved across the room toward her.

"As talented as ever, I see."

"Neill." Maggie shot to her feet, clutching the piano for support. His bright smile did not fool her for one minute. "What are you doing here?"

When she hadn't heard from him after that day in the park with Delia, she'd hoped he'd given up and returned home. And she'd foolishly put off telling her brothers about him.

"I've come for you, as I promised." Neill moved so close she could detect the faint smell of peat moss and sea brine that still clung to the fibers of his coat. "It's time to come home where you belong and become my wife."

Her fingers tightened on the smooth wood. She forced herself to breathe normally. "You seem to have forgotten that you are no longer my fiancé." She bent to retrieve the scattered sheets of music, anything to avoid looking at him.

"That's not true. We had a spat, is all. Now it's time to kiss and make up."

A wave of nausea rushed up Maggie's throat as she became aware of their surroundings and how alone they truly were. She edged across the room toward the door. "I'm sorry, Neill. But as I've told you numerous times, I have no intention of marrying you."

He came toward her, his eyes twin pools of rage. "You will not reject me again."

Cold fear welled up inside her, spurring her to escape. She whirled away from him, her feet slipping on the floor in her haste.

Neill yanked her back by the hair. Maggie cried out in pain as he twisted the strands at her scalp, bringing her face within inches of his own.

His breath puffed out over her face, the sour waft of ale repulsing her. "We can be wed right here in New York, if we have to. And have our honeymoon on the voyage home." A near-fanatical light glowed from the depths of his eyes.

Panic crashed through her, escalating her fear so that she couldn't breathe. In that moment, she came to understand the full scope of Neill's obsession.

He would never give up. Never leave her in peace.

Dear Lord, help me.

15

Adam strode down the main corridor of the orphanage. A wave of tension seized his neck muscles at the unnatural stillness of the building. If Maggie had followed her usual routine, she would be playing the piano while everyone was out. Yet as much as he strained his ears, he couldn't hear the familiar tones.

As he rounded the corner, however, the sound of raised voices drifted toward him. His pulse began an uneven rhythm in his veins as he ran in the direction of the noise. Without pausing, he burst into the common room and froze at the sight before him. A glowering Fitzgerald held Maggie much too close, his fingers a vice around her upper arm.

Maggie's disheveled hair sat in disarray about her shoulders, her wide eyes trained on Fitzgerald.

Adam balled his hands into fists at his

sides. With supreme effort, he drew on the skills he'd learned in prison, calling upon rigid self-control to hold his anger in check. "Maggie? Is everything all right?" As he moved closer, he noted that her slim frame shook — whether from fear or anger he couldn't determine.

Her gaze swung to his, and the relief in her expression told him all he needed to know. "Adam." That one breathless word filled him with purpose.

"Is this man bothering you?"

"Aye."

Adam pulled himself up to his full height, glad he stood a full six inches taller than Fitzgerald. "I think you'd better leave now."

An oily smile slid over Fitzgerald's face, though he released his grip on Maggie. "This is all a simple misunderstanding. My surprise arrival has shocked my fiancée, hasn't it, love?"

Maggie shifted away from him. "You're not my fiancé, or anything else to me."

When Fitzgerald made a menacing move in her direction, Adam stepped in front of him.

"I'll give you five seconds to walk away, or I'll be forced to assist your exit."

Fitzgerald waited a beat before moving, his focus trained on Maggie. "I'm not giving up, Maggie. You'll be my bride yet."

His patience at an end, Adam grabbed Fitzgerald by the arm and hauled the thrashing man along the corridor and out the front door. Only at the bottom of the stairs did Adam loosen his grip. He leveled Fitzgerald with an intimidating glare. "If I see you around here or anywhere near Maggie again, you'll be traveling back across the ocean in a pine box. Do I make myself clear?"

Pure hatred shot from the man's steely eyes. "We'll see about that." He buttoned his suit jacket, adjusted the angle of his hat, and strode down the road.

Adam watched until Fitzgerald turned onto a side street, and when several minutes passed with no further sign of him, Adam headed inside to make sure Maggie was unharmed.

He found her slumped on the piano bench, her dark hair tumbling about her face, her whole body shuddering.

Adam banked a jolt of concern. "Did he hurt you?"

Her head flew up as she emitted a strangled cry, giving him a second of remorse for startling her. Before he could say a word, she launched herself into his arms. He caught her and cradled her against him. Her breath came in shallow pants, her rapid heartbeat pulsing through the wool of his jacket.

A surge of protectiveness rose in his chest. He would do whatever it took to ensure her safety. "It's all right. He's gone." Adam lowered his voice to soothe her, but her face remained pressed to his shoulder, her fist clutching his shirtfront.

He raised a hand, hesitated for a moment, and then allowed himself the luxury of stroking her silky hair. The faint scent of jasmine wafted to his nose. Slowly, after several minutes, the tremors eased, and her muscles began to relax.

"I still can't believe he followed me here," she whispered.

"Is he really your fiancé?" It jarred him just to utter the word.

She stiffened and raised her head to look at him. "We were engaged for a short time, but I broke it off before I left Ireland. I knew he'd taken it hard, but I never dreamed . . ."

Adam's focus moved from the tempest of emotion in her eyes to the fullness of her lips, which quivered slightly. The temptation to taste their sweetness shook him to his core. With great effort, he pulled his attention back to what she had told him. "Was he harassing you back home?"

She nodded. "That's partly why my brothers agreed I should come to America. To give Neill time to get over the breakup."

The mention of her brothers brought stark reality crashing in on Adam, destroying their intimate moment. If Rylan or Gabe caught Maggie in his arms like this . . . Adam shuddered to think of the consequences.

He shifted and set her gently away from him. "As much as I'd love to stay here for the duration of the day, I think I'd be wise to take my leave — before Rylan gets back."

Maggie clutched his arm, her fingers a band of steel. "Please don't go. I — I don't want to be alone." Her gaze darted nervously to the door.

Adam released a long breath, and as she turned beseeching eyes to his, he knew that no matter the consequence, he could not refuse her plea. Especially since no one except old Mr. Smith was around to defend her. "Very well, but for propriety's sake, you'd best keep me company out front while I work."

Maggie nodded. "The fresh air would be most welcome."

Adam's shoulder muscles loosened the moment they exited the building. He gestured to the bucket and tools lying on the walkway below. "The cement will have hardened by now. I'll have to fix a new batch."

"I'll come with you." The nervous way she kept glancing up the street tore at him.

"Don't worry. I doubt he'll be back today."

"You don't know how unrelenting Neill can be."

"Come on, then. You can tell me more about this loathsome fellow while I prepare the cement."

She trailed behind him to the shed in the rear corner of the yard. The dog trotted up to greet him, sticking his wet nose into Adam's palm. He forgot he'd left the mutt at the back door when he went in to look for Rylan.

Maggie crouched beside the animal to pat him, a smile hovering on her lips. "Have you given him a name yet?"

Adam straightened and grabbed the supplies from a shelf in the shed. "That's a job for its new owner." He scraped the unusable cement out of the bucket, rinsed it, and mixed a new batch.

"Well, someone has to name the poor creature. I think Chester will do nicely. What do you think, boy?"

The animal gave a quick bark, almost as if he understood what Maggie had asked.

She laughed. "I'm glad you agree. Chester it is."

Adam glanced up as he stirred the cement. If Chester could make Maggie smile and chase the worry from her eyes, Adam would do his best to find him a nice bone later as a reward.

Once the mixture had reached the desired consistency, Adam led the trio out to the front staircase. Maggie and Chester perched on the top step while Adam worked below. Despite the unpleasant scene earlier, a sense of contentment washed over him. He found himself wishing this could be his life. Working on the house he shared with Maggie while she and their pet looked on.

"Before my father died, he and Mr. Fitzgerald made an agreement that Neill and I would marry." Maggie's soft voice pulled Adam's attention from his daydreams.

"I was only eight at the time, Neill about twelve. But years later, when both our fathers were deceased, Neill came to make good on Da's promise. Mum thought Neill a fine young man and allowed him to court me."

Adam's hand stilled on the trowel as he waited for her to continue.

"We'd been seeing each other for about a month when Neill declared us betrothed and started behaving in a more . . . forward manner. I did my best to avoid him. When I couldn't, I made sure we were never alone. To say he was frustrated would be a huge understatement." She let out a long sigh. "If that had been his only flaw, I might have gone along with the plan to marry him."

"Did something else happen?"

A soft breeze lifted the ends of her hair, making them dance over her shoulders. "One day I went in to the village to shop, and I saw Neill escorting another woman. The way they stood with their heads touching seemed far too intimate for a mere acquaintance." She shrugged. "Apparently he was soothing his frustrations with several willing girls in town."

Disgusted, Adam tossed the trowel in the now-empty bucket. "Any man who would cheat is not worth the dirt on your shoes."

She rubbed her hands over her arms. "Believe me, I told him so, in quite a colorful manner."

The sound of footsteps brought Adam's head whipping around. In his present mood, he could happily knock Fitzgerald into the harbor. Colleen and Rylan appeared with the children following two abreast behind them. Colleen halted the pram with a questioning look. Adam forced his face muscles to relax, not wanting to intimidate the children with his scowl.

Rylan stopped at the base of the staircase, looking from Maggie back to Adam. "Why are you out here, Maggie? I thought you wanted to practice the piano." Accusation laced his tone.

Maggie rose from the step, her hands gripped together in front of her skirt. "Neill Fitzgerald is here. He tried to force me to leave with him. If Adam hadn't intervened, I don't know what would have happened."

Rylan's jaw hardened. "Colleen, please take the children in while I speak with Adam and Maggie in the parlor."

Maggie tapped a toe on the carpet in the orphanage sitting room. From Rylan's serious expression, she imagined he would likely overreact, as her brothers always did. As soon as she saw Gabe, she would have to fill him in, as well. She suppressed a sigh, thinking of his reaction to finding out the man they'd crossed an ocean to avoid had followed them here.

Absently, Maggie patted Chester's head. The dog must have slipped inside without anyone noticing. She appreciated the feel of the beast's warm side pressed to her leg, as though he sensed her need for comfort. She raised her head and caught Adam watching her. He gave her an almost-imperceptible nod and shifted his attention to Rylan, who closed the parlor door with a distinct *snap.*

Maggie wished for her sister-in-law's presence to run interference between Adam and Rylan. But it seemed Rylan had made a point of keeping Colleen out of the conversation.

Rylan settled on the sofa. "Now tell me the whole story from the beginning."

For the second time that day, Maggie relayed her complicated history with Neill Fitzgerald.

When she had finished, Rylan rose to pace in front of the fireplace. "Now I see why Mum was so insistent on a lengthy visit." He paused and gave her a long look. "You two were engaged. Did you love him, Maggie?"

She sensed Adam tense beside her. "I was fond of Neill, since we all grew up together, and I hoped I would grow to love him one day. But too many differences made that impossible."

Adam shifted from his position near Maggie, his expression grim. "I feel this is partly my fault." He looked at Rylan. "I told Maggie I'd noticed a man lurking around lately.

But I should have told you sooner. I'm sorry."

A wave of guilt swamped Maggie. "Actually, this is my fault." She stared at her hands. "I knew Neill was here, but I didn't tell anyone."

A tense silence followed. Maggie's gaze darted from Rylan to Adam. Both men wore dark expressions.

"How did you know he was here?" Rylan finally asked. "Did you speak with him before today?"

"Yes." Maggie let out a sigh. "He approached me not long after we arrived, apologized for everything, and asked for another chance." She met Rylan's gaze. "I turned him down. When I didn't hear from him again, I assumed he'd gone home. But he found me again another time in the park with Delia." She hesitated. Her actions sounded incredibly foolish now. "I told him he was wasting his time and to go home."

Rylan paced to the fireplace and back. "Why did you not tell us, Maggie? I think we had a right to know." The hurt in his eyes tore at Maggie more than any heated words ever could.

"I know. I'm sorry."

"We only want to protect you."

"Aye. But sometimes being protected feels

akin to being a prisoner."

Rylan's throat worked up and down, and Maggie feared she'd hurt her brother's feelings.

He let out a long breath. "I'm only glad Adam was there to intervene in my stead. Thank you for that."

Adam stiffened, muscles cording in his forearms. "I'd protect her with my life, if necessary."

Maggie's heart seemed to stall in her chest at Adam's hoarse admission. The tears she'd held at bay all afternoon now stung her eyes, and she blinked to hold them back.

"All of us need to be on guard," Rylan continued, "until we can figure out what to do about this."

The door opened, and Colleen slipped inside, eyes darting to her husband.

Rylan ran a hand over his jaw. "If Gabe agrees, I think it might be wise for you both to go home as soon as we can make the arrange—"

Maggie shot to her feet. "No. I'm not going back." She hadn't wanted to tell her brother of her plans yet, but she refused to alter the course of her life one more time for the likes of Neill.

Rylan frowned. "You'll just be leaving a few weeks earlier than planned."

"No, Rylan. I'm staying in New York. Permanently."

The room went still. Only the ticking of the mantel clock broke the silence.

Rylan looked ready to explode, whereas Adam's expression proved unreadable.

Colleen moved to her husband's side and gently touched his arm. "Perhaps this is not the time to make hasty decisions. When Gabe gets back, we'll fill him in on what's occurred, and together we'll decide what's best."

A measure of relief trickled through Maggie's system. Colleen would temper her husband's reaction. She'd make Rylan see reason.

He gave his wife a thin smile. "Aye, that sounds like the sensible thing to do."

Adam uncrossed his arms. "I'd best clean up and be on my way. If you need me at any time, call John McNabb at the church. He'll get word to me."

Rylan stepped toward Adam. "I fear I owe you an apology. At the orphanage, I'm bound by regulations, but in my own home I should have been more welcoming. We're family, after all." He held out his hand. "I hope you can forgive me."

Adam didn't hesitate to accept his hand. "No apology needed."

Maggie's heart swelled with pride at Adam's honorable attitude. He would be well within his rights to harbor a grudge against Rylan, yet he bore her brother no ill will. Perhaps now her brothers would see Adam's true nature.

Adam pointed at Chester, still sitting by the chair Maggie had vacated. "It seems this fellow has taken a shine to Maggie. It might be timely to keep him as a guard dog. I can build a shelter for him outside, if you'd like."

Rylan nodded. "That sounds like a fine idea."

16

"Miss Hastings, may I speak with you, please?"

Aurora looked up from the book she'd been reading aloud, surprised to see Dr. Reardon in the doorway to the children's ward. Her heart gave an unwelcome lurch at the sight of his frowning countenance. Had she done something to displease him?

She handed the book to one of the older children. "Constance, will you continue the story? I'll be back in a minute."

With a quick nod to the floor nurse in charge of the youngsters, Aurora followed Dr. Reardon out of the room and closed the door behind her. "Yes, Doctor? Is there a problem?"

"I've just had a call from Mrs. Montgomery at St. Rita's. It seems several of the children have contracted a fever."

"Oh, dear. I'm sorry to hear that."

"They want me to come over and examine

them. Would you be able to accompany me?"

She frowned. "Are you sure you don't want a trained nurse to go with you?"

A flush rose up his neck. "Not until I assess the situation. If it's more serious than I anticipate, I can always bring someone else in." He gave a rueful smile. "The children respond far better to you than to me and are more likely to be cooperative if you're there to calm them."

There was a grain of truth in what he said. Some of the children were fearful of the doctor, especially since he usually administered shots or ill-tasting medicine. And they did seem to enjoy Aurora's presence. "Very well. I'd be happy to come with you."

"Good. We'll leave right away. I only pray we can keep the illness from spreading to all the children."

Adam trudged up to the front door at Irish Meadows, praying for courage to confront his mother in a calm and fair manner.

After finishing his day's work at the orphanage, Adam had found himself dwelling once again on his parentage and realized he had to take action or go mad from all his speculation. And so he had taken the train to Long Island. The fact that it was his father's evening at the men's club made it a perfect time to catch his mother alone.

He entered the foyer of his childhood home, and seconds later, Mrs. Johnston appeared.

"Master Adam. This is a surprise. Is your family expecting you?"

Adam almost smiled at the housekeeper's attempt at subtlety. "No, this is a spur-of-the-moment visit. Is my mother in?" It suddenly occurred to him that Mama may have gone out herself.

"She's in the parlor. One moment and I'll let her know you're here."

Adam wanted to protest that he had no need to be announced, but the reality remained that this was no longer his home.

Footsteps sounded seconds later. "Adam, what a wonderful surprise." A slight wariness accompanied his mother's welcoming smile. "What brings you here?"

He bent to kiss her cheek, the familiar scent of her lavender perfume bringing him back to his childhood. "I needed to talk to you about an important matter."

"Of course. Come in. Alice, please bring us coffee and some biscuits."

"Right away, ma'am."

Adam followed his mother into the parlor. The smoky odor from the fireplace blended with the smell of lemon furniture polish, unleashing a flood of memories of the times spent in this room with his siblings.

He swallowed hard and focused on the purpose of his visit. Once Mama had settled in her chair, he seated himself on the sofa near her.

"So what is this important matter you wish to discuss?" Mama picked up her needlework and rested it in her lap.

"I'm afraid it's a somewhat unpleasant topic, Mama, but one that needs to be addressed — once and for all."

"Well, that sounds ominous." Mama's nervous laugh echoed in the room.

Adam looked down at his clasped hands and prayed for the right words. He let out a slow breath. "First, I want to apologize for the disappointment I've caused you over the years. I know my relationship with Father has been a source of strife in your marriage." He held up a hand to halt her protest. "Don't deny it, Mama. It pained you that we never got along. That I never measured up to his expectations." He paused to regain his focus. "Over the past years, I've done a lot of thinking about why my father preferred Gil, another man's son, over his own flesh and blood."

"Oh, Adam. That's not true." Sympathy

glistened in his mother's eyes.

He shook his head. "You know it is, Mama. And the only conclusion I could come to is that I'm not James O'Leary's flesh and blood." He softened his voice and looked her in the eye. "Am I, Mama?"

A startled noise, half gasp, half moan, escaped her lips before she covered her face with her hands. Quiet sobs wracked her body, causing pangs of guilt to shoot through Adam's chest. This was exactly why he'd never broached the subject before. The idea that he could cause his mother even more grief tore at his soul.

"Here, here. What have you done?" Mrs. Johnston practically dropped her laden tray on a side table, and with a disgusted glare at Adam, rushed to her mistress's side.

"I'm sorry. I didn't mean to —"

"You never do, yet destruction lies in your wake wherever you go." She laid a hand on Mama's shaking shoulder in a protective gesture. "You'd best leave before your father gets back. He'll not take kindly to you upsetting your mother this way."

Adam rose, gripped by the strong desire to flee this house and never return. Yet the need to know the answer to his question held him frozen in place. Mama's reaction told him he had hit on the truth, but he had

278

to hear it from her lips.

He handed his mother a handkerchief. "I'm not leaving until I get the answers I came for."

Mama dabbed the cloth to her face, seeming to compose herself. "It's all right, Alice. Please leave us."

"But Mrs. O'Leary —"

"Now." The authority in Mama's voice made the older woman snap to attention.

"Very well. You've only to ring if you need me." Her stiff words spoke of the hurt his mother had inflicted.

Adam shoved his hands in his pockets, fingering the coins there while waiting for his mother to speak.

She gestured to the sofa. "Sit down, son, and I'll tell you what you want to know."

Stiffly he lowered himself to the edge of the settee, wishing he could do something to ease the pain on his mother's face.

"You're right," she said at last, her gaze fixed on the carpet. "James is not your natural father. I . . . I was expecting you when we married."

A horde of emotions surged through him. Relief, anger, disappointment, and regret all balled into one huge lump in his throat. He tore the top button of his shirt open, clawing to bring more air into his lungs.

"How . . . ? Who?" He didn't know what to ask first.

Mama let out a long-suffering breath. "His name was George Drake. I was betrothed to him before I met your father." She paused as she reined in her emotions.

Adam stared across the room as he tried to process the news. "Did you love him?" he asked quietly.

She must have loved him, to do what she'd done. But how could she have switched her affections to James so quickly?

"I loathed him." Her nostrils flared, and tight lines pinched the corners of her mouth.

"I don't understand. Then how could you . . ." He clamped his mouth shut, unable to ask such a personal question of his mother.

She lifted her chin, which quivered. "When George learned of my affection for James and my intention to cancel our betrothal, he . . . forced himself on me."

Adam lurched to his feet, shock reverberating up his spine. His mother had been violated?

"George thought by being . . . intimate with me . . . that James would no longer want me, and being a ruined woman, I'd be forced to marry him."

Adam paced the carpet in front of the

fireplace, trying to absorb the horrific revelation. "Did you have him arrested?"

She lowered her gaze and shook her head. "I was too ashamed to tell anyone at first."

"But you did tell James . . . and he married you anyway?" Disbelief stabbed at Adam. Even knowing how much James loved his mother, he couldn't imagine him simply accepting the situation.

"I didn't tell him right away," she said quietly. "I knew James would kill George."

Adam understood that feeling. If anyone ever violated Maggie, it would take an army to stop him from destroying the man.

"So you married him and then told him you were with child?"

His mother leveled him with a steely glare. "Do you really believe me capable of such a deception?"

Adam spun around, anger ripe in his chest. "I find it a distinct possibility since you've lied to me my entire life."

He regretted the words the moment they left his mouth — the moment his mother's features crumpled with grief.

The parlor door crashed open. James charged into the room, stopping inches from Adam's face, nostrils flared. "You will apologize to your mother at once, or so help me, I will throw your sorry hide out of this house for good."

The anger left Adam in one great whoosh, like air deflating from a balloon. He dropped to one knee before her and took her hand in his. "Forgive me, Mama. I had no right to speak to you that way."

She lifted sorrowful eyes to his and placed a tender hand on his cheek. "I never wanted you to know," she whispered. "Never wanted you to feel shame over your conception. That's why I hid the truth."

The sickening reality seeped through Adam like a toxin. He squeezed his eyes shut, the soothing contact of her palm unable to ease the pain radiating from his soul.

"When I found out I was expecting, I had no choice but to tell James. He loved me enough to marry me anyway and accept you as his own."

Adam rose stiffly then and faced James. "Except you never did accept me. No wonder I could never do anything right in your eyes."

A muscle twitched in James's jaw. "Lord knows I tried. But the older you got, the more you resembled *him.*"

No surprise there. All his life people had remarked on the lack of similarity between James and his oldest son. Mama had always laughed it off, insisting Adam took after her side of the family. "What happened to George? Did you confront him?"

Blue fire blazed in James's eyes. "I made sure he would never bother Kathleen again."

It didn't take much to imagine the type of punishment he'd inflicted. Adam frowned. "Why didn't he have you arrested for assault?"

"He didn't dare. I told him Kathleen would go to the authorities and make him pay for his crime."

Adam walked to the fireplace and peered into the ashes, as cold and gray as his tortured soul. He raised his head and looked around the room with changed eyes. The very walls seemed to mock him with fragmented memories of his childhood. "Did Drake . . . did he know about me?" He couldn't say why it should matter, but he had to know.

"No. He ran afoul of the law again and was thrown in jail." James's terse words left no doubt what he was thinking. *Like father, like son.* "He died in prison a few months before you were born."

Adam shook his head, his thoughts chasing around his mind like a cyclone. He was the son of a criminal who had died in jail — his existence the result of a brutal act. Although relieved to finally know the truth,

283

the searing pain remained — a festering wound that might never heal, knowing he'd been a source of grief for his mother since the moment of his conception.

Silent tears marred the complexion of his mother's pale cheeks. James stood behind her, one hand draped protectively over her shoulder.

"I'm so sorry, Adam," she whispered.

Adam straightened, pulling the last shred of pride around him like a suit of armor. "It's not your fault, Mama. You were the victim in all this."

"You were a victim, too. I should have tried harder —"

"Stop, please." He raised a hand and let it fall. "You did the best you could under the circumstances." Adam couldn't bear to look at James. Couldn't stand to see the contempt — or worse yet, the pity — that might shine there.

Fresh tears washed his mother's face. "I've always loved you, Adam. Please don't ever doubt that."

Threads of sorrow wound their way through Adam's chest, tightening to the point of pain. He couldn't stay in that room a moment longer or he'd suffocate. "I know, Mama. I love you, too," he said in a strangled voice.

Then, with her anguished features etched into his brain, Adam whirled around and strode out of the parlor, not stopping until Irish Meadows was nothing but a speck behind him.

17

The stillness of the house was Maggie's first indication that something was amiss. No sound of baby Ivy fussing for her morning bottle, no constant chatter from Delia as she prepared for school, no humming from Colleen as she cooked the family's breakfast.

Instead, the kitchen lay in cold, gray silence. A sense of foreboding sent shivers chasing up her spine.

After lighting the stove, Maggie moved to the parlor to start a fire there, in case Rylan hadn't yet done so. Disappointment weighted her steps. She'd hoped to speak with Rylan and Gabe this morning before they started their chores. It had been a few days since the incident with Neill at the orphanage, and Maggie wanted to find out what her brothers had decided. She hoped that Colleen had had a chance to make them listen to reason and decide that rushing to buy an early passage home would not be in anyone's best interest.

Not that it mattered what they decided, because Maggie was *not* going home. They'd have to hogtie her and haul her bodily onto the ship before she'd leave.

The faint glow from the parlor fireplace broke the darkness of the room. Maggie squinted in the dim light, vaguely making out a figure seated in the corner.

"Colleen? Is everything all right?"

Colleen shifted the baby from her shoulder, seeming to come out of a daze. "Oh, Maggie. I'm sorry. I didn't hear you."

"Where is everyone?"

With the stiffness of a much older woman, Colleen rose from her seat and placed Ivy in the basket at her feet. She brushed her hand over her wrinkled dress, which looked as though she'd slept in it. "Rylan's at the orphanage with Dr. Reardon and Aurora. There's a possibility that some of the children have contracted typhoid fever."

"Typhoid? That's terrible." Maggie had seen such an outbreak once before near their village. "Which children are sick?"

"Greta, Johnnie, and Felicia. Possibly a few others."

"What about Delia?"

"Not so far, thank the Lord. But I'm keeping her home for now. She's still sleeping.

Unlike Ivy, who's had me up most of the night." Colleen added a log to the fire and stirred the embers with a poker.

Maggie attempted to pull her thoughts together. "Don't worry about breakfast. I'll take care of it. You should catch some sleep while Ivy naps."

Colleen smiled. "Thank you. I think I will."

Maggie returned to the kitchen, took out the large frying pan, and set the tea kettle on to boil. She would keep it simple with bacon and toast, not sure when anyone would be ready to eat.

The bacon was almost ready when Gabe entered the kitchen. He came up behind her and kissed her cheek. "Good morning, love. Where is everyone?"

Maggie handed Gabe a mug of tea and quickly filled her brother in on the grim news.

A concerned frown marred his forehead. "When will they know if it's typhoid?"

She scooped out some bacon and biscuits and set them on the table for Gabe. "I'm not sure. Dr. Reardon and Aurora have been there all night."

Gabe's eyebrows shot up. "Aurora's there?"

"Yes. She's assisting the doctor."

Gabe set down his mug with a thump. "I'm going over to see what's happening."

Maggie frowned. "I don't think that's wise. Not until they're certain what they're facing."

Gabe plucked his cap off the hook on the wall. "I've likely been exposed anyway since I've been over there almost every day. Besides, I reckon Rylan could use my support."

Before she could protest again, Gabe strode out of the room, his breakfast untouched on the table.

Maggie wasn't sure what worried her more — the potential typhoid epidemic or Gabe's extreme reaction to Aurora's possible peril.

Aurora wiped the brow of five-year-old Greta and set the wet cloth in a bowl on the bedside stand. The girl's cheeks, red from fever, stood out like bright flags against the stark whiteness of the rest of her face. Her frame barely created a ripple under the quilt. Four other children slept in the spare room on the third floor, cramped quarters to be sure, but it was the only space they had available to care for the sick children away from the still-healthy ones.

Fighting waves of exhaustion, Aurora

slumped onto the side of the bed and bowed her head. "Dear God, send Your healing graces to these precious children. Use me as Your instrument to help them recover. In Your name I pray."

"Amen."

Sudden realization broke through her haze of weariness, propelling her up from the thin mattress. "Gabe, you shouldn't be here."

He stood at the foot of the bed like a guardian angel. The concern shining from his eyes made Aurora want to break down and weep.

She tried to grab his arm and move him toward the door, but he wouldn't budge.

"I'm not going anywhere, Aurora. Put me to work. I'm sure I can do something to help."

The relief that spilled through Aurora shamed her. Surely she should be made of sterner stuff if she were to work the long hours required to become a nurse. During the night, Aurora hadn't allowed any weariness or fear to show, but now the toll hit her full force.

She must have swayed, for Gabe wrapped an arm around her waist. "Easy now. Are *you* feeling okay?"

"I'm just tired."

He swiped the wisps of hair from her forehead and laid his hand there. "You don't have a fever, do you? We can't have you getting sick."

She could only shake her head, her throat had become so tight.

As if sensing her fragile emotions, Gabe squeezed her hand. "I'll go check in with Rylan while you find me a job to do."

He flashed her a smile that stole the air from her lungs.

"Thank you, Gabe."

"My pleasure, *cailín alainn.*" He winked and set off down the hall.

She had no idea what it meant, but his endearing tone warmed her heart.

When Dr. Reardon came in several minutes later, Aurora still had not recovered her equilibrium.

"Miss Hastings, are you well? You look . . ." He halted, as though realizing there was no good way to finish.

Aurora had to pull herself together. She might be a pampered rich girl, but she was determined to prove she could handle her duties. "I'm fine. Let's check on the children."

Gabe returned just as the doctor was finishing with Johnnie.

Dr. Reardon removed his stethoscope, a

scowl on his face. "What is he doing here?"

"Gabe came to help however he can," Aurora explained hastily.

The grim set to Dr. Reardon's mouth gave evidence of his displeasure. "May I speak with you both in the hall?"

"Of course."

He moved outside the room, likely so the children wouldn't hear his diagnosis. From his serious expression, Aurora feared the news would not be good. She and Gabe followed him out and closed the door.

Dr. Reardon didn't waste any time. "I'm afraid this has all the appearance of typhoid fever. I'm going to take some more blood and urine samples to have analyzed. We'll need stool samples, as well. In the meantime, we need to determine a possible cause. The likely sources of typhoid are a contaminated water supply or food tainted by a carrier." He tapped a finger on his hand as he spoke. "I'll need the water supply here tested. Until it is ruled out as a cause, water must be boiled before use. Proper hand-washing is of utmost importance. And all waste must be handled as per my instructions." He glanced at Gabe. "Until the outbreak is identified and contained, I am recommending a quarantine."

Aurora knew her dismay must show on

her face. "What is the incubation period, Doctor?"

"It averages from seven to fourteen days." Dr. Reardon folded his stethoscope and stuffed it in the pocket of his white coat. "I'll need a list of everyone who has been in the building over the past two weeks. In particular, anyone who may have eaten the food prepared here during that time."

Fatigue made Aurora's knees tremble. "I'll ask Rylan for help with that."

"Who is the cook here?"

Aurora shook her head. "I don't know."

Gabe stepped forward. "Mrs. Norton is the head cook. Miss Mary Brown was recently hired as an assistant. But apparently she left during the night," he said. "I stopped in the kitchen earlier, and unfortunately I believe Mrs. Norton has taken ill herself."

"Oh, dear." Aurora swiped the back of her hand across her forehead and attempted to pull her thoughts together. The situation seemed to be rapidly spinning out of control.

Gabe put a hand to her back, its warmth steadying her. "I'll help Rylan compile a list of any people who might have been exposed," he said.

Dr. Reardon nodded. "Good. Miss Hastings, I'd appreciate your assistance to take further blood samples."

"Of course." Aurora straightened her shoulders, but Gabe kept his arm about her.

He stared at the doctor. "Don't forget to check on Mrs. Norton, as well."

Dr. Reardon stiffened, and for a brief moment, Aurora sensed a strange tension between the two men.

After several seconds, Dr. Reardon took a step back. "Thank you, Mr. Montgomery. After you, Miss Hastings."

As Aurora followed the doctor into the sickroom, she wearily wondered if she'd be required to cook the meals now, as well.

18

The train ride back to Manhattan chugged by in a blur. Adam's tortured mind could do nothing but replay the events of the day over and over again. Try as he might, he could not erase the look of torment on his mother's face, nor the coldness on his father's.

Correction — *not* his father's.

Adam followed the line of exiting passengers through the train station and out into the dark night. A blast of rain-soaked air hit him full in the face. When had it started to storm?

Too late, he pulled up his collar, but not before a stream of cold water sluiced down his neck and back. Adam shivered and kept on walking. If only the rain could wash away the shame of his birth.

But nothing could do that.

Everything he knew about himself — about his life — had been a lie. His birth certificate was a lie, his father was a lie, his position in the family was a lie. No wonder he'd always felt separate from his family, like a ship moored in the wrong port. His brothers and sisters were a product of the love that existed between their parents. He was the result of a criminal act perpetrated against his mother. His conception had marred what should have been the happiest time of her life, when she married the man she loved. Instead of coming to James as a chaste girl, she'd been a fallen woman, carrying a terrible secret, bearing the sin George Drake had perpetrated.

How could his mother have kept him? Why hadn't she left him on the doorstep of an orphanage, as Jolene had, and continued on with her life — without the constant reminder of her violation? He would never understand that.

Now totally drenched, Adam arrived at John's church and headed to the back door, but once there, he couldn't face going in. Not even to his lowly cot in the basement. The long walk from the station had not drained the terrible anger pulsing within him. He needed physical labor to release it. Ignoring the rain, he stalked over to the pile of wood in the corner of the yard and retrieved the axe from the work shed. Heedless of the elements, Adam drove the axe over and over into the log until his shoulders ached — but even that violent action could not dispel his torment.

"Adam, is everything all right?"

Above the roar of the wind and slash of rain, John's concerned voice penetrated the haze of Adam's turmoil. Adam swiped the water from his eyes with the back of his free hand. "No, John. Everything's all wrong."

Sheltered by a black umbrella, John crossed the yard. "Come inside and we'll talk. You need to get dry."

The axe in Adam's hand shuddered. Looking down, he realized his whole body was shaking. He dropped the tool, which landed with a quiet thud on the ground, and silently followed John through the rear door of the church.

John closed the umbrella and led Adam to his tiny office on the main floor, where a fire glowed in the corner woodstove. "I was working on my sermon," he explained. He pulled a chair close to the hearth and gestured for Adam to sit.

Adam sank onto the seat and held his hands out to the warmth, barely conscious of the puddles pooling on the floor beneath him.

John reappeared moments later with two

towels and a shirt. He handed a towel to Adam and laid the other on the ground to soak up the water.

"Here's a spare shirt. I'll fetch some coffee from the kitchen."

John removed his own soggy cap and jacket, hung them on a hook behind the door, then left the room.

Adam rubbed the towel over his hair and face, then tore off his wet jacket and shirt. Now shivering violently, he scrubbed his chest and arms and tugged on the dry shirt John had left for him. Adam slumped on the chair, staring into the mesmerizing flames, almost incapable of moving.

John returned with the coffee minutes later. He handed Adam the mug, pulled a blanket from the back of an armchair, and draped it around Adam's back.

The warmth from the cup seeped into Adam's cold fingers. He sipped the liquid, grateful for the heat that spread from his throat to his stomach.

John pulled up a chair beside him. "You'll be lucky if you don't catch pneumonia. What possessed you to chop wood in such weather?"

What indeed.

"It was either that or drown my sorrows in whiskey. Chopping wood seemed the better option."

Concern shone from John's brown eyes as he watched him. "I can tell something has upset you greatly."

Adam inhaled and slowly let out a resigned breath. "I finally learned the truth about my father. And it was worse than I ever imagined."

John didn't blink. "It might do you good to talk about it."

The muscles in Adam's shoulders seized. What would John think of him now? Would he still be as accepting of him, knowing his dishonorable origin? Adam toyed with hiding the news but quickly discarded the idea. John deserved his honesty.

As succinctly as possible, Adam relayed the sordid tale of his conception. When he finished, John remained silent, staring into the fire. From past experience, Adam knew the man was praying for God's wisdom to guide his words.

"I'm so sorry, Adam. This must have been a terrible shock. Though it does explain a lot about James's attitude toward you."

"I suppose it's good to know that I didn't imagine his resentment. Still, it doesn't make up for my miserable childhood."

"No. It will take a lot of prayer and a forgiving heart. But I have confidence in you, Adam. I don't doubt for one minute that in time you'll be able to overcome this blow."

Adam raked a hand over his beard. "I'm not so sure, John. Right now I'm so full of anger . . . I don't know if I'll ever be able to face my parents again."

"Who are you angry at?"

Adam stilled. "The man who did such a despicable thing to my mother, for one."

"Who else?"

"I'm angry at James for the way he treated me. It wasn't my fault I resembled my father."

"Of course not." He paused. "Still, I'd like you to consider one thing, if possible."

Adam knew from past dealings with John that these seemingly banal requests usually ended with Adam feeling he was somehow in the wrong.

"How would you feel if the woman you loved was violated in such a manner and found herself with child? Do you think you could do what James did? Marry her and raise the child as your own?"

Adam jerked from his seat, his mind filled with images of Neill Fitzgerald abusing Maggie in such a manner, of her growing large with Neill's unwanted child. Would Adam be able to forgo his anger and accept

Maggie carrying Neill's offspring?

He stalked to the small window behind John's sparse desk and peered out at the deluge falling on the darkened ground. "I don't know if I could, John."

"It must be hard to imagine. You've probably never experienced the self-sacrificing type of love that thinks only of another's welfare." A warm hand came to rest on Adam's shoulder. "The kind of love God has for each one of us."

Adam let out a sound somewhere between a growl and a sob and then rested his forehead against the cold pane of glass. "What kind of love could God have for a man who would do something so horrendous to a woman?"

"We are all sinners to one degree or another. God doesn't love one of us more than another. We are all precious in His eyes, no matter how many times we fall under the weight of sin." John squeezed Adam's shoulders and gently led him back to his seat. "What's important is how we seek His forgiveness, how we pick ourselves up and carry on again."

Adam closed his eyes against the storm of emotions flowing through his body. How would he pick himself up after this? Could he even begin to unravel the events of his life, knowing what he did now?

"You need time, my friend. Time to pray. Time to process this information and discern God's will for your life. I'm a firm believer that nothing happens by chance. There is a purpose in this that only time will reveal. Surrender your anger and sorrow to the Lord, and let Him help heal your wounds."

Adam remained silent, glad his friend didn't seem to expect a response.

John bent to stir the embers in the stove and closed the iron door. "Feel free to sleep here tonight if it's warmer. It tends to be damp in the basement." John moved toward him. "I'll be praying for you, Adam. Remember the verse I always quote. 'All things work together for good to them that love God, who are called according to His purpose.' "

A reluctant smile tugged at Adam's mouth. "I remember." He looked John in the eye. "Thank you, my friend. You got me through prison. I hope you'll get me through this crisis, as well."

John thumped him on the back. "I'll do my best or die trying. Now get some sleep. Things are bound to appear better in the morning."

But as Adam dragged his blankets and pillow from the cot in the basement up to John's warm office, he doubted anything would be different come the morrow.

The next morning, after tidying John's office and moving his belongings back to the basement, Adam dragged his bone-weary body outside to the shed. In the damp morning air, he surveyed the strewn pieces of wood he'd hacked the night before, lying like fallen soldiers on the battlefield. In his rage, he'd damaged some wood he might have crafted into decent furnishings. Now in the cool light of dawn, he cleared the evidence of his destruction.

With a few salvaged logs in tow, he opened the shed and stepped inside, drinking in the soothing scent of hewn wood. When he bent to place the pieces in a corner bin, an uneasy feeling niggled his subconscious. Upon closer inspection, he discovered several of his creations were missing. A small cabinet, a stool, and two chairs, to be exact. Thankfully the cedar chest and the cradle remained where Adam had left them. Why would anyone take a few pieces and leave the two best behind?

He raked a hand through his hair, still damp from his morning ablutions, and decided he'd ask John for permission to start locking the shed. Couldn't be too careful, especially with flammable material like varnish that could start a fire in the wrong hands.

Adam returned to the woodpile and stacked the remaining pieces for use in the woodstove and fireplace. Later, when the McNabbs were busy with their day, Adam would deliver the wood to the rectory. He straightened and wiped the dirt from his hands, not surprised to see John crossing the grass. Likely checking to see that Adam hadn't done something crazy overnight.

"Good morning, Adam. Did you manage to get any sleep?" As usual, John was freshly shaved, his brown hair combed back from his face. Unlike Adam's wrinkled clothing, John's shirt and pants were crisply ironed.

"A little."

"Good. I have a matter to discuss with you. Are you up for a walk?"

Adam tried hard not to scowl at his friend's good cheer. "As long as it won't take too long. I have work at the orphanage today."

"Won't take long at all." John nodded as Adam fell in step beside him.

They made their way in silence, save for John's jaunty whistle, until they turned onto 14th Street, where several shops lined both sides of the road.

Adam blew out an exasperated breath, his patience worn thin. "What are we doing here, John?"

"There's something I want you to see." With a maddening smile, John stopped in front of an empty property sandwiched between a general store and a haberdashery. From the thick grime on the windows, it was evident the business had been closed for some time. A crooked sign, decorated with an anvil and tongs, hung over the door.

"You want to show me an old blacksmith's shop?"

"Correct." Undaunted, John pulled a key from his pants pocket and fit it into the door. After a few hard tugs, the door creaked open.

Reluctantly, Adam followed John inside, brushing cobwebs from his head as they passed through the opening. The interior proved as grim as the exterior, empty now except for a long counter against the left wall, a set of wooden shelves behind it, and a stone hearth where the smithy must have heated his tools.

"What's this about? Does someone need work done in here?" Perhaps one of John's parishioners had a job for him, after all. He studied the area more closely. With a good cleaning and a polishing of the wood, the place showed promise.

John turned to face Adam, hands on his hips. "As a matter of fact, yes. I'm thinking of opening a store."

Adam frowned. This seemed strangely out of character for his friend. "Aren't you busy enough with your church and your work at the prison? When would you have time to run a store, as well?"

"I won't be running it. I'll be a silent partner and leave the day-to-day operation to the store manager."

Goosebumps of awareness traveled up Adam's back. "What type of store are you opening?"

John quirked a brow. "A furniture shop." He regarded Adam steadily. "I thought we would make a good team. What do you think?"

Adam swallowed hard and walked to the counter to run his fingers slowly over the wood, mentally picturing how he would restore it. "Did you buy this property?"

"Rented it. I know the owner, and he's happy to have someone use it again. Gave me a very fair price."

Adam's pulse thrummed. He wanted to jump at this chance, but his pride rose to bar the path to his dream. "I appreciate the gesture, John, but I can't let you do this. Your family needs that money."

John held up a hand. "Hear me out, please. I'll pay the rent until you start making enough with your furniture sales to cover it. Think of it as a leg up until you can ride alone."

A tiny bud of hope began to unfurl in Adam's chest, but once again, cold, hard reality took hold. "It won't work. People aren't going to want to do business with a man who's been in prison."

"I don't see the need to tell anyone of your history."

"Your parishioners don't know?"

"I only told them that you had fallen on hard times and were looking for work. I've already taken the liberty of showing your work to several people who seemed quite interested."

So that's where his missing pieces had gone. "What if someone who knows me spills the beans?"

"Hopefully by then you'll have established a good reputation, which is what people will value." John paused. "Don't you think it's worth the risk?"

The bud of hope uncurled further. He'd always wished for this type of opportunity. Now that it was being handed to him, how could he refuse? He walked to the rear of the building and through a set of swinging doors, where he found a spacious back room — the perfect work area where he could build his inventory. At the far end, a narrow staircase led to an upper level.

John leaned against the doorframe, watching him.

Adam pointed to the stairs. "What's up there?"

"I believe a small living quarters. Go take a look."

Adam climbed the steps to a dusty but serviceable living area. A woodstove served as a source of heat and a place to cook. The space held a table and chair, a narrow bed, and a wardrobe. He returned to the main level, where John waited for him.

"Well?"

"It's perfect." Adam blew out a long breath. "I guess if you're willing to take a risk, then so am I."

Grinning, John shook Adam's hand. A rare burst of excitement filled Adam. Perhaps, despite the terrible news of his parentage, things were turning around, after all. If he could make a success of the shop, maybe it would be enough to overcome the disgrace of his past so that he might one day be worthy of a woman like Maggie.

For the first time in years, hope glowed brightly in Adam's heart.

19

Maggie walked briskly down the street, pulled her shawl more securely about her head, and allowed the fresh air to revive her soul. She needed this outing, needed to escape the confines of Rylan's house and feel the freedom to enjoy the hustle and bustle of the city.

Over the past few days, she'd felt like a prisoner, only getting outside for a few minutes a day to play with Delia and Chester in the yard.

The outbreak of typhoid had everyone in a dither. Rylan and Gabe were holed up at the orphanage, while Colleen seemed obsessed with not letting Delia or the baby out of her sight, lest they, too, be stricken with the disease. Maggie had been helping Colleen care for the girls, but there was little she could do to ease Colleen's anxiety. Other than cooking and cleaning, the only thing Maggie could do was pray that God would bring Colleen a measure of peace.

With not enough to occupy her restless mind, Maggie feared she'd go mad if she didn't get out of the house, even for an hour. After all, she and Colleen weren't under quarantine. As long as they showed no symptoms and were fastidious with their cleanliness, they posed no risk to anyone.

Or so Maggie told herself as she walked toward the cathedral, pushing the small prickle of guilt away. A telephone call earlier in the day from Mr. Unger had presented an opportunity she couldn't let pass. He'd asked to see her and hinted that he might have news for her. She didn't dare put off this meeting or she might miss out on the possibility of employment. Even if nothing came of it, she'd at least have a change of scenery for a few hours and perhaps the chance to play that grand organ again.

Though initially thrilled at her little adventure, the farther away from the house she got, the more aware she became of every noise. Knowing how furious Rylan and Gabe would be if they discovered she'd gone out alone put a slight damper on her excursion.

For the last several blocks, Maggie had the sense someone might be following her. Persistent footsteps sounded behind her, increasing in pace as she did. Her pulse sprinted in keeping with her breath. Two more blocks and she'd reach the cathedral. She crossed the street, thoughts of sanctuary spurring her onward. She'd been foolish to risk her safety. But she couldn't imagine that Neill would spend all his time lying in wait on the off chance she might walk somewhere alone.

Please Lord, let this be a random person out for an evening stroll.

Maggie quickened her stride once again. As soon as she reached St. Patrick's, she'd be safe. Neill wouldn't dare accost her inside one of God's holy churches. Still, her hand trembled when she lifted the latch on the great brass door. Once inside, she moved to the shadows of an alcove at her left, waiting to see if someone followed her in. She pressed her spine against the wall and willed her heart rate to lessen.

Several seconds later, the door creaked open, and a pair of men's boots entered her line of vision. She held her breath until the man moved farther into the entry and removed his cap. At the sight of auburn curls, accompanied by a muttered oath, Maggie's temper flared into full boil.

She charged out of her hiding place. "What in the name of all that's holy are you doing, Adam O'Leary? Following me around town, scaring the daylights out of me."

He whirled around to face her, his brows pulled together in a thunderous expression. "What am *I* doing? What are *you* doing sneaking off by yourself?" He moved closer, towering over her. "You're lucky I was on my way to see Rylan when I saw you leave."

"Lucky, am I?" She poked her finger into his chest. "Lucky to be watched over like a child? Delia has more freedom than I do." Maggie realized she sounded ridiculous, but the mixture of nerves and repressed anxiety from the past few days bubbled up, rendering her powerless to stop her tongue.

"Maybe Delia is more deserving of freedom because she heeds her parents' wishes and doesn't purposely set out to worry them."

Maggie's mouth flapped open as she searched for a scathing comeback.

"Excuse me, Miss Montgomery. Is everything all right?" Mr. Unger stood in the archway, a frown creasing his forehead. "Your voices are carrying."

In the church behind him, several people had gathered to gawk.

Her anger withered as fast as a candle's flame in a gust of wind. "I'm terribly sorry,

Mr. Unger. My . . . friend and I were just having a difference of opinion."

She ignored Adam's snort.

Mr. Unger gestured toward the small door leading to the loft. "Are you available to talk right now?"

"Aye. That's why I'm here." She turned to Adam. "Thank you, Mr. O'Leary, but as you can see, I'm fine. You may go back to your previous activities."

Adam shot her a dark look. "I'm in no hurry to leave. In fact, I believe a few prayers are in order."

"Suit yourself." She spun on her heel and followed Mr. Unger upstairs.

Although still thoroughly incensed, Maggie breathed easier knowing Adam would be there when she finished her conversation, saving her from having to face the long walk home alone.

In Adam's present state of mind, prayer was not exactly his top priority. He needed to get his temper under control before he spoke to the Lord. There was no telling what might come out.

In an attempt to walk off his foul mood, he paced the large foyer of the cathedral, his face and chest hot with annoyance. The one thing he could offer the Lord were words of gratitude that he'd come to Colleen's in time to see Maggie sneaking out alone. He hated to think what type of trouble she could have found herself in had he not been there to follow her. Adam had no doubt that Fitzgerald still lurked in the shadows, waiting for the chance to get Maggie alone. And she'd almost given him the perfect opportunity tonight.

Adam leaned against a wall near the stairs, poised to watch anyone who might enter the church. His thoughts drifted to another unpleasant topic — George Drake. For several days, Adam had ruminated on the fact that his natural father was a criminal and that Adam appeared to have inherited George's criminal tendencies. Any residual hope that Adam might one day be worthy of Maggie's affections had withered and died like a dehydrated plant. She deserved an upright man, someone without his tarnished heritage. Just as well that today she'd whipped him into a fine temper. Anger seemed to be the best weapon to keep his feelings for her from blossoming.

The beginning strains of a song on the pipe organ barely penetrated Adam's reflections at first. Then, as the music reached a powerful crescendo, he straightened against the wall. Maggie was playing. He'd bet his last piece of pine on it.

Adam didn't notice the newcomer stalk past him until the man stopped to look furtively from side to side, as though seeking someone in particular.

Fitzgerald. Adam jerked away from the wall. The mongrel *had* been watching Maggie. Did he know Adam was here, as well?

Adam slipped behind a statue to remain undetected. The moment Fitzgerald's gaze moved toward the loft, Adam froze. From the smug look on his face, Fitzgerald knew it was Maggie on the organ.

Adam's hands tightened into fists, his heart thrumming. He considered confronting Fitzgerald, but he didn't wish to create a scene in the middle of a church. Instead, he strode to the stairs and took them two at a time, following the vibrations of the music to the monstrosity of an organ where Maggie sat, her fingers moving over four massive rows of keys.

He moved toward her, ignoring the frown on Mr. Unger's face.

"Maggie, I need you to come with me. Right now."

Her fingers hit a discordant note, and she scowled at him. "I'm not going anywhere —"

"He's here, Maggie." Adam pinned her

316

with a pointed stare and nodded when her eyes widened. He turned to Mr. Unger. "Is there another way out?"

Mr. Unger looked at Maggie, then back to Adam, obviously sensing her distress. "There's another staircase on the opposite side."

"Thank you." Adam held out his hand to Maggie, who remained frozen on the bench.

Mr. Unger leaned forward. "Is it safe to let you leave with this man, Miss Montgomery?"

She stood up and reached for her shawl. "It's fine, Mr. Unger. The man downstairs is the problem."

"His name is Neill Fitzgerald. Tall. Dark coat. Claims he's Maggie's fiancé, but he's not." Adam helped Maggie wrap her shawl around her head and shoulders. "If you could distract him and give us time to leave, I'd appreciate it."

The man nodded. "Certainly." He turned to Maggie once again. "I'll be awaiting your answer to my offer, young lady."

"Thank you so much, Mr. Unger. I'll be in touch soon."

Footsteps echoed on the stairs.

Adam took Maggie's arm and led her to the back staircase while Mr. Unger went to

317

intercept Fitzgerald coming up the other side.

They made their way to the foyer below, exited the main door as quietly as possible, and started along Fifth Avenue.

Maggie walked in silence, her profile rigid. For once, Adam coveted her reprimand. Even her sharp tongue would be better than her silence.

"Go ahead. Say it," she finally spat out.

Adam took in her pinched features. "I don't need to. You know you made a poor choice coming out alone."

She pulled her wrap tighter around her and huffed out a shaky breath. The tremor of her hands told him how helpless, how powerless she must feel, and he reined in the urge to scold her further. "Promise me you won't take such a chance again."

She pressed her lips into a tight line, then she nodded. "I promise."

As they continued walking, Adam searched for a way to change her focus. "So, what kind of offer was Mr. Unger talking about?"

She clamped her lips together again and quickened her pace.

"He didn't offer to marry you, did he?"

She stopped in her tracks, mouth agape. "Don't be daft. He's sixty if he's a day."

318

"Then . . . what?"

Her nostrils flared. He waited while she seemed to wrestle with her response. "If you must know, he offered me a position as assistant organist."

"You must be happy."

She quickened her pace. "I am. Although the wage won't be enough to support me. I'll have to teach, as well."

The backdrop of noise from traffic in the streets created a buffer around them. Horses *clip-clopped* down the road, while the occasional motorcar honked for right of way.

Adam took her elbow to cross a street. "Why are you so set on staying in America? Won't you miss home?" His heart gave an uncomfortable thump at the mere thought of Maggie being an ocean away.

She sighed softly. "I do love Ireland. But ever since Rylan left for America, I've wanted to travel, to see more of the world."

"You're looking for adventure?"

"No. Just something different. I'm tired of everyone in our village knowing my business. Tired of all the boys I grew up with, none of whom I'd want to marry."

"You want a home and family of your own, then?"

She bristled. "Of course. Don't most women?"

"I suppose they do." An ache spread through Adam's chest, for he couldn't be the one to fulfil her heart's desire. The one thing he could do was protect her.

They walked on again in silence, with Adam occasionally casting glances behind him to make sure Fitzgerald wasn't following them.

"Adam, is something else bothering you?"

He looked over to find her studying him and frowned. "Fitzgerald isn't enough?"

She scrunched her nose at him like she'd hit a bad note. "I think something else has you preoccupied."

The fact that she could read him so well disconcerted him. He clamped his mouth shut and kept walking.

"Has Rylan —"

"It's nothing to do with you or Rylan."

She walked in silence for several moments. "Is it Ivy's mother? Has she contacted you?"

"No."

"Is it your —"

"Enough." Adam scrubbed a hand over his beard, regretting his harsh tone. Perhaps he should just tell her about his wretched background. Maybe then she'd quit haunting his dreams. The disgust on her face would surely cure him of any romantic delusions.

They reached the Montgomery house and came to a halt at the foot of the stairs. Adam turned to her. The sadness on her face sent arrows of guilt shooting through him. "I'm sorry for snapping. It's just . . ." He sighed. "I've had some disturbing news that's taking some time to process."

Her eyes lit with sympathy. "It might help to talk about it."

"There's nothing to talk about." He clenched his jaw until his teeth ached.

She took him by the hand, her warmth radiating through his fingers. "Come inside. It'll be safer than standing out here if Neill is following us."

He blew out a breath. "All right. Just for a minute." He'd go in long enough to make sure everything was secure. Long enough to tell her about his sordid beginnings and disillusion her completely.

They entered the house, doing their best to be quiet. Maggie hung her shawl on a hook, and he removed his cap. By mutual accord, they went into the parlor. Though the room was empty, the remnants of a small fire still burned in the grate.

"So what is this disturbing news?" She smoothed her skirts as she sat.

Why did he find her every action so fascinating? He tore his gaze away to stare at the pattern on the carpet. "What I tell you must remain confidential, especially from Colleen."

"You have my word."

Pressure built in his chest until he could no longer remain seated. Adam pushed to his feet and crossed the room to stand before the mantel. "I found out James O'Leary is not my true father."

He heard her soft gasp. "I don't understand. Who is your father, then?"

Adam stared into the fire, wishing his life hadn't been shrouded in secrets and shame. Wishing he could be a paragon of respectability for her. But there was no point in wishing for the impossible.

He turned to face her. "A criminal by the name of George Drake." He paused for effect. "The man violated my mother. My conception resulted from an act of violence."

Her hand flew to cover her mouth. "Oh, Adam."

"Drake spent his last days in prison, which proves the old saying is true. The apple doesn't fall far from the tree." He barked out a harsh laugh. And then, to avoid witnessing her disgust, he bent to stir the embers in the hearth with a poker.

Acutely aware of her every breath, he

heard her rise from the sofa, felt the vibration of her nearness. When he rose, wiping his hands, she stood before him, tears glistening in her eyes.

"You are not at fault, Adam."

"I'm a product of my father's criminal act. No wonder James can't bear the sight of me."

"Adam —"

He pulled away from her. "Now you see why you need to stay far away from me, before I contaminate you, as well. Goodbye, Maggie."

"Wait."

The pressure on his arm halted his retreat before he reached the door. He paused and closed his eyes, praying for the strength to leave.

"I don't care who your father is, Adam. I know you're a good and decent man. Nothing will convince me otherwise."

He opened his eyes, prepared to argue, but the sheer emotion on her face stole the words from his mouth. Before he realized her intent, she moved forward and laid her lips on his.

A jolt of electricity could not have jarred him more. He froze for a second, until the sweet essence of her being flowed through her lips, searing his soul. She moved closer still, wrapping her arms around him, enveloping him with her touch, her scent. Heat curled in his stomach. His chest vibrated along with his thudding heart, until a low whimper in her throat finally broke his stupor.

With great effort, he tore his mouth from hers. "Maggie, no. Don't you see how wrong this is?"

Her fingers grazed his cheek, and she shook her head. "I only see how *right* this is. You are not your father, Adam."

A groan of protest rumbled through him. He did not deserve her faith, her loyalty.

Yet reflected in her beautiful eyes, he saw the man he wished to be.

Dark tendrils of hair caressed her cheek. The softness of her skin beckoned to him, begging for his touch. He needed to get away from her intoxicating nearness, but his feet refused to cooperate. His gaze fell to the rosy moistness of her lips.

"Maggie." Without thinking, he lowered his head until his mouth found hers and drew her closer in his arms. Her fingers wound through the hair at the base of his neck, while her mouth matched his, the faint taste of honey tripping his pulse. Finally, before he lost complete control, he drew back to rest his forehead on hers.

With one finger, he traced the smooth curve of her cheek and released a sigh of regret.

"Maggie?" Colleen's voice drifted toward them. "Who are you talking to?"

Panic leapt into Maggie's eyes.

"We've done nothing wrong." He kissed her fingers and stepped into the hallway. "It's only me, Colleen."

His sister looked as though she'd just tumbled out of bed, her auburn hair in a long braid over her robe. "What are you doing here at this hour?"

Adam smiled. "It's barely nine o'clock. Not everyone goes to bed with the babes."

She clutched her arms around her frame. "I must have fallen asleep. It seemed much later." She straightened. "But my question remains — why are you here?"

"I came by earlier in the hopes of speaking with Rylan and met Maggie on her way to the cathedral. I made sure she got back safely."

Colleen moved farther into the room. "Maggie, why would you risk your safety like that?"

Adam expected Maggie's Irish temper to unleash at any moment.

Instead, she lowered her head and folded her hands in front of her skirts. "I'm sorry,

Colleen. I was desperate to get out of the house for a while. It won't happen again."

Colleen crossed to Maggie and enfolded her in a hug. "I couldn't bear it if anything happened to you." She turned to Adam, weariness etched in her features. "I guess you haven't heard about the typhoid out-break. Rylan and Gabe are at the orphan-age until the temporary quarantine is lifted."

Adam snapped to attention. "I'd heard about the illness, but nothing about a quarantine. Do you mean to tell me you two are staying here alone?"

Colleen nodded.

Alarm licked through him. "Fitzgerald was at the cathedral, lying in wait for Maggie. He could break in here and no one would be able to stop him." Adam's breath came faster, and his fists curled.

Maggie sank onto one of the chairs, her face drained of color, as though she only now fully realized the danger she faced.

Colleen plucked at the belt of her robe. "I've been so worried about the children, I never thought —"

Adam straightened, a decision cementing in his mind. "I'll stay here until Rylan or Gabe returns."

Colleen clutched the lapels of her robe together. "I don't think —"

"No arguments, Colleen. I'll take Rylan's anger over the possibility of harm coming to any of you."

Colleen sagged, the breath whooshing from her. "To be honest, I haven't been able to sleep without Rylan here. That must be why I dozed off when I put Ivy down." Tears formed in her eyes, a rarity for his vivacious sister. She must be past exhausted.

A movement at the open parlor door made Adam spin around.

Little Delia wandered in, her cheeks as red as the cloth of her nightgown. "Mama, I don't feel good. My tummy hurts."

As Colleen gathered Delia in her arms, Maggie exchanged a worried look with Adam. He gave a brief nod to reassure her. He'd do everything in his power to help his family through this crisis.

And he wouldn't rest until Maggie's world had become safe once again.

Early the next morning, Maggie placed the kettle of water on the stove and turned her attention to the ham and eggs frying in the skillet. Any moment now, she expected Adam to appear for breakfast. After a nearly sleepless night, staring at the ceiling where Adam slept above her, reliving the thrill of his kiss, Maggie's every nerve seemed on edge.

By all accounts, she should be ashamed of her brazen action, kissing Adam like that, but she couldn't make herself regret something that felt so right. Knowing that Adam would never act on his feelings — that his perceived unworthiness and his rigid self-control would forever hold him back — she'd taken matters into her own hands to show Adam where her heart lay. She only hoped she hadn't done irreparable damage to their relationship.

Maggie flipped the eggs, trying to determine how many she should cook. She doubted Colleen would be down anytime soon. After sending for Dr. Reardon, Colleen had sat up most of the night with Delia.

Heavy treads sounded on the staircase, and shivers of anticipation raced along Maggie's spine. Would Adam talk about the kiss they'd shared, or act as if it had never happened?

"Good morning, Miss Montgomery."

She turned from the stove to find Dr. Reardon in the kitchen doorway. "Good morning, Doctor. I'm surprised to see you."

From the weary lines on his face and the tousled mat of his brown hair, it appeared he'd been up all night.

"I thought it prudent to keep watch over Delia. I didn't want to move her in the middle of the night, but this morning, I'll transfer her to the infirmary at the orphanage. Her mother is getting her ready."

A slither of fear wound around Maggie's heart. "Delia will be all right, won't she?"

The doctor didn't meet her eyes. "We'll do our best. A few of the other infected children have shown slight signs of improvement."

"Please have a seat while you wait. I'll get you some breakfast."

He gave a wan smile and pulled out a chair. "Thank you. It's been a few days since I've had a hot meal."

Maggie used a cloth to grab the kettle and poured the strong coffee into a mug. Come to think of it, they hadn't received any of Mrs. Norton's biscuits lately. "Mrs. Norton hasn't left because of the illness, has she?" Knowing the woman's devotion to those children, Maggie couldn't imagine it.

"I'm afraid Mrs. Norton is ill herself. And the assistant cook has disappeared."

"That's a shame." Every time Maggie turned around, it seemed a new crisis arose. She slid a plate of eggs and ham in front of the doctor. "So who is making the meals?"

"The nuns are pitching in as much as possible." He dug into his food like a starving man.

Maggie returned to the stove and cracked three more eggs onto the hot skillet. "Have you determined the cause of the outbreak yet?"

Dr. Reardon shook his head. "It's baffling, to be sure. There's no real reason why some of the students are affected while others are not. We ruled out the drinking water, so we suspect it happened through food contamination. We're questioning everyone to determine the common factors." He chewed a mouthful and swallowed. "In the meantime, you all must be diligent about proper handwashing and hygiene."

The cold swath of fear returned. "Aye. But what about the baby? Is Ivy at risk?"

The grim set to his mouth told Maggie the answer. "We'll have to wait and see," he said, "but little Ivy is one of the reasons I think it best to remove Delia from her home."

Oh dear Lord, what will Colleen do if she loses both Delia and the baby to this illness? Maggie couldn't even begin to imagine it.

Dr. Reardon patted a napkin to his mouth and rose. "Thank you for the breakfast, Miss Montgomery. And please keep watch for any symptoms. Malaise, fever, stomach pain. If you start to feel unwell, you'd be wise to come right over to the orphanage."

Adam appeared in the doorway. Maggie startled, amazed she hadn't heard him come down the stairs. For a large man, he could be very quiet when he chose.

"May I ask why these patients are not being taken to the hospital? Surely they could be treated much more efficiently there." The challenge in Adam's voice was unmistakable.

Dr. Reardon stiffened. "And you are?"

"Adam O'Leary. Colleen's brother and Delia's uncle."

Maggie busied herself getting Adam a cup of coffee.

"Well, Mr. O'Leary, I understand your concern. However, we don't want to spread the contagion, if we can help it. Moving them to the hospital would risk an even greater outbreak there."

Adam gave a curt nod. "I suppose there's logic in that."

Maggie set a plate of food on the table and motioned for Adam to sit. A noise in the hall delayed him from doing so. Colleen moved into view of the doorway, carrying Delia.

Dr. Reardon rushed to assist her. "Mrs. Montgomery, you should have told me you were ready. I'd have carried her down."

Plastered against Colleen's shoulder, Delia's face appeared even more flushed this morning, her eyes glassy.

Colleen's alabaster skin now appeared gray, her hair pinned in a quick bun at the back of her neck. "You said you have a motorcar parked outside?"

"That's right, but Mrs. Montgomery . . ." He laid a hand on her arm. "I feel it would be wise for you to remain here. We will take good care of Delia, I can promise you that."

Something akin to panic flew across Colleen's face. "I won't let her go alone. She needs her mother." Delia's whimper only served to strengthen her argument.

"And what of the infant? We can't risk further exposure by bringing her with you."

Tears sprang to Colleen's eyes.

Feeling Colleen's anguish at the terrible choice she had to make, Maggie wiped her hands on her apron. "I'll take care of Ivy, Colleen. You go with Delia."

Colleen looked from Maggie to Adam and shook her head. "It won't be proper — you two here alone without a chaperone. Rylan and Gabe will be furious."

Adam moved up beside Maggie. "Then send one of them back here if they're so worried. I won't leave Maggie and the baby unprotected."

Dr. Reardon frowned. "Unprotected from what?"

"A man has been harassing Maggie. He poses a danger every bit as grave as the fever."

Colleen seemed to gather her strength. "I'll find someone to come and stay. Perhaps Brianna. In the meantime, let's be on our way, Doctor."

"I'll be praying for you all," Maggie called as they exited.

The band of stress across her shoulders threatened to snap the moment the door closed. Maggie inhaled deeply and turned to find Adam watching her in his usual intense fashion.

"Well," she said briskly, "I'd best go and get the baby. Eat your breakfast before it gets cold."

Adam reached out to halt her. Silently, he drew her to him and wrapped his arms about her. "It will be okay, Maggie. We'll get through this . . . together."

Despite her best efforts, a lump rose to block her throat. For a moment, she allowed her eyes to close and drank in the comforting scent of him, gaining fortitude from his solid presence. "Aye. We will. Along with God's grace and mercy."

20

Aurora descended the central staircase to the main floor of the orphanage. She could not get used to the stillness now pervading the building that once had bustled with activity and joy. Even the healthy children seemed subdued by the seriousness of the situation.

She brushed a weary hand across her forehead and tried to remember which day it was. Saturday? Sunday? How long had they been confined?

Her thoughts turned to her parents and the phone conversation she'd had with her mother. Although worried at Aurora's proximity to the illness, Mama had accepted the situation with good grace and had promised to try to temper her father's reaction. The last thing Aurora wanted was Papa to show up at the orphanage and create a scene.

An insistent pounding at the front door of

the orphanage pulled Aurora from her reflections. Why would someone knock despite the warnings posted on the exterior?

Warily, Aurora opened the door a crack. An unfamiliar woman stood on the stoop, agitation evident in the angle of her stance.

"Can I help you?" Aurora tried not to gawk at the heavily made-up face, which stood out in stark contrast to the drab brown hair and threadbare coat.

The woman lifted her chin. "I wish to speak to the director of the orphanage."

Aurora blinked. "I'm sorry, miss, but as you can see, we are under quarantine. You'd best try a telephone call instead."

The woman's pale eyes hardened. "My child is in there, and I will not have her exposed to this danger. She needs to come home with me."

Nothing about the woman's claim made sense. However, in her present state of agitation, Aurora doubted she would see reason. Best to see what Rylan wanted her to do.

"If you'll wait here for a moment, I'll see if Mr. Montgomery is available."

Aurora went directly to Rylan's office, where she found Gabe and Rylan involved in a serious conversation. The two men looked extremely grim as she entered.

"I'm sorry to bother you, but there's a distraught woman on the doorstep. She says her child is here and she wants her out of harm's way."

Gabe got to his feet. "How can that be? Aren't these children orphans?"

Rylan shook his head. "Not all of them. Some of them have a parent who can't afford to keep them." He rose from the desk. "Did she tell you her child's name?"

"No."

He let out a long breath. "I'll speak to her outside. Make her understand the severity of our situation and pray to God her child isn't one of those affected."

A flurry of activity beyond the office doors drew Aurora's attention. Rylan and Gabe preceded Aurora in the hallway. At the foot of the main staircase, Dr. Reardon stood, holding a child in his arms, speaking to Colleen.

Rylan surged forward. "Colleen, love. What are you doing here?" The slap of his shoes on the floor stopped the moment he saw the child. "Delia?"

Colleen flew to her husband and buried her face in his shoulder.

"I'm afraid she has the fever." Dr. Reardon shot Aurora a concerned look over

Rylan's head. "We're better to treat her here."

Gabe moved forward to lay a hand on his brother's arm. "You take care of your family. I'll handle the woman at the door."

Rylan nodded his thanks, while trying to comfort his distraught wife.

"I had to leave Ivy with Maggie," Colleen sobbed. "The doctor said the risk was too great."

"Shh, love. You did the right thing. Let's go get Delia settled."

The warmth of a hand on her shoulder brought Aurora's focus back. Gabe pressed a handkerchief into her hands, and she realized that she, too, was crying.

"Would you care to assist me with the woman outside?"

She dabbed the moisture from her cheeks. "Of course. Thank you."

When they opened the door and stepped outside, the woman whirled to face them. "I thought you'd forgotten me."

"Forgive us for the delay," Gabe said. "We had a slight emergency to handle first."

The woman's eyes widened. "What is going on in there?"

Gabe smiled at her. "First let me introduce myself. I'm Gabriel Montgomery. My brother runs this orphanage. And this is

Miss Hastings, who is tending to the children who are ill."

The woman took a distinct step backward and brought a gloved hand to cover her nose and mouth. "Is it smallpox?"

"Typhoid fever. May I ask your name?"

"Jolene Winters. I left my baby here a few weeks ago, but I've changed my mind. I want her back."

Aurora's insides turned to putty. The only infant at the orphanage was baby Ivy — the one Colleen had claimed as her own. She shot a nervous glance at Gabe, and from his expression, she knew he'd arrived at the same conclusion.

"You'll be happy to know your baby has not been staying at the orphanage. The director and his wife have taken her into their home."

Instead of being relieved, the woman appeared even more alarmed. "I demand to be taken there immediately."

To Aurora's great relief, Gabe stepped forward. "I'm afraid I can't do that," he said gently. "It's against the rules."

Aurora had no idea if that were true, but coming from Gabe, it sounded official.

Miss Winters lifted her chin. "Then I demand to speak with the director himself. Is he in there?"

Gabe hesitated, no doubt weighing the consequences for his brother. A breeze ruffled the hair on his forehead as his indecision played across his handsome features.

"If you don't tell me, I'll come back with the constable. I have a right to my baby." The woman's near hysteria rang in the air.

People passing on the walkway directed curious stares at them. St. Rita's prided itself on its sterling reputation. The last thing the facility needed on top of an epidemic was a scandal involving the police.

Aurora opened the front door. "If you'll come in and have a seat, I'll get him for you."

Miss Winters pointed to the warning sign. "What about the contagion?"

"You'll be safe in the waiting area."

"Fine." Miss Winters swept past them into the building.

Aurora turned back to Gabe. The sorrowful look on his face matched the dread that filled her heart.

How would Rylan and Colleen handle losing baby Ivy and possibly little Delia, as well?

So this was how it would feel to have Maggie as his wife, caring for their infant daughter.

Adam leaned back in his chair and watched Maggie rock the baby. The glow from the fire highlighted the expression of love on her face as she cooed and sang to the little girl. The poignancy of the moment, the contentment he felt at simply being in their presence, created a warm bubble in Adam's chest.

If only this were real, or even a distant possibility.

They'd spent a pleasant day together. Adam had fixed a few things around Rylan's house that needed repair, and Maggie cooked a wonderful meal of fried chicken and mashed potatoes while little Ivy dozed. For a brief moment in time, it seemed as though they existed in their own little cocoon — safe from the Neill Fitzgeralds of the world, safe from those who knew of Adam's criminal past, and safe from the threat of an epidemic.

A noise in the hall had Adam snapping to attention. He motioned for Maggie to stay put in her rocker as he headed into the hallway. The front door opened as Adam reached it, and Rylan entered. Words of greeting died on Adam's lips when he spied the woman standing behind his brother-in-law.

"Jolene. What are you doing here?" Though he asked the question, his gut told him the answer.

That and Rylan's stricken countenance.

"You two know each other, I see." Rylan made way for Jolene to enter.

"Yes. Why is Jolene with you?"

Rylan's ravaged expression told of the ordeal he'd been forced to bear. "She came to St. Rita's . . . to claim her daughter."

Adam's mouth went dry. Deep down, he'd suspected Jolene would eventually change her mind and regret giving Ivy away.

Jolene pushed forward. "Is my baby all right? Has she got the fever?"

"So far she's fine." Despite the emotions threatening to engulf him, Adam managed to keep calm.

"Where is she?" Rylan asked tightly.

"In the parlor with Maggie."

By the time the three of them entered the room, Maggie was on her feet, clutching the bundle to her shoulder. Her wide eyes moved from Adam to Rylan and then landed on Jolene. Maggie's arms tightened around the baby. "What's going on?"

Adam wished he could spare Maggie this pain. But no matter how much they disliked it, Jolene had a right to her child. "Maggie, this is Jolene. Ivy's mother."

"My baby." Jolene pushed past him across the carpet.

Maggie stepped back, protectively shielding the child, who let out a howl. Maggie began to sway. "Shh, darling. Everything's all right."

Though Maggie's tone was soothing, her glare was fierce. "You'll not be taking this child without Colleen here. She's mothered this baby from the moment you chose to discard her like a worn-out toy." Moisture rimmed her eyes, magnifying their pale beauty, as she turned to Rylan. "Does Colleen know about this?"

He nodded. "Aye, but she couldn't leave Delia."

Adam moved between the women. "Jolene, we won't know if Ivy's contracted the fever for a week or more. It would be in her best interest to let her remain here, where the doctor will come to check on her."

Jolene plucked at the top button of her coat, panic in her eyes.

Adam laid a hand on her shoulder, hoping to calm her apparent agitation. "If she hasn't shown any signs of illness in the next week, you can take her then." It wasn't much, but it would bide them time and give

Colleen a chance for a proper good-bye. He prayed Jolene's concern for her child would outweigh her desperation to take her now.

She wrung her hands together. "I know what you're doing. This is a trick to get me to change my mind. Well, it won't work." She clamped her thin lips together and lunged for Maggie. "Give me my child."

Maggie held her ground, not releasing her hold on Ivy. "If you care about your daughter's well-being, you'll leave her where she's better off. What will you do if she develops typhoid?"

A hint of fear flickered over Jolene's face before a hardness settled there. "If she needs a doctor, I'll find her one."

"And medicine? Will you be able to afford that? Do you even have a decent place to live?" Maggie's voice quivered.

Jolene lifted her chin. "It may not be as fancy as this, but I have a room. And a job. I've friends who will help me take care of her when I'm . . . working."

Adam's gut clenched, knowing exactly what type of work she'd be doing. He forced himself not to picture the saloon and the type of accommodation Jolene would have there. Adam didn't know all the legalities involved in this type of situation, but if Rylan was allowing Jolene to take the baby, it must mean she had the law on her side. Still, Adam would make it a point to see that Ivy was properly cared for, and if he found otherwise, he'd call in whatever authorities necessary to ensure the child's well-being.

Rylan seemed to come out of a daze. He turned to Maggie and released a ragged breath. "I'm afraid we have no choice, Maggie. Give her the child."

For a moment, Maggie remained frozen, as though she hadn't heard him, but then, with a quiet sob, she lifted Ivy from her shoulder. Her fingers trembled as she pushed the blanket away from the baby's face. "God be with you, little one." She kissed the top of Ivy's head, and then, instead of handing the baby to Jolene, Maggie held her out to Rylan.

Adam had seldom seen such anguish on a man's face as he lifted the still-whimpering infant.

"Good-bye, sweet Ivy. We were blessed to have you in our lives for a short time. We'll pray for you always." He kissed her and then handed her to Jolene, tears streaming down both cheeks.

Adam's throat tightened so that he could barely breathe.

In direct contrast to their sorrow, Jolene's

face lit with joy. "My sweet girl. It's okay now. Your mama's here."

Adam couldn't look at Maggie, couldn't bear to see her grief. Couldn't think of the almost-finished cradle Ivy would never sleep in. Or the pain his sister must be enduring. "I'll walk you to the streetcar, Jolene."

"Wait. You'll need another blanket. Ivy mustn't get a chill." Maggie rushed from the room, and seconds later her footsteps sounded on the stairs.

"If you'll excuse me," Rylan said in a strangled voice, "I'd best get back to the orphanage."

Moments after Rylan left, Maggie returned with a bonnet and a thicker woolen blanket.

"Thank you," Jolene said softly as she accepted the bundle.

Maggie's bottom lip quivered. "Just take good care of her."

Adam longed to stay and comfort her, but for the baby's sake, he wanted to make sure Jolene didn't walk the whole way to the saloon. The streetcar would be quicker and safer. "I'll be back soon," he said to Maggie. "Lock the door behind me."

Aurora paused outside the sickroom to lay a hand over her stomach. What could she say to a woman whose daughter was fighting for her life and who'd just lost the infant she'd hoped to adopt?

"Are you all right, Miss Hastings?" Dr. Reardon's voice sounded behind her.

"Yes." She straightened. "Just trying to determine what to say to Colleen."

The doctor touched her shoulder, and she turned to face him. "As a nurse, this is only one of the difficult things you'll be required to do. If you're having doubts, you may need to rethink your decision."

She straightened her back. "I can handle it, Doctor. I won't change my mind — no matter how difficult."

Approval lit his brown eyes, and he gave a slight nod. "Good to know. Now, let's go in and check on our patients."

With a swish of his white coat, he sailed into the room, confidence evident with every step. Eight small beds, four on each side, now swamped the room. If any more children fell ill, they'd have to use one of the dormitories or set up beds in the common room. Dr. Reardon was treating Mrs. Norton, and now two of the nuns who had fallen ill, but they were being treated in their own rooms.

Aurora fought back waves of weariness. How she longed for a full night's sleep. But even the thought brought a rise of guilt. How could she complain when the children were suffering so?

"Aurora."

Her heart lightened at the sound of her name, and she turned with a ready smile for Gabe. The only blessing in this nightmare had been spending so much time with him. Gabe had been a pillar of strength throughout this whole ordeal, quietly doing whatever tasks she or the doctor required of him. The fatigue was affecting him, too. She could tell by the shadows beneath his eyes and the lines bracketing his mouth. Still, he managed a grin as he came toward her. "You do realize the doctor is in love with you, don't you?"

She gaped at him. "What are you talking about?"

"The man can barely keep his eyes off you. Not that I blame him."

She smoothed the front of her apron, hoping to hide the heat rising in her cheeks. "You're talking nonsense when we've work to do."

He sobered. "That's why I've come. To see my niece. Any sign of improvement?"

"The doctor is checking Delia now. Why don't you come in with me?"

He nodded. "I've got a few minutes to

spare before I start moving beds into the common room. The doc needs a bigger area to work in."

They entered the room, and Gabe headed straight for Delia's cot. Colleen and Rylan hovered near the foot of the bed while Dr. Reardon examined the girl.

Aurora made a quick tour of her patients, making sure all the other children were comfortable before joining the group at Delia's side. The girl lay, eyes closed, unmoving beneath the blankets.

Dr. Reardon jotted a few notes on his clipboard and looked up, his expression grim.

"I'm afraid Delia is experiencing the worst of the illness. All we can do now is keep her hydrated, monitor her symptoms . . . and pray."

Colleen pressed her face into Rylan's shoulder, silent sobs shaking her frame. Gabe offered the pair his condolences and then grimly left the room, presumably to continue his tasks downstairs.

Aurora longed to go after him, but her patients here needed her attention.

She straightened her back and moved to the first bed. "Doctor, would you check on Felicia, please? Her temperature has risen and her pain seems worse."

"Right away."

Aurora accompanied Dr. Reardon as he examined all the children and made notations on their charts.

When he finished, he rubbed the bridge of his nose. "I'm worried about Johnnie and Felicia," he said quietly. "They don't seem to be responding as well as the others. We must watch them carefully for the next forty-eight hours."

Aurora nodded. She'd observed the same thing. If she thought she was tired now, the next few days would test the limits of her stamina.

Please God, help us all get through the worst of this disease.

21

Maggie finished packing a few articles of clothing and toiletries into her small valise. There would be no staying in her brother's home now that baby Ivy no longer needed her.

She scanned the room one last time and attempted to ward off the cloud of melancholy. Losing Ivy had hit her harder than she could have imagined. All along she'd feared Colleen and Rylan had become too attached to the mite, but she hadn't counted on becoming smitten herself. She ached for the sorrow her brother and sister-in-law must be experiencing, and for their worry over Delia on top of Ivy's departure.

Maggie closed her bag and descended the stairs to the main level. In the likelihood that she'd be gone for a while, she would empty the icebox and bring any perishable food with her.

As she finished tidying the kitchen, some-

one rapped on the front door. Maggie hurried to peer out the side window and, seeing Adam on the step, allowed him in.

The grim set to his jaw told her how hard
this evening had been for him, as well.

"Did Jolene make the streetcar all right?"

"She did." He twisted his cap between his
fingers, his brows slashing his forehead. "I
don't think you should stay here alone, now
that —"

She pointed to her bag in the hallway. "I
know. Just let me get the food from the
kitchen."

A few minutes later, they locked the house
and began the two-block walk to the orphanage. With Adam beside her, Maggie
had no fear for her safety.

She glanced sideways at him as they
walked. "What will you do now?"

"I've had no direct contact with the illness, so I should be fine. But I'll stay away
from anyone until I'm sure."

Maggie nodded, hating to think of him
relegated to the church basement. "You
could come to the orphanage, too. I'm sure
there's plenty of work to keep you occupied."

They reached the front steps at St. Rita's,
and Adam stopped, pinning her with a frank
stare. "I think you know why that's not a

good idea. Things have become . . . complicated between us. Being confined here will only heighten feelings that need to fade."

She'd wondered how he would act after their kiss. Now she had her answer. Maggie sighed. "Don't I have any say in the matter?"

Adam gave a sad smile. "I fear I must be sensible for the both of us."

For the second time that night, Maggie's heart squeezed with sorrow, preventing her from saying anything further.

"If you need me, you can reach me through John McNabb at the Shepherd of Good Hope Church."

The night breeze blew stray strands of hair about her face as she reached up to kiss his cheek, wishing she had the nerve to linger. "Take care of yourself, Adam," she whispered. "I'll be praying for you."

She lifted her skirts to climb the stairs and then, with a last lingering look at his anguished face, she entered the building.

Aurora's usual optimism had deserted her, leaving her clinging to a last thread of hope. Seated beside Delia's bed, she twisted a damp handkerchief between her fingers. No matter how many times she bathed the girl's face, her temperature refused to drop. She supposed she should be grateful it hadn't worsened, but to see a once-healthy child this helpless caused an irrational fear that overwhelmed the comfort prayer normally afforded.

She reached out to brush a stray lock of hair from the child's forehead. "Please get better, Delia. Your family needs you."

Once again, Aurora found herself fighting tears of helpless frustration that she could do nothing more to heal her. She blinked back the moisture, hoping to dispel the depression that plagued her.

"Miss Hastings, may I speak to you in private, please?"

Aurora reluctantly moved her hand away. "Right away, Doctor."

She made a deliberate effort to smooth the covers, then paused to check on little Greta before sedately following Dr. Reardon into the hallway. An unnatural hush hovered over the building, unnerving Aurora further.

"We can talk in Mr. Montgomery's office."

The grim lines on Dr. Reardon's face added to Aurora's dismay. Did he have bad news to impart? Or had she made an error with one of the patients?

"Please sit down."

Aurora complied while he took Rylan's chair and folded his hands on the desktop. Nothing about his manner eased her anxiety.

"I wanted you to know that I've engaged the services of a nurse from the hospital to assist here." He gave her an apologetic glance across the desk. "I resisted bringing anyone else into the situation, not wishing to expose anyone unnecessarily. However, Mrs. Patterson has already survived typhoid fever and has no qualms about coming. She'll arrive later today."

Aurora shifted on her chair. "Is there a problem with my work?"

He smiled, creating fine lines around his eyes. "No, no. You've done your best despite difficult circumstances. I fear it was my selfishness that got you into this unfortunate situation. I should never have insisted you accompany me before determining the extent of the illness."

A flush heated Aurora's cheeks under the directness of his gaze. "It's not your fault. You had no idea it would be so serious."

"Still, I can't help but feel guilty at the risk I've exposed you to unnecessarily."

"Nothing I won't face as a nurse." She rose and smoothed her apron.

The doctor rose, as well, and studied her

for several seconds, as if debating adding something further. At last, he nodded. "I'm certain Mrs. Patterson will prove an excellent role model."

"I look forward to meeting her."

Dr. Reardon came around the desk. "One more thing before you go. I neglected to mention that your father came by earlier today."

Aurora held back a gasp of dismay. She'd spoken to her mother several times on the phone, but always when Papa was at work. "What did he want?"

"To take you home." A touch of amusement lit his warm eyes.

Aurora's fingers tightened on the chair back. "How did you get him to leave?"

"I told him you had to remain until we're certain that you haven't contracted the illness."

"And he accepted this?" Aurora couldn't imagine anyone stopping her father when he was on a mission, especially when that mission concerned his only daughter.

"Not at first. But I convinced him I was looking out for your welfare and that you would be in touch with him soon."

She released a tiny sigh of relief, and the pressure on her ribs lessened. "Thank you,

Doctor. I hope my father wasn't too adversarial."

"Don't worry. I've handled worse in my time." A hint of a smile twitched the doctor's mustache. "Come. Let's get back to work."

As Aurora accompanied him back to the sickroom, an uneasy suspicion arose. Dr. Reardon appeared far too pleased with himself. And for Papa to leave without seeing her, something must have transpired. Aurora prayed it had nothing to do with an anticipated match to the esteemed doctor. For no matter who her father tried to pair her with, Aurora feared that only one man held the key to her heart.

And unfortunately it wasn't Philip Reardon.

"There's a woman on the telephone wanting to speak to Mr. or Mrs. Montgomery. I hate to disturb them. . . ."

Maggie turned from the sink to see an agitated Sister Veronica in the doorway. "It's all right, Sister. I'll take it."

Maggie dried her hands and made her way to Rylan's office, where she picked up the receiver and spoke into the mouthpiece. "This is Maggie Montgomery. May I help you?"

The woman on the other end identified herself as the O'Learys' housekeeper. "I'm afraid I'm phoning with unpleasant news." The woman hesitated. "Mr. O'Leary wanted Miss Colleen to know that her mother has taken ill with typhoid fever."

Maggie sucked in a breath. This was the first time they'd heard of any other case of typhoid outside of the orphanage. "What about the others in the family?"

"So far no one else has been affected."

"Thank goodness. Is there anything else you'd like me to pass on?"

"Please tell Miss Colleen we're praying for Delia and all the children."

"I will. Thank you for calling." Maggie hung up the receiver and remained seated at the desk. She hated to add to Colleen's burden with this latest piece of distressing news. Knowing Colleen, she'd want to be in two places at once. And she was already turning herself inside out over Delia.

Maggie found her thoughts turning, as they so often did, to Adam. Despite his strained relationship with his parents, Maggie felt certain he'd want to know about his mother. A pang of regret wrenched her heart. It had been over a week since she'd seen or heard from him. She missed the comfort of his presence, for whenever he was working on the grounds, she always felt safe.

Recalling his last words about how she could reach him, Maggie picked up the receiver of the phone again, waited for the operator, and then asked to be connected to the Shepherd of Good Hope Church. Nerves dampened her palms as she waited for an answer. At last, a man's voice came over the line.

"Hello. Reverend McNabb speaking."

"Good day. I hope you can help me. I'm trying to reach Adam O'Leary."

There was a subtle pause. "May I ask who's calling?"

"My name is Maggie Montgomery. I'm related to Adam's sister by marriage."

"Oh yes. Adam told us about the situation at the orphanage. I hope everything's all right."

It would be so easy to tell this man the news and let him impart it to Adam. But the selfish side of Maggie wanted to tell Adam in person — and be there to offer whatever comfort or support she could. "The children are holding their own. But I have something I need to discuss with Adam, if you don't mind."

"I'm afraid he isn't staying at the church any longer."

A cold ball of fear settled in Maggie's stomach. "Where is he, then?"

Silence hummed over the line for several seconds. "Adam is . . . doing some renovations at a store on 14th Street. There's no phone installed, but I could get a message to him, if you like."

Maggie paused to digest this new information and made an instant decision. "No, thank you. I'll make sure someone finds him and tells him the news in person. Where is this shop?"

"On 14th Street near the corner of 4th Avenue. Beside the general mercantile."

"Thank you so much for your help, Reverend." She hung up the receiver before he could ask any more questions.

Her heart beat a wild rhythm as her common sense warred with her emotions. By all rights, she should heed her brothers' advice and avoid Adam. Adam himself had made it clear that he would not entertain a romantic relationship with her. Yet she could not forget the power of the kiss they'd shared and the host of emotion it evoked within her. Never in her life had she felt anything like it. She had to believe something so intense could not be wrong, that God had brought them together for a reason. And so she would take advantage of this small opportunity to see Adam again, if only for a few minutes.

Leaving the orphanage should not be a problem, but she would check with Dr. Reardon to be sure. Then, once she was cleared, she'd set out to find Adam and this mysterious store.

22

After walking three blocks from the streetcar stop, Maggie paused to catch her breath, hoping she hadn't made a huge mistake by coming here. This area of town appeared rougher than Rylan's neighborhood, although perhaps the streets were merely unfamiliar, making them appear ominous.

Images of Neill Fitzgerald rose up to plague her. She hadn't thought of him in days, so consumed had she been with the epidemic at St. Rita's. She cast a furtive glance over her shoulder and across the street. None of the people appeared out of the ordinary.

She offered a quick prayer for protection and hoped Adam wouldn't be too angry with her for coming to find him on her own. Surely once he heard the reason, he'd understand.

Maggie crossed the road and hastened in the direction of the awning-covered stores farther down the avenue. She passed a woman's dress shop and a haberdashery before coming to the mercantile Reverend McNabb had mentioned. Next to it, a door had been propped open. Dust and dirt swirled out onto the walkway, forcing Maggie to stop before her shoes and skirt became soiled.

A second later, Adam emerged, wielding a broom like a weapon. When he turned and saw her, his eyes widened, and the handle slipped from his fingers. "Maggie? What are you doing here?"

He wore a burlap apron tied haphazardly at his waist, his plaid shirt rolled up past his elbows. Seeing him there in front of her, so solid and real, caused a mixture of relief and joy to rush through her. "What kind of welcome is that, Mr. O'Leary?" she teased.

A splash of pink stole across his cheeks as he retrieved the broom. "You shouldn't be out here alone. Have you forgotten about Fitzgerald?"

She lifted her chin. "There's been no sign of him for some time now. And I took the streetcar. I was perfectly safe with all the passengers."

His frown deepened. "How did you find me?"

"Reverend McNabb told me where you

were. May I come in?"

He scratched his head. "I . . . um . . . I haven't finished cleaning."

"A little dirt won't kill me." She laughed and brushed a hand over her skirt, hoping he wouldn't notice she'd worn one of her best outfits.

He shrugged and gestured for her to precede him. Once inside, she marveled at the rustic-yet-homey atmosphere. The building had a masculine quality that suited Adam. She could picture him working in such an establishment. The countertop gleamed, and the shelves behind it showed not a trace of dust.

"I can see you've been busy. I understand you were hired to renovate the interior."

Another frown creased Adam's brow. "John said that?"

Maggie hesitated. "Not in those exact words. Did I misinterpret his meaning?"

Adam stalked to the other side of the room, leaning the broom in a corner. "Why are you here, Maggie?" He whirled then, alarm evident in his eyes. "Is Delia worse?"

She shook her head. "She's holding her own for now. The doctor is optimistic that she'll recover."

The relief that spread over his features made Maggie want to hug him. But she knew he would not welcome her touch.

"Then why have you come? Does Rylan know you've gone?"

"No."

His intense stare, meant as a scolding, did not intimidate her.

She ignored his glower and moved to the rear of the room, inspecting the space as she went. Selfishly, she wanted to draw out this rare moment together. "This building has a lovely feel to it. What type of store will it be?"

When he didn't answer, she turned and pinned him with an arched look. "Well?"

"A furniture store," he ground out.

Understanding dawned, and a quiet joy filled her soul. "You're starting your own shop? That's wonderful." She swept out her arm. "How did you manage all of this?"

"John McNabb arranged to rent the building." Adam's scowl seemed permanently etched on his face.

"Where is the furniture? Back here?" Without waiting for a response, Maggie pushed through the swinging doors that led into a spotless work area, containing a long table and rows of neatly aligned tools hung on hooks. In the far corner, a large bin held piles of wood, ready for use. She gazed around in awe. Several chairs and stools in various stages of completion lined one wall. One piece in particular, a hope chest, made her breath catch. "These are beautiful, Adam. You have such a gift."

She turned to find him in the doorway, arms crossed, revealing corded forearms. Maggie couldn't tell from his guarded expression what he was thinking.

"It doesn't mean the business will be a success."

She ran her fingers over a few of the metal tools, all meticulously arranged. "At least you have the courage to try." She stopped in front of him. "I'm proud of you, Adam."

The muscles in his jaw tightened, and he moved behind the workbench, as though he couldn't bear to be near her. "You still haven't said why you've come. You must have a reason."

She repressed a quiet sigh. She'd been delaying, wanting to stretch out their time together, when in reality she had no right.

"I'm afraid I have some unpleasant news," she said at last, "and I wanted to tell you in person."

Adam grew still and fought for control over the tidal wave of emotion running riot through his system. Having Maggie so near was wreaking havoc with his senses. She looked so beautiful in a green dress and matching hat, her luxurious hair falling to her waist. With great effort, he pulled his attention back to her words and drew in a ragged breath. "What news?"

Her eyes clouded with sympathy. "Your mother has contracted typhoid fever. The housekeeper phoned to let us know." She skirted the work table and moved toward him. "I had to come and tell you."

The wood of the wall behind him bit into his back. "How bad is it?"

She moved closer. "Serious enough, or your father wouldn't have had Mrs. Johnston call."

A thousand thoughts invaded Adam's mind. What should he do? Would he be welcome at Irish Meadows after leaving on such terrible terms mere weeks ago? Worse yet, had his accusations against his mother contributed to her ill health?

A warm hand on his arm brought his head jerking up.

Maggie stood so close he could see the flecks of green and gold in her gray eyes. Smell the lavender of the soap she used.

"You must go to her, Adam. If anything were to happen . . ."

Bands of tension seized his shoulders. He needed air. Pushing past her, he strode through the main part of the store and out onto the walkway, where he leaned against a metal lamppost as if to draw strength from its solidity.

His mother could be dying. Maggie was right. No matter the consequences, he had to see her again and try to make amends before it was too late. With a deep breath, he turned and found Maggie watching him from the open doorway, her features awash in sympathy.

"I'm sorry to bring you such dire news." She held a handkerchief crushed between her fingers. "I know the type of fear you must be feeling. We've been keeping watch 'round the clock with Delia."

Adam took a closer look at her face, calling himself every kind of fool. How had he missed the dark circles under her eyes and the pinch of fatigue around her lips? She'd been through torture since he'd left, having to give Ivy back, worrying over Delia, tending the sick. Yet here she was, concerned enough about him to travel across town.

"Thank you for telling me, Maggie." He peered at her. "Are you keeping well yourself?"

She gave a thin smile. "Healthy as a mule, thank goodness. Though I wouldn't be adverse to a good night's sleep after all this is over."

He wanted to smile in return, to speak his heart to her, but he knew there was no point. Instead, he nodded. "I'd best lock the store. Then I'll accompany you back to the orphanage before I catch the train to Long Island."

Maggie entered the orphanage kitchen and found Sister Veronica already at work, pots of water heating on the stove, a mound of peeled potatoes sitting on the counter.

"I'm back, Sister. I'm sorry I wasn't here to start the potatoes."

The nun sniffed. "That's all right. I needed something to keep me busy anyway."

Maggie looked up from tying an apron around her waist, alarmed at the tears slipping down the woman's cheeks.

"What is it?" Maggie whispered.

Sister Veronica dabbed a limp handkerchief to her cheek. "We've lost another dear soul."

Please God, no. Maggie swallowed the swell of fear in her throat. "Not Delia."

The nun shook her head. "No, though she's had a setback. As did little Johnnie, and his poor heart couldn't take it."

Maggie clutched the counter for support. With his impish charm, Johnnie Feeney had been a favorite at St. Rita's.

Maggie sniffed back her own tears and moved to the sink. "Let's get the food cooking, and I'll go and set the table."

Sister Veronica gave a final wipe of her face, pocketed the piece of linen, and straightened her back. "You're right. We still have others in our care. There will be time to mourn later."

Maggie moved through her chores with swift determination, and when she found a moment to take a break, she went to check on Delia's condition.

She entered the hushed area and crossed to the far side of the room. The grief on Rylan's face made Maggie want to weep. Colleen's crumpled figure, twisted over the edge of the bed, spoke of tragedy.

Slowly she approached the bed. "Rylan?"

Her brother lifted his head, his normally luminous eyes now hollow and bloodshot. "Pray for her, Maggie. Aurora's gone to find Dr. Reardon at the hospital. We don't know if Delia will make it. . . ."

A strangled groan erupted from Colleen on the bed. "Why is God punishing us, Rylan? First He takes Ivy away and now Delia."

Rylan gathered Colleen to him. "We have to have faith, love. Delia is strong. She could still pull through."

Colleen's tangled auburn hair quivered as she sobbed on Rylan's shoulder.

For a minute, sorrow paralyzed Maggie, rooting her to the spot. She couldn't break further bad news to Colleen about her mother right now. She'd wait and see how Delia passed the night and make a decision in the morning.

Maggie stiffened her spine and crossed the room to the prayer corner the nuns had created. She lifted the Bible from the table, then returned and took a seat beside Delia's bed. She couldn't do much, but she could pray. In a strong voice, she began to recite Psalm 27. " 'The Lord is my light and my salvation; whom shall I fear? The Lord is the stronghold of my life. . . .' "

Gabe pushed out the rear door of the orphanage and strode across the back lawn. A forgotten baseball mitt, a skipping rope, and a rubber ball lay strewn across the grass, all evidence of normal children's lives that had been disrupted. An uncommon anger gripped him, almost crushing the air from his lungs.

Why had the Lord allowed this to happen to these innocent children who already had enough sorrow in their young lives?

Johnnie Feeney had been a happy soul, who, despite his orphan status, had tried to cheer the other children when they were sad. And now he was gone. Just like that. Just like Delia could be gone, as well.

Gabe bent to retrieve the mitt and ball, blinking back moisture that stung his eyes. Never had he seen his brother so helpless, so bereft of hope that even prayer didn't ease his mind. He loved Delia as much or more than any biological child he could have had. What would he and Colleen do if they lost their daughter?

Gabe sank down on an overturned crate and hung his head over his knees, wishing there was something he could do to help his family. Wishing he could find the words to pray.

The sound of material swishing over the grass barely registered in his brain until a warm hand landed on his shoulder.

"Is there anything I can do?" Aurora's sweet voice infused his soul with hope.

He looked up at her. "You can tell me Delia's regained consciousness."

Her sad eyes told him everything. "I wish I could," she said softly.

"Why could it not be me instead? Why these poor children? I ate here many a time, yet why has God spared me?"

"I don't have the answers, Gabe. No one does, except God himself."

He pushed to his feet. "I hate feeling so helpless with nothing to do but wait."

"It's the worst feeling ever, especially when it's someone you love." A tear rolled down Aurora's cheek.

"Ah, darlin', don't cry. Please." He pulled a handkerchief from his pocket and handed it to her.

"I'm sorry. I came out here to help and I've made things worse." She dabbed her face with the square of linen.

"Shh. You're doing everything you can to help your patients."

"It doesn't feel like enough."

A shudder went through her frame, and Gabe couldn't hold back. He reached out to pull her to him, rubbing his hands over her back. Her head rested on his chest, causing a bundle of emotion to riot through his system. For weeks now, he'd been fighting his feelings for this woman, so brave and beautiful and kind. Not once did she think of herself and her own welfare, but worked tirelessly to see to the children's comfort.

He pressed a kiss to the top of her head. "You're doing the best you can."

She didn't answer but held tightly to him, as if through their physical connection, they could share each other's pain and find the strength to carry on.

Behind them, the back door slammed, and Aurora jerked from his arms.

Dr. Reardon came down the stairs. "Miss Hastings, is everything all right?" The disapproving scowl on the man's face did not match the tone of his question.

She dashed the tears from her cheeks, splotches of red marring her delicate complexion. "I . . . I'm fine, thank you."

The desire to rush to her defense rose strong in Gabe's chest, but he held back, realizing she needed to handle this on her own.

"Is Delia . . . ?"

"The same, I'm afraid." He crossed his arms. "If you wouldn't mind, I'd like a word."

"Of course."

"Not you, Miss Hastings. I was speaking to Mr. Montgomery." His hard brown eyes pinned Gabe in challenge.

"As you wish, Doctor."

Aurora clutched Gabe's arm and shot him a look filled with anxiety.

"Don't worry. I promise we'll keep it civil. Why don't you go and check on my niece for me?"

She gave a tremulous smile. "I'd be happy to."

Once Aurora had gone inside, Gabe followed the stiff back of Dr. Reardon down the hall to his brother's office. The room hadn't been used much of late, with Rylan so preoccupied with his daughter.

"Have a seat," the man said as if he owned the office.

"I'd prefer to stand, thank you. What is it you wish to say?"

Dr. Reardon remained standing, as well. "I'll be blunt. I want you to leave. Your presence here is a distraction and is hindering Miss Hastings's work. Since you've passed the incubation period with no symptoms, I give you permission to leave the building. You may go back to your . . . firefighting." A definite swirl of animosity laced the doctor's tone.

Several rebuttals came to mind, but Gabe focused on the one that seemed the most rational. "I'm here first and foremost for my brother. With his daughter fighting for her life, Rylan needs all the support he can get. I'll not be leaving until the crisis has passed."

Dr. Reardon snorted. "I'm not a fool. I see your true motivation."

So he wanted to spar, did he? Gabe took

a step toward him. "Let's address the actual issue at hand, why don't we? You're in love with Aurora, and you can't stand that she seems to prefer my company."

The doctor's posture stiffened, his mouth a straight line beneath his mustache. "You are nothing but a passing fancy, a novelty. But you'll soon be back on a ship, an ocean away, whereas I'll be here for the duration."

Gabe's gut churned with that uncomfortable truth. "Aurora is a grown woman who makes her own decisions. My leaving the orphanage won't change our friendship."

Dr. Reardon crossed his arms and moved closer. "Just so we're clear, I plan to wed Aurora."

A stab of jealousy hit Gabe hard. "And how does she feel about this? Or have you even asked?"

"I don't have to. We have a solid connection — one borne of mutual respect and a shared love of medicine." His nostrils flared. "If you care about her, you won't dally with her affections when you'll be leaving soon and not returning."

The thought of never seeing Aurora's beautiful face again created a painful spasm in Gabe's chest. Could he really walk away forever? Suddenly his reasons for going home seemed to diminish in importance.

"Maybe I've changed my mind."

Something akin to fear flared in the man's eyes. "Go ahead and break Aurora's heart, Mr. Montgomery. I'll be here to pick up the pieces." He pushed past Gabe toward the door. "My initial request remains. Please leave and let us tend the sick."

The grip on Gabe's temper slipped, and he held back a growl. "Not until my niece is on the mend and my brother and Aurora no longer need me."

The door slammed behind the doctor, leaving Gabe with an uncomfortable sensation in his gut. He couldn't dispute most of what Dr. Reardon had said. Did Gabe have the right to disrupt Aurora's life, or should he do the noble thing and back away?

It was true that the doctor and Aurora shared a bond through their work, and with a doctor for a husband, she would be guaranteed a secure future.

And her father seemed determined to keep Gabe away from Aurora. If he pursued a relationship with her, he risked splintering her family.

He let out a long breath. For now, he'd keep his feelings to himself and concentrate on getting through the epidemic before making any life-altering decisions. Once the danger had passed, he would figure out how

Aurora felt about him, if he was indeed a passing fancy, or if they might share a more lasting connection.

He stepped out into the hall, at a loss as to what to do next. Quick footsteps sounded, and he turned to see Aurora rushing toward him. A clutch of anxiety hit him at seeing the tears streaking her cheeks.

"Gabe. Come quick," she cried. "Delia is awake!"

23

The beauty of the warm July afternoon did nothing to lighten Adam's mood as he climbed the grand staircase at Irish Meadows. The door to the master bedroom stood slightly ajar, and Adam paused to steel himself before entering. What would he find waiting inside?

The moment he stepped over the threshold, the gloom of the interior surrounded him like a shroud. Heavy curtains were drawn over the large window, with only a small crack of light casting a beam across the carpet. The stench of sickness, mixed with a sweet medicinal odor, permeated the space.

Please Lord, don't let me be too late.

James sat beside the bed, his head bowed over the still figure beneath the covers. Regret weighed like a two-ton load on Adam's shoulders at the sight. He hesitated, unsure what do next. Would James allow him to stay or throw him out? He waited for him to acknowledge his presence.

At last, James raised his head and directed a bloodshot gaze to Adam. "So you came."

"Of course I came. She's my mother."

James straightened and slowly rose from the chair. *Haggard* did not begin to describe his appearance, making Adam wonder if he'd turned to whiskey to ease his distress. His stained shirt hung out of his trousers, suspenders laying limply at his sides. His dark hair looked gouged from dragging his hands through it.

Adam watched him approach, inwardly bracing for a fist to the jaw. But James only stared at him. "If your presence will do her any good, then I thank God for bringing you." He pointed to the chair he'd vacated. "I'll give you a few minutes alone."

James didn't wait for a reply but walked out the door. His heavy footsteps thudded down the carpeted hall, leaving Adam alone to watch over his mother.

He pulled out the chair and perched on the edge, forcing himself to look at Mama's wan face. Her labored breathing made her chest rise and fall beneath the thin sheet.

Never had Adam felt more helpless, except for the time he'd found Danny floating in the pond. Though he'd tried to breathe life back into the boy's tiny body, nothing could be done to revive him. The sight of his little brother's blue lips and white face had haunted him ever since.

That couldn't happen again. This time he had to find a way to help.

Adam lifted one of his mother's hands and warmed it between his own. "I'm here, Mama. You've got to fight this illness. You're the cement that binds this family together." He rested his forehead on her hand. "Please don't give up now. We haven't had a chance to work things out between us."

He searched her face for a sign she'd heard him, but her features remained unchanged.

Adam hung his head in prayer and settled in to the vigil he would keep until his mother either got better — or didn't.

"I'm sorry, son. I wish I had better news." Dr. Shepherd, the family physician since Adam had been a boy, folded his stethoscope and placed it back in his battered leather bag. "There's no change."

Adam nodded, not surprised by his words. "But she's no worse?"

"No. She's the same, which for now we'll take as a good sign."

"Thank you, Doctor."

Two days had gone by in a blur, with the family keeping watch in the room. Adam, James, and the others took turns so Mama was never alone for a moment.

"Kathleen hasn't reached the critical point yet. If she makes it through the next forty-eight hours, she might have a fighting chance."

Adam swallowed the ball of fear in his throat. "You'll be around in case we need you?"

"I will. I have a few more patients to see today, but I'll be back."

James, who had been standing silently to the side, moved forward. "Let me walk you out, Doc."

The moment they left the room, Adam sank onto the chair, no longer having to maintain his façade of strength. He bent over the side of his mother's bed and closed his eyes. "Mama, you have to hang on. You're the strongest woman I know. You can make it through this."

Someone pressed a cup into his hand. "Here, you haven't eaten all day. At least have a sip of tea."

Adam looked up to see his sister. He blinked and wrapped his fingers around the warm mug.

Brianna rubbed a hand over his back.

"Mama always said a cup of tea could fix anything."

Adam's lips twisted. "Yes, she did. I think it made *her* feel better, to make the tea for us." He rose and offered Brianna the chair.

She took his place, picked up a cloth, and wiped Mama's face. "She has to get better, Adam. I can't imagine a world without Mama in it." Her voice caught, and she bit her bottom lip.

"She is going to recover. We all have to believe it, so she will, too."

Brianna turned her head to study him. "You've changed since you were . . . away."

"It's okay to say the word *prison,* Bree."

A flush colored her cheeks. "I mean it. You seem more at peace. Less angry."

Adam held back a snort. Ever since he'd learned of his true parentage, he'd been angrier than ever.

"Now that we're alone," she said quietly, "I want you to know Mama and Daddy told Gil and me . . . everything."

"They told you?" Shock stung Adam's senses. Remembering the shame and guilt on his mother's face, Adam couldn't imagine her telling the rest of the family.

"Yes. And it doesn't matter to us. You're still our brother, and we love you."

She held out a hand to him, and he

grasped it.

His throat constricted. "Thank you, Bree. That means more than you know."

She squeezed his fingers and let her hand fall to her lap. "It must have been quite a shock."

"Not totally. In a way, it's a relief to know the truth at last."

"It does explain a lot about Daddy's attitude. Not that I'm excusing his behavior, but I can see how hard it would have been for him."

Images of their childhood flashed in his memory. His gentle sister, ever the peacemaker, always managed to see both sides of every story. "Right now nothing matters except Mama regaining her health. The rest can be sorted out later."

"Bree, Adam —" James entered the bedroom, his face even more drawn. "Deirdre and Connor are both showing symptoms. Dr. Shepherd never got out the front door."

Maggie gave Colleen another full day before broaching the subject of her mother. By that time, Dr. Reardon had assured the worried parents that Delia had indeed turned a corner and was expected to make a full recovery. Maggie and Rylan had finally managed to coerce Colleen into one of the now-empty beds to get a decent sleep. She'd barely eaten or slept in the days since Delia had taken ill, and the toll it had taken on her body was obvious. Maggie only prayed she would regain her strength at the same rate as Delia.

The news she'd kept from Colleen now became a heavy burden on Maggie's conscience. She could not keep it to herself any longer.

When Colleen came into the orphanage kitchen that morning, Maggie set aside the mound of dough she'd been kneading. "You sit. I'll fix the tea."

"I've been sitting far too much. It will do me good to get back to normal again." Colleen tied an apron around her and began to inspect the cupboards. "We will need to get in a good order of staples. I'll try to do that tomorrow. When is Mrs. Norton expected back to work?"

"The doctor said a few days' more rest should do it." Maggie washed and dried her hands, then crossed the kitchen. "Colleen, there's something I must tell you now that Delia's on the mend."

Colleen closed a cupboard door with a frown. "Neill Fitzgerald hasn't been around again, has he?"

The worry on her face gave Maggie a pang

of guilt. "No. Nothing like that." She twisted her hands together. "There's no easy way to tell you this. . . . Your mother, Connor, and Deirdre have contracted typhoid fever. When the housekeeper phoned, I didn't want to add to your burden."

Colleen pulled out a chair and sank onto it. "How is that possible?"

Maggie took a seat across the table from her. "The doctor said the disease could be passed from tainted food. Did your family ever eat here?"

Colleen nodded. "Mama brought Connor and Dee-Dee one day. Mary had made a batch of peach ice cream, and they all had some." A stricken look came over her. "Delia had some, as well."

"And you?"

"No, I . . . By the time I finished tidying the classroom, it was all gone." She put a hand over her mouth.

Maggie nodded. "I remember that day. Rylan and Gabe complained that they'd missed the treat. And I gave my portion to Johnnie."

Colleen sat back with a thud. "How bad is Mama?"

"Her condition is quite serious." Maggie paused. "I let Adam know. He's gone to be with her. He was there when Connor and

Deirdre fell ill."

Colleen gripped her hands together on the tabletop. "I should go, too. But how can I leave Delia? She still needs her mother." Tears glistened in her eyes.

Maggie covered her hands with her own. "Your mother has the whole family there, but Rylan and Delia need you here."

Maggie hesitated. Now that Delia was on the mend, she felt she had to go to Adam. "I'm going to Irish Meadows tomorrow," she said quietly. "I could deliver a letter for you."

Colleen stared at her. "Why are you going there?"

Maggie lifted her chin. There was no point in keeping the truth from Colleen. Too many life-and-death events in the past weeks made hiding her feelings seem foolish. "Knowing how strained things are between Adam and your father, I want to be there for him. He needs someone in his corner." She held herself steady under Colleen's scrutiny.

"Maggie, you can't get involved in Adam's life. No good can come from it."

Maggie gave a rueful smile. "You sound like your brother . . . and mine. But I'm afraid it's too late for your warnings. Come what may, I have to follow my heart."

Sympathy oozed across Colleen's face. "Oh, Maggie. I know you feel compassion for him. Perhaps you're confusing that . . . sentiment . . . for something else."

With quiet determination, Maggie rose and went back to her dough. "I'm not confused, Colleen. Adam may have given up on himself — but I haven't. And neither has God."

24

Walking past the racetrack toward the barns, Adam inhaled the aroma of manure and grass. After days confined to the stuffy upstairs bedroom, the need for fresh air lured him outdoors. Though Mama hadn't yet regained consciousness, she had passed the crucial forty-eight hours mentioned by Dr. Shepherd without her condition worsening, and for that alone he needed to give thanks. He could think of nowhere better than out in nature where the pure essence of God lived.

He headed to the pond at the rear of the property, where the tragedy had occurred many years ago. Maybe by being where Danny had departed this world, he could feel close to his brother again.

Adam stood beneath the drooping willow, looking out over the deceptively innocent body of water, but he could no longer conjure the hatred and self-loathing it used to evoke. He had to believe God had a purpose for calling Danny home at such a young age, just as he had to believe his mother's life was safely in God's hands, as well.

Adam bent to pick up a couple of flat rocks and skipped them out over the water, watching the ensuing ripples skitter toward the shore. Events in his life resembled these stones, cast out into new territory, each creating its own set of ripples and consequences. Adam might not understand the way God worked in his life, but he had to trust it was all for the greater good.

One of John's favorite verses came to mind. *All things work together for good to them that love God, and to them who are called according to His purpose.* Adam had clung to those words during his time in prison, gleaning hope from the promise there.

He bowed his head and offered words of praise to his Heavenly Father.

Thank You, Lord, for your mercy upon our family. Please pour Your healing graces on my mother and my sister and brother. Bless Colleen and Rylan. Give them strength to deal with the loss of baby Ivy and little Delia's illness. I pray You see fit to grant healing unto Delia. They need her, Lord. Please use me as

Your instrument to help in both these situations to the glory of Your name. Amen.

Feeling steadier, Adam retraced his steps toward the house. He'd stop by the kitchen to see what leftovers Mrs. Harrison had, since he'd missed the midday meal.

As Adam crossed the property, the grass soft beneath the tread of his boots, he found his thoughts turning to Maggie, as they always did when he had too much time on his hands. How he'd hated leaving her at the orphanage that day. Did she suspect how badly he'd wanted to kiss her? To hold her close and bury his face in the silk of her hair?

He thought he'd seen a similar longing in her eyes as they'd said their good-byes. But he'd steeled himself to let her go. It wouldn't do them any good to ignite a passion that should be left to lie. It would only make them yearn for something that could never be.

He followed the white fence that surrounded the racetrack, intending to enter through the rear door near the kitchen. When he turned toward the house, though, he forgot to breathe. An apparition stood by the stairs leading to the porch, her long hair lifting in the gentle breeze.

Maggie. Had he conjured her from his

imagination?

His feet seemed rooted to the rich earth at his feet. He blinked, thinking to banish the image from his mind, but she remained, her blue skirts billowing out behind her.

With effort, he forced his feet to move forward, while his heart beat an unsteady rhythm in his chest. Sudden alarm filled his mind. Had something happened to Delia or Colleen?

"Maggie. What are you doing here?"

"Hello, Adam." She clasped her hands together in front of her. "How is your mother doing?"

She appeared nervous, her usual unflappable nature missing today.

"She's holding her own for the moment. What news do you have from the orphanage?" He hardly dared hear the answer, yet he sensed no grief in her spirit.

She smiled, wreathing her face in a beauty that blinded him. "Dr. Reardon says Delia will make a full recovery."

Relief rushed swift and fierce through his system. "Praise God. He's answered our prayers."

Maggie came closer, the hem of her skirt swishing the grass as she walked. "Indeed He has."

As though drawn by a magnet, Adam

continued forward until he was mere steps away. So close that her lavender scent surrounded him. "But why have you come? Surely a phone call would have sufficed." He knew the answer he wanted to hear, yet the futility of it all hovered in the recesses of his mind.

A cloud of uncertainty passed over her features. "I came to offer whatever support I could." Her fingers twisted in the fabric of her skirts. "Colleen wanted to be here, but she couldn't leave Delia yet. I offered to come in her stead and bring a letter for your mother." She lifted one shoulder. "If I can be of any assistance — cooking, washing, whatever needs to be done . . ." She trailed off, a slight frown wrinkling her perfect nose.

Adam held himself rigid, determined not to let his disappointment show. She'd come here to work. In all likelihood, Rylan had suggested it to make Colleen feel better about not being able to come herself. He straightened. "Come in. I'll find out what tasks you can help with."

"Thank you." She fell in beside him, crossing the grass to the back stairs.

Adam opened the door for her, and they entered through a narrow hallway into the kitchen.

Mrs. Harrison sat at the large wooden table, a plate of food in front of her. She jumped up when they entered. "Master Adam. What can I do for you?"

He gave a mock scowl. "You can sit and finish your meal. This is Maggie, Rylan's sister. She wants to help in whatever way she can."

Mrs. Harrison beamed at Maggie. "Lovely to meet you, dear. Any relative of Rylan's is welcome here."

Maggie's light laugh echoed through the kitchen. "I see my brother has worked his considerable charm on you. He knows how to keep anyone who cooks his meals happy."

"That he does." Mrs. Harrison settled her plump frame back on her chair. "I must rest my feet while I can. Though I'd be glad of your help later in getting ready for dinner."

"I'd be happy to."

"Thank you, Maggie. Help yourself to the leftovers if you're hungry."

"I'm fine, thank you."

Remembering his initial intention, Adam snagged two biscuits and an apple from a basket on the counter. "Could you let Mrs. Johnston know we have a guest staying overnight?" He peered at Maggie. "You *are* intending to stay?"

Maggie fixed him with a solemn gaze.

"I'm here until your mother is on her feet again."

Mrs. Harrison chuckled. "I think you're just what we need around here, Maggie. Nothing like a fresh dose of optimism, I always say."

Maggie nodded. "From your lips to God's ears."

In the Irish Meadows kitchen, Maggie's nerves lessened, and she breathed easier. At least Mrs. Harrison seemed grateful for her presence. Adam's unwelcoming manner had added to her initial anxiety, yet deep in her heart, Maggie believed she'd done the right thing by coming. Still, if it became apparent Adam didn't want her here, what would she do?

"Did you bring a bag?" Adam's voice jarred Maggie out of her thoughts.

"Aye. I left it by the front door."

"I'll get it and then take you to one of the guest rooms. You can freshen up before Mrs. Harrison puts you to work."

Adam led Maggie down another hallway to the front foyer, and she waited while he retrieved her bag. In silence, they began to climb the impressive, curving staircase.

Her mind searched for ways to keep him talking, to keep him from shutting her out.

"How have things been between you and your father since you got here?"

Adam shot her a hard look. "Strained. But we've struck a truce for now."

They reached the second floor, and a flurry of footsteps sounded on the carpet.

Brianna rushed toward them. "Adam, come quickly. Mama is asking for you."

He dropped the bag on the floor. "She's awake?"

"Barely. It's not good, Adam." Tears brimmed over Brianna's lower lashes. "She wants Colleen, Dee-Dee, and Connor. I don't know what to tell her." Dark smudges gave her wide green eyes a hollow look.

Maggie followed the pair down the hall, pausing when Adam entered what had to be his parents' bedroom. She stood, torn with indecision. She didn't feel entitled to be part of this scene, yet she ached for the pain Adam must be feeling. She walked to the open doorway and peered inside.

In the dimly lit room, Kathleen's body made barely a ripple under the quilt. They had propped up her head with pillows, and her eyes followed Adam across the room until he reached her side.

He fell to his knees and reached for her hand. "I'm here, Mama."

"My son." The tortured whisper hung in

the air. "Thank the Lord."

"You need to save your strength. You can talk when you're feeling better."

"No. Must talk now. James." She twisted her head to find her husband standing at the end of the bed. She reached out a hand, and he moved forward to take it.

He brought it to his lips and then held her palm to his cheek. "I'm here, too."

Kathleen looked at Adam. "You two must make peace. I need to know, in case I don't recover."

James shook his head. "Don't talk that way, Katie. You're going to get better. You have to."

She labored to draw a breath. "Promise me. Please."

Adam raised tortured eyes to James. Maggie could see only the man's back, which seemed as stiff as one of the bedposts. A sagging of his shoulders, along with a whoosh of air, signaled his capitulation. "Aye, Katie. I promise."

Adam turned back to his mother. "I promise, as well, Mama. Now you have to get well, because we might need a referee."

A hint of a smile touched Mrs. O'Leary's lips. "I've been doing that all our married life." Her expression burned with intensity. "Forgive me, Adam. I never wished to hurt you. I was only trying to protect you."

"There's nothing to forgive, Mama. I love you." Adam's voice cracked, and he laid his head on her arm.

Tears ran freely down Mrs. O'Leary's cheeks.

"Come now, love. You mustn't upset yourself. The doctor will have our hides for wearing you out." James gripped Adam's shoulder. "You'd best go and let her rest."

"Wait." Kathleen's gaze darted around the room. "Where are my babies? Connor and Deirdre. I want to see them. And Colleen?"

The panic in Mrs. O'Leary's voice tore at Maggie's heart. She sounded like she was two steps from heaven's door and couldn't leave without a final good-bye to her children.

Brianna leaned over to brush a few wisps of hair from her mother's forehead. "Colleen is caring for Delia, and Connor and Deirdre . . ." She glanced at Mr. O'Leary, who gave a tired nod. "I'm afraid they're sick, too, Mama."

"Noooo." The moan lingered in the air. "God, please don't take more of my children. I couldn't bear it." Her body shook beneath the bedcovers.

Maggie fought back tears of her own. Adam's head remained bent, shielding his expression from Maggie's view, yet the sight of his stooped shoulders told her of his pain.

As much as she wanted to be in the room to help him bear the sorrow, she knew she had no right. Before any of the family caught her witnessing such an intimate scene, Maggie found the stairs again and descended to the main floor. Sadness weighed upon her spirit. How would the family cope with the death of their dear wife and mother? Maggie feared they would fall apart without the one person who seemed to hold them together.

Maggie's sorrow led her to the place that could provide her a measure of solace. She entered the parlor, hushed and cold. Light shone in from the French doors, where the curtains had been pushed back. In the corner sat the baby grand piano, the one Mrs. O'Leary had played so beautifully the night of Brianna's party.

Maggie pulled out the wooden bench and sat before the instrument. She flexed her fingers, rested them softly on the keys, and began to play the hymn that always brought her consolation. She hoped that if the notes drifted upward, they would bring the others the same comfort.

As she played, the words of the hymn begged to be sung, and ever so softly she added her voice to the piece. " 'The Lord's my shepherd, I'll not want . . .' "

25

Adam drew in a ragged breath as he exited his mother's sickroom. The nurse James had hired had asked for a few moments with her patient. Adam walked the hallway, fighting to corral his grief, and his gaze fell on Maggie's forgotten bag. He remembered then that he'd abandoned her upon hearing Brianna's dire message. Where had she gone?

The sound of music penetrated his consciousness. He didn't have to guess who was playing the piano. He descended the stairs, cracked open the parlor door, and paused to listen. A pure, clear voice rang out over the room.

"The Lord's my Shepherd, I'll not want.
He maketh me down to lie
In pastures green; He leadeth me
The quiet waters by."

Adam's fingers tightened on the door handle until the metal seemed fused with his flesh. How could Maggie know this was one of Mama's favorite hymns? Forgotten memories from his childhood swamped his emotions for the second time that day — visions of his family standing in the pew on Sunday, of his mother's sweet voice ringing out above the other worshippers'. Would she ever have the chance to do so again?

His knees almost buckled at the thought that she might never rise from her bed.

Please Lord, don't take her from us. We need her here.

He wanted to escape the torture of Maggie's song, but his feet remained fixed to the spot as though held by an invisible force. At last, the song ended, and her fingers stilled on the keys. Without him saying a word, she seemed to sense his presence, for she turned and looked at the door.

"Adam." She pushed the bench back from the piano and crossed the room, concern shining on her luminous face. "Your mother?"

He dragged a hand over his face, stunned to find his cheeks wet. "I fear we're losing her, Maggie. She's so weak . . ." Adam swayed, not knowing what to do with the incredible grief that roared through every cell in his body.

Maggie wrapped her arms around his waist and laid her head on his chest. "It's in God's hands now. But no matter what happens, it will be all right. I promise."

The warmth of her body seeped into his. He tightened his arms around her, allowing his cheek to rest on her hair. The effort to repress his surging emotions made him shudder. In response, she moved soothing hands up his back, whispering Irish words he didn't understand.

The meaning wasn't important. She was in his arms, and despite the fear and grief that clawed at him, he felt safe. Comforted.

She lifted her fingers and wiped the dampness from his cheeks. He tried to move away, ashamed to be caught shedding tears, but she held him fast. "It's good to let your sadness out. You can't keep your emotions bottled up to fester and infect your soul. Let them out now, so you can be strong for your mother later."

"Maggie." The word strangled in his throat. If only he could stare into her beautiful eyes forever and forget the war that raged around them. Forget the past. None of that mattered in this moment.

Nothing mattered but Maggie.

He lowered his head until his lips found

hers, tasting the salt of her tears. She raised a hand to cup his jaw and kissed him with a sweetness that humbled him, soothing the pain in his soul like a balm. At last, with great reluctance, he pulled back. It wasn't fair to take from her this way, to accept the comfort she offered, when he could give her nothing in return.

"I'm sorry, Maggie. That was unfair of me."

"Hush. You've no reason to apologize. Kissing you is no hardship." She gave him a gentle smile. "I came to share your pain and to offer whatever consolation I'm able."

He brushed a finger down the silk of her cheek, studying her intently — the clear skin, the pert nose, the full lips. "Why, Maggie? Why do you care?"

A blush spread across her cheeks, and she lowered her lashes.

A gentleman would take back the question and relieve her apparent discomfort. But Adam needed to know.

She straightened and looked him in the eye. "I don't know how or why this has happened, Adam, but I *do* care. Very much. I believe God has a plan for me, and I'll bide my time until it becomes apparent. In the meantime, I choose to trust my heart. I can do no less."

Her honest admission astounded him. No games, no flirting, no hedging the truth. How did he respond to that?

He lowered his forehead to hers. "Maggie, you know why this is not possible. I have nothing to offer but a criminal record and a blemished bloodline. You deserve so much better."

She shook her head, sorrow filling her eyes. "Why do you insist on denying yourself happiness because of a man who died before you were born? He has no bearing on your life." Her tone held no anger, simply frustration.

Adam took a deliberate step back. "No bearing? His genes run through me and will run through any children I may have. I won't subject anyone to that." He raked a hand through his hair. He had to make her understand the importance of this once and for all.

She walked to the fireplace and stood staring into the cold, gray ashes. When she turned back to him, she lifted her chin. "Adam, what do you think of little Ivy?"

He frowned at the complete change in topic. "What do you mean?"

"Would you have any qualms about Colleen adopting her? Raising her as her own?"

"Of course not. She's an innocent babe."

Too late, he sensed a trap in her questioning.

"So Ivy's fate is not sealed by her mother's? Not tainted by her blood?"

The trap snapped shut. He grappled for a way out. "If Ivy is reared in that lifestyle then, yes, she will be corrupted by it."

"But if she were raised in a loving home by respectable parents, like Rylan and Colleen?" Maggie's slim brows rose.

"If the parents loved her and treated her as their own, then she'd be fine."

She walked up to him, her eyes earnest. "You had such an upbringing, Adam. You were raised in a loving home with upright parents, with a mother and siblings who adored you."

Adam snorted. "And a father who loathed the very sight of me." He stalked to the French doors and peered out over the garden.

The swish of fabric told him Maggie had followed. "Did your father beat you, mistreat you, punish you with cruelty?"

Adam's fingers twitched on the door handle, itching to push out into the open air. To keep walking, far from this house, away from these questions probing into areas he wished left alone. A flare of irritation pulsed through him, and he spun around to face her. "Is neglect not mistreatment? Is withholding affection from a child not cruel?"

She winced, and he instantly regretted the harshness of his tone. But if it took such frankness to make her see the truth, then so be it.

"A father withholding love from a child *is* cruel. But it doesn't mean the child will become a criminal, that his life has no worth." She moved so close he could see the mesmerizing flecks in her eyes. "You cannot allow the absence of affection from one parent to override the love of your mother and your siblings, not to mention" — she waved a hand around the room — "being given all the luxury a child could want. Other children have been raised in far worse circumstances and turned out fine." A flash of pain passed over her features. "A child whose father died in a mine, for instance, forced to live in a small cottage with her widowed mother and four brothers." Tears glistened on her lower lashes. "That child could have turned out many ways." She inhaled deeply. "But I believe she'll do quite well for herself."

"Maggie —"

"And you'll be fine, as well." She raised a hand to stroke his cheek. "But unless you can believe that, unless you believe in your own worthiness, none of that will matter." Her fingers fell away. "You have choices to make, Adam. I pray you make the right ones." Her eyes held his, professing the depth of her affection.

He longed to say something — anything — to reassure her, or if nothing else, to crush her against him and kiss her again. As he wavered, Maggie stepped back.

"Go and be with your mother. She needs you. And I have to help Mrs. Harrison."

With quick strides, she crossed the room, and at the door paused to look back. "I'm here if you need me, Adam. Don't be afraid to accept the gift that's offered — with no expectations attached."

26

Aurora stripped the sheets off another bed, free now due to little Greta's recovery. Dr. Reardon had finally deemed the child well enough to return to the girls' dormitory, leaving only three children in the common room. Delia, Felicia, and Anthony had been the most compromised by the illness and were taking longer to bounce back. But with time and care, Aurora felt certain they would regain full health.

Across the room, Colleen rose from Delia's bedside. She stretched and rubbed a hand across the base of her spine. Quiet alarm wound its way through Aurora's system. For the past few days, she'd noticed Colleen's pallor and lack of energy. Despite Colleen's protests, Aurora had managed to take her temperature, relieved to find it normal. Still, an underlying fear nagged at her that Colleen wasn't well.

Colleen crossed the room and stopped to

help Aurora fold the blankets.

"A couple more days and Delia should be able to go home." Aurora picked up a bundle of laundry to take to the basement.

Instead of smiling, Colleen's expression became somber. "I have a favor to ask, Aurora."

"Of course. What is it?"

"That phone call I received earlier was about my mother. She's taken a turn for the worse and is asking for me. My father and sister want me to come home."

Aurora set the laundry down. "I'm so sorry, Colleen." Aurora couldn't imagine Mrs. O'Leary, such a vital, energetic woman, lying close to death. "What can I do?"

"Take care of my daughter." Tears shone in Colleen's eyes. "As much as I hate to leave her, if Mama dies, I'd never forgive myself for not going."

Aurora impulsively wrapped her in a tight embrace. Any old resentment she held toward Colleen and her family had vanished — one good thing to come out of this shared crisis. "You know I'll look after Delia like she was my own."

"Thank you." Colleen's whisper was barely audible. "I'd better go. I have to freshen up and pack a few things. Rylan will take me to the train."

"I'll be praying for your mother."

Colleen nodded and left the room.

Aurora talked to each of the children and made sure they were resting comfortably before gathering the bedding and hurrying out into the hallway. She descended the stairs, heading toward the basement utility room, still preoccupied with Colleen's troubles. She rounded a corner and smacked straight into a hard chest. The pile of laundry slid to the floor. At the same time, a hand grasped Aurora about the waist to steady her. She looked up into Gabe's twinkling eyes.

He grinned. "Most girls don't fall quite so literally into my arms."

A blast of heat warmed her cheeks. "Gabe. I . . . I'm sorry. I didn't expect anyone to be down here."

He held up a toolbox with his other hand. "Rylan asked me to fix a clogged sink."

"I see." She knelt to gather the fallen linens, and he immediately set the tools aside to help her.

In the dimly lit corridor, with their heads bent together, the space seemed much too intimate. Their hands tangled in the sheets as they rose. Gabe freed one hand and lifted it to cup her chin. She raised her eyes to his. The twinkle had disappeared, replaced with an intensity that caused Aurora's heart to bang hard against her ribs.

"Aurora, *mo ghrá.*" His husky voice sent shivers down her spine. "I want to kiss you. I've wanted to for a long time."

She couldn't seem to move, her gaze focused on the cleft in his chin.

He lowered his face toward her. "If you want me to stop, say so now."

Fleeting thoughts of her father's disapproval flashed through her mind, but she pushed them away. For weeks she'd dreamt of this moment. She was not about to let her father ruin it.

"Don't stop," she managed to whisper.

When his lips met hers, the force of emotion that coursed through her nearly melted her bones. His arms tightened around her, capturing her close to his chest. The warmth of his lips sent thrills rioting through her body.

At last, she pulled back to catch her breath, unable to squash a wave of regret. "We shouldn't be doing this. You're heading back to Ireland in a few weeks, and I'm starting nursing school."

He caressed her cheek with his thumb, making coherent thought virtually impossible.

"What if I told you I'm reconsidering my departure?" Desire darkened his eyes.

"But you love your homeland. I know from all the stories you've told me. And what about your mother? You said you couldn't leave her."

"Maybe I've found something I love more."

His lips claimed hers once again, erasing all reasons for her protest. When he drew away at last, her head spun.

His gaze held hers. "I think I fell in love with you before I even knew your name. The moment I spied you across the room at the O'Learys' party, I was mesmerized by your beauty. Then once I met you, I became captivated by your kindness." He brushed a kiss to her temple. "Now after seeing you with these children, I know you're the most amazing woman I've ever met."

He lowered his head toward her again, and though she knew she should resist, everything in her yearned for the warmth of his lips on hers. Nothing had ever felt so thrilling, so right.

"Miss Hastings? Are you down there?" Dr. Reardon's disapproving voice broke the silence.

Aurora jumped back, bumping into the wall behind her. She glanced at Gabe, sending him a silent plea to remain hidden. If Dr. Reardon found them here together . . .

Gabe kissed her hand, which sent goosebumps racing along her arm. "You go. I'll take care of the laundry. Remember, you've done nothing wrong."

She longed to kiss him again, but instead she whirled around and ran up the stairs, smoothing her hair and apron as she went.

She emerged from the dark stairway onto the main floor, where Dr. Reardon paced the carpet. "I'm here, Doctor. Is anything wrong?" She hoped he took her breathless state as a result of climbing the stairs.

His forehead creased in an unbecoming manner. "Where have you been? I've been searching the building for you." His mustache practically quivered with indignation.

Aurora fought to keep the heat from her cheeks. "I was bringing the linens to the basement. What did you need me for?"

He stalked toward her, then scanned the hallway. Mrs. Taft was seated at her position at the reception desk, and two nuns stood talking nearby. "Perhaps we'd better continue this conversation in private. Please follow me."

Like a student about to be chastised by the principal, Aurora reluctantly followed him to Rylan's office. He ushered her in, and she took a seat across from the large desk. He, however, crossed to the window and remained standing.

"I am very disappointed in you, Aurora."

Aurora's mouth dropped open, but she quickly closed it. She had done nothing she could think of to merit his disappointment. However, the use of her Christian name made her feel it must be a personal issue.

"For what reason?" Her voice sounded clipped and cool to her own ears.

"Your growing . . . obsession . . . with Mr. Montgomery has interfered with your work."

She schooled her features to hide her outrage. "I have no idea what you're talking about."

His head whipped toward her. "I doubt the laundry is responsible for your disheveled appearance. The fact that I saw Mr. Montgomery go downstairs mere minutes before you leads me to a very natural conclusion." He folded his arms and leaned toward her. "Do you deny you were together?"

Aurora gripped her hands together on her lap to keep from throwing something. How dare he besmirch such a beautiful moment in her life? The kisses they'd shared were a sacred expression of their sincere feelings.

414

She pushed up from her chair and tilted her head in imitation of the ladies in her mother's social circle. "My relationship with Gabriel is none of your business. If that is all, I must be getting back to work."

"I'm afraid I'm having second thoughts about recommending you for the nursing program."

Aurora's feet stalled. She tensed and shot him a frown. "That is not fair. My personal life has no bearing on my abilities as a nurse."

"I must disagree. The way you conduct yourself in private has a direct bearing on it."

She whirled and marched back to the desk, slapping a palm down on the polished surface. "I will not stand here and let you insult my morals. Gabe and I shared a kiss, that is all. I find your jealousy far more suspect."

His cheeks reddened, but he did not respond.

"I suggest we forget this conversation and continue to serve our patients." She straightened. Then with a flick of her skirts, she bustled out of the room.

As she headed back to the common room, she congratulated herself for not backing down. For once, she had stood up for herself in the face of male dominance. At the same time, she prayed she hadn't ruined her chance at achieving her dream, for without Dr. Reardon's endorsement or, worse yet, with his disparaging remarks concerning her conduct, she might never get into nursing school.

27

Never had a night stretched out as incessantly as this one. Adam's muscles seized in painful spasms, stiffened from the hours spent sitting on the hard chair beside his mother's bed. He must have dozed off in an unnatural position that left his neck screaming for relief. If he didn't get up and move, he feared his limbs would freeze in place. The sound of Mama's labored breathing brought momentary relief, for at least it meant she was still alive.

Adam rose and stretched his back. In the semi-darkness, he scanned the room. Brianna and Gil must have left for a small respite. Perhaps to check on Deirdre and Connor, who were still fighting the illness themselves, though by no means as severely stricken as Mama.

Adam's gaze fell on the prone figure of James, half lying on the bed, his arm splayed out over the quilt to grasp Mama's fingers.

With his eyes closed, lines of grief etched into his face. A measure of sympathy rose in Adam's chest. How would he feel if Maggie were lying in that bed, at death's door with Adam powerless to help her? His gut clenched at the mere thought.

During the night, he'd listened to James murmur words of encouragement, of love, and finally of pleading for Mama not to leave him. To fight to get better, for her family's sake.

These past few days, Adam had witnessed the deep love and undying devotion James had for his mother. What would her death do to him? Send him spiraling into a despair so dark he might never emerge whole again? Adam prayed God would not allow that to happen.

He moved to the window and held aside the curtain to look out over the front lawn, where the soft pink hue gave evidence of the sun about to rise. For a moment, Adam tried to picture his mother as a young woman, pregnant and scared, worried that the man she loved might reject her. Yet James had loved her so much, he'd been willing to marry her, give her his name, and even raise her illegitimate child as his own.

Was Maggie right about Adam being ungrateful for what he'd been given in life?

That by focusing solely on the lack of love from James, he hadn't appreciated all the other incredible gifts he'd been given?

Adam hung his head. *I'm sorry, Lord. I've been so blinded by hatred and bitterness that I couldn't see Your blessings.*

Years of resentment and hostility began to seep away, while the need for repentance burned hot in his veins. His anger seemed so pointless now, as Mama lay fighting for her life.

A muffled cry sounded behind him. He spun around. "Mama?"

But except for the faint rise of her chest, she remained still. James's face was buried in the pillow beside her, his frame shaking.

Adam froze by the window, paralyzed by his father's weeping. Part of him wanted to slip unseen out the door. The other part, filled with compassion, wished to ease James's pain.

He walked to the bed and laid a hand on his father's shoulder. James stiffened at the contact, as though he hadn't realized anyone else was in the room.

"Would you like to pray with me?" As soon as the words left Adam's lips, he waited for the cold rebuke, remembering how his father had only endured church services to please Mama. He doubted James had any real faith, but simply bowed to his wife's wishes.

James lifted his head, hair a tangled mess, three days' growth of beard making him appear vagrant-like. He didn't even attempt to wipe the moisture from his face, but merely nodded. "Would you begin?"

Adam held out a hand to the man who had raised him. James hesitated for a brief second and then sat up on the bed. He grasped Adam's hand as though it were a lifeline, the one thing saving him from falling apart.

With his free hand, Adam entwined his fingers around his mother's limp hand and bowed his head. He emptied his mind and allowed the Lord's words to enter his soul. Immediately the words from the hymn Maggie had been playing came to him.

" 'The Lord is my shepherd, I shall not want.' "

With perfect recall, he recited the twenty-third Psalm. When he neared the end, he became aware of the door opening and other people entering the room. His heart swelled with love and gratitude for his family — a family he had failed to fully appreciate. From now on, he would work hard to reestablish broken bonds and repair the fragile relationships. Family, he realized, consisted of more than blood or genes. It was made up of love and respect and shared experiences. As he prayed for his mother's recovery, he also prayed silently for his family's forgiveness, that they would give him the chance to make amends for the past.

When their prayers ended, James raised his head again, his focus landing on Adam. A host of emotions passed over his features.

"Thank you, son," he said. "I've never been a religious man, but those words brought me a great measure of peace. Katie would have loved to hear you pray that way."

Adam swallowed, unused to words of approval from James. "The best thing that happened to me in prison was meeting John McNabb. He taught me the true meaning of being a Christian."

A hand squeezed his shoulder. Adam looked up to see Brianna's gentle smile, her green eyes brimming with unshed tears.

"We're so glad to have you back, Adam. I hope you won't stay away from home as much now."

"I'll do my best." His gaze moved past his sister to Gil, the man she would marry in a few weeks. Adam was astounded to see admiration shining on Gil's face. He swallowed and rose to face his former nemesis.

"Gil, I hope you can accept my apology for my past behavior. It's taken me a long time to understand that my resentment was a result of misplaced anger — totally unwarranted by you."

Gil fixed him with a solemn look. "All I've ever wanted is for everyone to get along." Gil held out a hand to Adam.

Astounded by the ease with which Gil accepted his long-overdue apology, Adam shook his hand. "Thank you. It's more than I deserve."

"I only hope we can move forward from here as a family." Gil tilted his head toward Brianna. "Especially with our wedding approaching."

"I second that." A voice from the hallway joined the discussion.

"Colleen!" Brianna whirled around to embrace their sister. "How long have you been there?"

Colleen gave a shaky smile. "Long enough to hear Adam's beautiful prayer and his apology. I'm just sorry it took Mama's illness to bring about this family reunion."

She pulled away from Brianna and moved to kneel by the bed, grasping Mama's hand in hers. "I'm here, Mama. I'm sorry I couldn't get here sooner, but I've been busy nursing Delia back to health. She wants to see her grandmother soon."

For a second, Mama's eyelids flickered. Adam, along with everyone else in the room, froze, but other than a raspy breath, she remained the same.

A knock echoed in the room as Dr. Shepherd entered. "May I have a moment with my patient, please?"

Grateful for a momentary escape and for time to recover his equilibrium, Adam strode out into the hallway and straight into Maggie.

Maggie gave a cry of surprise as Adam barreled into her, practically knocking her out of her shoes.

Adam grabbed her arms to keep her from toppling over. "I'm sorry. I didn't see you." He scowled. "How long have you been standing out here?"

She swiped at the telltale moisture on her cheeks. Dare she admit that she'd overheard the entire conversation?

"Long enough." She rubbed her hand across his upper arm, attempting to convey the depth of her emotion.

He avoided her eyes. "If you'll excuse me, I need some air."

She swallowed a rush of disappointment and stepped aside to allow him by.

She had no time to process his reaction before the rest of the family filed out of the bedroom. Gil and Brianna crossed to another room, likely to check on their siblings. Mr. O'Leary paced the carpeted corridor, appearing almost ill himself, his clothing and hair disheveled, a growth of beard hugging his jaw.

Colleen came up beside him. "Daddy, why don't you go and rest a while? We'll all be here with Mama."

He shook his head. "If I'm gone, it might give her the chance to slip away."

His dazed stare fell on Maggie, and he frowned. In all the confusion, he probably hadn't realized she was in the house. Now that Colleen had arrived, Maggie no longer had the excuse of being here in her stead. And in light of Adam's reunion with his family, he no longer needed her support. Yet, how could Maggie leave until she knew the outcome? If, God forbid, Mrs. O'Leary passed on to her heavenly reward, Adam would be stricken with an inconsolable grief, one Maggie felt compelled to help him through.

"What are you doing here?" Mr. O'Leary practically barked at her.

Maggie flinched and stumbled for a suitable answer. She must seem like an interloper at this intimate family time.

Colleen put an arm around her shoulders. "I asked Maggie to come in my stead when Delia was still so ill. I knew she'd be a help to the family, just as she was at the orphanage."

Mr. O'Leary's frown eased slightly.

Colleen squeezed Maggie against her. "Maggie is as dear to me as Brianna and Dee-Dee. I don't know what I'd have done without her."

Maggie smiled. "I'm glad to be of help. Can I do anything for you now?"

Mr. O'Leary studied her. "I heard the piano playing some time ago. Was that you?"

"Aye."

"My Katie loves the piano. If anything other than her family will help her recover, it will be music. Perhaps you could play again for a while."

"I'd be happy to."

28

Maggie's fingers cramped as she ended the song. How long had she been playing? Her aching back and numb extremities told her she'd gone on far longer than she'd intended. Some time outdoors and a bit of exercise would do her good.

The house sat in unnatural silence, its grim aura permeating the entire dwelling like a suffocating cloud. Maggie crossed the thick carpet to the French doors and let herself out onto the balcony. She walked to the railing and inhaled the fresh air, tinged with the scent of flowers from Mrs. O'Leary's garden. Despite the still-warm August temperatures, Maggie shivered and wrapped her arms around her middle. The sight of dark clouds roaming across the sky warned of an impending summer storm.

A blur of movement caught Maggie's attention. She leaned over the railing to see Adam striding across the lawn toward the barns. Everything about his countenance alarmed her. He hadn't taken the time to don his usual cap, leaving his hair to blow in disarray around his head. One suspender hung limply from his waist; the other cinched the linen of his shirt against his frame. But it was the storm of emotion on his face that caused her the greatest distress.

Dear Lord, no. Had his mother passed on?

Before she realized it, she had descended the stairs and started after him. The wind, now whipping into a frenzy, tore at her skirts as she ran down the path. Instead of entering the barn, Adam kept going, past the racetrack and across the far meadow. Keeping him in her sight, Maggie followed at a discreet distance. Where could he be headed?

She crested a hill and scanned the landscape before her. The moment she saw the pond, she knew it was his intended destination. Adam had told her the story of his younger brother's drowning and how he had tried in vain to revive the lad. The only reason she could think of that he'd come here was to relive the sorrow of losing yet another family member.

Soft drops of rain began to patter her shoulders and face. She continued walking, slower this time, now that she knew his goal.

Beneath the overhang of a large willow tree at the side of the pond, Adam dropped to his knees. His hands came up to cover his face, and his entire body shook.

Her own tears mingled with the rain on her cheeks. *Oh, Adam.* Her heart cried out for the greatness of his pain. Should she leave him to grieve in private or offer him comfort?

Haltingly, she approached the tree, skirting the low-hanging limbs. Underneath the canopy, a measure of shelter held the rain at bay. With his face still buried, Adam did not see her. In his cocoon of pain, she doubted he'd even heard her footfalls.

When she could no longer stand the sight of his weeping, she went to him, knelt beside him, and laid a hand on his shoulder.

"Adam," she whispered, "I'm here."

His head lurched up, and he swiped at his reddened eyes. "Maggie."

For a moment, she thought he might be angry, that he wanted to grieve alone. Then, astonishingly, he threw back his head and laughed out loud.

Was the man delirious?

He rose, lifting her with him. "Mama's going to be all right." He twirled Maggie in a circle before the understanding of his words seeped into her brain.

"She is?"

"Her fever broke, and she's awake. When she started issuing orders to my father, I knew the crisis had passed."

She laughed with him, realizing she'd never seen him so carefree. The tightness around his jaw had softened, and his eyes brimmed with joy.

She threw her arms around his neck in an impulsive embrace. "Thank You, God, for answering our prayers."

He buried his face in her hair, and they clung to each other, reveling in this rare moment of joy. A minute or two passed, and the mood shifted. Slowly, Adam pulled back, and the intensity of his stare stole the air from Maggie's lungs. His hands came up to cup her face on either side, and he lowered his mouth to hers.

Every one of her senses heightened. She tasted the coffee lingering on his lips, felt the thrum of his heart against her chest. The fragrance of summer rain drifted around them, blending with the masculine scent of his soap. In the shelter of his arms beneath the canopy of the willow, Maggie gloried in the feeling of being safe and protected and . . . cherished.

His lips trailed from her mouth to her temple, and he released a slow breath that fluttered her hair. "I couldn't have gotten through these past few days without you, Maggie. How can I ever thank you?"

Her heart expanded with his praise. "Your happiness is thanks enough."

He shook his head. "I don't know what I did to deserve you. But I thank God for bringing you into my life."

She stilled, waiting for him to remind her once again that he wasn't worthy and that she needed to leave him.

Instead, he smiled and traced her bottom lip with his thumb. "Maybe my life has turned a corner, as well. I've started to make amends with my family, and my store will open soon."

"What are you saying?" she whispered.

A shadow of doubt flickered across his rugged features. "I'm no prize, Maggie. But would you ever consider . . . ?" He trailed away, a frown wrinkling his brow. "Do you think Rylan might give me permission to court you?"

She scowled and lifted her chin. "Do I not have a mind of my own? I don't need my brother to tell me who I can or cannot love."

His eyes widened, then narrowed. "Did you just say you love me?"

She adored the fierceness in his voice that matched the expression on his face.

"Tá tú mo chroí go deo." She smiled at his confused look. "It means you have my heart forever. Whether you like it or not."

He let out a low growl and grabbed her by the waist, lifting her feet off the ground again. Her head brushed a branch above, unleashing a torrent of water that rained down on both of them. She squealed at the cold wetness that cascaded over her face and neck. When she opened her eyes, Adam's stunned expression beneath his dripping hair made her burst into laughter.

He set her on her feet and swiped the moisture from his face. His soaked shirt lay plastered against his chest, outlining the muscles beneath as his breath rose and fell. Maggie swallowed and raised her head. Adam's eyes darkened to midnight as he claimed her lips in a kiss that seared her soul, binding her to him for eternity. She returned his kiss with every ounce of emotion in her, until they both were breathless.

When he released her, she sighed with pure bliss. No matter what the future had in store for her, Maggie would remember this magical moment beneath the willow tree forever.

The day Aurora had both prayed for and dreaded had arrived. The quarantine had been lifted. All the patients were well on the road to recovery, and no further outbreaks had been reported. With the ever-efficient Nurse Patterson in charge of the last few children, Aurora's services as a caregiver were no longer required.

It was time to take her leave of the orphanage . . . and of Gabe. Time to go home to face her father's disapproval and relieve her mother's anxiety before moving forward with the next phase of her life. She was more convinced than ever that nursing was her destiny.

Aurora studied her reflection in the mirror of her small room as she pinned her hat in place. The hardest part would be leaving Gabe. She'd grown to love being around him every day for the past three weeks. Loved expecting his wink or his grin, his good-natured teasing, his unconditional support.

But despite the strong feelings of attraction between them, and despite the delicious kisses they'd shared, she feared a romance with Gabe was not the path meant for her. Gabe would be traveling back to Ireland soon, and she would start nursing school. Gabe would resume life in his village and find a nice local girl to share his life. The thought of him happily married to another woman should have comforted Aurora, but it only added to the weight of her regret.

She squared her shoulders and headed downstairs to find him. No point in putting it off any longer. She'd said her farewells to the others already. Dr. Reardon had returned to the hospital with a promise to check on the patients again in a few days to make sure no one had suffered a setback in their recovery.

Aurora entered the dining room, knowing Gabe would be sipping his second cup of tea while he read the morning news, as he did most mornings once the nuns and the children had cleared out. Sure enough, he sat at the end of the long dining table, the newspaper held out in front of him, hiding his face. The aroma of eggs and fresh bread teased her, adding to the homey atmosphere of the room. On the floor beside Gabe's chair, Chester raised his head from his paws, his tail swishing a silent greeting. How she'd love this to be the routine of their daily lives.

She took in a fortifying breath and attempted a smile. "Good morning, Gabe. I've come to say good-bye. I'm off to Long Island to see my parents."

He lowered the newspaper. Instead of his

usual cheery countenance, his expression radiated grief. His glassy eyes barely registered her presence.

Alarm pulsed in her veins, and she rushed forward. "What's the matter?"

Gabe rose from the table, shaking his head. "While we've been cocooned here in this building, terrible things have been happening in the world." He brushed his fingers over the newspaper.

A spurt of annoyance rushed through her. She'd thought someone had died, and he was stewing over a news article? Still, the information must be dire from the look on his face. "What sorts of terrible things?"

He trained bleak eyes on her. "War."

She grasped one of the chairs to steady herself. The strong aroma of lilies from the arrangement on the sideboard turned her stomach. "What are you talking about? We're not at war." How could they be? There hadn't been a whisper of unrest in recent months.

"Not your country. At least not yet." He slid the front page of *The New York Times* toward her. "But my country is at war."

England Declares War on Germany. British Ship Sunk.

Aurora frowned at the headline. "I don't understand. What has this to do with Ireland?" *What has this to do with you?*

Gabe expelled a weary breath. "I don't suppose many people here are aware of the complicated situation back home." He came forward to take her hand. "Ireland has been experiencing a state of unrest for some time now. I greatly feared civil war would break out while I was away. Many Irish want to break ties with England, to regain control over our land. I doubt that will happen now."

She struggled to understand the situation, embarrassed she knew so little about foreign lands. "Ireland is ruled by England?"

"Aye. And now I fear our men will be commandeered to fight for her. My brothers . . ." He broke off and swallowed. On a deep inhale, he looked her in the eye. "I have to return home. My family needs me."

Aurora's thoughts swirled as she attempted to make sense of this catastrophe. "But will they make you fight, too?" She couldn't bear the idea of Gabe in uniform, marching into battle.

"I don't know." His voice softened, and he raised her hand to his lips.

A last desperate notion surfaced. "Surely travel will be restricted, if there are battles raging."

"Possibly. But since England only declared

war last night, they may not have had a chance to enforce any changes yet. That's why I have to go now. While I still can."

A fissure of pain split Aurora's heart. "Does Rylan know?"

"I'm sure he's read the news. He doesn't know I plan to leave, though." Sorrow shadowed his gray eyes. "I can't tell him. He'll try to stop me from going. As will Maggie. This has to be our secret."

A sob stuck in Aurora's throat, making speech impossible. She shook so hard, her hat slipped over her forehead. With trembling fingers, she wrenched it off, mangling the brim from the force of her grip. "Please . . . don't go. It's not safe." She released the hat to flutter to the ground and grasped his arm. Tears blurred his precious face before her.

"Don't cry, darlin'." He pulled her against his chest. The soft cotton of his shirt absorbed the onslaught of tears that wouldn't stop.

When she'd thought of Gabe leaving to return to Ireland, she'd never imagined the reality of the moment. The finality of it. Her body quaked with sorrow, thinking that this might be the last time she ever saw him.

How would she bear it?

■ ■ ■ ■

Gabe pressed kisses to the top of Aurora's head, inhaling deeply to try to memorize the scent of her beautiful hair. This was not how he'd envisioned his future, but once he'd read the news, he knew he had no choice — he had to go back.

His country was at war, his family in upheaval. His conscience would never allow him to stay here solely to pursue a romance with the incredible woman in his arms.

"Hush, sweetheart. Please. You've been so strong these last weeks. Draw on that strength again. God will be with us both and help us through these difficult times."

She lifted her face, blue eyes framed by spiky lashes. "But I may never see you again. . . ."

He couldn't help himself. He pressed his lips to hers, drinking her in like a parched man. "I promise I'll come back for you. As soon as I can."

She hiccupped. "A war could last for years. You could be injured . . . or k-killed."

"I love you, Aurora. And as long as I have breath left in my body, I will come back for you. You have my word." He kissed her again.

"I love you, too," she whispered.

He wiped the tears from her cheek with his thumb. If he didn't go soon, he'd lose the willpower to leave her. Bending, he retrieved her hat and handed it to her. "You must go now. I have to pack my things and head to the docks. I promise I'll write as soon as I can."

She stood staring at him, tragedy etched in every line of her face. He was hurting her — the last thing he ever intended. He'd hoped — well, it didn't matter any longer what he'd hoped. He had to accept the reality of the situation and trust God to see them through.

Her small hand cupped his cheek. "We won't say good-bye. Only farewell for now. Until we meet again." She gave a wavering smile. "I know you to be a man of your word, Gabriel Montgomery, and I'm going to hold you to your promise. Come back to me." She pulled his face to hers for another kiss.

He wound his fingers through the fall of hair at the back of her neck. She clung to him as though she'd never let go. At last, when he thought he couldn't stand it another second, he released her.

"You own my heart, Aurora Hastings. And I'll be back one day to claim it."

With a last tender kiss to her forehead, he rushed from the room, not daring to look back, lest her sorrow keep him from doing what he must.

29

Maggie left Irish Meadows to return to the orphanage, floating on a bubble of happiness. She entered the main hall, pausing to remove her hat before going in search of Rylan. The news that she and Adam were officially courting should come from her. Rylan would need time to accept the inevitability of her future with Adam.

She couldn't keep the smile from her face as she recalled their parting kiss. Adam planned to stay with his family for a few more days, until he was certain his mother was fully on the mend, and then he would work day and night until his store was ready to open.

He was doing it all for her, Maggie realized. With a respectable business behind him, he would feel worthy to court her. Once the O'Leary Furniture Emporium opened its doors, she would bring Rylan and Gabe to see his accomplishment. Then any objections Rylan might still harbor would surely be abolished.

She paused outside Rylan's office and knocked.

"Come in." The tone of his voice did not inspire optimism.

She opened the door to find him staring out the window.

A thread of worry momentarily stole her joy. Surely Delia hadn't relapsed? "Rylan?"

He turned to face her, his expression bleak. "Maggie. It's good to have you back. Colleen tells me her mother is doing much better."

She nodded. "Aye. The Lord is good. First Delia and now Mrs. O'Leary." She was almost afraid to voice their good fortune. Especially when Rylan's countenance did not match the happiness within her.

She needed to get her news out before she lost her nerve. "I have something to tell you, Rylan, and you probably won't be pleased."

One dark brow rose. "Oh?"

She clasped her hands together in front of her. "Adam has declared his feelings for me and has asked to court me."

Rylan straightened, a scowl forming.

"I love him, Rylan. And I intend to become his wife. Though I would appreciate your support on this, know that I will continue to see Adam even if you object." She kept her chin tilted, her gaze level, waiting for his explosion.

But instead of anger, Rylan sagged like a leaky tire. "You're a grown woman, Maggie. Entitled to your own mistakes. I'll not stop you."

Concern shot through Maggie. His anger, she could handle. His defeat, she could not.

"What's wrong, Rylan?"

"It's Gabe. He's gone."

A whisper of fear invaded her heart. "What do you mean, gone?"

Rylan ran his hand over his face. "I guess you've not heard the news. England is at war. The moment Gabe heard, he set out for home."

The room swam before her. She knew the day would come when Gabe would sail back without her, but not so soon. And not without her bidding him farewell. "He left without saying good-bye." Her chest constricted. "How could he do that?"

Rylan moved to put his arm around her. "Aurora said he knew we'd try to stop him. And in fact I did, but I was too late. One of the workers said a man fitting Gabe's description booked passage on a steamer heading to Queenstown. Traded in his liner ticket."

Maggie's knees weakened, and she sank onto a chair. "Is he planning to join the war?"

"I don't know. Aurora only said he felt his place was with our family at this time of crisis."

"Why was Aurora privy to his plans?"

For the first time, a smile quirked Rylan's lips. "It appears both you and Gabe have fallen in love during your time here."

Maggie's mouth gaped open. So her suspicion of Gabe's interest in Aurora had been right. "Then why did he leave?"

"You know Gabe. His sense of duty overruled his feelings for Aurora. Although she said he promised to return one day."

A cold thrust of fear twisted Maggie's stomach. Her country was at war and her brother was headed right into its path. "What is happening to the world, Rylan? It feels as though God has lost control."

Rylan tipped her chin up, his brown gaze serious. "You know better than that, love," he said gently. "We have to trust in God to see us through these rough spots. But don't ever doubt He knows exactly what He's doing."

For the first time in her life, Aurora entered her family's summer home on Long Island without her usual joy at being back in the country. Instead, a deep sense of dread invaded her heart as she removed her hat and set it on the marble table. She paused for a moment in the hallway to bring Gabe's beloved face to mind. The thought of him crossing the sea on a steamer, all for the love of his country and family, made her determined to be just as courageous in facing her own situation.

Aurora bolstered her resolve, pasted on a smile, and sailed into the parlor.

Her mother dropped her needlework. "My darling girl, is it really you?" She rose and rushed to gather Aurora in a hug.

"Yes, Mama." She returned her embrace, drinking in her mother's comforting scent of Parisian toilet water with the realization of how much she'd missed her. "The epidemic is over at last."

Aurora allowed her gaze to move across the room to her father. Seated in his leather armchair by the fireplace, his usual before-dinner drink in hand, he slowly rose. "So you finally decided to grace us with your presence."

Aurora bit back a sigh. He wasn't going to make this easy for her. She moved toward him and planted a quick kiss on his leathery cheek. "Hello, Papa. How have you been?"

"I'm fine, but your poor mother has nearly worried herself into a pine box."

Aurora kept her features calm as her parents resumed their seats, and she sat beside her mother on the sofa. "I'm sorry you were worried, but I'm sure you understand the need to keep the typhoid outbreak contained."

Mama laid a hand on her arm. "Of course. But what we don't understand is why you were involved in the first place."

A twinge of guilt pinched Aurora's conscience. Perhaps keeping so many details of her life from her parents hadn't been the wisest choice. "That's one of the reasons I'm here now. To explain a few things to you both."

"This sounds serious." Her father took a cigar from the inside pocket of his suit jacket.

"It concerns my future, so for me it's very serious." She clasped her hands on her lap. "You know I've been volunteering at the hospital for some time now. The reason for that was more than charitable. I wanted to determine if I'm suited to become a nurse."

Papa's hand stilled on the box of matches, and his eyes narrowed.

Aurora fought the nervous urge to twist her fingers. "Dr. Reardon, whom you met at the orphanage, Papa, has been acting as a mentor of sorts. He's allowed me to accompany him on rounds at the hospital and to the orphanage when treating the children. Dr. Reardon asked me to help out before we realized the nature of the outbreak."

Mama's hand fluttered at her neck. "My word."

Papa stormed up from his chair, his cigar forgotten on the table. "No daughter of mine is going to be dealing with illness and bodily waste. It's outrageous."

Aurora stiffened her back. "Nursing is a noble profession. One I intend to pursue." She paused. "I've applied to Bellevue's nursing program for the fall."

Papa's mustache twitched, a sign he was distinctly displeased. "You should be putting all your energy into finding a husband. What man will want you now that you'll be training for such a distasteful profession? Unless . . ." His gaze zeroed in on her. "This Dr. Reardon seemed to hold you in high regard. He acted very protective when I came to the orphanage. I can respect a man like that."

She swallowed. Time for the rest of her admission. "I'm afraid my affections lie elsewhere." *Aboard a ship on the ocean.*

Papa's brow rose with undisguised interest. "Do tell, daughter. What man has captured your fancy at long last? Someone from a good family, I hope."

Aurora managed to hold back a burst of nervous laughter. "A very good family. In fact, his brother is the esteemed director of the orphanage."

Papa's high color vanished. "Not that blasted Irishman."

"Yes, Papa," she said softly. "Gabe and I are in love, and when he returns from Ireland, I'm hoping he will ask me to marry him."

Mama squeezed her hand, her expression a mixture of happiness and sympathy.

Papa stalked across the room to the fireplace. "He's gone back to Ireland in the midst of war? Is he mad?"

"Only worried for his family, as I'm sure you can understand."

Papa grunted. "With the way things are shaping up overseas, I doubt he'll be back. He'll probably be drafted into the fighting."

"Arthur!" Mama's voice quivered with mild outrage. "Don't talk that way. Aurora must be worried about him."

"I am. But I have to trust God to keep him safe and bring him back to me." Aurora got to her feet and walked over to stand before her father. "And when he does, Papa,

I expect you to treat him with decency and respect. He's the man I love. The man I choose to spend my life with. And I'll not hear otherwise."

"I'm not sure I like this defiant attitude." Papa crossed to the table and picked up the cigar. He rolled it between his fingers, as though contemplating her words, and when he turned, his expression proved unreadable. "If this Irishman ever shows up again, I'll decide then how to handle the situation."

Aurora held her ground, not breaking eye contact. "There won't be anything to handle, Papa. Because when Gabe comes back, nothing is going to keep me from him."

Instead of the expected anger, her father studied her with an unreadable expression. "I guess we'll see, won't we?"

Despite Aurora's bravado, a niggle of fear invaded her heart. Why did her father seem certain that Gabe wouldn't return? Papa might be a powerful man in New York, but surely his reach didn't extend to the other side of the ocean.

If only Aurora could be sure.

30

Adam whistled cheerfully while he chiseled away at the piece of wood on the table in his workshop. For the first time since he could remember — since his early childhood, really — his heart was filled with optimism for the future.

His hands stilled, and he looked around his work area with a sense of wonder. A prayer of gratitude lifted from the depths of his soul — gratitude for the opportunity to do the work he loved, gratitude to God for bringing his mother back from the brink of death, and gratitude for the love of Maggie Montgomery.

Less than three months ago, when he'd walked out of the penitentiary a free man, he never could have imagined receiving such an abundance of blessings. Adam resumed his work, making a silent vow to honor the Lord in all ways and prove himself worthy of His gifts.

The heavy tread of boots thudded across the floorboards in the outer store. Adam looked up to see the smiling face of John McNabb in the entrance to his workshop.

"You've done wonders with this place, Adam. I never imagined you could be ready to open for business so soon."

Adam wiped his hands on a towel and moved to clap a hand on John's shoulder. "Thanks to you, O'Leary's Furniture Emporium will have its grand opening next week."

They moved into the store, and as Adam viewed the area through John's eyes, pride inflated his chest. The pieces he had ready to sell all exhibited the quality of his workmanship. He hoped it would be enough to entice customers to return on a regular basis to view the new stock he would be adding.

"How did you manage to get so much inventory ready to sell?"

Adam straightened one of the high-backed chairs. "I restored some older pieces. You'd be surprised how many people discard furniture for a broken leg or drawer. Easily fixable by someone who knows how."

"I must say I'm very impressed." He paused to look Adam in the eye. "And very proud. You've come a long way, my friend."

Adam swallowed the swell of emotion in

his throat. "I couldn't have done it without you, John. You have my undying gratitude."

John's mouth quirked up in a grin. "Maybe now I can convince you to attend one of my services. I promise my sermon won't put you to sleep."

Adam laughed out loud. "As a matter of fact, I intend to come this Sunday. I have a great deal to give thanks for."

The front door opened, and Maggie entered with a swish of skirts.

Adam couldn't suppress a foolish grin at the unexpected sight of her. "Maggie. What a nice surprise."

Upon spying John, she hesitated. "I'm sorry. Is this a bad time?"

"Not at all. I'd like you to meet my friend, John McNabb."

Her blinding smile lit the room. "It's a pleasure to meet you, Mr. McNabb. Adam has told me so much about you and everything you've done to help him."

John bowed over her hand. "Funny, he hasn't told me much about you at all." He shot Adam a smug look before smiling at her. "Please, you must call me John."

"And I'm Maggie." She turned to Adam. "I came to see how the store's progressing. I can't believe how much you've done since I was here last." She ran a finger over an oak dining table. "This is beautiful."

Adam's gaze followed her as she moved, unable to tear his eyes from her. In her blue-and-white dress, she mimicked a summer sky. Her ebony hair flowed in mesmerizing curls over her shoulders.

John cleared his throat, grinning. "Well, I must be going. I have a few parishioners to visit. It was nice to meet you, Maggie. I hope to see you again soon." He lifted a brow. "Perhaps you'll accompany Adam to church this Sunday. He's finally agreed to attend one of my services."

A flash of regret crossed her beautiful face. "I'd love to, but this Sunday is my first day playing the organ at St. Patrick's."

John's eyes widened. "The cathedral? How did you manage that?"

Adam strode forward to steer John toward the door. "That's a story for another day, my friend."

John chuckled. "I can take a hint. See you on Sunday."

When Adam turned back to Maggie, a tinge of pink colored her cheeks in a most becoming manner. He could hold his longing in check no more and swept her into his arms.

She gasped. "Adam! What are you doing? Anyone could come in."

"Let them." He lowered his head to capture her lips with his.

Though she gave an initial squirm of protest, she soon melted against him and returned his kiss.

When they parted, he gazed down into her flushed face. "I don't think I'll ever grow tired of holding you in my arms."

"You, sir, are far too adept at kissing. You make me forget everything around me." She disengaged herself and smoothed the bodice of her dress.

"Did you really come to see the store, or did you have an ulterior motive?"

"Other than kissing you, you mean?" Her eyes sparkled with mischief.

"Ah, so you admit the real reason for your visit."

Her laugh tinkled out over the shop. "I came to see you . . . to ask a favor."

"Another kiss like that and I'll do anything," he teased.

Though she smiled, a hint of anxiety loomed on her face.

"What is this favor?" Anything to make the joy return to her countenance.

"I'd like you to take me to check on Ivy. I thought it would make Rylan and Colleen feel better to know she's being properly cared for."

Though he dreaded returning to the saloon, Adam had been meaning to check on Jolene and make sure she was keeping her promise. Mama's illness, not to mention his fixation on the woman before him, had derailed many of his plans.

"I'll go later today." He lifted her chin with one finger. "But you will not be accompanying me." Under no circumstances would he allow Maggie to enter such a seedy place. Nor did he want her to witness the type of life he'd led before his conversion.

She scowled at him, tiny ridges forming over her nose. "You listen to me, Adam O'Leary —"

"Yes, Miss Montgomery?" He bit back a grin at her famous temper, which made her Irish lilt all the more pronounced.

She poked a finger into his chest. "Just because you're courting me does not give you the right to dictate what I can or cannot do."

He captured her hand in his and rubbed his thumb over her palm. "Does the fact that I care about your welfare mean anything?"

She paused. "Of course, but —"

"Then trust me on this, Maggie."

She stared at him for a moment before

huffing out a breath. "Very well. As long as you promise to let me know what you find."

"I promise." He twisted one of her curls around his finger. "It will give me a good excuse to drop by and see you later."

She laughed and stepped back. "I suppose I'd best go and let you get on with your work. I'm off to St. Patrick's to practice."

He walked her to the door and paused to give her another lingering kiss. A shadow of movement across the street caught his attention. Memories of Neill Fitzgerald flashed into his mind, filling him with guilt. How had he gotten so lax with Maggie's safety?

"Wait." He untied his work apron and hung it over a nearby chair. "I'll walk with you."

She appeared ready to argue, but his grim expression must have given her pause. Instead, she winked. "Face it, Mr. O'Leary, you can't get enough of my company."

Adam repressed a shudder later that day as he entered the door of the Lucky Chance Saloon. Fortunately it was early enough that the place was essentially empty. Marty leaned on the counter of the bar, perusing a newspaper.

He looked up as Adam crossed the room.

"Back again, O'Leary?"

Adam gave a brief nod. Marty would be more likely to cooperate if Adam tried to be friendly. He pointed at the newspaper. "What's happening in the world today, Marty?"

The man gave a weighty sigh and flipped the paper to the front page. "Nothing good. Hope the war doesn't spread to this side of the world."

"You and me both."

"So what brings you by again?"

Adam placed a foot on the brass rail and attempted to keep his tone casual. "I've come to talk to Jolene. Is she around by any chance?"

Marty's gaze shifted toward the back hall. "She's probably sleeping, like most of the girls at this hour." He straightened his large frame. "If you want to see her, you should come back when she's working."

Adam held back a grimace of distaste. The last thing he'd do was come when the bar was in full swing. "Guess you're right. How's Max handling her having a baby?"

Marty jerked, sloshing coffee from the cup on the counter. "Keep your voice down. How do you know about . . . it?"

"Long story." He narrowed his eyes. "What are you hiding, Marty?'

He dragged a cloth across the bar. "Look, Max doesn't know about the kid. We're all helping Jolene so he doesn't get wind of it."

Suspicion soured Adam's stomach. "Who watches the baby while she's working?"

Marty's face hardened. "If you want to know more, talk to Jolene." He turned away to wipe the ledge behind him, where the bottles of liquor stood.

Frustration hummed through Adam. Marty had clammed up tighter than a vise grip. He'd get nothing further from him. And Adam couldn't afford to hang around the bar until Jolene happened to come down. He'd have to come back another time. Disappointment ran through him at the thought of having no news for Maggie.

He tugged on his cap, about to head for the door, when a distinctive cry sounded from the rear of the building. Adam whirled, noted the panic on Marty's face, and barreled down the hall to Marty's office. He pushed open the door, and the wailing grew louder. Adam rushed in, eyes scanning as he went. In the far corner, wedged between the desk and the wall, the rim of a wicker basket was visible. Conscious of Marty's heavy footsteps, Adam crossed the untidy room and peered down at the squalling infant. Wrapped in an old towel, Ivy's little face, red and puckered, howled at him. An arrow of hot rage seared Adam's chest. What kind of mother left her infant holed away in a filthy room all alone?

He reached into the basket and lifted the baby, frantically trying to remember how Maggie had held her.

"O'Leary, what are you doing?" Marty huffed and puffed, his stomach rising and falling with his heaving breath.

Adam pushed past him. "I'm taking this child to its mother." He strode down the hall, his boots slapping the floor.

"Wait. You can't go up there."

"Watch me." For all his bravado, Adam's insides roiled. He'd sworn he'd never climb those stairs, but there was nothing else he could do at the moment. "What room is Jolene in?"

"Max will kill me if he finds out . . ."

The baby screeched louder.

"Either tell me, or I start opening doors until I find her."

Marty blanched, nervously fingering the strings of his apron. "All right, but make it quick. Third door on the right."

Adam charged up the stairs, trying not to jostle the babe. When he reached the third door, he steeled himself for what he might find, and then knocked.

Someone mumbled a few choice words on the other side.

"Open up, Jolene."

Rustling noises came from inside. "I'm sleeping. Go away."

"I'll give you to the count of three or I'm coming in."

"Wait."

More scurrying could be heard. At last, the door opened, and Jolene stepped out into the hallway, belting a thin robe around her. Her hair sat in a tangled mess on her head, and smears of black makeup streaked her face. Jolene scowled. "Can't you get her to be quiet?"

Adam held the baby out to her. "I believe that's your job. Why isn't she in the room with you?"

Jolene made no effort to take the baby from him. "I need my sleep so I can function at work. Marty said he'd watch her for me."

"Well, she was shoved in a back corner of Marty's office all alone."

"Probably because she was asleep. Take her back to Marty." She moved toward the door, but Adam barred her way.

"You're awake now. Take care of your daughter, Jolene. Or do I have to call someone from Children's Aid?"

Right then, Ivy chose to screech at the top of her lungs.

The door to Jolene's room opened, and a paunchy, middle-aged man in an undershirt peered out. "What's all the noise out here, Jolene? I'm trying to sleep."

Jolene's eyes darted from Adam to the man. "It's all right, Harry. This man has the wrong room. Go back to bed."

A full-blown rage roared through Adam. "Since when do your customers spend the night?"

She glared at Adam. "Harry's not a customer, he's my boyfriend."

Adam stared. "Is he Ivy's father?"

"No, I met Harry after I started back to work here." She jutted her pointed chin at him. "I don't know which of my customers is the baby's father." Jolene clutched Adam's sleeve then, eyes darting to the door. "Look, I think I made a big mistake taking the baby back. I'm just not cut out for motherhood. And besides, Harry doesn't like kids."

Adam stared at her ragged state of disarray and clamped his lips together to keep from shouting at the woman. God had given her an amazing gift, yet she chose this life and that man over her baby. He patted Ivy's tiny back and jiggled her on his shoulder. Thankfully, she began to settle.

"Would you be willing to let my sister and her husband raise her?"

Jolene gazed at the back of Ivy's head, and her chin wobbled. A single tear ran down her cheek, trailing through the black makeup. "I think it would be best for the baby."

Adam's heart rate quickened, but he kept any expression from his face. "You have to be sure. There's no changing your mind again. I won't do that to Colleen a second time."

"I understand."

"Then you'd be willing to sign papers waiving your rights?"

Jolene's shoulders drooped, and she sighed. "Yes."

Adam purposely softened his manner. "You're doing the right thing for your daughter. She'll have a good home with Colleen and Rylan."

"I know." More tears fell. She raised a hand and laid it on the baby's back. "Good-bye, sweet girl." She swiped a sleeve across her cheek. "Just a minute and I'll get you the rest of her things." She disappeared into the room and emerged a few seconds later with a blanket and a few pieces of clothing.

Adam accepted them. "We'll have a lawyer draw up papers and bring them by for you to sign."

Jolene wrapped her arms around her too-thin frame. "Fine." She regarded him with weary eyes. "Will you promise to let me know how she's doing?"

Though he hated the idea of ever returning to this God-forsaken place, Adam nodded. "I can do that. Good-bye, Jolene."

Before she could change her mind, Adam headed back downstairs, clutching the precious bundle to his chest.

31

Maggie looked out the parlor window at Colleen and Rylan's, scanning the street below for any sign of Adam. She'd assumed he would be here before the evening meal, but it was now long past eight o'clock.

Perhaps his plans had changed. Perhaps he needed to get straight back to the store to finish a repair for one of the people John had recommended to him.

She sighed and replaced the curtain at the window. No point in stewing. He'd come when he was able. Maggie only prayed the wee girl was faring well with her mother.

Maggie walked to the fireplace and stirred the dying embers, her thoughts turning to Gabe. She wished she'd had the chance to say good-bye, for she feared she might never see him again. She straightened and whispered a quick prayer for her brother's safety, wherever he might be.

Voices sounded in the hall, and Rylan and

Colleen entered the room. Maggie turned, relieved to see Colleen looking much more like her old self now that Delia was home and well again.

Colleen took her chair by the fireplace. "Sorry to take so long. Delia insisted on three stories."

Rylan grinned. "We don't have the heart to deny her anything right now."

Maggie laughed, pleased to see her brother's sunny nature returning. "I hope she doesn't ask you for a pony, or you'll be in real trouble."

Rylan shook his head, the glow from the table lamp reflecting merriment in his brown eyes. "Bad enough she has Chester sleeping by her bed all the time."

Maggie took a spot on the sofa beside him, smoothing her skirts beneath her. "I always knew Chester was meant for this family. It's clear he adores Delia."

And Adam, she added silently. She hadn't told Rylan or Colleen about the mission she'd sent Adam on, just in case Ivy wasn't thriving in her new home. Maggie didn't want to burden Colleen and Rylan with any more bad news.

When a loud knock sounded on the front door, Maggie's heart gave an excited leap. "I'll get it."

Rylan exchanged a look with Colleen that told Maggie he suspected why she was so eager to get the door. He wasn't thrilled with the new state of her relationship with Adam, but Maggie felt confident Adam would win her brother over in the end.

At the front entrance, Maggie took a moment to smooth her hair before opening the door. In the waning evening light, Adam stood on the doorstep, holding a bundle against his shoulder.

Maggie's hand flew to her mouth. Instant tears sprang to her eyes.

He grinned. "May we come in?"

Silently, she moved aside and allowed him into the narrow corridor.

He held out the baby to her. "Hold her for a minute? I need to get something."

Maggie gladly cuddled the baby in her arms, hardly daring to think what this might mean for her brother and sister-in-law. Above the tiny face, Ivy's shock of dark hair peeked out from the blanket. Other than the lingering scent of cigarette smoke, the child didn't seem any the worse for wear.

Adam returned carrying a wooden cradle. "I stopped by the shop to pick this up. I made it before Jolene came to claim Ivy." He shrugged. "I didn't have the heart to give it away."

"Maggie, who was at the door?" Rylan strode into the hall. When he spied the baby, he stopped dead. "What's this?"

Adam removed his cap. "Maggie asked me to check on Ivy. I discovered she wasn't being properly cared for . . . so I brought her back."

Instead of the joy Maggie expected, Rylan's eyebrows thundered together. "I won't put my wife through the grief of losing this child again."

Adam held up a hand. "I made that very clear. Jolene has agreed to sign legal documents to allow you to adopt her."

Maggie held the child out to Rylan. "Why don't you go and give Colleen the most wonderful surprise?"

Rylan hesitated a second, then took the baby into his arms. "Hello, Ivy. We're happy to have you home again. I'm sure you want to see your mama."

Maggie clamped her lips together to contain her emotions as she and Adam followed Rylan into the parlor. Busy with her knitting, Colleen didn't look up right away. Only when Rylan stopped in front of her chair did she raise her head.

A strangled cry escaped her. She leapt to her feet, the wool falling to the floor.

"Ivy has come back to us, love." Rylan

held out the bundle to Colleen.

"Can this be true?" She gazed at the infant with absolute awe, then bent to kiss each cheek. With a sob, she hugged the baby to her neck and rocked her back and forth.

Maggie's own eyes misted with tears of joy.

Adam set the cradle on the floor beside Colleen's chair. "I told Jolene you'd have a lawyer draw up the necessary papers for her to sign, waiving her rights. Taking legal steps should ensure that she won't change her mind again."

"Adam, how can I ever thank you?" Her eyes awash with tears, Colleen leaned over to kiss his cheek.

He laid a hand on Ivy's head, so large yet so gentle. "This is all the thanks I need." His rough voice gave away the extremity of his emotions. He cleared his throat. "Um, the poor thing was in a bit of a mess. I tried to clean her up, but you might want to check the diaper."

Maggie choked back a giggle at the astonishment on Colleen's face, as though she couldn't imagine him changing a baby.

Colleen laughed. "I'll do that right away. Care to help me, Rylan?"

"Nothing would make me happier."

On the way out, Rylan paused in front of

Adam. "There are no words to thank you for what you've done. To see Colleen so happy again, after nearly losing both girls . . ." He broke off, unable to continue. Instead, he pulled Adam into a hard hug.

Adam blinked and gave him an awkward pat. "She's my sister. I'm glad I could do something for her."

When Rylan excused himself, Maggie chuckled at Adam's bewildered expression. "I see you're not familiar with my brother's exuberant expression of emotion."

"*Exuberant* is one way to describe it." Adam grinned, the lines on his forehead easing. "At least he's not scowling at me anymore. I still can't believe he's allowed me to court you."

Maggie moved close enough to see the variation of color in his beard. "I think he has his reservations, but this has definitely helped." She tilted her head. "When I asked you to check on Ivy, I didn't dare hope for this outcome. I only prayed you'd find her safe and healthy."

Adam's expression darkened. "It's a good thing you weren't there. No child should have to live like that."

Images of filth and degradation invaded her thoughts, and she breathed a prayer of thanksgiving that Adam had saved Ivy from such a fate. "Thank you for bringing her home."

His eyes shone an intense blue. "I'd do anything within my power to make you happy, Maggie."

She reached up on tiptoes and brushed a soft kiss across his lips. He wrapped his arms around her and kissed her back, his strength and gentleness enveloping her.

With God's blessing — and her brothers' — Maggie prayed she could stay safe in Adam's arms forever.

Adam's feet barely touched the ground as he made his way home. Not since his days as a young boy had such a sense of happiness saturated his heart.

Thank You, God, for Your blessings. For allowing me to bring Ivy back to Colleen, and for Maggie, who for some unfathomable reason loves me.

A grin stretched his face from ear to ear, and though he must look a fool, walking the streets of New York smiling at nothing, he couldn't seem to stop.

His thoughts turned to the gift of his mother's unexpected recovery. It amazed him how God had used a bad situation to bring about good. Mama's illness had been terrifying, yet it had given Adam a chance to see James in a different light, as though the blinders had fallen away and the truth had been revealed. In those uncertain days, they'd come a long way toward healing their relationship. A feat he'd never dreamed possible.

Now if he could just make a success of his shop, perhaps he'd achieve respectability in his father's eyes — at last.

The warmth of his newfound happiness carried him all the way to the corner of his street — until the sound of alarm bells and people yelling pulled an icy chill through his veins. A crowd had gathered in front of the mercantile. Smoke billowed upward from the roof of the buildings. Old Mr. Sampson, the proprietor, stood in the road, waving at the firemen jumping from the truck.

On a rush of adrenaline, Adam raced forward. If the mercantile was on fire, he needed to help put it out and make sure it didn't spread.

When he reached the next corner, his feet faltered. The horrible truth smacked him in the face like a bucket of cold water. *His* shop was on fire. The firemen aimed their hoses at the flames and smoke pouring out of his store.

Alternate currents of heat and ice raced

from Adam's head to his toes. He tried to rush past the crowd, but Mr. Sampson grabbed his arm. "You can't go in there, son. It's too far gone."

"I have to save the furniture."

"It's too late." The man stood with his shirttail flapping. "We thought it was our store at first. By the time we sounded the alarm —"

A high-pitched buzzing in Adam's ears drowned out the words. He had to do something before all was lost. Adam sprinted down the side alley of the mercantile toward the back entrance to his workshop. Furious thoughts pounded through his brain. If the fire was mostly in front, maybe he'd have time to save some inventory.

Sweat poured off Adam's forehead as he pushed through the rear door. A thick cloud of smoke immediately encircled him. He coughed, covered his face with his arm, and forged on, relying on his memory to guide him. Like a blind man, he felt his way across the room, grabbed what felt like a cabinet, and hefted it onto his shoulder. As quickly as possible, he made his way outside to the back lane. Eyes stinging from the smoke, he dropped the cabinet and fell to his knees, fighting to get air into his lungs. After a fit of coughing, he pushed to his feet and headed back inside. Whispers of panic threatened to overwhelm him. He wouldn't — couldn't — allow himself to think he might lose everything.

This time the smoke was thicker, and intense heat blasted him from the store. Flames licked the wall between the front room and the workshop, but Adam pressed on. If he could rescue another few pieces, maybe all his work wouldn't have been in vain.

Barely able to open his eyes, he made his way to the bench, feeling his way until he hit a large solid object — the table he'd been sanding. He lifted it and inched his way back through the intense smoke. Flames hissed and crackled, as if warning Adam of their approach. His lungs screamed for air. Where was the opening?

He gasped in a breath, but his lungs seized in a fit of coughing. He crashed to his knees, ramming the table against his chest. Heat engulfed him from all sides. He had to get up.

Lord, help me!

With his last surge of energy, he crawled across the floor in the direction of the door. Flames scorched the air around him. The floorboards vibrated as he crawled on, an inch at a time. In the distance, voices shouted. He kept his face low to the floor, but his lungs spasmed, attempting to steal oxygen. When he thought he could go no farther, hands clamped on his arms and dragged him outside.

Blessed coolness bathed his face. He sucked in great gulps of air, yet his body failed to register the fact that he could now breathe.

His chest seemed to collapse as darkness overtook him.

32

The morning sun streamed in through the kitchen window, bathing Colleen and little Ivy in an almost angelic light. A thrill of delight slid through Maggie as she watched Colleen rock the child after her morning bottle. Despite the upheaval of the previous day, Ivy seemed in fine spirits. Bathed, dressed in clean clothing, and now with a full tummy, she dozed contentedly in Colleen's arms. Colleen gazed at the babe with such tenderness that silly tears brimmed in Maggie's eyes. Tears of happiness.

Thank You, Lord, for seeing us through the typhoid crisis with our loved ones unharmed and for the added miracle of Ivy's homecoming. Rylan and Colleen deserve this happy ending.

Maggie hummed to herself as she washed the breakfast dishes, looking forward to getting back to work at the orphanage. Maybe she'd have a chance to give a few piano lessons today, if the children's schedule allowed.

She turned from the sink, wiping her hands on a towel, as Rylan entered the kitchen. Words of greeting died on her lips at the distressed lines around Rylan's eyes.

"I'm afraid I have some bad news."

Maggie stilled, praying Mrs. O'Leary hadn't suffered a relapse.

But Rylan wasn't looking at his wife. His sympathetic brown eyes were trained on Maggie. "You'd best take a seat."

She sank onto a kitchen chair, her heart thudding in her chest. "What is it?"

Rylan crouched beside her, his face even with hers, and took her hand in his. "There was a fire last night. Adam's shop burned down."

Maggie's blood ran hot then cold. "No."

"Adam was taken to the hospital."

The air whooshed from Maggie's body, and she sagged like a rag doll. The room swam around her.

Colleen leaned over the table to clutch Maggie's other hand. "Dear God. Is he all right?"

"I don't know, love. His friend, John McNabb, called to tell me. He was about to go up to the hospital to see him."

On a burst of frantic energy, Maggie

pushed up from her chair and lunged toward the door. She tore off her apron with shaking hands. "Which streetcar do I take to get to the hospital?"

Colleen rose with little Ivy in the crook of her arm. "Rylan, you must take Maggie and find out how Adam is."

Rylan straightened and nodded. "All right. Let me get my hat."

The trip to the hospital went by in a blur, with Maggie only vaguely aware of the streetcar ride. She thanked God that Rylan was with her to ask all the pertinent questions at the hospital reception desk when they arrived. Maggie's brain seemed frozen, incapable of one coherent thought, other than to pray for Adam.

A nurse ushered them to a large ward in the main wing, consisting of many beds, most of them with the curtains drawn. She motioned to a seating area. "You can wait here. The doctor is in with him now. He won't be long."

Maggie couldn't sit. She paced the floor, trying to ignore the moans of the patients. The strong medicinal scent of antiseptic and cleanser seared Maggie's nostrils, forcing her to cover her nose with her handkerchief. At last, the curtain around Adam's bed moved and a nurse emerged carrying a tray

476

of medical supplies.

Maggie moved to intercept her. "Excuse me, can you tell us how Mr. O'Leary is?"

The woman stopped. "Are you a family member?"

Rylan stepped up beside Maggie. "Yes, we are."

The nurse glanced back at the curtain. "The doctor is finishing his examination. I can tell you that Mr. O'Leary suffered a few burns, and his lungs have been somewhat compromised from the smoke. But other than that, he should be fine."

Maggie's legs went limp. Rylan's hand under her elbow was the only thing that kept her upright. "May we see him?"

"You'll have to wait for the doctor to determine that."

"Thank you." Maggie pressed the handkerchief back to her mouth. Loose strands of hair clung to the moisture on her cheeks. Adam was going to be okay. *Praise be to God.*

Rylan guided her to a nearby chair.

Maggie sat, twisting the handkerchief between her fingers, fighting to hold back tears of gratitude and frustration. How could God let this happen to Adam just when he was turning his life around?

She swallowed hard, determination

straightening her spine against the hard metal chair. She had to stay strong for Adam.

Maggie's gaze darted to the curtain, where Dr. Reardon now exited. She jumped to her feet.

His eyebrows rose when he spied her. "Hello, Miss Montgomery." He looked past her and must have noticed Rylan. "Mr. Montgomery. I hope all is well at the orphanage?"

Rylan stepped forward to shake his hand. "Yes. Everyone is recovering nicely. But we're here to see about Adam."

Maggie had no time for pleasantries. "How is he, Doctor?"

Dr. Reardon shook his head. "He's a lucky man. If not for someone pulling him out of the building, he would have died."

Maggie pressed her lips together to keep from crying out.

Rylan wrapped an arm around her. "Is he able to go home, or does he need treatment?"

Dr. Reardon tapped the chart in his hand. "I'll discharge him later today. He'll have to take it easy for a day or two and come back to have the burns re-bandaged."

Maggie didn't wait to hear anything else. She pushed aside the curtain and found

Adam lying on top of a narrow bed, covered by a thin, white sheet. Black smudges marred his cheeks and nose, accentuating the pallor of his skin. Thick gauze bandages covered his hands and areas of his forearms.

She rested her palm on his cheek. "Adam? Can you hear me?"

His eyes fluttered open. For a moment, he blinked at the ceiling before he turned his head to focus on her face. The bleakness of his stare caused the blood to freeze in her veins.

"It's all gone, Maggie. The shop . . . everything's destroyed."

The complete lack of hope on his face tore at Maggie's composure. Tears spilled down her face. "It's okay, my love. As long as you're alive, nothing else matters." Even as she spoke the words, she knew they were not true for him.

He shook his head. "This was my chance to start over. Now it's gone. All the furniture I created, the restoration pieces, every-thing . . ." He closed his eyes, his mouth pressed into a hard line.

Maggie ran her hand over his hair, mur-muring soothing words to him, wishing she could think of something to ease the pain in his soul. The burns would heal, but she feared he might never recover from losing his dream.

"The doctor says you can leave soon. Come back with us to Colleen's. Let us take care of you."

"No." The anguish fled from his demeanor, replaced with a cold, shuttered look. "I'll go back to my cot in the basement, where I belong." The bitterness of his words tore a strip from Maggie's already bleeding heart.

He shoved up from the bed. The sheet slipped off to reveal his bare chest, where angry welts were visible through the mat of his hair. He grabbed his shirt from a chair and stuffed his arms into the sleeves, then yanked on his boots and pushed to his feet.

Icy prickles of fear pierced Maggie's heart. "Wait. Where are you going?" She scrambled to follow him through the ward.

Rylan spied them and moved to intercept Adam. "Slow down, lad. You've been through a terrible ordeal. Colleen and I want you to come and stay with us."

Adam shoved past him, fastening his shirt buttons as he went. "Thank you, but I'll be fine at John's." His words spat out like bullets.

Maggie flinched with the sting of his rejection. Why would he turn away from his family at this time of crisis — right when he needed their support the most? She rushed over to him. "Please, Adam, let us help you."

He looked at her fully for the first time, his eyes as dead as the wood he carved. Slowly he shook his head. "I should have known this was all too good to be true. I'm sorry, Maggie, but you're better off without me."

With that, he charged down the hall, each step reverberating in the now-hushed space, leaving Maggie feeling more bereft than she'd ever been before.

33

Adam stood in the street before the blackened shell of his shop, the burns on his
hands and arms throbbing a painful rhythm
that matched the ache in his soul. The horrible stench of burnt wood lingered in the
air, a bitter reminder of the destruction of
his dreams. On stiffened limbs, he walked
into what remained of the store. His lungs
— not yet recovered — wheezed in response
to the acrid smoke that inhabited the space.
Though scorched, the main walls remained
standing, but little else had survived.

Blackness had invaded Adam's heart, and
he barely resisted the urge to shake his fist
at the heavens. Clearly this was God's
punishment, giving Adam a taste of happiness only to wrench it away.

With the toe of his boot, he kicked at a
pile of debris, unearthing a metal handle
from one of the cabinets. He picked it up,
wiped the soot from it, and stuffed it in his

pocket. A grim souvenir of everything he'd lost.

Adam forced himself to continue on to the workshop, to the place where he'd almost lost his life. His muscles tightened to the point of pain at the unrecognizable sight before him. Nothing remained but the charred skeleton of his workbench and the outer walls. His inventory had turned to ash. A harsh laugh gurgled in his throat. What a naïve fool he'd been to think he could start over.

Adam grabbed a stick and thrust it into the rubble. From the midst of the wreckage, an oval piece of wood jutted out. He pulled it free and stared down at the sign he'd created to hang out front. *O'Leary's Furniture Emporium,* carved and ready to paint. Now only a disfigured letter *O* remained visible.

The charred remnant of his ruined dreams.

Rage spread like a toxin through his system. With an unholy roar, he spun around and hurled the useless piece at the blackened wall. It hit with a sickening crack and splintered into several chunks before falling to the dirt below.

The thunder of his fury, as loud and as blistering as the howl of the flames the night before, buzzed in his ears. He stumbled across the area to what was left of his workbench, raised it above his head, and heaved it with all his might through the back door, shattering what remained of the frame. Like a madman, he careened around the shop, hurling planks and chunks of debris, destroying every piece of usable wood. When at last his muscles burned worse than his battered hands, and his lungs screamed from the exertion, he sank to his knees in the midst of the ash and rubble and wept.

Maggie wrapped her shawl about her shoulders as she left the choir loft and descended to the foyer below. A distinct chill pervaded the vestibule, a sign that summer would soon turn to autumn. Or perhaps the chill lived only inside her — a chill that nothing could chase away. If she hadn't made a commitment to Mr. Unger that required practice time, she never would have left her room today. Would have wallowed under the covers until her heart stopped aching.

Mr. Unger crossed the foyer toward her, the movement causing the votive candles to cast eerie shadows against the walls. "That was some intense playing, young lady." He folded his hands over his ample belly, where the buttons of his vest pulled a little too tight. "I think something has made you either very mad or very sad." He chuckled at his own remark but quickly sobered when she did not join his laughter. "Oh, my dear, you seem greatly troubled. Can I help?"

Maggie swallowed hard. "I'm afraid not, Mr. Unger. But thank you. I'd best be on my way. As usual, I lost track of the time."

"Would you like me to accompany you to the streetcar?"

Maggie pulled her shawl tighter and shivered. Though she didn't relish having to make polite conversation, she couldn't turn down his protection. "That's kind of you, thank you."

"Mr. Unger?" A voice echoed through the cavernous area, preceding the swish of a priest's robes. "I'm sorry to interrupt, but there's an urgent phone call from your wife."

Mr. Unger turned, creases etched in his forehead. "Miss Montgomery, will you wait while I take the call?"

Maggie hesitated, hating to delay, but what else could she do? "Of course."

She waited at least fifteen minutes, but as each moment passed, her nerves edged higher. The afternoon was slipping away. She wanted to get home before Colleen and the children returned from the orphanage, in time to help with the evening meal.

When five more minutes had passed, Maggie could stand it no longer. She pushed out the main doors and onto the street, hoping Mr. Unger would understand. The fresh air was a welcome balm to her nerves as she walked down Fifth Avenue, until a few blocks later, when the amount of pedestrians thinned. She hoped there would be more people once she reached the streetcar stop.

Nerves as taut as the strings of a piano, Maggie rushed to step off a curb. A man grasped her by the elbow, pulling her away from a carriage that careened around the corner, barely missing her.

"Be careful, darlin'. The streets aren't safe — especially for a woman alone."

Icy fingers of fear raced up her spine at the familiar lilt. "Neill." She tried to pull her arm away, but his steely grip was unbreakable.

"Good thing I'm here to walk you home."

"I'd rather be alone, thank you." She did her best to sound haughty, to hide the alarm building inside her.

"Where is your friend today? The one who usually guards you like a vicious hound?"

She whirled on him, fear turning to rage. "Adam is none of your concern."

One brow arched in a mocking manner. "I beg to differ. A man who insists on kissing my fiancée is most definitely my concern."

Maggie's insides went cold. Neill must have been watching her all this time. Plotting, planning, obsessing . . .

The grip on her arm tightened. Neill forced her down a less-populated street, his stride quickening. "I doubt he'll be a problem any longer. Unless he's not smart enough to understand the message I sent him last night."

Goosebumps rose on the back of Maggie's neck at his menacing tone. Her heart thudded so hard she feared it would fly from her chest. "You caused the fire?"

He shot her a scathing sideways glance. "What do you think?"

Dear Lord, is the man insane? He'd been spying on her and Adam, and now, because of his obsession, he'd destroyed Adam's dreams for the future.

Maggie searched for someone who might help her, but other than a horse and carriage in the distance, they were alone.

"None of that matters any longer," Neill said, "since we're leaving for Ireland tonight."

Maggie's terror mounted, leaving her

momentarily without words.

A gust of wind blew dirt and debris around their feet. "If you cooperate, I'll allow you to stop at your brother's first. You can pack a few things and leave them a note saying that you've decided to marry me, after all." He turned hard eyes on her. "If you don't cooperate, we will bypass the house altogether and head straight for the docks. You can mail them a letter from the ship."

She wrenched her arm free. "You're mad. I'm not going anywhere with you." Surging forward, she managed to get a few strides away from him before he caught up with her.

"Oh, I think you'll change your mind — once I make my intentions clear."

Her footsteps faltered, the sinister quality of his voice rattling her so that she could barely think. "What do you mean?"

"I've taken care of your friend. Don't make me take similar measures with your family."

She shivered and pushed away the fear that gripped her. Would Neill really harm Rylan or Colleen or the children? She couldn't take the chance that he might.

"Oh, and in case you think you can out-smart me, I have one more incentive to consider." He pulled a pistol from the folds of his overcoat. Light from a store window gleamed off the cold metal barrel. "Don't think I won't use it on anyone who gets in my way."

Maggie's insides solidified into a ball of terror. For now, she had no recourse but to play along until she saw an opportunity to escape. She squared her shoulders. "I'll come with you, if you promise to leave Adam and my family alone."

With a smug smile, Neill shoved the gun back into his pocket. "I always knew you were a smart one. Come. We'd best hurry. The ship won't wait for us if we're late."

Gabe stood on the upper deck of the steamship and hunched his shoulders against the biting wind. After numerous long days at sea, today he would reach his home, yet the surge of joy he'd expected on returning to Ireland was missing.

The pallor of war had cast a shadow of gloom over everyone on board the ship, passengers and crew alike. That and the ache in his heart over missing Aurora weighed heavy on Gabe's soul.

He walked to the railing and peered out over the vast expanse of unending water, hoping for a small glimpse of land, a beacon to welcome him home. A silly gesture, for it would likely be hours before the appearance of any shoreline. Nothing but the grayness of the sea, as well as a creeping fog, met his eyes. As dull and hopeless as his present mood.

Gabe had no clear picture of what his immediate future held. Other than getting home to his mother and brothers and finding out exactly how the war was affecting his countrymen, his plans seemed as murky as the waters below him. What would he do if the British army demanded he and his brothers enlist to fight with them? Before he'd left Ireland, he'd itched to join a war that would ensure the freedom of his country from British rule. But now, to be forced to fight as a British soldier? The thought brought a wave of nausea through his system. Or perhaps the rough seas were responsible.

Gabe pulled the collar of his coat up around his ears and turned to head back to his cabin. If he were lucky, he could escape his tortured thoughts for a few hours of sleep before they docked.

Shouts and frantic footsteps sounded from the captain's deck, followed by a loud explosion. The ship gave a sudden lurch, sending Gabe hurtling across the wooden boards.

He grappled to find purchase but crashed into a wall. Pain shot through the back of his head as he slid across the floor. A deluge of water sprayed over the deck, saturating him instantly, filling his mouth with salty brine.

Through the haze of his vision, Gabe noted that the deck remained tilted at a strange angle.

"We've been hit!" A crewman crawled by him on the slanted surface.

"Man the lifeboats!"

His heart pumping at a furious pace, Gabe grasped the railing and attempted to pull himself up. He had one last glimpse of a wall of water descending before another explosion sent him flying.

His last conscious thought before the waves swallowed him was of Aurora.

34

When Adam's emotions had been spent, leaving his insides as hollowed out as his shell of a store, he pushed bleakly to his feet. His knees ached from the time spent on the hard ground, and he stumbled until his joints started working again. A coughing fit hit him, so intense it seemed his body was determined to expel his very lungs. When the spasms finally eased, Adam became aware of noises in the outer room.

Was someone out there?

He swiped his face with the sleeve of his smoke-laden shirt and made his way to the front. Two lit lanterns hung from blackened nails on the remains of a wall, brightening the area. When had it become dusk?

Clad in a long, black apron, John whisked a straw broom over the floor, a cloud of soot almost enveloping his tall frame.

"What are you doing? This isn't your job." Adam could not even regret the harshness of his tone.

John, however, kept sweeping. "I'm helping a friend who would do the same for me if I were in trouble."

Adam fought another rush of emotion that threatened to close his throat.

John glanced over his shoulder. "There's another broom over there if you care to join me."

At a loss, but not about to let John work alone, Adam picked up the tool. In silence, they swept the debris into piles, then, using a shovel, began to fill the large barrels John had brought with him.

"I spoke with Chief Witherspoon last night after you'd been taken to the hospital." John leaned on his broom for a small respite.

Adam looked up. "You were here?"

"Who do you think helped drag you out of the building?"

Adam sucked in a breath. "You? But how did you even know about the fire?"

"A parishioner called to tell me. I came straight over. Never expected to find you risking your neck for a piece of wood."

John's amused look tempered his scolding, yet the enormity of the danger he had faced for Adam's sake brought about a wave of shame. What if he'd lost his life on Adam's account?

"I don't know what to say, John. You've rescued me more times than I can count."

John's unrelenting gaze held Adam's. "The only thing I want to rescue is your soul. Don't let this misfortune define you, Adam. Trust God to help you pick up the pieces and carry on. He won't forsake you."

Adam swallowed the bitterness on his tongue. "Right now I'm not sure I can believe that." He resumed sweeping with the vigor of his anger.

"Then it's my job to keep reminding you." John moved toward him. "I wasn't sure if I should mention this or not . . ." He hesitated. "Since the building is leased to me, the chief gave me some information I think you should know."

At the seriousness of his tone, Adam stopped working. "What is it?"

"The chief believes this may be a case of arson."

"Arson?" The word slammed into Adam with the force of an anvil. Who would do such a thing? It made no sense. Could someone have gotten wind of Adam's past and objected to an ex-convict opening a shop here? Someone who believed he might be bad for business?

Adam heaved the shovel into the trash pile, bitterness leaving an acidic taste in his mouth. Would this be his fate for the rest of his life, constantly dodging a barrage of prejudice and hatred, all because of a past mistake? God might forgive him, his family might even forgive him, but many others would not.

"Did I hear you say *arson*?"

Adam looked up to see Mr. Sampson picking his way across the debris. A flare of unease surfaced. "That's right. Why?"

The old man tugged at one of his suspenders. "Like I told the constable last night, I noticed a stranger on the edge of the crowd. Seemed real interested in what was going on. Asked about you in particular."

Adam's blood turned cold. "What did the man look like?"

Sampson moved closer, chewing on a toothpick. "Decent enough. Had a pretty nasty scar on his jaw, though. Imagined he was a friend of yours at first, but he seemed almost disappointed when the reverend here got you out."

Adam's heart stalled. "Fitzgerald."

"Who?" John came up beside him.

Adam paced the floor, kicking up a cloud of dust as he moved. "Maggie's former fiancé." Adam clenched his fists at his sides. What did this mean? Was Maggie in danger, or was this message aimed solely at Adam?

Suddenly the loss of his shop and all its contents faded in importance. The only true thing that mattered was Maggie's safety. As long as she was all right, Adam could bear any misfortune.

"I'm sorry, John. I have to go and warn Maggie. I'll see you later."

After pounding on Rylan's door for what seemed like several minutes, Adam startled when the door yanked open. Colleen stood on the threshold, baby Ivy in her arms.

"I need to speak with Maggie. It's urgent."

"You're too late." She stared at him with a dull look. "Maggie's gone."

The hair on his arms stood on end. "What do you mean? Gone where?"

Sorrow drifted across her features. "Back to Ireland . . . with Neill Fitzgerald."

White flames of terror exploded through his torso, and his breathing thinned. "That's ridiculous. She'd never go anywhere with him, especially not back to Ireland."

Without a word, Colleen walked into the parlor. Adam forced his feet into action and followed her. She laid Ivy in her cradle and moved to the desk in the corner, where she picked up a piece of paper. "When I got home from the orphanage this afternoon, I found this." Her accusing glare challenged

Adam. "Maggie said you broke her heart and she could no longer bear to stay here."

Adam took the page and scanned the hastily penned note. "This says they're leaving tonight." He raked a hand over his jaw, his brain whirling to take in the magnitude of the situation. He looked up. "Where's Rylan?"

"Gone to look for her, of course. But it's been over an hour now." His sister's brows slashed her forehead in obvious concern.

"Fitzgerald's dangerous, Colleen. I believe he caused the fire at my shop. He must be forcing Maggie to go with him." Adam jammed his hat on and headed to the door.

Little Delia and Chester appeared in the hall. Traces of moisture shone on the girl's tiny cheeks. "Uncle Adam, Aunt Maggie left without saying good-bye. Will you bring her back, please?"

The sight of her blue eyes awash in tears twisted like a knife in Adam's chest. He knelt down to hug her. "I'll do my best, sweetheart." He kissed the top of her head, nodded to Colleen, and dashed out the door.

All the way to the waterfront, Adam begged God to spare Maggie, to save her from the maniac's clutches, and prayed that, by some chance, Rylan had already found her.

But an hour later, after scouring the docks of the Hudson River without finding Rylan or Maggie, Adam's hope began to fade. He stopped to scan the fleets of ships lining the harbor. How would he know which one of these boats they were on? The distinct possibility that they may have already left haunted him, as did the certainty of what Fitzgerald would do to Maggie once they'd set sail.

Helpless fury pulsed through his veins, adding to the throbbing of his wounds. Dusk had turned to full inky blackness. Dampness from the mist hovering over the water sank into Adam's bones. He blew on his stiff fingers, his desperation mounting.

Please Lord, help me find her.

Shoring up his determination, he doubled back toward the ships' offices. Maybe one of the men there would remember something. A woman as beautiful as Maggie would surely stand out. . . .

The sound of raised voices caught Adam's attention, spiking a rush of adrenaline. Maybe Rylan had found Maggie and needed his help. He sprinted off toward the ruckus, dodging crates and barrels, until he saw two men arguing near the steamship office.

The man with his back to Adam raised a hand. "But I have two tickets here already paid for."

"Nothing I can do about it, mister." The second huskier man moved away, revealing a woman standing to one side.

Adam's heart screamed to a halt in his chest.

Maggie.

35

Standing on the dock, Maggie winced as the sharp bite of wind tore through her clothing. She clutched her cloak tighter around her in a vain attempt to ward off the dampness, yet nothing stopped the cold press of fear that invaded her soul. The scent of rotting fish assaulted her senses, adding to the nausea that roiled her stomach. While Neill negotiated with a steward about their passage, she recited every prayer she knew, even resorting to bargaining with God, in a desperate attempt to procure a miracle. Anything to keep from boarding that ship. As time went on with no such miracle in sight, an overwhelming sense of the hopelessness threatened to drown her.

She blinked back tears, forcing her mind away from the imagined hurt and confusion on Rylan and Colleen's faces when they read her letter. Only the knowledge of the type of terror Neill was capable of unleashing on them — as well as the reminder of the gun in his pocket — had given Maggie the strength to pen the note and leave. The fact that she'd had to use Adam's rejection as an excuse filled her with guilt. Rylan would no doubt pay Adam an unpleasant and undeserved visit to let him know exactly what he thought of his treatment of Maggie.

How would Adam react to learning that she had left the country with Neill — after all he'd done to protect her from him? Pain radiated through Maggie's heart at the thought of adding one more misery to Adam's life.

Loud voices brought her focus back to her present surroundings. Neill shook his fist at the steward outside the office, leading Maggie to believe that things weren't going as planned. What would happen if they couldn't get on a ship tonight? She scanned the area around her. Surely Neill wouldn't expect her to stay in one of the filthy boarding houses meant for sailors. Yet if he did, might it offer her a chance to escape?

A flash of movement farther down the dock claimed her attention, and she froze.

Dear God, it can't be.

"Maggie!" Adam sped toward her at a flat run, his jacket flying out behind him as he dodged men loading crates onto a wagon. "Maggie, wait."

Her initial leap of joy at the sight of him changed to terror when Neill whirled around. The moment he spied Adam, Neill yanked her to his side, holding her captive with arms like iron bands.

"Remember what I have in my pocket," he hissed into her ear. "I'll have no qualms about putting a bullet in him."

Her knees shook beneath her skirts. How would she ever convince Adam she was leaving willingly with Neill? She stiffened her legs and steeled herself to do what she must to ensure his safety.

"Come to wish us *bon voyage,* O'Leary? How very civilized of you." Neill's deceptively pleasant tone sent shivers across Maggie's spine.

"Let her go, Fitzgerald. She's not going anywhere with you." The wind whipped his hair across his forehead. His eyes glinted like blue steel.

Maggie's arm ached from the increased pressure of Neill's fingers. She clamped her lips together to keep from crying out. A ship's horn gave a mournful blare that matched the bleakness of her soul.

"I'm afraid you're mistaken. Maggie begged me to take her home, and I'm more than happy to oblige."

"You lying piece of filth." Adam charged forward.

Neill held out his hand. "Stop right there. Maggie, tell him I speak the truth. You're coming home to marry me."

She could feel the weight of Neill's stare boring into her as she kept her eyes trained on Adam. Neill shifted so that the hard press of the gun bit into her side. She swallowed hard and lifted her chin. For Adam's sake, she had to make him leave. "It's true. There's nothing left for me here."

"You're going to marry *him*?" His hoarse question tore through Maggie's heart like a dagger — ripping, rending, destroying.

"Yes," she whispered, her lie barely audible above the noise on the dock. Her eyes burned from keeping them open, certain that if she blinked, something unspeakable would happen.

He crossed his arms over his chest, his gaze never leaving hers. "I don't believe you. He's forcing you to go with him." He stepped toward her, his face wreathed in agony. "Don't do this, Maggie. Come with me."

Her heart shredded further. If only she could.

She opened her mouth to say something,

but the words wouldn't shake loose.

Neill shoved her behind him. "She's made her choice, O'Leary. I suggest you accept it. Go back and rebuild that shop of yours while you still can."

Adam clenched his hands at his sides until his knuckles ached. The temper he'd been suppressing whipped into a haze of rage, threatening to break free of its shackles, yet still he held back. He needed to be smart to outwit this piece of scum.

Adam had never known Maggie to lie to him, but she was lying now. The panic on her face told him so. Short of killing the man, what could Adam do to free her from his clutches once and for all?

Time seemed to stand still. Maggie struggled against Neill's grasp as he pushed her behind him. She stumbled, tripping over her skirts, and hit the dock with a sharp cry.

Anger became a living beast inside Adam, roaring for release, urging him to rid Maggie of Fitzgerald forever. Yet if he did so, Adam would surely hang for murder or, at the very least, face a life term in prison.

A price he'd willingly pay to save Maggie from an even worse type of prison.

Fitzgerald stepped toward him, silently

daring him to take action, and the ugly truth hit Adam hard. He would have to sacrifice his freedom to ensure hers.

Despite the chill in the night air, beads of sweat banded under his cap and dripped down his temple. He dared not move or break eye contact with the enemy.

Behind Neill, Maggie scrambled to her feet and attempted to push past him, but he snagged her around the waist.

Adam charged forward a second time.

"Adam! No!" she cried. "He's not worth it."

Adam met her frantic gaze. "You're right, Maggie. He's not worth it — but you are."

"Come on then, coward." The taunt in Fitzgerald's voice matched the sneer on his face. "Show her what you're made of. Defend her questionable honor."

Adam exploded forward and plowed his fist into Fitzgerald's arrogant face. The cad flew backward, crashing into a mooring post. Before he could regain his senses, Adam grabbed him by the front of his jacket and hauled him up. Blood oozed from Fitzgerald's nose, dripping onto his fancy overcoat.

The scent of blood added to the rush of violence surging through Adam's veins, begging him to obliterate this sorry excuse for a human. But the roar of a more powerful force vibrated between his ears.

Love your enemies, bless them that curse you, do good to them that hate you.

Adam could hear John's clear voice in his head, citing the passage from Matthew he'd made Adam memorize. Words of wisdom that had held him in good stead during his incarceration and helped him keep a cool head in the prison yard.

Adam fought to calm his erratic breathing and slow his pulse rate. Fought to control the anger that still hungered for release.

He pushed Fitzgerald away from him with a snort of disgust. The lout stumbled against the rope fence that surrounded the water.

Adam moved quickly to Maggie's side. Tears stood out in her wide eyes, and she clutched the lapel of his jacket. "Be careful. He has a gun."

Adam jerked. A gun changed everything. "Run, Maggie. Go find Rylan. He's out looking for you."

"I'm not leaving you."

Adam turned to find that Neill had risen to his feet and was fumbling to pull something from his pocket.

Adam had one chance to act. With an enraged bellow, he charged. Maggie's scream pierced the air, sending the gulls into a frenzy of fluttering wings.

The second before Adam reached him, triumph flashed in Neill's eyes. An explosion shattered the night. Searing heat blasted through Adam's chest and radiated out through his torso. He glanced down at his shirt, stunned to see a crimson stain seeping through the material. His legs turned to rubber. Clutching his chest, he turned to find Maggie. "Run." The word came out as a croak. Had she even heard him?

Fat tears spilled down Maggie's horrified face. He wanted to comfort her — tell her not to cry, tell her he loved her — but his eyes fluttered closed, breaking their connection.

Then the world went black around him.

36

Maggie stared in horror as Adam crumpled to the ground. Behind him, gun in hand, Neill rushed toward her. She didn't care if he pulled the trigger. If Adam died, she wanted to die, as well.

Maggie dropped to her knees beside Adam's body. She pulled the shawl off her head, wadded it into a ball, and pressed it against Adam's wound.

Shouts and footfalls drifted toward her, as though coming from a great distance. She looked over in time to see a burly dock-worker swing at Neill with a club. Neill raised a hand to ward off the blow and the gun flew across the ground.

"Somebody get help!" Her shout seemed too weak to garner attention, yet she heard others take up her plea.

"Get a doctor."

"Call for the ambulance. A man's been shot!"

Around her, snatches of conversation and shouts from onlookers buzzed in the background of her consciousness. Her sole focus remained on keeping Adam alive. From his shallow breathing, she determined he hadn't left her — yet.

When Maggie glanced up again, a familiar face came into view, one that brought a rush of emotion to her throat. She waved her free arm.

Winded, Rylan rushed over and crouched beside her. "Maggie! Are you all right?"

"Aye, but Adam's been shot." Her voice broke on a sob.

"The steward has called for an ambulance. They'll be here soon."

A tear fell from her chin and landed on Adam's neck, sliding down to his collar. "Hang on, Adam. Help is coming."

Please God, don't let him die.

Rylan pried her cold, stiff fingers away from the blood-soaked shawl. "Let me take over."

She conceded, realizing he could apply better pressure than she. She laid a stained hand on Adam's cheek, silently willing him to live. Beneath his beard, his face had turned a deathly shade of gray. Just when Maggie thought she'd go mad, a murmur went through the crowd of onlookers, and two men came forward carrying a stretcher.

They moved Adam onto it with Rylan still pressing the wound. Together, they rose as one and made their way to the horse-drawn ambulance waiting at the foot of the docks.

Clutching her skirts, Maggie followed, standing helplessly by while they loaded Adam into the back of the vehicle. She went to climb in after them, but one of the men stopped her.

"I'm sorry, miss. You'll have to find your own way to the hospital."

Maggie's temper flared. "I'm going with him. Someone has to make sure he doesn't bleed to death on the ride."

The second man had taken over from Rylan, holding Maggie's shawl to staunch the blood flow.

"Fred will do that, miss. Now we'd best be on our way. The sooner the doctor sees him, the better chance he'll have."

Rylan gently pulled her back so the men could close the gate at the back of the wagon.

"Come on, love. We'll find a way there."

"Not yet, sir. I'm afraid I need the young lady to come with me." A police officer stepped out of the crowd. "I'm Officer O'Brien of the New York Constabulary. I understand you witnessed the shooting."

Maggie only nodded. Her attention remained fixated on the ambulance as it pulled away. Fear wrenched her heart, turning and twisting in her chest. Would she ever see Adam alive again? She pressed a fist to her mouth to keep from sobbing.

Rylan's arm came around her shoulders. "My sister was kidnapped by the man who shot Mr. O'Leary."

The officer pulled out a notebook. "Then the sooner you provide us with the information, the sooner you can get to the hospital."

Now that the excitement was over, the crowd dissipated. The dock workers returned to loading barrels onto the cargo ships. A few stragglers murmured to themselves about the dangerous people trying to get passage.

A type of numbness invaded Maggie's limbs, spreading through her body. The ambulance had moved out of her sight. She couldn't do anything for Adam right now except help to catch the man who'd harmed him. She sucked in a long breath. "Will you provide us a ride to the hospital when we're finished?"

The officer nodded. "Agreed."

"Very well," she said. "Let's go."

The cold light of dawn crept through the

window in the hospital waiting room where Maggie stood, staring out. She'd hoped the coming of morning would erase the bleakness from her soul, but the light did little to ease her fears. She'd spent most of the night pacing the room, unable to rest. Each time she closed her eyes, all she could envision was Adam's lifeless face as the ambulance took him away.

After she'd given all the information she could to the constable, he had kept his word and driven her and Rylan to the hospital. Partway through the night, she'd sent Rylan home, insisting that Colleen would be frantic and that Maggie would be fine on her own. Adam had been taken into surgery, leaving her with nothing to do but wait . . . and pray.

Pray that Neill hadn't killed him.

A sob caught in her throat, but she pushed it back. She had to stay strong. If Adam made it through the operation, he would need her strength to help him recover.

Maggie stared at her discolored hands clasped on her lap. She hadn't wanted to wash away that last contact with Adam — the visible reminder of his sacrifice, of the precious blood he'd spilled for her. Adam had lost everything — his shop, his dream for the future, perhaps his very life — all because of her. She'd brought nothing but disaster to the man she loved.

In the stillness of the empty room, Maggie fought to hold on to her faith. To feel that God cared what happened to her and to Adam. That He had everything under control.

Where are You, Lord? I need You. Adam needs You.

Only a hollow echo of footsteps in the corridor broke the silence.

Unable to stand her own thoughts any longer, Maggie left the waiting room and walked out to the nearest nurses' area.

A woman raised her head from the sheet of paper where she was recording some information. "May I help you?"

"Could you tell me how Adam O'Leary is doing? He went in for surgery hours ago."

The plump, motherly-looking woman scanned Maggie's face and clothing, halting at her blood-stained hands. "Are you a relative, dear?"

Maggie nodded, hoping the woman didn't ask her to explain their relationship. She didn't know if any of the other O'Learys had been informed of the shooting, and if so, whether anyone would come. Colleen would likely arrive soon, but Maggie couldn't wait any longer to find out if Adam was alive.

"Just a moment," the nurse said, "and I'll see what I can find out."

"Thank you," she whispered.

Exhaustion tugged at Maggie's limbs, attempting to pull her down. If she didn't keep moving, she feared she would collapse. She paced the long hallway, trying to ignore the strong medicinal scents that hovered in the air. Several minutes later, the woman returned with a doctor in tow.

"This is Dr. Plimpton. He can tell you about Mr. O'Leary."

The doctor stepped forward and peered at her over his spectacles. "Are you Mrs. O'Leary?"

Maggie wet her dry lips. "No. I'm related . . . by marriage."

"I see." He frowned but let out a sigh. "Mr. O'Leary survived the surgery. The bullet went clean through his left shoulder. Luckily it missed hitting anything vital. It was a tricky procedure, but we feel we were successful in repairing the damage."

"Will he be okay?"

"It's too soon to say for certain, especially given the extreme amount of blood loss. But we are cautiously hopeful."

Maggie's legs wobbled like a marionette whose strings had suddenly loosened. "May

I see him?"

The man gave her a concerned look. "For now I've restricted him to no visitors. He needs complete rest. However, you may check back later in the day to see if his status has changed." He looked pointedly at her tarnished hands. "In the meantime, I'd suggest you go home and get some rest yourself, ma'am."

"Thank you, Doctor," she whispered.

He gave a nod and continued down the hall, leaving Maggie a quivering mass of relief and despair.

Adam had made it through the night. God willing, he'd make it through the day.

Adam struggled to fight his way to the surface through murky water. He must have fallen from the docks into the river. His limbs seemed confined, as though tied down, impeding his effort to move. He took in a long breath and coughed, his throat raw and aching. When he attempted to sit up, searing heat shot through his chest, forcing him down.

Where was he? He blinked, trying to focus his vision.

"Easy does it, Mr. O'Leary." The syrupy female voice jolted Adam.

He glanced to the right and saw a large-boned woman bending over him, a white nurse's cap pinned to her head. He must be in the hospital — again.

White-hot pain shot through his upper torso, bringing the events of the night rushing back.

Maggie! Had Neill spirited her away once he'd gotten rid of Adam?

A gray-haired man in a white coat entered the room. "Hold on there, son. Don't be undoing all our hard work."

Adam winced, furious at not being able to rise. "Is anyone asking for me?"

The doctor ignored his question until he'd lifted the sheet, poking and prodding the gauze on Adam's chest. "Good. The bleeding hasn't started again. Try not to move unless absolutely necessary. And then wait for the nurse to assist you."

Grinding his teeth together to fight the pain, Adam shot out a hand to grasp the doctor's sleeve. "Maggie . . ." He wheezed, trying to get air.

The doctor disengaged his arm. "A woman has been asking about you. I'll see if she's still here."

When he left, the nurse continued to fuss around him and administered a dose of laudanum. Adam swallowed, grimacing at the bitter taste. He wanted to bark at her to leave him in peace, but his eyes drifted closed.

When he opened them again, Maggie's face filled his vision, concern and sorrow flitting over her features. A burst of relief coursed through his body. She hadn't left for Ireland with that madman.

"Maggie." He tried to raise a hand to touch her, but the effort proved too great.

She grasped his hand and held it to her cheek.

"You're . . . all . . . right?" The effort to speak left him weaker than a newborn.

"Yes. But don't talk or the doctor will make me leave." She pressed a kiss to his palm.

"Fitzgerald?" he managed to wheeze out.

"The police caught him. He'll be going to jail for what he did to you." She laid a hand on his arm, its warmth penetrating the sheet that covered him. "I'm so sorry, Adam. For the fire, the shooting — all the terrible things that have happened because of me." Her voice cracked.

"Not . . . your . . . fault."

"Aye, it *is* my fault. I've brought you nothing but harm since we met." Tears flowed freely, bathing her beloved face.

Adam wished he had the strength to wipe them away. "Not true." His lids drooped as the medicine took effect. "Safe now, Maggie."

Her fingers squeezed his. "Aye, I'm safe, and so are you. Rest now and get your strength back."

"Stay." He felt himself drifting.

"I'll be right here when you wake."

37

Seated in the dining room at her family's Long Island home with her cat Petunia dozing on the floor beside her, Aurora sipped her coffee and opened the morning paper. It had been three weeks since the start of the war in Europe, three weeks since Gabe had left, yet Aurora still couldn't quite believe it had happened. She scanned the newspaper for articles about the war, almost as though she could find word of Gabe on the pages. Yet any news concerning the fighting did little to reassure her.

She turned the page, attempting to suppress the melancholy that plagued her so often of late. Gabe had promised he would come back one day, and she believed he would keep his promise if it was in his power to do so. But in reality, it could be years before the war ended, before he was able to make his way across the ocean again. And what if something terrible happened to him before then?

"Aurora, you have a visitor." Papa entered the room, a smile beaming under his handlebar mustache.

She sighed and lowered the newspaper. "Who is it?"

"It's Dr. Reardon. He's waiting in the parlor."

Aurora's heart climbed into her throat. "What is he doing in Long Island?"

"He came to see you. Don't keep the good man waiting, daughter."

Aurora hadn't seen Dr. Reardon since the end of the epidemic. Holed up here at her parents' home, nursing wounds of her own, she hadn't been able to face going back to the city just yet. He must wonder what had become of her.

She smoothed her hair into the knot at her nape, adjusted her skirt, and made her way to the parlor.

Philip stood at the window, gazing out over the gardens. He whirled around at the sound of her entering the room. In a gray suit and tie, he cut a very handsome figure, quite different from his usual white coat. The sight of him brought both comfort and pain, for he, too, reminded her of Gabe.

"Hello, Aurora. You look lovely as always."

Aurora hid her surprise at his compliment

with a gracious nod. "What brings you all the way out here, Doctor?"

He inclined his head. "Surely you could call me Philip since we're not at work?"

She nodded. "Very well, Philip. Won't you sit down?" She gestured to the sofa along the far wall.

They each took a seat, keeping a respectable distance between them.

Aurora forced her mouth into a smile. "You haven't answered my question. What brings you here?"

"I have news for you from Bellevue, and I wanted to deliver it in person." He pulled an envelope from inside his jacket. "It came to my office since I was the one who sponsored you."

Her heart thundered against her ribs as she accepted the envelope. "Do you know what it says?"

He smiled. "I have a fair idea, but why don't you open it and find out?"

With trembling fingers, she ripped open the flap and pulled out a folded sheet of paper. She scanned the words on the page.

Congratulations on your acceptance into the Bellevue Nursing Program.

The rest of the words faded away. She looked up at Philip, blinking back tears of joy. "I've been accepted."

"I had no doubt you would." He beamed at her like a proud teacher. "Congratulations, Aurora."

Gratitude swelled in her chest. "Thank you, Philip, for everything. Without your mentorship and recommendation, this would never have been possible."

In the rush of joy, she leaned over to kiss his cheek. However, he misread her intention and pulled her to him, kissing her fully on the lips.

Shock stiffened her spine, the paper fluttering from her fingers. She pulled away from him as if scorched and jumped to her feet. "Forgive me, Philip. I merely meant to thank you . . ."

He rose and took her hand in his. "Please don't apologize. I've wanted to do that for a long time now. In fact, I came here to do more than kiss you. I came to ask you to marry me."

Aurora's mouth gaped open. Several emotions struggled to gain hold of her. "I . . . I don't know what to say."

"First, let me be clear. I fully support your schooling. We can wait to be married until you've finished."

His earnest expression shamed her. He'd been nothing but kind and supportive of her. How could she turn him down after everything he'd done? Yet how could she accept him when her heart belonged to another?

"This has all happened so suddenly, Philip. I'm afraid I don't —"

He held up a hand as though anticipating her refusal. "Please don't answer right now. Take some time to think about it." He gave her a smile tinged with disappointment. "Again, my sincere congratulations on your achievement." With a lingering kiss to her cheek, he picked up his hat and left the room.

After he'd gone, Aurora leaned her head against the back of the settee and blinked back tears that came too easily these days. Somehow she'd have to find a way to let Philip down gently and pray that he could accept her refusal without it affecting her career.

Oh Gabe, I wish you were here.

Just over two weeks after the shooting, the doctor deemed Adam improved enough to leave the hospital. Gil and Brianna arrived to pick him up in their father's auto. Adam accepted their assistance down the long corridor, mildly disappointed that Maggie wasn't there to see him walk out of the hospital on his own steam.

Colleen and Mama had fought over where he would recuperate, but Adam had decided it would be easier at Irish Meadows, with plenty of room and servants to assist in his care. Plus it would give him a chance to solidify his new relationship with his father.

Brianna helped Adam into the backseat of the motorcar. Gil stowed his bag, then came around to the driver's side, started the car, and pulled away from the curb.

While Gil maneuvered the car through the crowded streets, Adam tried to find a comfortable position where his injury didn't pain him. He peered at the back of Gil's and Brianna's heads. "Why didn't you send Sam to get me? You two must have better things to do now that your wedding is almost here."

Brianna twisted to give him a sad smile. "Actually, we've postponed the wedding for a few weeks so Mama will have longer to regain her strength."

Adam nodded. "Probably a wise decision." He winced as the car hit a bump and jostled his shoulder, wishing he'd taken a last dose of laudanum.

His stay in the hospital had given him many hours to ponder his future. Almost dying, and almost losing Maggie to that madman, had put things in perspective for him. His shop, the furniture he'd created — they didn't define who he was, didn't measure his worth. His worthiness came from God, from belonging to Him and living a life according to His word. Perhaps Adam had to lose all his material possessions to see what truly mattered.

Loving God, loving his family . . . and loving Maggie.

His sweet, brave Maggie. Adam's heart squeezed at the thought of the sacrifice she'd been willing to make for him — leaving with Fitzgerald in order to keep Adam from harm. If by some miracle she still wanted him after he recovered, Adam wasn't going to be foolish enough to turn her away again.

Adam swiped the moisture from his eyes and turned his focus to the streets outside the car window. He frowned at the sight of the familiar surroundings. "What are we doing here?"

Gil slowed the car to a stop across from Adam's shop and pulled up the parking brake. "A small detour before going home."

He scowled. "There's nothing to see but rubble."

Brianna opened the door for him. "Why don't you let us be the judge?"

With little choice, Adam followed Gil and

Brianna across the street, only to stop dead in front of his shop. The bricks still bore the scorch marks of the fire, but a new door and windows graced the front.

"Who did this?" His voice rasped like a rusty pipe.

"You'll have to go in and find out." Brianna winked at him.

Gil held the door for Adam to enter. He stopped just inside, scarcely able to believe what he was seeing. Gleaming wooden floors shone in the interior. The walls and ceiling had been restored, along with a new counter and shelving, very similar to the ones that had been there before. The whole room smelled of freshly cut wood and varnish.

Shockwaves coursed through his body, leaving him reeling. Only the faintest scent of smoke gave evidence of the fire that had all but destroyed the place.

"How is this possible?" Adam spoke almost to himself as he moved toward his former workshop.

Inside, leaning against a wooden workbench, John grinned at him. "Welcome home."

Adam stared around the room at the assortment of tools hanging on pegs, at the pile of wood neatly stacked in one corner, and at the few pieces of furniture he'd managed to rescue, which now sat against the wall.

His stunned gaze returned to John. "You did all this?" He couldn't believe so much had been done in such a short amount of time. It would have taken an army.

"Not quite." John straightened. "You've heard of barn raisings? Well, we had a shop raising." He let out a shrill whistle, and the back door opened.

A flood of men poured in, cheering and waving their hats.

John gestured to them. "Thanks to your fellow parishioners, who all came together to help, we have the basic structure restored. Ready for you to make more furniture."

Adam fought the onslaught of emotion that clogged his throat as he scanned the group of men. Some he recognized, some he'd never met before. "H-how can I ever thank you for this?"

One man stepped forward, grinning. "No thanks needed. Unless you let me place your first order. My wife needs a rocking chair. She's expecting our first babe around Christmas."

"And I could use a dining table."

More remarks flew around as the men came forward to shake Adam's hand. He thanked each one, his mind a haze of disbelief.

Slowly they all trooped out the rear door, except for John — and one man who had lingered against the back wall. The air seized in Adam's lungs as he stared at his father.

"When were you going to tell me you'd started your own business?" For once his father's blue gaze held no disapproval, no censure, only curiosity.

Adam cleared his throat and attempted to banish the fog from his brain. "Once it became a success."

A dark brow rose. "That could take years."

Adam shifted his weight, at a loss for something to say.

"Wait here." James went out the back door and returned moments later with a small table — one Adam recognized from the parlor at Irish Meadows.

"Your mother's been after me for years to refinish this for her." His father shrugged. "Turns out, unless it's repairing a paddock fence, I'm not much good at woodworking." He set the table on the floor. "I know she'd be thrilled if you'd restore it for her."

Adam swallowed against the tightness in his throat. "I'd be happy to."

John came up and clapped a hand on Adam's shoulder. "James was a big help in getting this place repaired. He supplied most of the materials and put in some hard labor, as well."

His father came forward, hand outstretched. "I hope this will mark a new beginning for both of us."

Adam's chest constricted with an ache completely unrelated to his injury as he shook his father's hand. "I have no words to thank you both for what you've done." He turned to shake John's hand, as well.

His friend gave him a broad grin. "There's someone else who deserves your thanks. She's the one who got this project started. James and I simply rounded up the workers."

Adam's heart gave a hard lurch. "She?"

John gestured to the staircase leading up to the living quarters. "I believe she's waiting for you."

Adam swallowed and turned to his father. "Will you tell Bree and Gil that I'll be out in a minute?"

His father chuckled. "Certainly."

Adam made his way to the staircase and slowly climbed the steps. When he entered the room, he couldn't believe the transformation. The walls had been whitewashed, the restored woodstove sparkled, and a new table and chairs sat against the wall. Instead of the narrow cot he'd been using, a metal-framed double bed dominated the space, with his blue quilt from home covering the mattress. He reached out to finger the soft fabric and blinked back the moisture that stung his eyes.

Maggie appeared out of the shadows, light glowing on the dark hair framing her face. "Your mother insisted I bring it for you as her contribution to your new home."

He moved toward her like a magnet seeking true north. "You're responsible for all this?"

She folded her hands in front of her green linen skirt. "I only made the suggestion. John and your father gathered the people to do the work." She waved a hand. "Though I did paint these walls."

His throat tight, he reached out to draw her to him. "I don't know what to say. You've given me back my hope, my purpose, my future."

A smile softened her features. "That was my intent, since it was my fault you lost everything."

"Not everything." He ran a finger down the silk of her cheek and then, unable to hold back a moment longer, he kissed her, his heart nearly bursting from his chest with love.

She eagerly returned his kiss, until at last she pulled away with a shaky laugh. "So, do you like your new bed? A dear lady from John's church donated it, since she and her husband are moving across the country to live with their son."

A lightness he'd not felt in ages invaded his being. "It will do, though I'm not sure it's big enough."

She frowned at him. "It's a far cry from the cot you had before."

He tugged a tempting curl hanging over her shoulder. "But is it big enough for two?"

Delicious color bled into her cheeks along with a look of outrage. "What are you insinuating, Adam O'Leary?"

He couldn't keep the amusement from his face. "Only that my wife may want something bigger."

"Well, if your wife is any kind of decent woman, she'd be happy just to have you."

With his good arm, he crushed her to him and captured her lips for a kiss that left no doubt as to whom he wished to marry.

"Maggie Montgomery, I love you more than my very life, and I'll spend every day from now on making you happy — if you'll agree to become my wife."

Her eyes became shimmering pools of heather. "I love you, too, Adam, and I'd be proud to be your wife." She threw her arms around his neck with such vigor that he groaned.

She gasped. "Your shoulder. I'm sorry."

But he held her fast. "It's worth the pain."

His lips sought hers once more, until a loud bang from below interrupted the embrace.

"Adam?" Brianna's voice floated up the stairs. "I hate to rush you, but Mama will be frantic if we don't get you home."

"Be right down." He paused to steal one more kiss. "How would you feel about a double wedding?"

Maggie laughed and shook her head. "A lovely thought, but I would never intrude on Brianna's day. She's waited too long for it."

"You're right." He grinned. "How about a Thanksgiving wedding, then?"

"Why don't you concentrate on recovering from your injury and we'll discuss this later?" Her eyes overflowed with love. "Thankfully we have all the time in the world."

38

Peering into the grand foyer mirror, Aurora adjusted the angle of her large floral hat and re-tied the sash of her pink gown, the perfect outfit for Brianna and Gil's wedding. If only Aurora could share in the joy of the day. But such a romantic occasion made her yearn for Gabe all the more.

The fact that she'd had no word from him chipped away at her confidence. Perhaps he'd joined the fighting and couldn't contact her. Or perhaps he'd forgotten about her, after all.

Approaching footsteps alerted Aurora to her parents' presence.

"Come, daughter. We mustn't be late for the wedding of the year." Her father's voice echoed over the tiled entry.

Her mother moved to the mirror. "You look lovely, dear."

"Thank you, Mama. So do you." Aurora did her best to smile, knowing how worried her mother had been about her. The typhoid epidemic had taken its toll on everyone involved.

Papa threw Aurora a sullen glance. "You could be basking in the glow of your own upcoming nuptials, if you'd accepted Dr. Reardon's proposal." He pulled his ornate walking stick from the stand in the corner. "Just how long do you intend to wait for this Irishman with not even a word from him?"

A stabbing pain invaded the region of Aurora's heart. Papa had touched on the very core of her fear, that if Gabe were alive, surely he would have sent some word to her. Or had being back in his homeland caused his feelings to fade? She swallowed her insecurities and stiffened her spine. "I'll wait as long as it takes, Papa. Until I know for certain one way or another."

Before her father could comment further, she walked out the door to the waiting car.

Thankfully Papa remained silent on the drive to the church. As the chauffeur pulled up in front of the quaint stone building, Aurora gave herself a stern lecture. This was Brianna and Gil's big day. After countless setbacks, they would now see the fulfilment of their dreams. Aurora was relieved that her long-held bitterness toward the couple had disappeared, and she would do nothing to take away from their joy. She only prayed that one day she, too, would experience such a wondrous occasion.

Her father held out a hand to help her alight from the automobile. She straightened and inhaled the crisp air. The first hint of color had begun to tint the leaves. A mild breeze teased the ribbons on her hat and blew the hem of her dress around her ankles as she turned toward the church.

At the base of the stairs, a shaggy-haired man leaned on a crutch. Aurora squinted. Surely this vagrant wasn't one of the wedding guests. The man moved away from the railing, and something about his demeanor made Aurora's heart stutter in her chest.

"Do I look that bad that you don't recognize me?"

She stifled a cry with one gloved hand. Was she dreaming?

Crutch under his arm, Gabe limped toward her, gazing at her with an intensity that left her knees weak. Tears blurred the sight of his beloved face.

On legs as wobbly as a new colt's, she darted forward. He dropped his crutch and caught her in his arms.

"Aurora, *mo ghrá*. How I've missed you." He crushed her to him.

"Is it really you?"

"No one else." His Irish lilt was even more pronounced after being home.

She pulled away and bent to retrieve his crutch. "You're hurt. What happened?"

"It's a long, sad tale, which I'll save for later."

"But why did you not send word you were coming?"

His eyebrows rose. "Did you not receive my telegrams?"

She shook her head.

"None of them?"

"No."

He wiped her tears away with his thumb. "Ah, darlin', I'm sorry to cause you such worry. I don't know what could have happened."

Suspicion dawned, and she glanced over her shoulder to where her parents stood watching. "Papa, did you intercept telegrams intended for me?"

The color heightened in his cheeks, but he said nothing.

She stalked across the grass to confront him. "You knew how worried I was. How I longed for word of Gabe to be certain he was alive, yet you kept that knowledge from me. How could you do that?" Her hands shook with a combination of shock and anger.

"I only had your best interest in mind. I truly believed the man would never return. . . ." Her father waved a hand in the air as if that was explanation enough.

Gabe appeared beside her. "You couldn't be more wrong, sir. I would have moved heaven and earth to come back to her." Gabe turned and took her hands. "Nothing except my death would have stopped me."

"Oh, Gabe." The intensity of the love in his gaze turned Aurora's insides to warm pudding.

"I hope it's not too soon to make my intentions known," Gabe said, his eyes still on her, "but I'm asking for Aurora's hand in marriage. If she'll have me."

More tears bloomed, and she didn't wait for her father's reply. "Yes, I'll have you."

"The saints be praised." Gabe grinned down at her. "There's only one more thing I need." He cupped her face with both hands and very deliberately kissed her.

Eagerly, Aurora drank in the familiar scent of his aftershave and the warmth of his lips, relishing the shelter of his arms surrounding her. How many weeks had she longed for this moment?

Moments later, they drew apart.

Gabe smiled and held out his arm. "May I escort you inside?"

She laughed out loud. "I'd be delighted."

Together, they entered the church, his crutch making their progress slow but steady. The joyous strains of piano music accompanied them as they moved up the aisle. Never had Aurora felt such happiness in her life.

Smiling through tears of joy, she lifted blissful prayers of gratitude to a most gracious and loving God.

Thank You, thank You, for bringing Gabe back to me!

On a wave of near euphoria, Maggie drifted through the crowded parlor filled with wedding guests. Brianna and Gil's reception was being held at Irish Meadows, as per the bride's wishes. Mr. O'Leary had spared no expense, ordering dozens of roses to grace the interior of the house, as well as the balcony outside. Maggie inhaled the delicious floral fragrance and sighed with delight.

Today had been the happiest of days for the O'Leary family, one they richly deserved after all they'd been through. Thankfully Mrs. O'Leary had recovered enough to participate in the activities, although she still tired easily. Deirdre and Connor had also regained their health, due in part to the resilience of their youth.

With the festivities fully underway and Adam busy with his duties as best man, Maggie exited onto the balcony, intent on finding Gabe. Another burst of gratitude radiated through her at the surprise she'd found upon waking. Though injured from an accident at sea, her dear brother had returned, arriving in the middle of the night. She'd hardly dared believe it when she'd spied Gabe in Colleen's kitchen that morning. But with the flurry of preparations for the wedding, they'd had no chance to speak. Besides which, Gabe's sole intent had been getting to Aurora. Now that the couple had spent a few hours together, Maggie needed to find out about her family and how the war was affecting them.

She stood for a moment at the balcony rail, looking out over the colorful array of guests on the lawn below, and simply drank in the glorious scene. The breeze teased Maggie's hair and gown, calling to mind when she'd stood at another railing. Was it only a few short months ago that she'd looked upon the Statue of Liberty for the first time as their ship made its way into the New York Harbor? The excitement and trepidation she'd experienced then could not compare to the joy and peace that flowed through her soul today. She lifted a prayer of immense gratitude to God for bringing her across the ocean to her new home and for granting her the freedom to find the love of her life. Both she and Gabe had been truly blessed to find their hearts' desire in America.

Thoughts of her brother brought her back to her initial purpose for coming outside. Gabe and Aurora had gone for a walk in the garden some time ago. Surely they'd returned by now. Maggie scanned the sea of people below her and, not spying the couple, headed down to the garden. She soon found the lovebirds on a bench near the water fountain and waited until a fairly passionate kiss ended before she made her presence known. "Hello, you two."

Aurora blushed. "Maggie, it's lovely to see you again."

"And you, as well. I hope you don't mind the intrusion, but I haven't had a chance to talk to my brother."

Gabe rose and gestured for her to sit down. "I'm afraid I was somewhat pre-occupied when I arrived." He winked at Aurora, who blushed again.

Maggie took his spot on the bench. "So

tell me everything."

Gabe crossed his arms, his eyes darkening. He glanced from Aurora to Maggie. "I still don't know exactly what happened, but our ship went down. There were rumors of a torpedo attack. In any case, I woke up in the hospital with a concussion and a broken leg. I got off easy compared to some."

The distress on Aurora's face mirrored Maggie's feelings. "Why didn't you let us know?"

"I didn't want to worry everyone. After I got out of the hospital, I stayed at Tommy's so Mum and the girls could fuss over me. She sends her love, by the way."

"What about the war?"

"So far, Tommy and Paddy haven't enlisted, and they won't unless they're given no choice." He scowled, and Maggie knew better than to get him started on his views of the British army.

"The rest of the clan is fine, but everyone misses you terribly."

A twinge of sadness pinched Maggie's heart. "I miss them, too."

Gabe plucked a flower from the bush beside him and twirled it between his fingers, a pensive expression on his face. "I had a lot of time to think while I was recuperating, and I knew what I had to do once I got well enough." He handed Aurora the bloom with a smile. "I had to keep my promise to this lovely lady. As soon as I could, I got on the next ship."

A tear slid down Aurora's cheek as she raised the flower to her nose.

Maggie tried to imagine how hard it had been for her mother to let Gabe go. "How did Mum take the news that we're staying in America?"

Gabe tweaked one of her curls. "You can stop worrying. Mum suspected all along you were destined to stay."

Foolish tears clogged Maggie's throat. "Did she seem upset?"

"A little, now that three of us are here. But she understands."

Maggie pulled a handkerchief from her reticule. "Tomorrow I'll write her a long letter."

"That's a grand idea. Now if you don't mind, sister dear, I'd like at least one dance with my fiancée, if she doesn't mind my limp."

"I'd love to." Beaming, Aurora rose and took his hand.

With a quick wave, they set off toward the house.

Maggie sat for a few seconds longer, allowing her emotions to settle. Today was not a day for sadness or regret.

"Are those tears I see?"

Maggie looked up to see Adam, and once again her heart stuttered at the handsome figure he cut in his tuxedo. She'd never seen him dressed in such finery. For the first time since she'd met him, he looked like the heir to the O'Leary estate.

He came to sit beside her on the stone bench and laid a hand over hers. "What is it, sweetheart?"

The tenderness in his question made her throat tighten. She wouldn't mar his happiness with any talk of homesickness. She smiled at him. "It's nothing. Weddings always make me sentimental."

He peered at her, then tipped up her chin for a light kiss. "We'd best get inside. I believe the best man has a speech to make."

She wound her fingers through his. "Did I tell you how proud I am?"

"Once or twice." He winked at her, warming her heart. Then he sobered. "I'll never understand why you had such faith in me, despite everyone's warnings."

Love shimmered inside her like a beautiful dream. "I believe God brought us together — to help each other through some difficult times, and to love each other."

"And I promise to spend the rest of my

days doing just that." He pulled her tight to his chest and kissed her again.

Her soul sighed with pleasure, her earlier euphoria returning to erase any lingering sadness. She would always miss her mother, but she wouldn't trade her happiness with Adam for anything.

The patter of feet on the garden path, along with a high-pitched giggle, had Maggie and Adam pulling apart.

Delia stood beside them, her white-and-pink dress swishing about her legs. "Uncle Adam, Aunt Maggie, Daddy sent me to find you." Her blond curls bobbed around her flushed cheeks.

Maggie smiled, another wave of gratitude arising for Delia's restored health. "We're coming now, sweetie."

"Good, 'cause Daddy didn't want you to miss the 'nouncement.'"

"What announcement?"

Delia covered her mouth with a tiny gloved hand. "It's a secret. You have to come now."

She grabbed Adam's hand and tugged. He grinned over his shoulder at Maggie, who tried not to laugh.

They followed the noise of the crowd into the dining room, where the bride and groom stood poised to cut the wedding cake. Brianna looked resplendent in her ivory lace gown.

After they shared the first bite, Gil turned to address the guests. "Brianna and I wish to thank everyone for sharing this special day with us. I'm very proud of my wife for graduating from Barnard College earlier this summer. But I must say, I am looking forward to our honeymoon and having her all to myself."

Maggie joined the laughter that rippled through the crowd.

"Before the toasts begin, I've been told that Rylan wishes to say a few words."

Rylan came forward with Colleen, Delia, and the baby. "It's grand to be here for this wonderful occasion." He smiled out over the room, then gazed at his wife. The intimate look they shared made Maggie tingle down to her toes. "We hope Brianna and Gil don't mind us stealing their thunder with good news of our own. In addition to our beautiful daughter, Delia, Colleen and I are adopting this lovely girl — Ivy Kathleen Beatrice Montgomery."

When the crowd stopped clapping, Rylan grinned again. "I must say God has a most interesting sense of humor. Not to mention incredible timing." He gave a low chuckle. "We've just learned we're expecting a baby of our own next spring."

More applause erupted, and Maggie squeezed Adam's hand, her heart overflowing. "God is so good to us, Adam."

He dropped a kiss on her head. "That He is, my love. Now, excuse me, I need to say a few words myself."

Adam pushed back a rush of nerves as he picked up a glass of champagne from the table. "As best man, it is my duty to toast the bride and groom. Before I get to that, I hope you'll indulge me for a moment." His hand trembled slightly while he paused to collect his thoughts. "Most of you know about the recent time I spent in prison. While there, I met a good Christian man who helped me face a few harsh truths about myself and who urged me to reconcile with my family." Adam swallowed hard, picturing John's face. "With his guidance, I have learned to appreciate the true importance of family." Adam looked to the place where he'd seen his parents standing. To Adam's astonishment, his father had pushed through the crowd and now came forward to wrap Adam in a tight hug. The unexpected action caused a host of emotions to riot through Adam's system. He clamped his jaw tight so as not to break down in front of everyone.

His father faced the guests. "As most of you know, we've been through some trying times of late. Almost losing my Kathleen has made me appreciate all that God has given us." He glanced at Adam. "I'm very impressed with the way Adam has turned his life around . . . and I'm proud to call him . . . my son."

He shook Adam's hand, and they embraced once more. Adam glanced over at his mother, smiling through her tears of happiness. He didn't dare look at Maggie or he might lose his last thread of control. Instead, he raised his glass. "To Gil and Brianna, may your love endure forever, and may God bless your marriage with great joy and many children."

"Amen." The guests applauded and lifted their own glasses.

Adam added a silent prayer of thanks for the second chance he'd been given with his father. For the first time in his life, Adam felt he truly belonged.

Some time later, when the party began to wind down, Adam sought Maggie in the crowd and pulled her off to an alcove for a little privacy. He'd been waiting for the right moment to give her his surprise.

She nestled into his arms with a contented

sigh. "Brianna loved her cedar chest. Will you make me one as a wedding present?"

He gazed down at her, wanting to promise her the world. "I'll do better than that. I'll build furniture for our whole house."

"Just where do you plan to find space for more furniture?"

He chuckled at her incredulous expression. "You don't imagine I'd let you live in that tiny room over the shop, do you?"

She regarded him with a serious stare. "I'd live anywhere with you, my love. As long as we're together."

He caressed her cheek. "I love you more than the air I breathe, Maggie, and I hope one day to be worthy of your heart."

She smiled tenderly. "You don't have to earn my heart . . . or my love. They're yours — now and forever."

Adam's heart soared with a magnitude of love and tenderness he never dreamed possible. "I have something for you." He reached into his jacket and pulled out an envelope. "An early wedding gift."

Fascinating creases wrinkled her nose. "But our wedding's not for months."

He only smiled. "Open it."

His pulse rate sprinted as she pulled up the flap and removed the contents. The paper shook in her hand. "Tickets to Ireland?"

He grinned. "I thought we might honeymoon in Cork, and you could show me your hometown."

"Oh, Adam. This is the most wonderful gift ever." Moisture shimmered in her eyes. "But how can you afford this?"

"Because of the war, steamer tickets are not much in demand at the moment, and I got a good price."

She opened her mouth as if to object, but he held up a finger.

"One more thing." He made sure he had her full attention. He'd seen Maggie's sadness when she'd thought he wasn't aware and knew she missed her mother terribly. "If your mother is willing, I thought we could bring her back here . . . to live with us."

With a strangled cry, Maggie threw her arms around him.

He held her as she wept on his shoulder, satisfaction warming his insides. Happy tears he could handle. "Of course, our trip will depend on the war. After what Gabe went through, we may have to wait." He pulled back to look at her. "In the meantime, how would you feel about moving up our wedding date?"

Her beaming smile fairly knocked him over. "Will tomorrow do?"

Adam laughed at the light in her eyes and then bent to kiss her again. He gave thanks to God from the depths of his being for the precious gift of her love, for freeing him from the shackles of his past and bestowing on him the promise of a bright future ahead.

With Maggie by his side, he would continue to build the O'Leary legacy and create a most worthy heritage — one that would make his family and his God very proud indeed.

A NOTE FROM THE AUTHOR

A Worthy Heart was a challenging story to write — and even more challenging to edit. Yet in some ways, it makes the end result even sweeter.

First of all, I have a confession to make. In the beginning, I did not like Adam O'Leary, not one little bit. In fact, during the writing of *Irish Meadows,* I had initially intended for him to play more of an antagonistic role in Gil Whelan's story. Instead, I basically banished him from the book altogether, hinting that he was on the outs with his father and was potentially involved in some "less than legal" undertakings.

How on earth was I going to make him the hero of *A Worthy Heart* when I didn't even like him?

But then an amazing thing happened. The more I delved into Adam's backstory and his true nature, the more I came to love Adam! I only hope I did his character justice and that readers will fall in love with him, too. It took a strong woman like Maggie to see past his mistakes and love him anyway, mirroring the way God loves all His children unconditionally.

I want to thank the wonderful team at Bethany House for all their hard work on my behalf. In particular, thank you to Dave Long and Charlene Patterson for their excellent editorial input and advice! Thank you also to Noelle Buss and Amy Green for helping this newbie navigate the promotional aspect of publication. Their patience and generosity are greatly appreciated!

Once again, I owe a huge debt of gratitude to my wonderful critique partners, Julie Jarnagin and Sally Bayless, who went above and beyond the call of duty with many quick turnarounds! I am most grateful for their friendship and support.

And of course, I have to thank my family — my husband, Bud, and my children, Leanne and Eric — for their continued love and encouragement!

I am so happy to be a part of the Bethany House team of authors. I feel blessed to be able to share my stories with you all!

Warmest wishes,
Susan

ABOUT THE AUTHOR

Susan Anne Mason describes her writing style as "romance sprinkled with faith." She loves incorporating inspirational messages of God's unconditional love and forgiveness into her characters' journeys. *A Worthy Heart* is her second novel in the Courage to Dream series, which features the O'Leary family. The first book in the series, *Irish Meadows,* won the Fiction from the Heartland contest sponsored by the Mid-American Romance Authors chapter of RWA.

Susan lives outside Toronto, Ontario, with her husband, two children, and two cats. She loves red wine and chocolate, is not partial to snow even though she's Canadian, and is ecstatic on the rare occasions she has the house to herself. In addition to writing, Susan likes to research her family history online and occasionally indulges in scrapbooking. Learn more about Susan and her books at www.SusanAnneMason.com.

The employees of Thorndike Press hope you have enjoyed this Large Print book. All our Thorndike, Wheeler, and Kennebec Large Print titles are designed for easy reading, and all our books are made to last. Other Thorndike Press Large Print books are available at your library, through selected bookstores, or directly from us.

For information about titles, please call:
  (800) 223-1244

or visit our Web site at:
  http://gale.cengage.com/thorndike

To share your comments, please write:
  Publisher
  Thorndike Press
  10 Water St., Suite 310
  Waterville, ME 04901